"Ha," Nathan cried. "I've got you now!"

Rachel laughed and so did he, but their amusement suddenly gave way to something more intense. Her pulse quickened; her senses came alive. He stared down into her eyes. And she couldn't have broken from his gaze even if she'd tried. He would kiss her now, she thought. She wanted him to kiss her very much.

Instead, he loosened his hold on her. "I...we..." He pulled away abruptly, turning from her. "I can't believe I did that, given what you've been through today."

"A kiss from you would have nothing to do with what the general did earlier," she assured him.

But he stood stiffly apart from her and rubbed the back of his neck. "Maybe we should call it a night," he suggested.

She raised her arm and slid her fingers through his hair, encouraging him with every subtle shift of her body.

His eyes flashed with desire. But instead of kissing her, as she wanted him to, he spoke softly. "I want you, Rachel. There's no denying it. But I need you to think about what *you* want first.... Don't say anything now. Go back to the hotel. If this is really what you want, it'll still be what you want in a little while."

If he said more, she didn't hear it. She forced her legs to move her toward the bright lights of the hotel. Once there, she would have to decide—without lust drugging her, without the heat of the moment coaxing her....

Dear Reader,

While the traditions of honor and integrity that make up
an officer's training usually produce the most trustworthy
individuals in society, there are a few without scruples
who slip by the rigorous oversight of their superiors.
They usually don't go unnoticed for long. Eventually,
even a general gone bad will be thwarted by those who
are determined to maintain the sanctity of the officer
corps. But the cost of bringing down an amoral general
can be very high.

So it is with Chief Warrant Officer Rachel Southwell and
Captain Nathan Fordham, who must put a stop to their
commanding general's sexual harassment. If things go
wrong and the general dodges their attempt to bring him
to justice, they could lose their careers and they could lose
each other. But nothing will keep them from doing what
honor demands. The general must be stopped. Together
they take on the daunting task, embarking on one of the
most challenging missions of their military careers—and
find themselves victims to love even as they triumph over
staggering odds.

I hope Rachel and Nathan's story means as much to you as
it does to me.

Elizabeth Ashtree

Books by Elizabeth Ashtree

HARLEQUIN SUPERROMANCE

A Captain's Honor
Elizabeth Ashtree

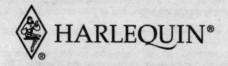

TORONTO • NEW YORK • LONDON
AMSTERDAM • PARIS • SYDNEY • HAMBURG
STOCKHOLM • ATHENS • TOKYO • MILAN • MADRID
PRAGUE • WARSAW • BUDAPEST • AUCKLAND

ISBN 0-373-71089-5

A CAPTAIN'S HONOR

Copyright © 2002 by Randi Elizabeth DuFresne.

This edition published by arrangement with Harlequin Books S.A.

® and TM are trademarks of the publisher. Trademarks indicated with ® are registered in the United States Patent and Trademark Office, the Canadian Trade Marks Office and in other countries.

Visit us at www.eHarlequin.com

Printed in U.S.A.

To the men and women of the United States Armed Forces,
who put their lives on the line every day
to keep all of us safe at home.

And to every person standing against sexual harassment
in its many forms.

CHAPTER ONE

CAPTAIN NATHAN FORDHAM stood under the blazing sun and scanned the confidence course at Fort Bragg, North Carolina. He needed only seconds to spot her. Though tall for a female, she was much smaller than every other soldier out there. Yet what she lacked in stature, she clearly made up in fortitude. She hadn't hesitated even a moment before scrambling up the thirty-foot incline on all fours and then rappelling down the other side with grace and agility.

Watching her, Nathan felt a warmth inside him that had nothing to do with the relentless heat. For here was a woman who dazzled him with her contradictions and intrigued him with her complexity. And when she grinned at one of her teammates, showing white teeth that stood out against her mud-covered face, he couldn't take his eyes off her.

He'd seen a photograph of her before departing his duty station at the Pentagon, but the photo hadn't done her justice. The officer in it was delicate and slim, with a heart-shaped face. At five feet seven inches, she could be described as willowy and feminine—the kind of woman men fall all over themselves to protect. Major General Walter Cornelius Donner would enjoy toying with Chief Warrant Officer Rachel Southwell. Nathan was here to make sure he never got the chance.

"C'MON, YOU GUYS, MOVE IT!" Rachel shouted from the far side of the stream she had just crossed. One team member had followed her lead and stood nearby.

Two men dangled from the solitary rope stretched tightly over the water. Their legs were loosely slung over it as they hauled themselves hand over hand along its length. Two other teammates awaited their turns.

Her six-man team was ahead by several minutes, but Rachel was eager to increase their advantage. As always, she was driven to prove to everyone that she could compete as well as most men, that she would not hold anyone back, that she was an important member of the team. So she'd led the way over the river, showing these young men how easily a body could travel on the rope by staying relaxed and fluid. And now she urged them to hurry, spurring them not only with her words but with the fact that she herself had crossed with such alacrity.

"You made it look easy!" cried Private MacDonald as he completed the obstacle. "How the hell did you do that so quick?"

Rachel shook her head in disgust. What the young soldier really wanted to know was how a *woman* could manage it so fast. "Just get moving!" she barked as the last man dropped to the ground beside her. "Up and over!" she called as she followed the men toward the seventh grueling event of the course.

HER STAMINA WAS AMAZING, Nathan observed. If anyone was up to the challenge of dealing with Donner, it was Rachel Southwell. Provided she fully understood the risk to herself. He'd already decided weeks ago that the danger to himself was nothing compared with the damage Donner could inflict in others. Witnessing what the General had done to Sergeant Sheila Walker had been all the persuasion he'd needed.

"I'm not the first and I won't be the last," Sergeant Walker had muttered one day after she'd been with the General in his office for a while. "It's like being a prisoner of war, working here." After that, she'd pursued reassignment doggedly until she finally PCSed, glad to make an unpopular permanent change of station to Korea even in the midst of America's war on terrorism.

There had been other soldiers upon whom the General had preyed. In the six months since Nathan had become General Donner's aide, he'd seen him destroy too many lives. Hating to involve his own brother but knowing of no one else who could help, Nathan had gone to Julian in the Army Criminal Investigation Division, or CID, on Fort Belvoir, Virginia, not too far from the Pentagon. Newly promoted to major, Julian had been more than willing to help. His plan had involved finding an office worker with the emotional strength to join in the effort to stop Donner. They needed a person who would press charges even against a general—someone with the fortitude to stick with the prosecution even through the inevitable scandal. Julian's connections had led him to the transfer request Rachel Southwell had submitted.

"Her father is sick and she wants to move closer to her parents to help out. She's a 420A," Julian said, reading her MOS, or military occupational specialty code. "As she's a personnel technician, the opening in your office is just about her only chance of coming north. This warrant officer is perfect, both for the job and for stopping Donner. Look," he said as he tossed some stapled sheets from the dossier toward Nathan, "her personnel records show she's unmarried with no dependents. We agreed we'd need someone without a family."

"Donner doesn't hesitate to silence his victims by threatening to drag spouses and children through scandal," Nathan noted. "We definitely need a dependent-free female on this mission."

Of course, Donner could still use his other tactic to control the Chief—threaten to transfer her to a tour in Somalia to keep her silent. Somehow, Donner had managed to employ such threats successfully for a very long time. But watching the tough, unmarried and childless Chief Southwell as she ran the confidence course, Nathan felt a surge of hope. As much as he hated putting her in harm's way, this particular woman appeared to have the strength of character to help him end Donner's reign of terror.

THE NEXT CHALLENGE on the course was Rachel's least favorite because of the immense amount of stamina required to scale the swaying rope netting. The rope wall stood forty feet high. Private MacDonald, whom Rachel could see had a little problem with heights, stopped dead in his tracks as his gaze went up, and up, and up.

"Go, go, go!" she shouted. She gave the young man a little push in the right direction. There was absolutely nothing like being shoved by a female to spur the male ego into overdrive. MacDonald put his hands on the ropes and hauled himself up a few feet. His teammates had already ascended a third of the way. Rachel took her place beside the Private, knowing he'd need all the encouragement he could get.

Whenever she'd done this obstacle in the past, her muscles had trembled with fatigue by the time she got to the top of the net and she'd barely had the strength to get down the other side. But she didn't let herself think about that now. She focused only on grasping firm handholds and where her booted feet needed to be. Like Spider-Man, she climbed—first her left hand and foot, then her right. It was tiring. The only way she knew to accomplish the feat was to keep moving steadily.

About halfway to the top, MacDonald came to a complete stop again.

"Private! What are you doing?" she called from just above him. Then she saw what was happening. She groaned. "Soldier, look at me when I'm talking to you!"

The Private had his eyes glued to the ground—a long way down. He'd looped his left arm through the net and was clinging to the rung for all he was worth. In the rope beneath her hands she could feel the tremors that radiated from his quaking.

Rachel swore under her breath. She would have to go down to him and then climb up again, repeating all those vertical feet. Looking up, she saw that the other men on her team were too far ahead to be of assistance. The burden of helping Private MacDonald fell to her whether she liked it or not. So she descended, cursing softly.

"MacDonald!" The eighteen-year-old didn't seem to hear her. She could see him trembling. Her own limbs shook, but not from terror. As always, the other events on the course had taken their toll and she was nearly spent.

Rachel adjusted her hold on the ropes so she could spare one foot. She wished she could think of another way to deal with the problem, but nothing came to mind. This young man needed immediate help or he'd embarrass himself and earn the scorn of his teammates. So she hauled off and kicked Private MacDonald in the butt.

"Ow!" He gazed at her, shocked, and when his eyes threatened to gravitate back to the ground, she nudged him again with the rounded toe of her black-and-green jump boot.

"Up," she said. "Only look up. Or at me. Got that?"

"Yes, ma'am," he said, staring at her with an intensity born of fear.

"Now, you do exactly what I do, you hear me? If I can do it, so can you. Right?"

He nodded, started to glance down again, must have noticed her boot preparing to swing toward him again, and decided to turn his face up to the hot sun, instead.

"Here we go," she said as she began to climb again.

It was slow going, what with having to check on Mac-Donald's progress every few minutes. But at last they were both at the top. The hardest part of the climb was just ahead. And suddenly, MacDonald realized it.

"I can't do it. I can't do it," he began to chant. He was back to clutching the ropes.

She didn't spare him a glance but kept her eyes on the

goal. She had to get over the top, and that took a great deal of strength and concentration.

"I can't do it," MacDonald whined again. He quaked so violently the ropes shook hard.

"Shut up." She licked her dry lips and tried to still her own trembling limbs. "I told you to watch me and to do what I do. You telling me you can't do something I can do?"

MacDonald didn't answer. He eyed the thick top rope dubiously, but at least he didn't look down.

"Watch me closely, soldier, 'cause I'm not doing this a second time."

NATHAN SAW HER MOVE EFFICIENTLY up the rope wall and whistled softly under his breath. Her movements were precise and elegant. But when she stopped to help her younger teammate, he could see that the climb was nowhere near as effortless as it appeared. She gazed longingly at the top of the net but didn't abandon the man clinging in fear about midway. Nathan couldn't hear her words, but he saw her wince when she kicked the soldier to get his attention away from the ground. Clearly, she wasn't as heartless on the inside as her action implied.

Once she got the soldier moving, he had the pleasure of watching her climb again. The pull of her camouflage pants on her thighs exhibited long, trim legs. Her T-shirt hid none of the flex and release of her shoulder and arm muscles, showing off her surprising strength with mouthwatering clarity. Nathan acknowledged right then and there that he was going to have a hard time dealing with his natural attraction to her. She was just about a perfect example of the athletic female he'd always found irresistible.

Yet resistance was paramount. There would be no room for romance once they joined forces against a two-star general.

Julian had summed things up nicely when Nathan had protested that Chief Southwell might not be right for what they had in mind. "She's Airborne qualified," he'd said, referring to the fact that she'd completed the Army's grueling parachute training. "They don't make 'em any tougher than that."

"Hoo-ah," Nathan had responded with an exaggerated lack of spirit, then said, "Tough or not, she deserves some warning about what she's transferring into. I'll need to go and talk to her before she makes the commitment to come to D.C."

"You can't be serious! You'll never find anyone else more qualified!" Julian exclaimed.

Nathan had slammed his palm on the top of Julian's desk in frustration. "You may be the only family I have left and you might outrank me, too, but I have to handle this so my honor remains intact when it's over. I can't let her walk blindly into Donner's clutches. She could turn out like all the others and refuse to press charges no matter what the depraved piece of shit does to her. That would be worse than her not coming at all."

"Watch yourself, Captain Fordham," Julian warned. "That depraved piece of shit is a two-star general. Make a mistake and he'll crush you. You want to bring him down, little brother? Put your efforts into gaining her cooperation. For God's sake, Nate, how long can you let him get away with it all?"

Nathan had been asking himself that same question since he'd gone to work for Donner. Again he recalled how he'd been shocked to see the hunted look in Sergeant Walker's eyes. She hadn't been willing to tell Nathan much about what Donner was doing to cause her to change from what her records described as a friendly and capable administrative assistant into a withdrawn shadow of a person. But it didn't take a rocket scientist to figure out what was going on. After a while, he'd gained her trust enough for her to confirm his suspicions.

Major General Walter Cornelius Donner had been sexually harassing her and he'd apparently made a habit of doing so with most of his female subordinates.

CHAPTER TWO

RACHEL GATHERED HER STRENGTH and climbed the last few feet until she could swing her body over to the other side. It was a tricky maneuver on the swaying net and losing her grip could mean a plummet to the huge air cushion below— not deadly, but definitely painful and embarrassing. "Up and over," she said, more for her own courage than for Private MacDonald's. When she was on the other side, she enjoyed the pleasure of success for less than a second before she looked sternly at her teammate. "Your turn."

God bless him, the Private closed his eyes before he did it, but somehow he ended up on her side of the net. There were a few cheers, and then demands to hurry from their other team members waiting below. She and MacDonald exchanged triumphant grins and then wasted no more time before scrambling downward. Down was immeasurably easier than up.

She had no time to catch her breath. The next team had reached the rope climb and several members were already ascending. Two more obstacles lay ahead of Rachel—a belly crawl under planks that could really knock some sense into you if you held your head too high, and a twelve-foot wall that required teamwork to get everyone over. Being smaller than the other soldiers, she wiggled through the crawl faster than most. That put her first of her group to get to the wall. She didn't think twice before getting on all fours so the next soldier could use her back to vault to where he could grasp the top of the wall and pull himself up. One, two, three, four, five grown men put a booted foot on her spine for the split second it took to spring aloft onto the wall. She barely felt it. And the instant the fifth man had passed, she jumped to her feet and held her two arms straight over her head. Strong hands grasped her wrists and in seconds she was hauled skyward.

There came an upwelling of triumph as she balanced on the pinnacle of the wall and realized her team would come in first in this confidence course exercise. With a grin, she dropped to the ground and sprinted the final yards to the finish line where her teammates gleefully clapped her on the back, exactly as they'd slapped one another.

Once again, her gender had not been a hindrance. More than that, her expertise had been the deciding factor in their win. And they all knew it. Rachel reveled in the thrill of conquering prejudice against female soldiers—a huge pride of accomplishment that never seemed to lessen, no matter how many times she proved herself. She'd had to prove herself many, many times since she'd joined the Army seven years earlier.

Even today, the memory lingered of that first time through an obstacle course when her teammate had failed to reach down and lift her over the top the way he should have. That move had automatically put them in last place and the idiot who had failed to help her over the wall never finished basic training. But Rachel had paid an even dearer price. Every time she held up her arms to be lifted over, she wondered if she'd be left behind again.

"Chief Southwell?" said a voice from behind her as she gulped water from the bottle she'd left on the side of the field. "Sorry to bother you out here, but we had an appointment today." The man impugning her ability to keep her calendar straight wore captain's bars on his epaulettes and had a very nice smile.

So nice that Rachel did something she hadn't done in many years. She glanced down and assessed her appearance. Her BDU—battle dress uniform—was caked with mud. The dark stains on her brown Army-issue T-shirt indicated profuse sweating. She knew her damp hair hung in limp clumps below her filthy camouflage cap. But she quickly pushed aside the unexpected concern for her looks in favor of addressing the implication that she'd missed an appointment.

"Sir, I have no meetings scheduled for today," she said calmly. She swept her hand out to take in the soldiers all around her. "This exercise has been on the calendar for months."

He smiled and nodded. "Our administrative assistant tended to confuse things. More often than not she'd make appointments for Wednesday the tenth when Wednesday was on the eleventh. She's gone off to a tour of duty in California now."

The man was so amiable Rachel found herself smiling back at him. She glanced at his name tag. It read Fordham, and she remembered a hurried phone conversation with a woman who'd said Captain Fordham would like to meet with her to discuss her upcoming PCS to the Pentagon. All at once, she recalled that Fordham was the military aide for the man who was soon to be her new boss, Major General Donner.

Though she couldn't help but recall how strange it was for Captain Fordham to want to meet her prior to her transfer, she knew she could not afford to be anything but gracious. She'd have to work with this man for the next couple of years.

"Sir, I'd be glad to talk with you, if you can wait until I get cleaned up," she offered.

"Thanks. The flight from D.C. to North Carolina wasn't too bad, but making my way from Fayetteville Regional Airport to the fort was a nightmare. I'd hate to have to do it again another time. So if you don't mind…" He said this with that ever-so-charming smile of his and Rachel felt her heart do an unexpected little dance.

"Um, it's a bit of a drive to the gym where I can take a shower. How did you get out here to the course?" She looked for a car next to her own and the bus the troops came in on. She didn't see one. He stood on the grassy hill as if he'd materialized there, very dashing in his crisp class B uniform and black beret tilted at the proper cocky angle. He appeared cool and comfortable, despite the humidity-thickened air.

"I hitched a ride with Specialist Stewart from your office. It wasn't too far out of his way. He said your car was out here with you and you could take me back after we talk."

"Yes, that's right," she admitted reluctantly. The last thing she wanted was to be in the confines of her car smelling as pungent as a horse after a long gallop while this man sat in the passenger seat as fresh as though he'd just stepped out of the shower.

"Okay, then," he said, and swept his hand forward like a gentleman allowing a lady to precede him.

Defeated, Rachel waved goodbye to the men she'd run the course with. They responded with a hearty "Airborne!" in unison. Then she led the way to the nearby parking lot. As she approached her car, she realized for the first time that the vehicle was nearly as dirty as she was. Without ceremony, she opened the unlocked door, got behind the wheel and dug the keys out from beneath the floor mat. Captain Fordham settled in beside her.

"That was pretty impressive out there," he commented. "Your team came in first."

She straightened her spine and started the engine, wondering if he was surprised that a female could manage to keep up. "I've had a lot of practice. I like to volunteer to be one of the seasoned soldiers when the new guys first come through. Keeps my skills sharp."

"Yeah, well, you've clearly got skills," he said with admiration. "I don't think I could make it through the first five events."

As she turned onto the road that led to the gym a mile or so away, she glanced at him, secretly assessing his honed physique. Clearly, he was no softy. "Didn't you have to do a confidence course in basic training?"

He scratched at the back of his head and squinted slightly, as if trying to remember. "Honestly, it's all a blur. I'm not really cut out for the grunt-and-groan military stuff. I guess my skills are more mental than physical."

She couldn't decide whether to be amused that he was making himself out to be a wimp or insulted by the implication that she might not be much of a thinker. Somehow, she knew that the man beside her was not a lightweight, but his lack of arrogance about his physical capabilities was refreshing. She had yet to meet a man who didn't feel the need to compete with her athletically. Perhaps Captain Fordham would be the exception.

She pulled into the parking lot outside the gym and paused. "You want to go back up to my office again and wait for me there? I won't be long." Her building sat a few blocks down the road.

He looked at her, then out at the landscape, thick with North Carolina foliage. "It's a nice day. I'll just wait for you here, if you don't mind." He got out of the car when she did and then settled himself in a shady spot on a ledge by the steps to the building that served as a physical training center for the troops at Fort Bragg.

"I'll be back in ten," she said, then she went through the door and headed for the women's locker room.

Getting to her locker without passing a mirror was impossible, and even though she would never have admitted it to a soul, she felt compelled to glance at her reflection. The sight made her groan. She looked like a monster in camouflage. She could scare children, curdle milk, stop clocks.

Unable to remember the last time she'd cared about being attractive to a man, she couldn't quite put her finger on why she would care now. Something to do with Captain Fordham's clean-cut good looks, no doubt. She gave herself a mental shake. If she let herself become interested in Captain Fordham, it would be the worst in a long line of bad decisions about men. He wouldn't be her supervisor, but he still outranked her and they'd have to work together day in and day out at the Pentagon. She could not afford to give him more than polite, professional cordiality. And for that, her looks didn't matter in the least.

Still, she took considerably longer than the ten allotted minutes to clean up and get herself in shape. By the time she finished, however, she was satisfied that the Captain would no longer recognize her. Her brown hair was clean and shiny and blown dry in a neat, chin-length bob. Her cheeks were pink from washing in the hot water. Her light green short-sleeved shirt was pressed; her dark green skirt, hemmed to regulation length. And she stood quite a bit taller in her black patent-leather heels. Placing the maroon beret of the 82nd Airborne Division on her head and adjusting it to one side of her brow, she decided she might have to introduce this new woman to Captain Fordham all over again.

Yet the instant she appeared on the steps in the sunshine, he stood up. "Now you look like your picture," he said with that lethal smile. Her expression must have given away her surprise. "In your official file," he added.

He'd accessed her file from electronic records, she realized. How had he acquired the authority to do that? He wasn't going to be directly in her chain of command, so normally he shouldn't have been granted the right to look over her personnel records. That he'd come all the way to her current duty station to talk with her about a future assignment was odd enough, but to also have read her file… Things were becoming stranger by the minute.

A head-on approach was called for. "You looked in my file?" she asked.

Captain Fordham suddenly appeared less comfortable. "Well, yes. I know this all seems out of the ordinary." He hesitated and glanced around the sun-sprayed area in which they stood. "Can we go somewhere to talk privately?"

"That leaves out my office. I sit in the main reception suite with six other people. How about the coffee shop?" She checked her watch. "At this hour, we might get lucky enough to find a booth open."

"That sounds perfect. Is it far from here?"

"Everything is far from everything else inside Fort Bragg. But we can drive it in a couple of minutes."

Once again, he climbed into her car with her, but at least she smelled like shampoo this time instead of the inside of a locker room after a big game. "I apologize for coming here on the wrong day," he said. "This is one of the many reasons we need you at the Pentagon. It would be great to have someone in charge to get things organized. From the looks of how you handled your team on the field, I can already tell you'd have our operation whipped into shape in no time at all. But before you make the commitment to come to D.C., I want to tell you more about the position."

For the first time since Rachel had met him, Captain Fordham's voice lost some of its warmth. She glimpsed his face from the corner of her eye and saw that his jaw was set and his eyes glinted with some darker emotion. Daunting determination etched his expression.

"Somehow, I have the feeling there's a great deal you need to tell me about this job that isn't in the written position description," she ventured as she passed through the doorway of the newly opened Fort Bragg coffee shop.

"You've got that right," he said grimly.

CHAPTER THREE

NATHAN WAS HONEST ENOUGH with himself to recognize that his weakness for the type of woman sitting across from him in the coffee shop would keep on growing the more he got to know her. But he also recognized that the case he hoped to build against the General would be shattered if he pursued her. This was not the right time to discover whether or not Rachel Southwell could be the woman of his dreams. His dreams would have to wait until the nightmares were taken care of.

Yet, even as he waited for her to order her coffee, those wide amber eyes, so openly curious, drew his gaze. If he hadn't seen her lead a team of burly men through a brutal course in record time, he would not have believed she could. She was just too damn cute. He wanted to flirt, ask her on a date, see if the spark went both ways. But none of that was possible, he reminded himself. Besides, he was a confirmed bachelor who could sense that this particular woman might expect more from him than he could give.

"Well, Captain Fordham, what can you tell me about the position at the Pentagon?" she asked after he'd made small talk until it became obvious he was stalling.

He shifted slightly, finding it difficult to begin now that he had to. "This won't be easy to explain. Any chance we can do this off the record, nonattributionally?"

Her eyebrows shot up and she leaned back in her chair. "Yes, sir. If that's what you want."

"Let's start by scrapping the 'sir.' I'm Nathan." He held out his hand to shake as if he were just meeting her.

Her eyes lit with amusement and she put her hand into his. He liked its warmth and feminine strength. "Then I'm Rachel," she said.

"The thing is, Rachel," he said, enjoying the robust flavor of her name, "General Donner isn't an easy man to work for." He needed to say this carefully. She'd promised she wouldn't attribute these revelations to him, yet he would be foolish to trust her completely right away. He couldn't let himself forget how much damage she could do to his career if she didn't believe him and decided to tell someone about his allegations. He leaned forward a bit and added, "He's especially difficult for women to work for."

Nathan paused to let that sink in. The coffee arrived and he stirred in cream and sugar while he awaited her reaction.

"So, he's another one who doesn't like females in his man's Army," she said with resignation in her voice.

He could see she'd faced that old prejudice before. If only the situation were as simple as that. "No. Actually, he likes women in his Army a little too much. A lot too much, if you know what I mean."

Nathan watched her process the implication. Her eyes wavered slightly as she pondered his words and read between them. After a few seconds, her gaze came to rest steadily on his face again. "Harassment?"

He nodded. Now that she'd said the word, he'd have to spell out the situation, taking the risk of trusting her. At least she seemed to be taking him seriously. "Maybe even sexual abuse," he said. "We've had quite a rapid turnover of female personnel in our office."

She rolled her head to one side for a moment in a defeated posture that spoke volumes. She clearly did not want to tangle with that kind of man. And Nathan didn't blame her. Major General Donner, Chief of Human Resources and Readiness for the Army National Guard and world-class pig, could be the ruin of a career she had obviously worked hard to maintain.

She straightened back up quickly and looked him in the

eyes. He could see the cold determination in the set of her features. "I'll just make certain he knows I won't tolerate any such nonsense."

A huff of exasperation escaped him. "That's what the last personnel technician said. She was completely convinced she could handle him. She was wrong."

Her lips compressed as he saw her frustration mount. She blinked at him. "Are you trying to scare me off? Don't you need someone to straighten out your systems regardless of the General's behavior?"

"Yes, we need you badly. It's never easy to get people to voluntarily transfer to the Pentagon and it's been even harder since the terrorist attack." He leaned forward and looked into her eyes. "But I need to make certain you understand what you'd be getting yourself into."

She said nothing, and instead focused on turning her coffee mug slowly in a circle and watching the steam rise from the surface of the liquid.

"If you're still determined to come to the Pentagon, I'll do everything in my power to help you deal with him." He paused and wondered if he dared to say more than that.

"Why don't you just report him anonymously to Criminal Investigation Division?"

"My brother's with CID. He advised me against it until I find someone willing to testify. The culprit here is a two-star general, after all. But not a single one of Donner's victims has been willing to press charges."

"I would," she said with the same level of determination he'd seen her use on the confidence course. "If what you're telling me turns out to be true." She added this last part with a sensible measure of skepticism in her voice. He couldn't blame her for doubting his story.

"I've had to watch what he does to the women who've come to work with us. I've tried to protect them when I'm physically present, but I can't do much else on my own. Who would believe me without any corroboration?"

"So why should *I* believe you?"

"I can't give you a single reason to trust me." He smiled ruefully and held her gaze.

She nodded and turned her cup slowly around two more times. At last she took a sip, and Nathan wondered how she would take his admission. The only thing he had going for him was that he'd gone to all this trouble to see her without any apparent benefit to himself.

"Why won't the victims testify?" She looked truly bewildered by the idea that women would allow such behavior to go on without consequences.

"You'd think I would know the answer to that, just coming off a tour in psychological operations in central Asia, but I don't understand it very well myself. The local shrink on post—who never realized I was telling him about a two-star general—says it has something to do with the effect his behavior has on the victim's self-esteem. Donner wears the women down, uses threats against their careers or families to convince them it's hopeless to charge him. Truthfully, I'm not certain how or why he manages to get away with what he does."

"So what will you do if I refuse, too?" A glint in her eyes that told him she was testing him, but he couldn't imagine what she hoped to learn.

"The truth is, Chief, if you aren't willing to help me deal with him, I hope to God you find somewhere else to PCS. I do not want to have to stand by and see him hurt you."

"I can take care of myself," she asserted, but he could see a measure of doubt wavering in her eyes.

"I read your file and I saw you on the confidence course, so I won't argue about that. But this guy is not playing fair." He took a swig of coffee while he tried to get a grip on the anger that threatened to surface whenever he thought about Donner's behavior. "It's one thing to train for war and learn ways to survive abuse from an enemy. It's a whole other thing to be tormented by your own commander. If you think you'll be able to simply endure it for your entire tour without trying to put an end to it, then I have to beg you not to come."

"Well, you can forget about begging, because I'm taking the job at the Pentagon." Clearly, she was not going to be swayed easily from this decision.

Nathan took a deep breath and let it out. "Then help me stop him," he urged softly. "I've had enough psych classes to understand that the hope of ending his reign of terror might help you hang on to your self-esteem." He watched her expressive face as she considered his plea.

"Look," she said after a while, "I don't know you. You seem sincere and I appreciate that you came all the way here to warn me, but I'm going to have to make my own determination regarding General Donner."

He nodded. Her caution was admirable. "Just do me one favor before you pack up and head north," he said as he pulled out a folded paper from his pocket. It had Sergeant Walker's name and number on it. "Call her and ask what it was like to work for Donner. She probably won't tell you a whole lot, but I think she'll try to warn you off as best she can. That should help you decide whether I'm telling you the truth."

"It's not that I don't believe you, sir..." she began.

He held up his hand to ward off her protest. "I'm glad you aren't willing to just take my word for it. What I'm alleging is serious stuff. It makes sense that you'd want to see how things are for yourself." He slugged down the last of his coffee. "If you change your mind about taking the position, I'll understand. But if you come to the Pentagon, I hope you'll give some thought to helping me stop him."

RACHEL THOUGHT ABOUT IT for days. The last thing she needed when she finally returned to her hometown of Annandale, Virginia, was to be distracted by a general with groping hands. But even if half of what Captain Fordham had said turned out to be true, she'd be up to her eyeballs in trouble at the office she needed to transfer into. According to the bits and pieces Sergeant Walker had been willing to share by phone, Captain Fordham had not exaggerated the situation.

Without a doubt, Rachel wouldn't be able to silently put up with harassment for long. She hadn't made it this far in the U.S. Army by letting men walk all over her. And when she butted heads with the General, her career would be as good as over. But how could she turn down the opportunity to transfer after waiting so long for something to open up? She could wait months, even years, for another chance to transfer home. That was something she was not willing to do. She'd already told Adam she'd be coming home to stay by the end of June when her tour at Fort Bragg finally concluded.

Sighing deeply, she headed to the kitchen of her Army-issue apartment. The clock told her she had ten more minutes to wait until she would see Adam's smiling face light up her computer screen through their respective video phones.

She put water on for tea, foraged in her cupboards for cookies, then waited for the tea to steep and for the minutes to drag by. It was a ritual she'd been following every day for three years, ever since she'd first figured out how to set up the video-phone system through her Internet provider.

At last, she heard the delightful chirp of the computer alerting her to an incoming call. Before she could scurry into the living room and set herself in front of the camera, she heard a youthful voice call out, "Mom?"

"Here I am," she said with a smile as she skidded to a halt in line with the camera eye. And her heart sang with joy to look upon his eight-year-old face. "How're you doing, Adam Ant?"

"I'm okay," he said in a world-weary voice that alerted Rachel that something was amiss.

"Just okay?"

"Well," he said, holding her gaze from the computer

screen, "I had to sit out from dodgeball in gym class again today."

"Having some trouble breathing again?"

"Yeah." Clearly, he was very unhappy about this.

"When I'm home for good, we're going to get you in to see a specialist. We'll figure out how to fix you up, I promise."

His eyes brightened. "Only one more week, right?"

She matched his grin. "Yup. Only one more week." Then she'd be home to live with her pride and joy after seven long years away. Even the prospect of dealing with General Donner couldn't dampen her enthusiasm for this long-awaited PCS.

"I can't wait!"

"Me, neither. Hey, how are the grandparents?" She asked this cautiously, wondering how he would express the changes he'd seen lately in the man he looked up to as a father.

"Grandma's okay. She bossed me around yesterday, making me do a thousand chores."

Rachel smiled at his beleaguered tone. "And Grandpa?" she prodded.

Adam pursed his lips to one side of his face, a quirk that told Rachel he was thinking about something important. "He talks better now. Grandma makes him walk a little every day. He says he needs to get his land legs back so he can play ball with me again," said her son.

Rachel wondered if her father would ever be able to play much with Adam. "I'm glad he's working at it." When she'd visited him a few months ago, right after his stroke, he hadn't seemed predisposed to giving recovery much effort. This was Bernard Southwell's second stroke, the first one being right after Adam had been born. Eight years ago, he'd tried hard to get back to normal. But this one had really knocked the spirit out of him.

Adam nodded thoughtfully. "He didn't try very hard at first. Grandma said so. But then he said he saw me playing outside and decided there was still some fun left in him after all. Will he stay stuck this way?'' he asked.

Rachel smiled reassuringly but didn't want to make false promises to her son. "Depends a lot on him. You just keep reminding him of all the fun he has left in him, and I bet he'll keep on improving.''

"Grandpa's getting old.'' Adam made this observation with the seriousness of a sage.

She nodded. Her father had been a little older than most dads, but he'd loved his only child to distraction. She'd been the apple of his eye, until her last year in high school when she'd screwed up big-time. Even then, he hadn't condemned her. He'd just grown a little quieter and sometimes he'd ask her if he could have done things better by her. "Yes, he's getting older now,'' she agreed.

"I liked him better the other way,'' Adam said. "I miss playing basketball with him.''

"I know, sweetie. Maybe in time you'll think of other things you can do together. We love him no matter what, don't we?''

Adam nodded again and his eyes lit with mischief. "You love *me* no matter what, too. Right, Mom? Even if I got in trouble for chewing bubble gum on the school bus.''

She tried to look stern as she said, "You know you're not supposed to chew gum on the bus, Adam.''

"I forgot. And besides, I had to show Brian that I too could blow two bubbles at the same time.''

"Such talent,'' she said dryly. "Try not to forget again,'' she advised, even as she felt the tug of a smile overcoming her conviction that this was a moment for serious parenting.

They talked for another half hour, until Rachel's mother sent Adam to wash his hands for dinner. Then Virginia Southwell took her place in front of the screen, her expression tired and careworn.

"What did that Captain Somebody-or-other have to say about your new job at the Pentagon?'' she asked. Rachel had forgotten she'd mentioned Captain Fordham's pending visit to her mother the week before.

"He said I seem like the sort of person who can whip his office back into shape. They've been without a personnel tech for a while." Under no circumstances would Rachel confess the true nature of Captain Fordham's message. The woman had enough to worry about right now.

"You've come a long way, Rachel," her mother said with a proud smile. But then her expression sobered. "Did that boy of yours tell you about the school bus problem?" she asked.

Rachel suppressed a grin. "Yes, he told me. What's the penalty going to be?"

"No gum for two weeks." Adam absolutely loved bubble gum.

"Very clever. That'll really get his attention." She and her mother had both become masters at devising consequences for Adam's occasional transgressions. Their creativity had been paying off. Adam was well behaved without lacking in spirit.

"So, you'll be home in a week?" Her mother liked to review information already received, just as Adam did.

Rachel nodded. "I'll be glad to get home to give you a hand. I know how hard it's been for you to care for Adam and Dad at the same time." Her mother had stoically dealt with everything dished out to her over the years. But when her husband had gone from a fairly robust seventy-year-old housepainter to nearly an invalid in a single day, she had lost some of her usual sparkle. Even months later, he couldn't do a whole lot for himself, and Virginia waited on him day and night.

"I'm just glad you can fix it now so Adam will be covered under your military benefits and we can get his asthma looked at. When your father stopped working, our health insurance got so complicated."

More than just their health insurance had grown complicated since her father had suddenly been disabled. Money was tight, too. Bernard Southwell had never planned on retiring.

Both her parents had been wonderful with Adam while she'd pursued her military career. But Rachel could no longer ask her parents to bear the burden of caring full-time for an energetic eight-year-old boy. As much as they loved Adam, Rachel needed to return home and pick up the responsibilities she'd been compelled to hand over to her mother and father seven years ago.

NATHAN SAT JUST BEHIND his commanding officer in one of the larger Senate hearing rooms on Capitol Hill. He watched Donner work the senators who sat around the semicircular table on the dais set imperiously in front of their own table on the floor of the room. From their higher vantage point, they pelted the General with questions. It was this sort of scenario that exposed Donner for the capable and amazingly effective leader he could be. With the aplomb of a seasoned politician and the spine of a hardened warrior, General Donner manipulated every response into a point of his own.

All for the betterment of the Army National Guard.

One of the more verbose senators spoke. "Now, General, you say you need to recruit more Guardsmen, and that you can't do that without better pay and additional benefits. Now, don't get me wrong here, because I'm a real supporter of our men and women in uniform, but as I see it, we're already spending a whopping big wad of money on your Guard—and for what? It's the Regular Army and the Reserves who are taking care of the real business with this war on terrorism."

"Sir," the General began, for he never forgot that these civilians believed that they outranked him by a wide margin and could be wooed easily by deference from a two-star general. "Let me draw your attention to your packets of information I had sent over for you last week." He shuffled through one such packet that he had at the ready in front of him. After bringing forth a particular sheet, he held it up. Even from their lofty perches on the dais, the senators would be able to read the bold title on the document.

"This is a brief list of some of the benefits our country reaps from a strong National Guard. And public sentiment toward the Guard has never been higher. As you can see…" He highlighted some of the data, taking particular care to note the humanitarian assistance the Guard had provided to recent disaster victims in the home state of one of the senators sitting before him. His delivery was such that it wasn't an obvious ploy, yet the senator who now remembered the heroic deeds of the military folks during the devastation could be seen nodding in agreement with whatever the General said.

One down, Nathan thought as he tried to guess how the General would shrewdly bag all the others in turn. He knew the material almost as well as Donner, having been the one to pull it all together in the current format to the General's specifications. But it was the manipulation of that data that made Major General Donner so damn good at what he did. He had to hand it to Donner; the man was a master. Nathan struggled with a grudging respect and admiration for this side of the man who could do so much good for the National Guard and yet abuse certain individual members without any apparent shred of conscience. This contrast made him seem doubly dangerous to Nathan.

"As you know, the Army National Guard of the commonwealth of Virginia was called up for duty during the recent security scare…" the General said next. He went on to enumerate what the Guard had done for Virginia.

Ah, so that was how he would do it. Donner would pick off the senators one by one, finding ways to work in some significant achievement of the Guard from each state. Or commonwealth, as the case might be. Nathan stifled a smile at the way Donner never seemed to slip up on small points that could impact one of these old-timers in a huge way. Mistaking a commonwealth for a state, or vice versa, would be the kiss of death in terms of seducing a senator into voting for whatever the General needed.

The only person on the panel at this hearing before the Armed Services Committee whom Nathan couldn't imagine General Donner luring to his point of view was the Honorable Barbara Zemin of Hawaii. As crusty and sharp as an old warhead left on the bottom of the sea too long, and just as dangerous, she wasn't moved one iota by General Donner's seemingly unrehearsed eloquence.

As if to prove that she wasn't, the Senator coughed loudly in the middle of one of Donner's sentences, and when the General paused for a split second, her voice plunged into the breach.

"General Donner, I'd like you to address the incident at Fort DeRussy," she said in a clear, no-nonsense voice.

Nathan stifled a groan. Of all the questions that could have diverted the General from his God-given talent as an advocate for the Army National Guard, this was it. And as the silence vibrated in the suddenly charged air of the Senate hearing room, he could almost feel Donner fighting the urge to utter the slur he'd called this particular senator before and tell the bitch to go straight to hell.

"I have not been authorized to speak to you today about that issue, ma'am. But I'd be glad to respond to written questions you—"

"You mean, you're not prepared, General. Not prepared to address an issue that the public is keenly interested in. Not willing, perhaps, to respond to the justified outrage of our citizens in regard to what apparently happened at Fort DeRussy, Hawaii."

General Donner shifted slightly in his chair. The movement would have been imperceptible, except that Nathan was seated directly behind him, ready to hand over papers or deliver some small fact that the General might request from the files the pair of them had brought to the hearing. The General's adjustment to his position was not for added comfort but in preparation for battle. Nathan knew this from experience. He dreaded what would come next if Donner didn't get a grip on his anger. As much as it could solve his problems if Donner ruined his own career right here in front of Senator Zemin, Nathan hoped he wouldn't. If his boss lost his cool, Nathan would have to mop up the mess afterward. That was what a general's aide did, after all.

"The facts are not all known yet in regard to the alleged altercation at Fort DeRussy." He delivered this calmly enough, but Nathan suspected the General clenched his teeth in his effort to hold back the blasting he longed to deliver to the woman confronting him.

"What we know, General, is that law-abiding women in uniform were mistreated and embarrassed by fellow soldiers—all men, some members of the regular Army and others who were members of your National Guard—and that civilian men came to their defense. What followed was a melee that hit the front page of the *Waikiki Times*. And you have nothing to say?"

Nathan was quite certain Donner had a great deal he would like to say. Among the comments a creep like the General might want to make would be one implicating the female soldiers as probable instigators who asked for trouble and deserved what they got, thus making the females at fault for the entire debacle. Or maybe not. Truthfully, Nathan hadn't yet figured out exactly what General Donner thought about women in the Army. Except for his inability to leave them alone sexually, he never indicated, by word or deed, that women should not be welcome in the military. In fact, he fought doggedly for benefits for female soldiers geared to put them on an even footing with the men. Just last month he had been working his circuit, advocating better methods of child-support collection for mothers in the Army dealing with deadbeat fathers.

"Indications are that tensions are high throughout the military, including at Fort DeRussy. I'd be glad to go out to Hawaii as soon as my other duties permit and investigate the matter personally. Before then, I will respond to written questions, ma'am,'' he said again, stonewalling now to effectively shut her down.

Before she could renew her onslaught, the Senator from the state where the National Guard had been working miracles grew impatient with Senator Zemin and said, ''He told you he'd investigate and respond to written questions, so let's agree that he'll do that so we can get back to the purpose or our hearing today. Shall we?''

Nathan relaxed his shoulders. He might think General Donner was a certifiable bottom feeder, given his mistreatment of subordinate females, but he did not want to be sitting behind him as his aide when a senator goaded him into a disastrous explosion. And besides, there was work to be done here—honest work for the good of the National Guard.

Oddly enough, General Donner was the very best man to get that work done on behalf of both the men and women of the Guard.

If only Donner would suddenly discover an ability to control his baser side, Nathan would work under the General with great pride. Instead, his ambivalence toward the man was driving him insane. Especially since Donner had already hinted—by slapping Nathan on the back after he'd reviewed Southwell's file and heartily approving of the choice—that the new personnel tech was slated to be his next victim even though she hadn't reported for duty yet. As Nathan listened to the hearing drone on, he half wished Senator Zemin would take the floor again and stick it to the General. The Guard would lose an advocate, but Rachel would be out of harm's way. And the more he thought about the Chief, the more important it seemed to protect her.

He looked toward Zemin, wondering if she could be of any use in his campaign to stop Donner. Then suddenly he realized the Senator was looking back. She held his gaze with that cunning stare she was so famous for and Nathan found it hard to avert his eyes. When he finally did, he felt a sheen of sweat on his brow. That woman saw too much. And the last thing he needed was to become one of her pawns.

Yet he found himself glancing surreptitiously at the older woman one more time, wondering if she could afford any protection to his career and Rachel's if things got rough with Donner. The possibilities bore further consideration, he decided. He would begin his research on Zemin as soon as he returned to the office.

A WEEK LATER, RACHEL BID goodbye to Iron Mike, the beloved statue that guarded Fort Bragg. The drive from North Carolina to Virginia was long, but she was glad to have the quiet hours in which to collect her thoughts regarding this move. Imagining what it would be like to live with her parents after all these years of independence was hard. The possibilities bore considerable analysis. If not for Adam, Rachel would have found a place of her own, near enough to help with her father but far enough to maintain her life without the scrutiny of her parents. But the house where she'd been raised was the only home Adam had ever known and she couldn't bring herself to uproot him. At least not right away.

As she drove, she also reviewed in her mind some of what she'd read at the Fort Bragg library on how to deal with sexual harassment. She'd already decided that she would turn the guy in if he tried anything. With or without the help of Captain Fordham. This thought prompted her to check the dashboard clock. It was not yet fifteen hundred hours. She decided now was a good time to give the Captain a call to let him know her schedule.

When she had him on the other end of her cell phone, he was all business. Nothing like the friendly, open individual with the smiling brown eyes she'd met before.

"So, you're really coming, despite my warnings," he said.

"I told you I would be, both in person and on the phone last week when my orders arrived."

"Don't get me wrong, Chief. We need you here."

"I'm looking forward to the work, sir."

"I just don't want this PCS to end up being the ruin of your stellar career," he added with more warmth in his voice. He seemed genuinely concerned.

"I'll be fine, Captain. I'm not new to the Army."

"Seven years and some amazing progress in that time." He sounded as though he was smiling now.

She smiled, too. "Been going through my personnel file again, I see."

She was certain she heard amusement in his voice when he said, "I need to learn all there is to know about you." His tone, and the slight pause that followed, seemed to fill those words with alternative meanings. "And everyone else who works for General Donner, of course."

Rachel felt a little tug in the region of her solar plexus. Was he flirting with her? Impossible! No, not exactly impossible. Sergeant Walker had volunteered that Captain Fordham wasn't married—not that a wife would necessarily stand in the way of some determined men.

A long-dormant part of her wished the Captain really was flirting. She hadn't forgotten the unexpected attraction she'd felt when she'd been in front of him physically. Knowing the danger of such feelings, to her career and to her heart, she pushed these uncharacteristic thoughts aside.

"I wanted to tell you I'll be in-processing first thing in the morning. I should be reporting to the office by Thursday, 0800."

"That'll be fine, Chief. You be sure to let me know if you need anything. I'm supposed to be your sponsor," he pointed out, referring to the practice of having a person already well established at the duty station take the new arrival under his wing. "You never told me if you have a place to stay or if you can find your way around."

"Yes and yes," she replied. "I have my living arrangements all squared away and I'm familiar with the area. If I have any trouble in-processing, I'll call you.''

On that promise, they ended their conversation, and Rachel spent the rest of her drive wondering if this rekindled interest in the opposite gender applied to all men or just Nathan Fordham. She hoped it wasn't the latter, because pursuing the charming Captain when they would be working so closely together wouldn't be wise.

Perhaps she should start dating on a more regular basis, she thought. Her career was as settled as it ever would be, and she wasn't likely to be required to PCS away from the area for a long time. She'd been out with men at her various duty stations in the past—there were always so many attractive men to choose from wherever she went for the Army—but nothing had ever come of any of those efforts. She'd been so busy with her career that she hadn't really been looking for anything serious then. And she understood her early experience with Adam's father made her wary of men and their promises. But maybe she should think about finding a decent relationship. For Adam's sake, as well as her own.

Before another hour had gone by, Rachel found herself pulling up beneath the overhanging trees alongside the curb in front of her parents' house. She spotted her Adam Ant immediately, playing a solitary game of basketball at the hoop over the garage door. He needed a haircut and he'd grown at least another inch since she'd last seen him, but there was no mistaking his full-tilt approach to the baskets he dunked. Rachel emerged from the car, then stood and watched him play for a minute. Her heart felt as though it would expand to bursting with love and happiness. She was home to live with her precious boy for the first time since he was a year old.

''Mom!'' Adam shouted, sighting her from where he had run for the basketball after swooshing a no-netter. He stood stock-still near the dogwood tree that decorated the slightly overgrown front lawn, almost as if he couldn't believe his eyes. Then he suddenly came to life again and ran toward her in an all-out sprint.

Rachel moved around the car and trotted in his direction, and when he was nearly upon her, she stooped and wrapped her arms around him so she could whirl him in a circle while he clung to her in a fierce embrace. He smelled like the outdoors and the earth and maybe a little like chocolate pudding, but underneath all that there was the hint of that scent that was uniquely Adam. In her mind it recalled the fragrance of his babyhood, and suddenly she remembered rocking him to sleep when he could still fit in the crook of her arm. Sometimes, when she was far away from him, she would wake up in the night with that scent in her nostrils and she would weep with longing. Even with him wrapped around her neck in a choke hold, she still felt that old yearning in her heart. She had last seen him in person only three months before when her father had suffered his stroke and she'd come home on leave briefly. But, as always, it seemed as if she hadn't seen her boy in aeons, as if she would never get enough of him, as if she would die if she were parted from him again.

This time there would be no parting. She was home to stay. And if another PCS was in her future and she found herself moving to another military post, she would have to take Adam with her. She simply could not bear another separation.

Letting him down so he could stand on his feet again, Rachel found she couldn't quit hugging him, so she dropped to her knees and forced him to endure many kisses all over his face. When she pulled back to look at him, she saw that he was laughing—and breathing a little hard. She wanted to ask about his asthma, but at the same time she didn't want to make him overly focused on this condition that had taken hold of him in recent months. It was Adam's breathing problems, even more than her father's stroke, that had urged her to return home as soon as possible. She watched him pop up and down on his toes in glee, noticed his breaths were even and not too labored. Her worry eased. For the moment, he would be okay.

"I'm so glad to be home," she said.

"I'm glad, too!" Then his eyes lost some of their initial elation. His expression grew deeply earnest. He braced her face between his two small hands to hold her still and capture her gaze with his own. "You're home for good, right? No more leaving." He said this as if speaking it once more would seal the promise she had made many times since her decision to return home.

Fighting tears that she longed to shed for the innumerable days and hours and minutes she had not been with him, Rachel nodded. "We're going to live together from now on, Adam. I promise."

"And we'll live here with Grandma and Grandpa, unless someday the Army needs you someplace else." The last part was said while he eyed her carefully. It was a test. She had gone away on orders from the Army so frequently, perhaps he couldn't quite believe she wouldn't do so again.

"If the Army wants me to move someplace else, then you'll just have to come with me."

He brightened at that. "We'll see the world!"

"Sure," she agreed, happy and a little relieved that he would be eager to live elsewhere with her when the time came.

"And Grandma and Grandpa, too!" He said this as if it were a foregone conclusion rather than a question and Rachel didn't have the heart to indicate otherwise. Parting him from them would not be easy and she refused to worry about it before she had to.

Adam was a shrewd child and—though she recognized she might be partial in this estimation—exceptionally intelligent. Nothing got past him. His suddenly pensive expression told her that he noticed that she'd failed to agree with him about his grandparents, but he was sensitive enough not to press the issue. Instead, he tugged on her a little and said, "Come on! We have to get all your stuff put away in the house."

She saw that this was important to him, perhaps because she'd always lived out of suitcases. "My stuff is coming by truck in the next couple of days. The Army is shipping everything here. So I'm afraid I only have a car full of luggage for now."

"But we can put everything in the drawers and then bring the suitcases to the attic, right?"

"Right," she agreed readily. She would agree to do almost anything he wanted if it would make him happy right now. No matter how tired she was from the long drive, she would fold away every last sock and stow those suitcases into the barely accessible attic if that was what her boy wanted. Nothing would spoil this homecoming for Adam if she could help it.

He'd waited his entire life for it.

CHAPTER FOUR

WHEN RACHEL ARRIVED FOR the first time at the Pentagon office suite she was assigned to, she stood in the doorway, stunned once again by that certain something Captain Fordham had. Focused on his computer with a studious expression, he looked almost ordinary with his basic brown hair and eyes and unremarkable features. Yet he held himself just so and his eyes were bright with intelligence. She knew that he would come alive with an abundance of charm and his lips would turn up into a glorious smile when he finally saw her. Luckily, she had a moment to prepare herself for the onslaught of that dazzling charisma she remembered all too well. She took a deep breath to compose herself, then she walked toward his desk. She was right in front of him before he glanced up.

And there it was. That heart-stopping grin curved his mouth and the light of interest danced in his eyes. *Get a grip, soldier,* she told herself just before she raised her hand for a precision salute. "Sir, Chief Warrant Officer Southwell reporting for duty." She was a little surprised her words had come out so clear and even.

With what seemed to be amusement on his face, he touched his fingers to his brow in a casual salute and Rachel dropped her hand to her side. She remained at attention, looking straight ahead. Looking anywhere but at his beguiling smile.

"At ease, Chief," he said. "Have a seat." He indicated the chair by his desk. His gaze fell to her left hand, which held her headgear. "Wearing the black beret now, I see. I was partial to the maroon one."

"Had to give it up," she said, trying not to be rattled by the admiration in his eyes. "I'm not with the 82nd Airborne anymore." Few men thought well of her ability to complete combat-type training. This man's obvious appreciation only added to his appeal.

She reminded herself that she'd been surrounded for seven years by the healthiest and hunkiest men the world had to offer—U.S. Army soldiers of every make and model. She had prided herself on maintaining a measure of detachment when on duty. Otherwise, she would have found it difficult to get any work done with so many masculine distractions surrounding her day in and day out. This man sitting in front of her should be no different from any of the others she'd worked with. That was what she needed to keep reminding herself.

"It's good to see you," he said, and something in his voice—or perhaps in her imagination—made it sound as though he meant more than a polite comment. "Despite your phone call en route a few days ago, I was a little worried you wouldn't actually show up."

She took in the suite, trying to get a feel for the place. There were three other desks in the reception area with Captain Fordham's. Two were vacant and one had a very youthful-looking male specialist sitting at it. He tapped continuously on a keyboard.

"Besides the things we talked about at Fort Bragg, the files are a mess," Nathan added. "You'll see for yourself soon enough. Let's just say you'll have your work cut out for you to get our records in shape. I think our predecessors were still using whatever the system was before MARKS," he said, referring to the modern army record-keeping system. It was one of the many information control systems in which she was an expert.

She smiled. She would enjoy setting things straight. "We'll get you squared away in no time at all, sir."

He nodded as though he never doubted that she would. "Guess you didn't need my help with in-processing," he said almost wistfully. "But at least I can show you around and introduce you to everyone." He hesitated, glancing at the closed door just behind his desk. The name above it indicated it was the General's office. When she turned her attention back to the Captain, his expression had lost all humor.

He appeared to grit his teeth as he stood, and she watched in fascination as the muscles tightened and released along his jaw. He faced the General's office as if it contained a man-eating lion instead of their commanding officer.

Getting to her feet again, she clenched her beret. "If it wouldn't be too much trouble, I'd like to meet the General sooner rather than later."

"Well, you're in luck," he said grimly. "He's awaiting your arrival." But instead of moving forward, the Captain stood in place. In a hushed voice he confided, "He probably won't bother you at first. He'll seem very charming and dignified. Enjoy it while it lasts. And at the first sign of trouble, you come straight to me and—"

"Sir, with all due respect, I know what to do at the first sign of trouble," she said gently, wanting to reassure him—and maybe herself, too.

He took it in the spirit it was intended. "I just bet you do," he said as he mustered a lopsided half grin for her. He rang the General on the intercom and asked permission to enter.

"Ready?" he asked as he put his hand on the doorknob and looked back over his shoulder.

Her heartbeat accelerated at the concern in his eyes. She remembered that this man was prepared to risk his career to help her if she needed him. That was an almost irresistible characteristic for a woman who had been on her own for so long.

Can't have him, she reminded herself. "I'm ready, sir." Then she followed him inside.

"General Donner, this is Chief Warrant Officer Rachel Southwell, our new personnel technician."

Rachel stepped up beside Captain Fordham and saluted her commanding officer. She did her best not to gape at the older man. She hadn't expected him to be handsome enough to grace a magazine cover. He put Nathan Fordham's good looks completely to shame. The General's hair was blond and only hinted at gray near his temples. He had the bluest eyes she had ever seen. In his youth, he would have been devastating. Even in his late fifties, he was exceptionally handsome. If this man was a sexual harasser, it wasn't because he'd have trouble getting attention from women through more dignified means.

The General returned her salute. "At ease," he said in a deep, slightly gravelly voice that would hold a person's attention. "Captain, I'll talk with the Chief for a while and call you when she's ready for a tour of the place," he said, effectively dismissing the younger man.

Fordham nodded once at Donner, then glanced at Rachel as he left the room. Their eye contact seemed deeply intimate for the split second that it lasted. They were conspirators, in a way. Internally, she felt repelled by the thought of plotting against her superior officer—something that directly opposed her years of military training—but she sensed that the Captain would not have suggested it if he'd known of any other way.

Nathan slipped through the door and quietly closed it behind him, as was clearly called for in this situation. But after what she'd been told about Donner, the click of the latch made her edgy. Looking back at the General, she felt perspiration crawl from her pores. But she worked at maintaining a neutral expression and kept her body very still, refusing to let the man see her sweat.

"Sit down, Ms. Southwell," he said, using the more formal salutation for a warrant officer rather than the casual

"Chief." "How was your trip here?" he asked congenially.

"Fine, sir. In-processing went smoothly, too."

He nodded and smiled, exhibiting perfectly straight white teeth. "So tell me a little about yourself. Family? Hobbies?"

Her tension went up another notch as she remembered from her reading on harassment at the Fort Bragg library that her family might be used to manipulate her. She wouldn't be foolish enough to tell him anything about her son or parents if she could help it. Instead, she responded to the second question. "I play basketball as often as I can. Actually, I like just about any sport. To play, that is. I'm not much for watching them on television."

"Ah, excellent. I'll have you show me what you can do when we do PT together," he said as he leaned back in his chair, eyeing her. For a moment she thought he was suggesting that they go out for physical training alone, just the two of them. But then he added, "The office staff members go running together in the afternoons when we can, but if it's hot or we feel like it, we go to the POAC to play volleyball or maybe shoot some hoops."

Rachel remembered that POAC was an acronym for the Pentagon gym, though she couldn't remember what the letters stood for exactly. "I'd be glad to join you," she said. And she meant it. The sheer physicality of military life was one of the many things that kept her signing on tour after tour.

"From the looks of your athletic record, seems we'll need you on our team when we have our annual face-off with the Reserves Office."

She had to smile at that. She knew she would be an asset to their team, especially when the game was basketball. She didn't like to brag, but her ability handling the ball as a point guard had been legendary at her previous duty station. "Just let me know when and where, sir."

She relaxed a little after that as they talked about the

work of the Human Resources and Readiness Office and
about her duties specifically. Then the General casually informed her that she would do just fine as long as she followed orders. This last remark brought her back to full
alert. She'd expected him to say that she would do just fine
as long as she did her job well. This was an office, not the
middle of a conflict—terrorist attacks notwithstanding.
There shouldn't be too many opportunities for Donner to
be delivering military-style orders. It seemed an odd thing
for him to say, especially given the way he looked right
into her eyes when he'd said it.

As she left the General's presence, she wondered if he'd
intended the comment as some kind of warning. But when
a concerned Captain Fordham appeared before her in the
outer office, asking how the meeting had gone, she momentarily forgot what she might have asked about the General's comment and what it might mean.

"Fine, sir," she managed to say, and the Captain looked
so relieved she decided Donner's comment wasn't worth
sharing.

"Conversation could become fairly burdensome if you
insist on 'sir-ing' me all the time, Rachel." Her first name
coming from his lips gave her a jolt. "Officers tend to use
first names with one another in the Pentagon," he explained
as she fought a blush that was creeping upward to where
it would soon be visible above her collar.

"Um, yes, sir," she said. When he huffed a little laugh
and shook his head in defeat, she realized her mistake. "I'll
work on it," she promised, sure she must be pink-cheeked
by now. Calling him Nathan felt so intimate. Doing so
would defeat that imaginary barrier she needed to keep between them in order to remain aloof. And if there was anyone in this vast, five-sided building she should remain aloof
from, it had to be Nathan Fordham.

"Time to introduce you to everyone else," he said as he
swept out his hand for her to precede him through the door.

With something very akin to the fear and thrill she used

to feel just before she jumped out of an airplane, she walked along the corridors of the Pentagon beside the Captain. But after a few hours of introductions and sightseeing through the complex corridors of the enormous building, Rachel realized that her efforts to think of the man as "the Captain" had failed miserably. He was friendly and unpretentious and everyone liked him. All the other officers called him Nathan.

And so did Rachel—at least, in her thoughts, by the time they had circled back up the wide ramped corridor that led to the cafeteria on the second floor.

"So just remember that the corridors are like spokes, and break the building into ten pieces," he said. "And there are five concentric rings, A being the smallest inner ring and E being the largest along the outer perimeter."

"Except that the rings don't go all the way around anymore since that plane took out one side of the building," she said. "That part is still under repair."

His expression grew serious at this reminder of America's nightmare the previous year. "I wasn't stationed here when that happened, but I was told that section had been under repair even before the attack. Most of the long-term civilians don't really notice much different about coming to work here every day. But the renovations make it harder than usual to find your way around. Nowadays, you can't just go to the A ring and keep walking along the circle until you're where you want to be."

"If I can parachute out of a plane and then find my way to the checkpoint in the middle of an unfamiliar forest, I guess I can figure this place out," she said, hoping she could. She would have to consider bringing a compass with her to work.

"Airborne!" he said playfully, and she found herself smiling back into his eyes, even though she knew she shouldn't allow herself this easy camaraderie with him. She sensed how swiftly it could turn into more than she could handle right now.

"Maybe tomorrow you can take one of the tours. They start down on the Concourse on the hour until 1300 hours and are worth the time. You want to get lunch?" he asked.

"Um, sure." She followed him into the cafeteria, wondering if he spent so much time with all the new staff members. Part of her hoped he was making a special effort for her, and another dreaded the possibility. Keeping her attraction to him under control was hard enough. If he returned the interest, resistance would be futile.

A WEEK LATER, NATHAN FOUND himself suffering under the weight of violently conflicted feelings over the presence of Chief Southwell in his office.

On the one hand, she took charge of the badly managed personnel systems, to his relief. He had tried to deal with the basic stuff but hadn't done any of it right, and most everything else had gone unattended. Her upbeat and proactive personality had become an inspiration to them all. In only a few days, she had cheered everyone's spirits with her can-do attitude and efficient attention to detail. Also, he couldn't say he minded having her to look at from his desk, which sat directly across the room from hers.

On the other hand, he had to look at her all day long, and it required a force of will to keep from being seriously distracted by her presence. As this contradiction formed coherently in his mind, he lifted his gaze and saw that she had gone down on her hands and knees to rummage beneath her desk for something. The dark green material of her uniform slacks stretched tautly over her tight little derriere, making his mouth water. He told himself to look away or else risk actual arousal, but he couldn't make himself do it. And he paid the expected price.

"What's the problem, Chief?" he asked, speaking a little more gruffly than he'd intended but forgiving himself considering the provocation.

She crawled backward, sat on her heels and blinked at

him. Her cheeks grew pink and he wondered if she realized the visual she had treated him to. "Sorry," she said.

Oh, how he wanted to assure her that *he* wasn't sorry at all, but he knew that such a comment could be taken the wrong way. Her thinking he was coming on to her and labeling him a harasser right along with the General would be unbearable. "Is something broken?"

"Uh, my mouse came unplugged," she explained, still on her knees. By way of proof, she held up the end of the cord, which she'd retrieved from the corner beneath her desk.

"I see. Well..." He hesitated. Should he tell her to go ahead and fix the thing, which would put her back in that provocative position? Or should he offer to do it for her? He rose halfway out of his seat to take charge of the situation, but she held up her hand.

"I've got it, really. Not a problem." She put her lovely backside on the seat of her desk chair, slid into position in front of her computer, reached to the back of her keyboard, where a loose extension wire hung limply over the tray, and deftly plugged the mouse cord back into the end of it.

Show over, his blood pressure began to drop back down to normal. At least, until he sensed that the General was standing in his doorway just behind him. Nathan glanced over his shoulder, wondering how long the man had been there. Long enough to see Rachel under her desk, if the General's interested gaze meant anything. The expression on the older man's face as he looked across the room toward Rachel, who was innocently tapping on her keyboard, made Nathan's skin crawl.

"You did well, Captain," Donner said with a leering grin. "She's going to work out very nicely here. You picked an excellent example of womanhood for me."

Resisting a shudder of revulsion, Nathan casually pointed out that he'd had nothing to do with Rachel's assignment to the office. "She wanted to come to the D.C. area and the regular Army HR folks matched her up with us," he explained. The last thing Nathan wanted was for anyone, especially Donner, to think he would get women into the office for the General like some sort of military pimp.

"Except that you went to all the trouble of visiting her at Bragg to make sure she took the job." Donner winked at him and eyed an oblivious Rachel some more.

Nathan felt the blood drain from his face, so he kept his eyes fixed on the papers in his hands and said nothing. How had the General found out about his trip to North Carolina? He'd been on personal leave and couldn't remember telling anyone except Julian about his plans.

"Why do you suppose she needed to move here?" Donner asked. "Find out, will you?"

"Yes, sir," Nathan replied, though he had no intention of telling him anything about Rachel's personal life.

"Get my wife on the line for me, Captain," Donner ordered.

"Right away, sir." Nathan thwarted a curse as he picked up the receiver. If the General paid more attention to his wife, he'd have less time to bother his female subordinates. Unfortunately, he treated Lydia Donner like dirt.

"Oh, and make sure Chief Southwell joins us for PT this afternoon," he added as his parting shot before shutting himself off in his office.

Nathan closed his eyes for a moment, containing his frustration. Then he dialed Lydia Donner's number.

"Hello, handsome," said the woman who answered. She had caller ID and this was a little game she liked to play with him because she could tell that the call originated from the General's office. He went along because he couldn't think of any way not to.

"Mrs. Donner, this isn't the General, ma'am. It's Captain Fordham." He was ready for what she would say next, but he'd never forgotten his embarrassment when she'd said it for the first time six months ago.

"I know," she drawled in that same slow, sultry voice

she always used when no one else could hear. "How are you, sweetie? Having a good day?"

"Yes, ma'am. Let me put the General on for you." He clicked the hold button and cut off her low, staccato laughter. She had explained once that he gave her a little thrill when he managed to remain so reserved and official even when she spoke inappropriately to him. Nathan knew the game would be over if he could just return the kind of talk she dished out, but he didn't dare. He wouldn't put it past the woman to have him up on charges if he tried. So he endured the teasing and tried not to let her antics make him blush anymore. "Sir, your wife is on line one," he said into the intercom.

Today's exchange with Mrs. Donner, a woman with children not much younger than his own age of thirty-one, had not been as bad as some. It was early in the day so she probably hadn't had time to do any serious drinking, which he suspected was her excuse for her behavior. That, and her marriage to Donner.

"Are you okay?" Rachel asked from her desk. She looked at him with concern and Nathan couldn't help but shake his head at the irony. He'd set himself up as Rachel's champion against the General, but perhaps he needed one against the wife. Harassment could go both ways. The difference was that while Mrs. Donner was merely annoying, what the General did was damn destructive.

"I'm fine," he said, purposefully blanking his expression. "Listen, you brought your PT clothes, right?" he asked.

Her face brightened. "Yeah, you wanna go running?" She glanced at the clock hopefully.

He'd only worked with her a week and already he knew that she performed best when she didn't have to sit still for more than two hours at a stretch. She was a dynamo right after some sort of physical activity, but that energy only lasted so long before she started looking for an excuse to run an errand or courier something to another office.

Though he hated to dash her hopes, he had to say, "Too early. But I need to warn you that the General wants group PT today and he specifically asked that you join us."

"That's okay," she said amiably. "Are we gonna run the perimeter of the north parking lot? I saw some of the other soldiers out their yesterday."

Nathan shook his head. "We start there, next to the day-care center. Then he usually takes us on a route to the edge of Arlington Cemetery and back. It's hillier, but prettier. Some shade along the way."

She nodded and didn't look even a little bit intimidated.

Gently Nathan reminded her, "You'll be the only female with us." Although they didn't all share the same office suite, twelve officers and soldiers made up the command group of the Human Resources and Readiness Office and Rachel was currently the only woman among them.

She gazed at him with her head slightly tilted to one side. "So?"

He got up from his seat and moved to the side of her desk so they could talk quietly. Fortunately, their other office mate, Specialist John Walinski, had gone to the cafeteria for coffee. They were alone, but he still chose his words carefully. He didn't want to be accidentally overheard and he didn't want to sting her pride.

"I know you run fast, but you'll be the slowest one in *this* group." Nathan remembered that her records said she could run two miles in something less than thirteen minutes—amazingly quick for a woman—but he was willing to bet Julian was right and it was a typo. Or maybe a one-time achievement, given how hard she could push herself if the confidence course was any indication. "The General might drop back to run beside you," he warned. "He's done that before, when I didn't realize what he was up to. The results weren't pleasant."

"Ah," she said with an understanding nod. "I see."

"So, if you don't mind, I'll stick with you on the run. I

can use the excuse that I'm still favoring the knee I injured last month."

"Sure," she said brightly. "That would be great."

Nathan had a funny feeling about her unwarranted cheerfulness. Something wasn't right. As if she knew something he didn't. "Yeah," he said warily. But then she got more into the spirit of what he was trying to tell her.

With a frown, she asked, "What did he do to the other woman he ran with while you guys went on ahead?"

"I honestly can't say. Sergeant Walker wouldn't confide in me. But that was the first time I began to wonder what the General was up to. She was a zombie for days afterward. She came up with a sprained ankle and refused to run again for weeks after that. Then she got a doctor to say she should swim or bike ride until the pain went away. I was pretty convinced the pain was never going to go away until she secured her transfer."

She eyed him for a full minute and he could tell she was thinking something over. "You know, he hasn't really said or done anything since I've been here."

He stood up straight from where he'd been leaning against the partition that surrounded two sides of her desk. Damn if she didn't doubt what he'd been telling her about Donner, Nathan thought. He opened his mouth to protest, but she held up her hand to stop him—a gesture of hers with which he was becoming very familiar.

"Not that I don't believe you," she explained. "I've seen his looks and he's said some odd things that make me certain your warnings were necessary. It's just that it's hard to wait for him to actually *do* something for real. I'm impatient for him to get on with it. It's as if I'm sure someone's about to jump out of the dark alley, but I don't know when."

He nodded, appreciating her description and hating that she felt perpetually threatened. But he tensed when he saw that stubborn look he'd come to recognize as belonging uniquely to Rachel.

"Well," she said, "I'm tired of skulking around hoping to avoid a situation with him. I think I should give him some opportunities to do his worst. I need to find out whether he's really going to target me or not."

"Shit," he said under his breath. He should have known. Chief Southwell wasn't the type to wait patiently for the enemy to strike in his own good time. Goading him into premature action was more her style. "Rachel," he said very firmly and quietly, "you can't do that. For one thing, you could be accused of asking for it. For another, I can't let you put yourself into a dangerous situation just because you're tired of waiting."

Her eyebrows shot up. "You can't *let* me?"

He closed his eyes briefly, searching for patience, knowing full well that the conversation would be a lost cause if she chose to dissect each of his words and twist their meanings. When he lifted his lids again, he tried a different angle. "I'm asking you to protect yourself and your career by avoiding unnecessary issues. If he starts harassing you and you can't avoid it, your case will be that much stronger against him. But if there's even a hint of a possibility that you didn't do everything in your power to steer clear of his abuse, then you'll lose in every way imaginable."

She twisted her mouth a bit to one side, looking sulky but clearly listening to his reasoning. "You're probably right," she admitted after he'd waited an eternity for her to respond.

That halfhearted admission didn't cause relief to wash over him, but it helped to ease his tension enough so he could muster a smile for her. "On that note, I vote that you go get some lunch. I'll take my break after you. That way, Specialist Walinski will be here with you when you get back." The thought of leaving her alone in the office when the General was here gave Nathan the chills. There was no telling what she might do if she got sick and tired of waiting for Donner to misbehave.

As he watched her go, his shoulders sagged. This was

going to be much more dangerous for her than he'd realized if she believed she could beard the lion. If she thought she could do that, Nathan could no longer hope that she would be able to come out of this with her career intact. The only thing left for him to do was to talk her into taking a transfer away from the General.

"IT'S A GREAT DAY FOR A RUN!" Rachel heard General Donner declare as he stretched his calf muscles and Achilles tendons. She had to agree with him. The sun was shining; the sky was blue; the humidity was bearable. Of course, she was used to North Carolina, so maybe she wasn't a very good judge of humidity.

Covertly, she eyed the others who were preparing to run the two miles. There was an even dozen men dancing in place like spirited stallions before a race.

"How 'bout them Os," one of them called to another, referring to the Baltimore Orioles. Rachel knew from the local talk-radio station she listened to on her way in to work that the baseball team had won their game last night.

"What do you think of that guy the Wizards picked?" another asked. There was general agreement that the young man would not be ready to play basketball to his full potential until he'd matured some more.

Specialist Walinski turned to Rachel suddenly and with a slight stammer said, "Hey, m-my sister said the Mystics won their exhibition game last weekend."

The way the young man made the effort to include her in the group's discussion of sports by mentioning how the women's professional basketball team had done was sweet, really. So Rachel smiled at him and nodded as if she really cared. "That's good," she said, but then she was glad that someone else picked up the thread about the Wizards so she could slip off to one side without appearing rude.

She chose a spot near a tree where she wouldn't be conspicuous and stretched her limbs, undecided yet whether she would push herself on the run today or take things easy.

The former would startle these arrogant men out of their preconceived notions about her, but the latter might give General Donner an opportunity she probably ought to avoid.

Nathan approached her just as she put her foot high up on the tree trunk so she could lean forward and stretch her hamstrings. She didn't pause, but a strange expectancy tripped through her as it always did when the Captain focused on her. She'd been sure it would wear off after a while, but even a week later there was no lessening of the flutter of anticipation that came over her when he neared.

"Don't give him an opening," he whispered, as if he knew she was still toying with the possibility.

"Is that an order, Captain?" she asked. Why couldn't he trust her to handle things on her own?

He squinted at her, pretending to be stern. "Yes, it is."

"Well, you just stick by my side like you said, okay?"

He nodded, but he didn't seem quite as certain of himself. She noticed he wore a support around his right knee and she felt a twinge of sympathy. She joined the others as they grouped to begin, letting the General decide when to get everyone moving. On cue she started off, with Nathan pacing her. Loping at a normal gait, she gauged his ability and assessed the others, as well. A half mile later, the pack had pulled a good distance ahead, the General at their flank. Obviously, this group didn't try to make Donner look good by letting him take the lead. Rachel saw the General urging his troop onward, and the better runners began to outstrip the less agile, including their commanding officer.

"Look," Nathan said, "I've been thinking." He wasn't panting, hadn't even broken a sweat yet as they jogged behind a group in the middle of the pack, where the General tried to remain.

"And?" She picked up her stride a bit, just enough to make it a little harder to chat.

"I think you should transfer out, find a different position."

She glanced at him to see if he was serious. His expression was grim and determined. The sharpness of her disappointment surprised her. When had she come to hope that he liked having her around? Why did it feel so bad that he wanted to be rid of her?

"I'm not going to do that," she assured him as she extended her gait slightly.

"Why not? I know about your father, but you could get an assignment to Fort Meade or Carlisle Barracks and still be close enough to help your mother with him."

Rachel didn't want to get into this discussion right now. Helping her mother take care of the formerly self-sufficient Bernard Southwell had been more time-consuming and difficult than she'd expected. And then there was Adam. Explaining herself to Nathan would lead to telling him things she still wasn't ready to confess. Maybe she never would be ready.

"You know what?" she said by way of reply. "I really have to get the blood pumping here today. See ya." And with that, she lengthened her stride and pulled ahead.

She thought she heard him mutter a curse, but she didn't stick around long enough for him to be more articulate. In no time, she'd caught up with the slowest of the front runners.

"Well, well," the General said admiringly when her legs carried her near him. "Looks like you weren't kidding," he said between hard breaths. "You're quite the runner."

"Yes, sir," she agreed, still restless and yearning to sprint ahead. They had gone a full mile now and she saw that they were returning the way they had come. That meant she no longer needed a guide.

The only thing holding her back was an unwillingness to seem like a show-off. Besting these men would not endear her to them. She especially wondered about the wisdom of outrunning the General. But then two things happened at once to change her mind. Donner said, "Let's have a chat about the position you'll play on our basketball team. You and me, tomorrow." And then Nathan caught up with her just in time to hear those last words. He shot her a disapproving look. Suddenly Rachel needed to be away. She pumped her limbs a little harder.

The General gave her a rakish grin and waved her forward. "Go ahead, Chief. Show 'em what you can do," he urged.

Rachel didn't need any more prodding than that. As soon as she had the Pentagon in her sights again, she took off. From this angle, she could see the portion where the plane had hit and the scaffolding used in repairs. To see firsthand what the terrorists had done made her even angrier and she let that energy surge into her legs. She wanted to escape, to stretch her spirit, and she didn't even care when she heard the General shout, "Look at the filly run, boys!"

Remembering that she had secretly compared the men to eager stallions just prior to starting off, she didn't think she had a right to take offense. So she just went faster, passing one surprised male after another until she couldn't hear them hooting and hollering behind her anymore. Her only regret was that Nathan's weak knee had prevented him from making the effort to keep up with her.

Not until she had showered and was back at the office to finish a database task she was determined to complete did she face the ramifications of her bold actions during PT. Thinking she was alone in the suite, she jumped a full six inches straight up from her chair when the General suddenly opened his office door.

"I didn't mean to startle you," he said as he sauntered closer.

To Rachel's dismay, he hitched one hip onto the edge of her desk and perched there in a casual pose that some women might have found sexy. Trying not to be too obvious about it, she slid her chair a few inches back and guardedly watched his every move. The office was deathly quiet. Even the normally well-traveled corridor beyond the entry was deserted.

"You're really a remarkable athlete, Rachel," he said, using her given name and smiling very handsomely at her. "And very attractive, too."

The *f* word shot through her mind, but she managed to keep the expletive from passing between her lips. Then a chant of *stupid, stupid, stupid* silently swamped all possibility of strategic thinking. Stupid she'd come back to the office on the assumption she'd be alone. Stupid she'd thought it better to face an overt assault than to endure the waiting. Stupid she'd believed she could single-handedly deal with this situation and this man.

"I like that," he added when she didn't respond. He continued to smile and she saw that his eyes twinkled with mischief as if his behavior were only slightly naughty instead of outrageous. Not to mention illegal.

Then, just as she took a breath to admonish him for saying such things to a subordinate, he lifted his hand toward her face, reaching out to caress her cheek but managing to remind her that he could just as easily strike her with force. She blinked and then froze.

"Don't be alarmed," he said in a soothing voice, still smiling. The back of his index finger made contact with her cheek when he gently tucked a lock of her hair behind her ear as though innocently correcting her appearance. "I just want you to understand that I admire you. We could be friends, you and I."

Rachel suppressed the urge to slap him and suddenly rolled her chair back several feet and surged to her feet. Things had gone far enough.

CHAPTER FIVE

THE GENERAL STOOD, TOO, AND Rachel realized how much bigger he was, even though she was fairly tall. He leaned forward a little in an obvious attempt to further intimidate her. Yet he retained that slight smile, as if this was all fun and games. Incensed, she forced her shaking legs to hold their ground.

"Sir, I'm obliged to warn you," she began, but lost her voice when she heard him chuckle. His amusement at her expense made her seethe. At the same time, she was cold with fear. What would he do next?

She glanced to her right and left, marking escape routes and assessing possible weapons. But as soon as her gaze returned to Donner's, he eased away from her just enough to let her breathe again. "You're obliged to warn me..." he repeated. Laughter laced his words.

Barely able to control her outrage and yet ever wary of his superior strength, stature and rank, she nodded. "I will not tolerate this behavior from you, sir."

He threw his head back and gave a few barks of outright laughter. "What behavior is that?" he asked, eyes glinting with mirth.

"The things you said, the way you touched my hair." She realized he'd skillfully put her on the defensive, but she was unable to think of a way to avoid it.

"Rachel, Rachel," he said, shaking his head as if correcting a wayward child. "I said you are a remarkable athlete. What harm is there in that?"

"You...you touched my hair," she said, floundering

now but unable to stop the effect he had on her. The silver stars on his epaulettes seemed to glow, reminding her of the man's power.

"Did I?" he asked, deftly pointing out that it would be her word against his. Then he shrugged as if nothing she said mattered to him. "I always enjoy a challenge, Rachel, and you certainly seem willing to provide me with one."

He grinned, showing his even white teeth, and Rachel couldn't hold back a shudder. But then she took a breath and said the necessary words, albeit in a less sure voice than she would have liked. "I will be forced to report your actions if anything like this happens again, sir."

"I wouldn't want you to feel forced, Chief." He glanced down at his wristwatch. "It's late. Why don't you go on home now. Monday morning will be soon enough for you to finish whatever it is you were working on."

And with that, he strolled back to his office. He didn't shut his door and Rachel could hear him gathering his things to depart for the day. In a flash, she grabbed her purse and bolted, willing herself to walk rather than run through the corridors of the Pentagon.

"JULIAN!" NATHAN CALLED to his brother from across the basketball court inside the air-conditioned gymnasium on Fort Belvoir. His brother waved but didn't stop passing the ball to the little boys shooting baskets in rapid succession from the row they had formed near the foul line. Nathan smiled. He counted ten kids today—an even number and enough to form small teams for an actual game. Up until now, there just hadn't been enough kids attending the Saturday-morning basketball program the brothers coached for the Army brats whose parents were stationed in the Washington Capital Region.

Setting an example for the kids, he dutifully stretched and ran a couple of laps. He spent the time trying to shake loose from the thoughts that had haunted him since the day before when he'd caught up with Rachel and the General

and overheard their commander's remark to her. He'd
needed immense control to keep from grabbing the son of
a bitch and beating the tar out of him. He still wasn't sure
he would have resisted if Rachel hadn't distracted him so
thoroughly by running like a gazelle toward the Pentagon,
effortlessly outpacing all the men. If he hadn't been furious
with the General, he might have laughed at his own arrogance as he remembered his offer to stay by her side and
the twinkle in her eye as she'd agreed. Rachel was full of
surprises, he mused as he jogged over to the boys, but he
was worried about what the General would do now that
he'd targeted her for conquest.

The eager faces of the young basketball enthusiasts
helped him put aside his troubled thoughts. Julian introduced him to the new kids: Eddy, Tyrie and Adam. Adam's
smile looked so familiar that Nathan asked if they'd met,
but the boy said he'd never been out to Fort Belvoir before.
A break for water followed because the boys had already
been working hard at skills practice for half an hour before
Nathan had arrived.

"Sorry I'm late," he said to Julian as they watched the
boys line up at the fountain. "There was new construction
on Route 1 and traffic was backed up a couple of miles."

"Not a problem. It's just great that you came all the way
out here at all. Today you can help me keep an eye on
Adam. He's having a little trouble breathing and I don't
want him to overdo it."

"What did his parents have to say about that?"

"Looked like a grandmother dropped him off and she
didn't mention it. You know how chaotic things can be
when these kids all arrive at once."

"Well, he seems happy. I think he can hold his own,"
Nathan said as Adam raced some other boys toward the
balls sitting idle on the court. "So, let's not make more of
it than necessary."

Julian nodded and then smiled mischievously. "I'll take
blue—you take red," he said, referring to the colorful tank

tops they used over the kids' clothing to tell one team from another. "I've already got them split as evenly as possible."

Nathan smirked. "I'll just bet you do. I suppose Terrance is on the blue team." Terrance was taller than his fellow eight- to ten-year-olds and had clearly played some basketball before joining this program.

Julian shrugged. "He has to play for someone." Then he clapped his hands to get the boys' attention. Gleeful hoots followed his instructions to put on the colored tank tops so they could play an actual game with ten-minute quarters.

Nathan spent a few minutes making sure he remembered the names of all five of the boys in his group. Then he gave a spirited pep talk, pointing out that teamwork was the key and reminding them to pass the ball to the person best set up to take a shot. Adam raised his hand.

"Yes, Adam?"

"On defense, should we practice guarding the opposite position or just defend against whoever's closest, seeing as how we don't have many players?"

Nathan's eyebrows shot up. How could such a complicated question come out of the mouth of someone so small? The other four boys eyed one another, silently inquiring whether anyone had understood anything the kid had just said. No one uttered a word. Adam continued to look at Nathan expectantly, oblivious to the effect he'd had.

"Um, we're not really into guarding positions yet," Nathan said. "Some of these guys haven't played much before." He glanced at the others and smiled to reassure them. "We'll just try to block the other team from making baskets however we can. Okay?"

All five yelled their agreement at once. Nathan doled out their positions, putting the precocious Adam at center even though he was the shortest. The boys piled their small hands on top of Nathan's larger one, shouted "red team" three times, then ran out onto the court to confront the blue team. Adam's face was a mask of concentration as he looked over the opposition, but then he gave Terrance the once-over and a gleam of excitement came into his youthful eyes. When Terrance lunged for the ball toss, Adam grinned and scooted beneath the taller boy's arm to take control of the ball.

He'd dribbled it down the court and swished it into the basket before Terrance had recovered from the shock of not claiming the ball.

Nathan shouted his encouragement as he chalked the points for the red team onto the blackboard at the sidelines. Catching Julian's eye, he grinned broadly. It was only a kids' game, but giving the overconfident Julian and his protégé, Terrance, a run for their money would be fun.

By the last quarter, the red team was still ahead, but not by much. Nathan could see that Julian was enjoying himself a great deal as he attempted to coach his boys into strategies with which they might steal victory out of the red team's clutches. Nathan laughed at his brother's efforts and just let the red team do their thing—which had been working pretty well so far.

"Way to go, red!" he called. "Great teamwork," he added as Eddy passed the ball to James.

Then Nathan's voice caught in his throat as he noticed the woman standing on the sidelines, observing the game.

Rachel.

His first sensation was one of relief to see her safe and seemingly unaffected by Donner's comments the day before. Then he noticed the smile she directed toward the court full of boys and his heartbeat stuttered. Who would she be watching on the court?

His gaze drifted to her civilian clothes—a snug T-shirt and denim shorts. Those athletic legs curved all the way down to her running shoes, once again making his mouth water. The blast of a whistle brought him back to his senses. When he looked to where Julian stood poised to throw the ball back into play, Nathan realized he'd missed a basket his team had made.

"Yeah! Great job!" he shouted to them even though it was far too late for such praise. Cheeks heating, he glanced toward Rachel to see if she realized the effect she had on him. She didn't seem to see him at all. Her focus was on the game.

And that was where his focus needed to be, too, he told himself as he urged Eddy to block a pass the other team had set up to execute. From the corner of his eye, he couldn't help but notice that Rachel gave a cheery wave to someone on the court. Unfortunately, he didn't see who waved back. Did she know one of the kids? A sinking feeling took hold of him.

The whistle blared again. Julian called the end of the last quarter and declared the red team victorious. "No thanks to you," he muttered with humor to Nathan as he passed.

"Line up to shake hands," Nathan shouted, and he set his mind to putting the kids in position so the two teams could run past each other, giving friendly pats to the opposing group as they went by. "Shirts in the box!" He pointed to where the tank tops had come from.

Nathan saw that Adam was breathing pretty hard as he moved forward to deposit the shirt. But just as he was about to approach the boy to ask him about it, Adam dropped the thing and pivoted toward the sideline.

"Hi, Mom!" he called with a wave. To Nathan's astonishment, the child trotted to Rachel and then hugged her around the waist. As Adam scurried off to exchange good-byes with the other boys by the door at the far end of the court, Rachel's gaze met Nathan's. Her eyes were filled with resignation as she waited for him to approach. He moved toward her without making any conscious decision to do so. His mind whirled. Rachel alone had been more worry than he could handle. Rachel with a child posed risks well beyond anything he'd imagined even in his worst nightmares about what could happen to her.

"So I guess my secret is out now," she said softly as he drew near. "It's quite a coincidence that you coach this group way out here at Fort Belvoir. I thought I'd be safe from recognition this far from the Pentagon."

"It's only a few miles," he replied. The inanity of his words struck him and he overcompensated with a thrust to the heart of the matter. "Your personnel records say you have no dependents. But you have a child."

She looked into his eyes for a long moment. "That's right," she agreed. "I had to give custody to my parents when I enlisted. I suppose only my medical records would reveal that I ever had a son. I guess even *you* couldn't have a peek at *that* file," she said, reminding him that he shouldn't have been poking into her personnel file, either. Glancing fondly at her son—whose smile was so familiar because it mirrored hers—she added, "You might as well know now that there's no husband, never has been." She paused, but Nathan's ability to comment had been stolen by his horror at the additional ways Donner could manipulate her if he found out about Adam. He stood frozen, with the sound of his own pulse throbbing in his ears.

"Does that make a difference to you, Captain Fordham?" she asked. Her gaze turned up to his once more and he saw the suppressed pain and subtle challenge there.

"Yes!" he blurted out before he could think. Deep, unfiltered hurt flickered in her eyes for the merest second. But Nathan saw it. Confusion swamped him as he tried to discern how he had caused her such pain with just one word. He opened his mouth to explain, to set things right, to erase that hurt that must still reside behind her now cool facade. "Rachel," he began, but Adam returned just then.

"You two know each other?" the boy asked. His expression was puzzled, but pleased, too.

At the same time, Julian approached. "You must be Adam's mother. He's quite a basketball player."

Nathan knew his brother wanted to broach the subject of Adam's shortness of breath on the court during the game, but that issue would have to wait. Finding his voice, he said, "Julian, this is Chief Southwell, who is assigned to my office at the Pentagon. Under General Donner," he added unnecessarily. "And Adam is her son." He stopped speaking after that, sure that his brother could figure it all out from there.

"Uh-oh," Julian muttered for Nathan's ears only. After a moment of awkward silence, Julian smiled and stuck his hand out. "Nice to meet you Chief Southwell," he said as he shook her hand. "Nate can tell you all about how the game went for Adam, and, well, I need to be going now." He shifted the box of shirts from one arm to the other as if it was heavy, then stepped back a pace, preparing to make a hasty retreat. "Good luck," he whispered to Nathan as he turned tail and walked swiftly toward the exit.

"Captain Nathan and Major Julian are brothers!" Adam said as though this was an amazing fact. "They coach basketball together. Isn't that great?"

Rachel smiled and nodded her agreement. "So your brother's in the Army, too?"

He ignored the question but remained mindful that Adam was watching and listening. "We need to talk."

Adam bounced on his toes as he said, "He could come home to supper with us and you could talk then." Turning to Nathan, the boy added, "Grandma's making pot roast. She puts potatoes and carrots and green beans in it." He smacked his lips to indicate his appreciation, and despite the dire situation at hand, Nathan's stomach growled. He'd only had a bagel for breakfast and it was now past noon.

Rachel seemed uncomfortable. Her gaze rested everywhere but on him. Clearly, she hoped to escape him as quickly as possible. Not a chance. "Pot roast sounds good to this starving bachelor," he said, wondering what she would do. "And we could talk after we eat," he added. "We really need to talk."

At last she looked up, and he saw curiosity overwhelm

whatever else she might feel toward him. "All right," she said.

"I'll need to wash up and change clothes first," he said, unable to take his gaze from hers.

"Supper isn't until about 1600."

"Oh, goody!" Adam exclaimed as he bounced some more. "Tell him how to get to our house, Mom. Did you know Captain Nathan is a black belt in tae kwon do? Major Julian said so. He told us we better mind Captain Nathan because he can break six boards with his bare hands and—"

"Hush, Adam," she admonished softly. "Let me give the Captain directions."

Five minutes later, Nathan stood unmoving as he watched Rachel walk away with Adam's small hand clutched in hers. He'd felt protective of her before, but now the need to keep her and her son safe filled him to overflowing. And fear that he might fail grew in equal measure. Inadequacy nearly choked him as he forced himself to start walking, too.

All the way home, he rehearsed his arguments for why Rachel simply had to transfer out from beneath Donner's command. Adam's existence made her patently unsuitable for the task of ending the General's harassment. If he had to stoop to detailing the ways Donner would use Adam against her, then he would do so, even if Rachel hated him for it.

RACHEL FELT LIKE EVERY KIND of fool as she carefully applied just enough cosmetics to enhance her features without overdoing it. And the pile of clothing on her bed made her groan with self-reproach as she realized how hard she'd searched for just the right outfit. She told herself repeatedly that she was not trying to make herself attractive to Captain Fordham. Such an attempt would be sheer stupidity given that they worked in the same office. Besides, she wasn't ready for anyone like Nathan. He made her feel too many things she hadn't felt in a long while. She wanted to start dating again, but she did *not* want a serious relationship yet, given how much she was needed at home.

She checked her reflection one last time. Staring into her own eyes, she had to be honest. Things could become serious with Nathan very quickly if she let them.

And if he was interested, she added as a reminder that he might not be. She'd noticed that he'd watched her sometimes in the office. There had been admiration in his eyes on a few occasions. But now he knew her secret. She'd learned from experience that Adam's existence could quickly transform admiration into disinterest.

It didn't matter, she told herself as she gave a final adjustment to her blouse. *He* didn't matter.

So why were there butterflies in her stomach? she asked herself. For that matter, why had she even agreed to invite him into her home for dinner? He'd said they needed to talk, but she could have come up with some other place. Or she could have saved him the trouble by admitting she already knew what his lecture would include. In that shattering moment on the basketball court when he'd said yes to her question about whether or not her unwed motherhood made a difference, she'd first assumed he thought less of her for it. But then Adam had begun to chatter about black belts and tae kwon do and she'd remembered that Nathan had sought her help with Donner partly because her records showed no dependents. Perhaps now that he knew about Adam, he would redouble his efforts to get her to transfer.

Descending the stairs and entering the kitchen to help her mother with supper preparations, she silently admitted that she had a perverse need to find out exactly why Nathan had said yes so promptly to her on the basketball court. Exasperated with herself, she let a heavy sigh escape.

"Are you okay?" her mother asked. "Is anything wrong?"

Rachel mustered a smile. "I'm fine."

She reached for the stack of plates that needed to be

distributed around the table in the dining room. Her mother put her hands over Rachel's, stopping her.

"You've been in a mood ever since you got back from picking up Adam at basketball. Is there something about this Captain Fordham that troubles you?"

"No, of course not. I told you—I work with him. He's very nice."

Her mother eyed her with that penetrating gaze that would have Rachel blurting the truth any minute. She searched for a diversion. "I think Adam had some trouble breathing while he was playing with the other boys today. I suspect that's what Captain Fordham wants to discuss with me."

"I see."

That her mother saw far too much was clear to Rachel. "I'm worried about how long it's taking for the Army to add Adam to my records as my dependent. It's been a week since I put in the papers, but I haven't got the documents to get him his ID card yet. I can't have him see a doctor until I have that ID card."

"You should ask your Captain to help you with that."

Rachel blinked. Then she felt a blush creep over her cheeks. "He's not *my* Captain." She looked away, hoping her mother wouldn't notice her high color. "For heaven's sake," she added as she lifted the plates from the counter and headed for the dining room.

She thought she heard her mother chuckle softly behind her.

An hour later, she met Captain Fordham at the front door, feeling like a schoolgirl as she let him in. Adam rushed down the stairs to them, saving her from awkward conversation.

"Captain Nathan, can you teach me some karate moves? Just a few, like maybe how to break a board or punch like a ninja?" He demonstrated with some childish but enthusiastic chops and kicks into the air.

She watched with a full heart as Nathan tousled her son's

hair and promised to teach him a few moves before the evening was over. Rachel hoped she'd get to look on, not only to see her son enjoying himself, but also to see Nathan Fordham doing martial arts. Her mouth already watered at the very thought.

The pot roast had the same mouthwatering effect, and not long after she introduced her colleague to her parents, they all sat down to consume the sumptuous meal her mother had prepared.

"You know, Captain—" her mother began.

"Please, call me Nathan," he interjected.

Virginia Southwell smiled and a hint of pink brightened her cheeks. "Nathan," she said. "You know, our Rae is quite a cook herself."

Rachel immediately choked on the piece of roast she'd been swallowing. She coughed and coughed, waving her hand to let them know she would be okay, but embarrassed to her toes. Not only had her mother just made an outrageous statement designed to attract Nathan's interest, but all the coughing had undoubtedly turned her face bright red. Nathan, seated to her right, moved toward her as if he thought he ought to whack her on the back or something, but at the last minute, he settled for splaying a hand across her shoulder blade and stroking her there while tears streamed from her eyes and the tickle in her throat refused to subside.

After what seemed like an eternity but probably only spanned a few seconds, someone handed her the water glass near her plate and a sip helped her regain control. "So sorry," she croaked, then she had to clear her throat one last time.

"Down wrong pipe," contributed her father, slurring his words a bit but making the effort to converse. "Happens to me a lot."

Nathan grinned at her father, and to Rachel's amazement, Bernard Southwell returned the gesture with a lopsided smile of his own. She realized that after months of slow progress to regain his speech and some semblance of independence, her dad had made a joke about his stroke-induced difficulties swallowing. And Nathan had understood.

First he charms me, then my son—and now my mother and my father! Rachel realized in that moment that she could easily fall hard for a guy like Nathan. The possibilities thrilled her and terrified her at the same time.

"So, you cook?" Nathan said to Rachel. When she looked up quickly, horrified that this topic had somehow been resurrected, she caught the twinkle of amusement in his eyes. Before she could come up with a response, her mom launched into a detailed story of her youthful escapades making macaroni and cheese. From there, it was only a matter of time before he knew all her kitchen exploits. There were many.

"But our Rachel stuck to it. Perseverence is her middle name," Virginia said as she served dessert. "After practicing and practicing, she taught herself to make the best sweet potato pie in the commonwealth."

"I'll bet Rachel Perseverence Southwell can accomplish just about anything she puts her mind to," Nathan said.

"Got that right," her father agreed. "Shoulda made pie."

"Now, Bernie, you know Rae was busy all day," Virginia said. "Besides, you like my chocolate cake."

Though his bites had to be small and his hand was shaky, Rachel watched with growing relief as her father ate the cake with gusto and cleaned every crumb from his plate.

"Can we go do karate now?" Adam pleaded with big, hope-filled eyes.

Nathan glanced her way and told her without words that he'd be willing if she permitted it. She nodded slightly and Nathan's smile broadened. "Sure, sport. Let's go break some boards."

"What?" Virginia said. "Boards? What boards?" But

the boy and the man were already heading out the back door.

Rachel patted her mother's hand. "They're not really going to break anything," she said. Then she stood to help clear the dishes.

"No, I'll do this," her mother insisted. "You go make sure your son doesn't get into mischief. And keep an eye on that handsome officer, too."

Rachel didn't need much arm-twisting before she joined Adam and his idol out on the expansive back porch. She sat on the swing and watched Nathan patiently explain a basic punch and block. Then he urged the boy to repeat it over and over.

"When do I get to break a board?" Adam asked as he thrust and blocked, thrust and blocked.

"There's a lot of practicing before you get to mess with boards. You have to learn the first three katas, too," Nathan said as he thrust and blocked alongside Adam. His white, button-down shirt snapped taut with each one, giving Rachel an excellent idea of what his lean body looked like beneath the cloth.

"What's a 'kata'?" Adam asked.

"A kata is a special pattern of tae kwon do moves. Each one is a little more complicated, but once you know the main ones, you'll be ready to try breaking a board."

"Is that enough for now?" Adam asked after dropping his arms in exaggerated weariness. Rachel hid a smile behind her hand. Adam had a longer attention span than most eight-year-olds, but even *his* had its limits.

"Sure, that's enough. You did great. I can teach you some other stuff another day. I need to talk to your mom now."

"Okay. I'll go watch TV until it's time for bed," he said as he began to skip toward the house.

"Hold on there, pardner," Rachel said, catching him with one outstretched arm as he was about to pass. "You can play Math Blasters or Reader Rabbit on the computer, but no TV.''

''Aw, Mom,'' he complained, but he gave her a peck on the cheek before he disappeared inside the house. She stared after him, her heart filled with the simple pleasure of being a mother, of having her child think to give her a little kiss.

Then Nathan's weight made the porch swing shift and creak.

She admired his profile as he settled next to her. There was a stir of expectation in her stomach as she realized she was all alone with the Captain, sitting on a porch swing under a dark blue sky already dappled with evening stars. Her pulse quickened slightly, and she knew this had little to do with the conversation at hand and everything to do with the man beside her and the inexplicable chemistry that drew her to him.

CHAPTER SIX

THE SILENCE WAS BROKEN only by the hum of the cicadas and the creak of the chains that held the swing. Then a dog barked, waking Nathan from the daydreams that had flitted through his head, one after the other, as he gazed at Rachel. None could become reality, he told himself. If he so much as stretched his fingers so they grazed the side of her hand, she would pull away and he would be no better than Donner.

"I'd like to learn tae kwon do someday," she said with a tentative smile.

"I could teach you a little, get you started." Her skin looked perfectly smooth in the light of the newly rising moon.

"Okay, that would be great. Maybe after PT or something," she suggested.

The mention of PT reminded him of the sight of her sleek legs when she'd outdistanced all the male runners the previous afternoon. And that reminded him of General Donner's comments to her as she'd gone by. His purpose in coming to Rachel's home this evening came rushing back to the forefront of his thoughts.

"We need to talk about Donner," he said softly, wishing he didn't have to mar this lovely night with unpleasant conversation.

"Yes." She stared off into space, and Nathan was sure she wanted to say something else. He waited, and his hunch was proved right a few seconds later. "I didn't know he

was going to go back to the office yesterday after we ran.
I went up to finish some work and he—''

When she broke off and studied her feet as though
ashamed, Nathan's whole body went hot with anger. If that
man laid a finger on Rachel, he'd…he'd… But beating the
tar out of the General was not remotely possible and frustration churned inside him. ''What did he do, Rachel?'' he
urged as gently as his rampaging feelings would allow.

She glanced at him sideways, as if to check his mood.
''Honestly, he didn't do anything so terrible. He didn't
grope me or make lewd remarks or tell me my officer's
evaluation report would suffer if I didn't sleep with him.''
Then she repeated word for word the disturbing conversation she'd had with their commanding officer and showed
him how the General had tucked a loose strand of hair
behind her ear.

''He touched you,'' Nathan said through gritted teeth.
But even as he said it, he saw the very same strand of hair
fall loose and fought the urge to tuck it behind her ear for
her, exactly the way Donner had done. He watched that
silky strand bob slightly as she nodded, affirming that the
creep had put his hands on her.

''The worst part,'' she said, ''was that when he reached
out suddenly, I realized he could just as easily hit me. I
jerked back and then froze. I must have seemed afraid. But
I'm not afraid of him.'' She said those last words with a
little extra force, and that told Nathan that the General
scared her shitless.

The man scared Nathan shitless, too. General Donner
was a powerful man with powerful friends. What hope did
they have of bringing him down?

''You have to find another job,'' he blurted, determined
to secure her safety even if that meant giving up his plan
to stop the General. ''You can't stay in the office. He's not
going to leave you alone. He'll destroy you.'' The depth
of his fear for her made him consider whether or not he
might be losing the battle to remain objective. He wouldn't

be able to keep a grip on his professionalism if he let this woman get under his skin.

She held his gaze fixedly for a few seconds. "I told you I'm not afraid of him." Nathan wondered if she was trying to convince herself as much as him.

"Damn it, Rachel, you're not the only one who matters in this. What about Adam and how he'll feel when Donner drags his mom to hell and back? What about your parents?"

She continued to stare at him and Nathan could tell that she was growing stubborn and solidifying her position, whether it made sense or not. He suspected that every argument he could make would only entrench her more deeply. But he had to try. "Please. Do this for me, for Adam, for your parents. Find another job. Do whatever you have to do to get out of Donner's way."

Her gaze shifted away and she seemed to be thinking it over. Nathan concentrated hard, willing her to see reason. But then she shook her head slowly.

"I can't," she said. "I can't let Donner control me. I can't let him do this to someone else. I did that once before. I'm never doing it again."

"Once before?"

Her chin went up a bit and she set her jaw. "Adam's father was a few years older than me—a secret lover I met at the mall where I worked during the summer. I was young and stupid and I just wanted to find a man who would love me and take care of me the way my father did my mother. At that age I hadn't been exposed to other options. And Paul had a lot to say about love and marriage right up until I got pregnant. He stuck by me for exactly one week while he tried to get me to abort the baby. I might have done it if he'd stayed, but when I needed time to think about it, he left town." She sighed heavily. "I drew the curtains in my room, curled up on my bed and cried for days. I was so confused. Mom thought I had the flu and I didn't say anything to tell her otherwise. After a few weeks of dragging myself through the time in a blind funk, an abortion wasn't an option anymore. The last day came and went and I hardly noticed. Talk about letting someone else control your life!''

Nathan didn't know what he should say to that. He found that he'd reached out and put his hand on her shoulder in comfort. She didn't draw away so he left it there. ''I'm sorry,'' he said. ''You were young. And Adam's father was an idiot to let you go.''

She gave him a sad, hesitant smile. ''That isn't even the worst of it.''

What more could there be? he wondered.

''About a year later, after Adam was born but just before I joined the Army, I found out that the creep did the same thing to another girl.'' Her eyes glistened with moisture. She swiped at her eyes roughly. ''I swore I would never shed another tear over that man.''

Thinking only of offering comfort, he slipped his arm around her shoulders and cradled her against his side. She didn't resist, and in seconds her head nestled into the space between his shoulder and chin and her hand gently rested on his chest.

He rocked them slowly on the swing. The cicadas had quieted, but the creak, creak, creak of the chains suspending the swing lulled him into believing that there was nothing wrong with holding her like this. She needed comfort, that was all.

Then she tilted her face up a little to look at him and he thought about kissing her, soft and slow. He moved his hand to stroke her cheek and would have eased his mouth to hers if Mr. Southwell hadn't chosen that moment to shuffle awkwardly out onto the porch.

''''Kay out here?'' he asked in a conversational tone as he came through the screen door haltingly, still unsure of using his walker.

Rachel eased to her side of the swing and Nathan withdrew his arm from around her shoulders as casually as possible. He felt like a sixteen-year-old caught stealing a kiss from a teenage girl; his cheeks went hot and his heart rate accelerated.

Bernie Southwell edged to one of the cushioned porch chairs and lowered himself into it with an effort. "Not chilly?"

"We're fine, Dad," Rachel said with both amusement and exasperation in her voice.

"Lookin' out for m' girl," he muttered. But Nathan heard and got the message loud and clear. As he relived how close he'd come to kissing Rachel, he recognized that while he was trying to protect her from Donner, someone had to protect her from him.

"I need to be going," he said, and got to his feet. "Thank you for dinner."

"I'll walk you to your car," Rachel offered. She stepped off the porch before Nathan could tell her she shouldn't. Nathan followed her over the grass to the curb, wishing he had better control over his attraction to this woman.

She stopped by his car and turned to him. "My father is overprotective because he thinks he must have been remiss as a parent when I got pregnant with Adam. He means well."

Nathan glanced back to where the older man sat, watching them placidly. "I'm glad he's looking out for you. Once Donner decides to start playing rough, you may need every ally you can find."

"Then you see why I can't run away from this fight?"

Reluctantly, he nodded. "But I won't promise I'll stop trying to talk you into a transfer. I seem to have this uncontrollable urge to protect you, just like your dad." Her smile did the strangest things to his insides and he longed to pull her into his arms again.

"Thank you for understanding. And...for not, well, judging me now that you know about Adam and everything."

He suddenly realized that she'd been worried his opinion

of her would change now that he knew she'd had a child out of wedlock. Nothing could be further from his mind. Her story made her even more beautiful and brave to him. And even more desirable.

But he couldn't say that. "I think Adam is a wonderful child and you're a wonderful mother. I only wish you weren't Donner's target."

She sobered at that. "Well, let's at least try to keep Adam's existence quiet for now. I had to give custody of him to my parents when I first joined the Army, and now that I can reclaim him, he still isn't showing up as my dependent on my records. Some kind of glitch in processing the paperwork. Maybe the General won't know about Adam until we figure out a way to stop him." She paused and then added, "I'd pull back Adam's paperwork, except I need to get him medical care for his asthma."

He nodded, certain that they wouldn't be able to keep that secret for very long. Donner had a way of finding things out about his victims. "We noticed his breathing on the basketball court. That was one of the things I was supposed to talk to you about tonight. Let me know if I can help with the personnel office and Adam's documentation. His health is the most important thing and I might be able to help get things squared away."

"Okay." She said it softly, then a long silence stretched into the stillness of the night. It was time to leave, but Nathan couldn't get going. If he tried to move, he felt sure he would sweep her into a kiss right there in front of her house. So he remained awkwardly standing in place for seconds that seemed to last hours.

To his relief, she took the initiative and stepped back onto the curb. "Good night, Nathan. Thank you for coming so we could talk these things over."

"Tell your mother the food was exceptional." He was grateful she couldn't see how much he fumbled with the keys. When was the last time he'd been so nervous around a female? he asked himself. Not since his sophomore year in college when he'd fallen head over heels in love with his best friend's girl. As he drove away from Rachel's house, he remembered that he'd gotten over his infatuation back then and he could do it now. Because pursuing Rachel while they were trying to stop a sexual predator was not an option.

If only his heart would cooperate by not falling in love with her, he'd be all set.

RACHEL COULDN'T STOP THINKING about the hour she'd spent with Nathan on the swing. Sometimes her thoughts were like daydreams, allowing her to relive the moments. Other times they were like nightmares, haunting her with what couldn't be. Mostly, she wondered what would have happened between them if her father hadn't come out onto the porch. Had Nathan really been about to kiss her, or had she imagined it? Certainly, in the three working days since that moment on the porch, he'd been polite, cordial, professional, distant.

Except when the General came out of his office. Then Captain Fordham bristled and did everything in his power to keep the General from having private moments with Rachel.

Today Nathan had exchanged benign pleasantries with her in the morning and then had focused on his own work, never even looking in her direction. She wished she didn't care.

At 1300 hours, Donner appeared on the threshold of his office and ordered Nathan to get Mrs. Donner on the phone. The minute the number had been dialed, the General sauntered in Rachel's direction. Clever of him to make sure Nathan would be trapped on the phone with the wife so Donner could prowl for conquest unimpeded, Rachel thought as she watched him approach her. She'd been wondering how long Donner would take to wise up to Nathan's protective strategies.

"Rachel, how are things going for you?" the General said to her. "All settled in?"

"Yes, sir," she said, casually sliding her chair back so she could stand up before he got too close. She knew from the times Nathan hadn't been available to interfere that Donner would come too near, ostensibly to look over her shoulder at her work on the computer screen—but really so that he could splay his hand over her shoulder blade. The heat of his palm through her Army shirt always made her skin crawl.

"No, no, don't get up," he said with a pleasant smile. "I don't want to interrupt." He held out his hand in a gesture meant to keep her seated.

Feeling she had no choice now, she stayed in her chair. But she swiveled so that at least she would face him. That seemed better than keeping her back to him and cringing with dread at his inevitable touch. He couldn't touch her if she was looking him in the eyes. Could he?

He stopped in front of her, crossing his arms over his chest and smiling benevolently down at her, his straight, white teeth showing and a little sparkle in those blue eyes. "You're tense today, Rachel. Is everything okay at home?"

"Yes, sir, everything's fine."

"Work, then—are things going well here at work?" He glanced toward Nathan as if to check that he was still occupied.

When he brought his gaze back to hers, she nodded because her mouth had gone dry. He stood close enough for her to smell his aftershave, to feel his heat, to sense his predatory intent. But her back was to the wall and she could retreat no farther. She could hear Nathan struggling to end the conversation he'd been trapped into with Mrs. Donner. The looks he shot in her direction told her he was frantic to call the General to the phone and get him away from her. Rather than await his rescue, she willed her tongue to work and said, "Work is going well. We've nearly finished reorganizing the files in compliance with standard operating procedures. We've got half the data input into the personnel database.''

The General looked briefly to the desk behind Rachel's when she said ''we.'' He knew that she and the new enlisted clerk had done the work together. Rachel wanted to share the credit for the progress the office had made. Specialist Allison Fitzpatrick had helped a great deal since she'd arrived to fill the administrative vacancy left by Specialist Walinski's departure on a standard PCS.

''That Allison—she's a sprightly one,'' he said with a grin that Rachel didn't like. Allison was very young and vulnerable. All Rachel's protective instincts came screaming to the surface. Allison's country upbringing had given her absolutely no ability to handle someone like Donner. Rachel wanted to tell him to leave the poor woman alone.

But that would be the worst thing she could do. If he knew it would bother Rachel, Donner might pursue Allison all the harder, using the younger woman in his attempt to manipulate Rachel. Or he might just stalk Allison for no other reason than the pleasure he got from wielding his power over a weaker person.

''She does good work,'' Rachel said in as calm a voice as she could muster.

''So do you,'' the General countered, swinging his gaze back to hers. ''On and off the job, I'm sure.'' He let that sink in a moment before adding the words meant to make his last comment seem innocent. ''There's that basketball tournament coming up in a couple of months. I need to see what you can do on the court so I can decide if I should make a spot for you on our league team. Let's you and me go over to the—''

Nathan rose to his feet with a squeak of chair wheels, drawing the General's attention as well as Rachel's. She noticed the pinkness of his cheeks and the twitch in a jaw muscle. She prayed he wouldn't say anything in anger that would get him into trouble. ''Sir,'' he said, ''your wife is on line three.''

"I'll call her back," he said, shifting his focus to Rachel again.

Nathan's eyebrows shot up and her heart beat a little faster as she wondered what he would say now. But just as she began to worry, Nathan's shoulders relaxed, as if he'd forced them to do so. Then that charming half smile quirked at his lips. She wondered if anyone else would notice that his smile didn't touch his eyes. "Sir, you asked me to get her on the line and she's waiting. From what she told me of her day, it might be better if you talk to her now." He gave the General one of those looks that men share sometimes about how difficult women can be.

The General huffed as if both amused and annoyed. "Thanks for the warning. I'll take that advice." He sauntered into his office.

The minute his door closed, Rachel sagged with relief and Nathan sat heavily into his chair. He stared across at her with eyes that said her encounter had been a close call. She knew as well as he did that the General had been about to insist on a private basketball tryout with her.

"Thanks for telling General Donner that I do good work, ma'am," Allison said.

Rachel turned to her and smiled. "He needs to know about your performance so he can give you an accurate enlisted evaluation."

"Well, he seems to like me and that's always a good thing," she said. Rachel wondered what had happened between them to give Allison the impression that the General already felt anything one way or the other about her. But she didn't ask. She didn't want to say anything that might cause Allison to be worried or afraid. There was still hope that Donner would keep his lascivious attentions trained on Rachel and away from Allison. She also didn't correct Allison's impression that having the General like her was a good thing.

"We need to decide what to do next," Nathan said. He'd chosen his words and tone so that Allison would not think anything of it. Only Rachel understood that he meant they had to decide what to do about the General.

"We should go—" She was about to say they should go somewhere else to talk, but General Donner reappeared in the frame of his door.

"Chief, I'll see you in my office a moment," he said. He sounded all business, but Rachel's heart began to race and a coldness slid over her skin.

Nathan stood up quickly. "Is there something I could help you with, sir?" he offered.

"No, thanks," the General said amiably. "The Chief and I just have some things to discuss." Then he smiled his terrible smile and gestured for her to enter his domain.

She had no choice but to comply.

CHAPTER SEVEN

RACHEL WENT INTO THE GENERAL'S office as wary as if going into a wolf's den. She didn't hesitate, but her senses were fully alert. She could smell her own fear and wondered if he could, too. His triumph as he watched her with unblinking eyes was nearly tangible.

"Have a seat," he said in a falsely casual tone, staring steadily.

She sat and said nothing. Something icy cold ran swiftly through her veins.

He smiled, losing his predatory gleam in favor of the charming, boyishness that didn't fool her for a minute. "This is really a bit awkward for me. I've never needed this sort of help before."

Determined that he wouldn't have the satisfaction of making her speechless, she said, "What sort of help, sir?" As soon as she uttered them, she knew those words led her right into his trap. He would be able to demand any number of lurid things from her and tell himself that she had asked him for details.

"Well—" he appeared somewhat sheepish now "—there's this female Senator with her panties in a wad over a little incident out in Hawaii. You hear of that?"

Rachel nodded. The story about Hawaii had been all over the newspapers. Some male officers, including some Guardsmen, started coming on to some uninterested females who turned out to be military officers. All of them were on a brief R and R before returning to Central Asia. They were drinking and socializing in civilian clothes, mostly bathing suits, which is common at the military's Waikiki hotel, the Hale Koa. One of the men tugged on a string that barely held together one of the bikinis and that was when the screams of outrage began. Pretty soon, name-calling turned ugly. When some civilian males stepped up to the plate to defend the honor of the women, the resulting melee provided plenty of photo opportunities, none of which did any good for the reputation of the Army or the National Guard.

"To shut up this Senator Zemin at the hearing where I was testifying, I told her I'd go out to Fort DeRussy to look into it," the General said. "But the thing is, I could use a woman officer's point of view so as to make sure I appear to do my investigation thoroughly. The last thing I need is to have someone accuse me of bias when the report comes out."

This was so far from what Rachel had expected the General to say to her and seemed so benign that she felt thoroughly confused. "But I work for you, sir. Won't people just suppose I would go along with anything you wanted to report about what happened there?"

"Yes, I suppose that's true, but who else should I pick? I'm a major general and there aren't any female officers I don't outrank, so I might as well take you with me. Truthfully, it's more for show than anything. It'll be a free trip to Hawaii for you and helps me out a great deal. I'd like to be able to say I had a woman on the team."

Rachel didn't like being on any team just for show, and something must have given away her thoughts. The General hastened to add, "But that doesn't mean there isn't real work for you to do on the case. I really *do* want your honest opinion of things. But most of your information will come from e-mailing the officers who are back with their units now." He smiled kindly and without any hint of ulterior motives. "What do you say?"

Rachel's mind whirled over how much turmoil such a trip would cause her family, but she couldn't really see a way she could refuse. Although he made it sound like a request, Rachel had no illusions. Still, she wanted to escape the trap he'd set if she could. "Of course I'll go if you need me to, sir, but perhaps staying here and getting started on corresponding with the people involved would be just as effective."

The General waved his hand in front of his face as though to sweep away her protest. "No, no, that won't do. Zemin will want you on site." He slapped his hand onto his desk and grinned. "So, that's settled. I'll make sure Nathan includes you in the travel plans." He stood up, still smiling amiably.

Rachel assumed the interview was over and also got to her feet. Then, when she was least prepared, he acted upon his baser desires. Moving quickly, yet without rushing, the General placed himself between her and the door. "Are we finished with our meeting already?" he asked with what would have seemed like a friendly smile if Rachel hadn't known better. "There's so much more I'd like to say, or even do...."

"Don't!" She took a quick step to the side, avoiding his outstretched hand. A fury rose inside her and she set her feet in a defiant stance and even leaned a little forward with her hands clenched at her sides. "General Donner, you must know that your advances are unwanted. I don't want you touching me ever again, even on the shoulder. I don't want to hear your suggestive remarks. There will be no relationship between us other than a purely professional one!" She didn't shout, but she gave her little speech with force and conviction just the way she had practiced in front of her mirror at home. "What you're doing is sexual harassment. You must stop."

He never lost his smile, which now looked almost gleeful. "Rachel," he said as though soothing an upset child. "You're making too much of it. I only want to get to know you better." He stepped closer. "How else can I assess your performance and worthiness for advancement?"

There it was—a threat to her career. Bitterness welled inside her where anger had blazed only a moment earlier. Her rage had no power over this man; her demands that he desist were meaningless to him. She knew in that moment that no matter how hard she tried, she would never escape the trap he had set for her. She would lose no matter what she did.

"You have nothing to fear from me, Rachel. I'll take good care of you." Donner advanced and Rachel stood still, unable to move. The gap between them constricted. "I could help you," he whispered. Then in a still softer voice he added, "We could help each other."

As if in a terrible dream, she couldn't make her limbs obey her. She watched in frozen horror as his hands came up to clasp her upper arms. The most she could do was force her tongue into action, but even that effort stumbled as she thought with revulsion that he might try to kiss her. "I...I'll be forced to...to report you." Then she steeled herself and delivered the next words with deadly calm. "No matter what the cost."

He must have believed her, because he dropped his hands to his sides again. But he laughed. "Ah, Rachel, you are such a wonderful person. So honest, so righteous, so controlled. I will enjoy testing all your convictions during these years we work together." Then he moved away from the door, benevolently granting her freedom.

She didn't bolt for the exit as her instincts urged her to, but waited until he'd sauntered over to his desk. When she was sure she would not be within his reach, she willed her trembling limbs to carry her away in measured paces. Somehow, she made it through the exit without running.

"My God, what happened!" came a male voice close to her left. But she didn't look toward the soothing, familiar sound. She just kept walking. "Rachel!" she heard him call as she passed into the ring of the Pentagon outside the office suite. She moved along the circle that would lead her to one of the spokelike hallways. Once there, she went on like an automaton toward the inner courtyard, blessedly un-damaged by the terrorist attack and currently full of sun-shine and blue sky and the powerful fragrance of mag-nolias.

Eventually, she realized she sat on a bench with her fore-head propped in her hands, elbows on her knees. She be-came aware that someone sat beside her, silently offering the comfort of his company. Having no idea how much time had passed, she lifted her head and looked at him. The bright sun emphasized the concern that etched thin lines around his mouth and eyes. Yet he had never looked so handsome to her.

"Thank you for following me out here, for sitting with me," she said. "It's really important for me to remember that I'm not alone in this."

"You're not alone," Nathan agreed firmly. "Can you tell me what happened?"

The scene within the General's office replayed itself in-side her head. Thinking about it now with Nathan at her side and the sunlight pouring over her, she recalled that nothing too awful had happened. "Once again, he didn't really do anything overt," she admitted, embarrassment creeping over her as she wondered if her revulsion might have made her overreact. If she nearly fell apart over *this*, how would she handle the creep when he did something serious?

"Words are powerful, Rae. Don't underestimate how much threats and double meanings can affect you. Look how terrorist threats have changed the behavior of Ameri-cans, even though we try not to let them get to us. Donner is using similar tactics all specifically directed at you."

"Yes. His threats have gotten to me. I have to find ways to stand up to them. Especially since I'll have to travel with him soon." Haltingly, she told him what he'd said about going to Hawaii.

"Shit!" Nathan said, then immediately apologized for swearing. "He just wants to get you alone on TDY with him." He looked off toward the hut that sold food at the center of the courtyard, still called the Ground Zero Café even though it had been spared in the terrorist attack. "I'll go with you, of course. I'm his aide, so it would be odd for him not to take me along on the trip. And maybe I can persuade Mrs. Donner that she should accompany her husband, too. *That'll* keep him busy while he's there."

Wearily, she smiled at him. "Thank you."

He appeared to be startled by her simple expression of appreciation. Then he smiled back at her. He gazed into her eyes for a long moment. "You're not alone in this, Rachel," he reiterated. "We'll figure out a way to deal with this guy."

NATHAN CALLED HIS BROTHER as soon as he got home that evening. "Julian, things are getting tense."

"You knew they would," the Major replied calmly.

"You don't understand."

"Yes, I do. You have a thing for the Chief Warrant Officer and it's killing you to see Donner prey upon her."

Nathan didn't respond to that directly. He couldn't deny what his brother had surmised. But he didn't want to admit it, either. "What are we going to do, Jules? This can't go on."

"Do you have any hard evidence yet?"

"No. He just keeps messing with her head, toying with her. If you're looking for bruises or the kind of evidence that would prove rape, I gotta tell you that'll happen over my dead body."

"If you could get some neutral party to overhear what he says, at least then we'd have Southwell's word corroborated by yours and another person's."

"That's harder to get than you think. He does everything behind closed doors. But I was thinking about going to this Senator I know of. She can't stand Donner. Maybe she could help us figure out what to do."

"You mean Senator Zemin, don't you?" Julian sounded

alarmed. "That's not a good idea. You'll end up turning this into a political thing. You know how this stuff works with those congressional types. You'll be halfway to where you want to be and then this Senator will cut a deal with someone and your career will be sacrificed for the greater good!"

Half amused by his brother's vehemence, Nathan said, "So, I guess you're against going to Zemin."

"Damn straight!"

"Look, Julian, I've got to do something! Give it some thought, will you? We need to come up with a way to wrap this up quickly. We can't let him continue to do what he's doing to Rachel."

"Your Rachel will need to tough it out until we get something solid. Her word won't be worth a dime against the word of a two-star general."

"On that grim note, I'll say good-night," Nathan said just before he hung up the phone.

"ADAM ANT! HOW'S MY BOY?" Rachel was glad to be home, glad to see her son and to let his sweet smile wipe clean any taint of Donner's behavior.

"'K." Several small, nonproductive coughs followed this single consonant. But he gave her a smile from his lounging position on the small sofa.

"Adam?" Her instincts told her something was wrong.

"Yeah—*cough*—Mom?" More little coughs followed.

Rachel sat beside her son and put her hand to his forehead. No fever. "Does your throat hurt?"

"No," he said, then put his hand over the center of his chest. "Feels heavy." There was a catch in his voice between the last two syllables.

Uh-oh, she thought. Another asthma attack. And this one seemed serious. "Hey, kiddo, can I listen to your chest a second?"

He nodded and lifted his chin. Rachel pressed her ear against his solar plexus. "Deep breaths," she urged, and then, in between the short coughs, she heard a faint whistle every time Adam exhaled.

She lifted her head and studied her son's features. His eyes were slightly bruised with allergic shiners. She'd read about them. "I think we should go see a doctor, Adam."

"Aw—*cough*—Mom! I'm watching—*cough*—Dragon Ball Z." But even though he protested, he scooted forward in the love seat as if he would go see a doctor right that moment if it meant he could get some relief.

"Let me call and see if I can get someone to take a look at you first. You can see the end of your show." She didn't usually let him watch television once she got home from work because he watched enough of it while her mother was busy taking care of her dad during the day. But this time, she'd make an exception in the hope that it would keep him still and quiet. Perhaps this attack, like all the others, would get better on its own.

An hour later, she had made little progress toward getting someone to see Adam. First a technician and then a nurse and then a doctor at DeWitt Army Community Hospital on Fort Belvoir assured her that Adam could not be seen there unless he had his dependent identification. Rachel's explanation about the Army losing his documents fell on deaf ears. They each urged her to take her son to a civilian hospital for his asthma, and no amount of protesting that the cost of an emergency room visit would be well beyond her budget made any difference.

Not to mention that both she and Adam were entitled to free medical care, she thought after she hung up the phone. Gritting her teeth in frustration, she went back to the living room to check on her boy, as she had done several times during her conversation with the DeWitt hospital staff. He'd fallen asleep and she took this as a good sign. His breathing sounded even, if a little raspy, so she decided to carry him to his bed.

Lifting him, she was reminded of how light he had been when she had done this on a regular basis before she'd joined the Army. Her baby boy would fall asleep in her arms and she would carry him easily to the crib that stood beside her bed in the room she'd slept in all her life. Now her son weighed enough to make her glad for all the strenuous physical training she put herself through during her military years. And he was deadweight, stirring only slightly from his slumber when she hoisted him to where his head could rest upon her shoulder. When she laid him on his bed and pulled the covers over his body, that cosmic yearning for her son's well-being came over her again, as it did so often. She swept his hair off his forehead and kissed him there, feeling a little reassured that his brow was still cool. Surely he would have a fever if he was seriously ill, she told herself as she tiptoed out.

She checked on him six times before she finally climbed into her own bed. Nothing had changed. When she rested her ear against his chest, she could hear the rasp and wheeze of the air sluicing through his constricted bronchial tubes, but he sounded no worse then earlier. Still, she couldn't seem to sleep, and tossed and turned for half an hour before she got up again and slipped down the hall to Adam's room once more. She stood by his bed a long time, just staring down at him, watching his blankets rise and fall with each breath. After a while, she began to sense a change. Was his breathing more labored or was she working herself into needless worry?

Just as she began to talk herself out of feeling alarmed, Adam's eyes fluttered open. "Can't breathe," he croaked as he attempted to inhale deeply. When he let the air out a sputtering whistle followed.

Rachel's pulse shot into overdrive. But she paid no attention, focusing only on Adam. "Okay, sweetie," she soothed as she ran her fingers gently through his hair. "I'm going to get you fixed up. We're going to go for a ride in the car and talk to the nice doctors now."

Immediately, Adam's face crumpled with fear and strain, though he clearly tried to control it. She thought he might start to cry and she wasn't sure she would be able to handle that without falling apart herself, so she did what she could to buck up his courage as she found his slippers and put them on his small feet.

"You'll like it where the doctors are, Adam. They have all sorts of cool stuff. You can listen to a stethoscope and maybe you can have a ride in a real wheelchair."

"Stethoscope?" he managed to say, sitting up now and cooperating with Rachel's efforts to get a sweatshirt over his head. His jammies and the slippers would have to be good enough for the trip to Fort Belvoir because Rachel refused to take the time for more. She was in her night-clothes, too—a T-shirt and shorts—but she didn't care. She would grab her mother's sweater hanging by the door on her way out.

Calmly, she tried to explain about stethoscopes and such, speaking in a hushed, easy voice that seemed impossible given the pounding of her heart. Then she lifted her son into her arms again. "Okay, big boy. I'm gonna carry you to the car."

"Can walk," he said, even as he wrapped his arms around her neck and tucked his legs around her waist.

"I know you can walk, but you're wearing your slippers so it'll be better if I carry you." Should she call an ambulance? No, doing that would take longer than driving him herself and would alarm Adam even more. One thing she remembered from all her reading was that if she could keep her son calm, his attack might not escalate.

He settled his head against her and she could feel the warmth of his breath against her neck. She took enormous comfort in that as she went to the kitchen, where she only paused to scribble a note for her mother in case she woke to find them gone.

Fort Belvoir wasn't far, she told herself. Getting him there wouldn't take long. Only a few minutes on roads empty of traffic at this hour. Yet an eternity passed as she strained her ears toward the back seat for the sound of every breath Adam took. Then, to her increased alarm, she realized she didn't have to strain her ears much at all given the wheeze that followed each exhale.

Almost there, she told herself. "You doing okay back there?" she asked cheerfully as she so often did when they were heading out on a normal day to a normal place at a normal hour.

Adam grunted, which was enough to keep her from completely losing her composure. He hadn't lost consciousness, at least. She kept on driving, forcing herself against all her instincts to maintain a reasonable speed. At last she saw the lights of the guard gate at Fort Belvoir. She slowed and presented her identification. The MP shined a flashlight into the back seat, right into Adam's eyes. He whimpered and Rachel cursed under her breath. She wanted to shout at the man, but knew that doing so would only delay her progress. Security was necessarily tight around all military posts and would remain so for the duration of the war on terrorism. So she spoke calmly. "I'm taking him to DeWitt," she explained, hoping he would just wave her through.

"Sure. Sorry about the light," he said politely. Adam continued to chuff softly, as if trying not to cry. "Go ahead, ma'am," said the MP.

She drove through the dark, tree-lined streets of the installation, trying to remember which turn would get her to the hospital the quickest. Adam started those soft, useless coughs again and Rachel thought she would come out of her skin with frustration and worry.

"Here we are, sweetie," she said as she pulled into a parking space clearly reserved for an administrator. She didn't care if the parking ticket was a thousand dollars; all she could think of was getting her son into the hospital, and this was the only empty space within sight of the emergency room door.

When she finally carried him inside, where the lights were so bright they made her squint, Rachel needed every ounce of her willpower to control the urge to scream for someone to come help her son. Somehow, she managed to walk instead of run to the admissions desk, carrying Adam's inert weight as if it were nothing.

"My son is having an asthma attack." She held out the Army ID card she'd shown to the MP at the gate.

"Yes, ma'am," said the young man in an enlisted uniform. He immediately pressed the intercom button and called for a nurse.

A woman in a captain's uniform appeared quickly and guided Rachel to where she could put Adam onto a hospital bed behind some curtains. Fear shot through her, cold and sharp, when she looked at her son's face and saw that his lips were the wrong color and his eyes were unfocused. She could feel her own pulse at her temples and wrists as blood pumped too hard through her veins. Suddenly, all the years she'd missed spending with her son caught up with her. With a tightness in her throat, she regretted every minute gone and wondered how many there would yet be. Somehow, they seemed numbered, finite, far too few.

What followed was a whirl of activity that alarmed her and relieved her at the same time. A nurse put something on Adam's finger and commented that his oxygen level was low. No surprise there. More people came—a doctor asking questions, a nurse explaining the nebulizer mask she put over Adam's nose and mouth, someone else telling her to sign the admittance form and to hand over Adam's dependent ID card. So many people trying to help Adam, yet Rachel felt very alone. Fleetingly, she thought of Nathan, who had promised that she wasn't alone in her fight against Donner. Would he come to her aid now? Certainly, she needed it badly. Because she had no ID card for her son.

What would these people do when they realized she couldn't produce the ID card? How long would they let her ignore the request in favor of paying rapt attention to the doctor's explanations of what would happen with Adam overnight?

"We need to put an IV into him so we can get the med-

icine working as quickly as possible,'' the youthful Major
said. He looked fresh out of medical school, but he appeared to be confident and Rachel was grateful to him.
''You might want to talk to him, hold him, while we put
in the IV,'' he suggested.

Rachel was glad for the opportunity to go to her son.
Only two feet away from her the entire time, he seemed
miles out of her reach until the doctor let her touch him.
But, oh, what a terrible task she'd been given—to keep her
son still and calm while the nurse stuck a needle into a vein
on the top of his hand. She did her best. And so did Adam.
His color had returned to normal even without the IV—a
result of the medicine he breathed though the mask over
his face, she presumed. And although he winced and his
eyes welled with tears, he played the stoic soldier and let
the medical team do what they had to do. He was rewarded
for his bravery by a great deal of enthusiastic praise from
these strangers who held her boy's life in their hands. Rachel kissed him on the cheek when the job was done and
promised him a big pile of ice cream the minute the doctor
said it was okay.

''We're going to take him to a room now, ma'am,'' said
the doctor, whose name tag read Fletcher. ''I need you to
go with this lady here and help her find your son's records.
He keeps showing up missing from the computer. As soon
as you get that squared away, you can come right up to
your son's room and even stay the night with him if you
want. It should only take you a couple of minutes. Okay?''

Swamped with a choking regret at the prospect of parting
from her son, Rachel nodded. She knew it would take more
than a couple of minutes to find Adam's nonexistent records, but what choice did she have? She would have to try
once more to explain that his documents were lost.

Again, she thought of Nathan. Glancing at her watch,
she realized it was 0100 hours. A dreadful time to call
someone for help. But she was beyond pride now. He'd
said he would help her and by God she would make herself

ask for it even though this had nothing to do with Donner. If he couldn't find Adam's documentation wherever it was buried in the dependent personnel office, at least he could corroborate her story.

A half hour later, after heated negotiations with the admissions staff, Rachel had a fragile agreement with those in charge that if she could produce Adam's birth certificate showing her as his mother, they would treat him here rather than shipping him off to a civilian hospital she couldn't afford. She would have to produce his ID card by close of business the next day. Though fatigue and strain made her hands shake, Rachel dialed the phone to talk to her mother, praying the woman knew where Adam's records were.

She explained the situation to her groggy mother, answering her many questions with a patience she wouldn't have believed she could still possess after what she'd been through this night. "No, Mom, don't come to the hospital and leave Dad alone in the middle of the night. I'd never forgive myself if something happened to him while you were gone. I'll have someone drive over and get the certificate from you soon. Just have it ready, okay? You're sure you know where it is? Good."

The next phone call was harder to make. She'd searched her purse and found Nathan's home number on the laminated phone-tree card she'd been given upon her arrival in the office. It was for emergency use. Rachel had no trouble thinking of this as an emergency even though it was hers alone. Shaking off the last shreds of her pride, Rachel dialed his number. When she heard his sleep-raspy voice, her heart skittered and her tongue tied itself in knots. She couldn't remember ever asking anyone for help since the day she joined the Army. Doing so now was harder than she'd expected. But somehow she had to—for Adam, who was probably scared to death and wondering what was taking her so long.

CHAPTER EIGHT

"WHAT'S WRONG?" NATHAN ASKED as dread coursed through him in hot waves.

"Adam's in DeWitt Hospital—asthma attack. But they won't keep him here unless I can get his birth certificate over here tonight. My mom can't leave my dad alone. So, I was hoping maybe…"

"I'll get right on it," he said as he brushed one hand through his hair and blinked the sleep from his eyes.

"And tomorrow, I need to produce an Army ID card for him. The paperwork still hasn't gone through. It must be lost. You said once that you might be able to help me with that if—"

"Consider it done. Does your mother know I'm coming for the birth certificate?" he asked.

"Yes, she said she knows right where it is."

"Okay." He looked at his watch. "It'll be about an hour before I can get to you. How're you holding up?"

The moment of hesitation before she answered made Nathan wonder if she spoke the truth when she said, "I'm fine. Really. If you could just get me the certificate…"

"I'm on my way, Rachel." And in five minutes, he was heading for her parents' house. In another twenty, he pulled into the driveway.

He'd half expected Mrs. Southwell to be standing on the porch, waving the required document so she could pass it off to him and he would be quickly on his way. Instead, he saw that every room in the house was lit. This was the hallmark of a frantic search and his heart sank. The birth certificate had probably not been found.

He walked straight into the house without knocking, but called out to announce his presence. He heard Rachel's mother shout for him to join her upstairs. He took the steps two at a time, then drew up short when he found her on her knees in a sea of white pages and an overturned desk drawer.

"Told you to file 'em," muttered Mr. Southwell from just inside what appeared to be the spare bedroom. "File 'em, I said." Leaning on his walker, he glared furiously at the mess. Mrs. Southwell seemed ready to burst into tears any moment.

Nathan shook off his immobility and stepped forward. "We'll get this squared away in no time at all, ma'am," he said calmly. "Is the birth certificate in with these papers?"

"I...I think so," she said.

Nathan heard the tremor in her voice. Catching her gaze, he willed her to retain control. She wouldn't be able to help him if she lost it. He put a reassuring hand on her shoulder and took heart when she put hers on top of his. "Well, if you could just give yourself a minute," he said, "and try to be sure, that would be a big help." He could not afford to waste time organizing these papers if the right one wasn't among them.

"It's there," said Mr. Southwell. "Put it there myself," he managed to say.

"And I looked everywhere else before Bernie heard me and told me to check in here. So I suppose it *must* be here."

Nathan had already begun sorting through the array. "Mrs. Southwell, could you put together some things for your daughter? She probably left here without a change of clothes or anything. You'd know what she might need." With a sigh of relief, the woman got to her feet and went to comply. Just as she returned with a loaded gym bag in her hand, Nathan said, "Found it!"

"Oh, thank you!" said Mrs. Southwell.

"Well, get going then!" her husband said.

Nathan didn't need to be told twice. He grabbed the bag and was halfway down the stairs before he called a reassurance. "I'll let you know how things are going for your daughter and grandson as soon as I can."

"Thank heavens she found you to look after her, Captain," Rachel's mother said as she followed him to the door.

All the way to Fort Belvoir, Nathan thought about that last comment. The idea of Rachel needing anyone to look after her seemed absurd. Still, she had asked him for help, and he was profoundly happy to come to her rescue. He suddenly knew that he would like to be Rachel's knight in shining armor at every possible opportunity.

When he finally made it to Adam's hospital room and saw her, his heart constricted and his throat went tight. She sat by her sleeping son and stared at him with weary, frightened eyes. He wanted to sweep her up into an embrace and tell her that everything would be fine; wanted to hold her and lend her his strength; wanted to take care of her so she could take care of her child.

Yet he hesitated on the threshold, feeling like an intruder. She was not his to reassure or hold or take care of, he reminded himself. And what did he know about providing that kind of comfort, anyway? There had certainly been little enough to observe about caring when he'd been growing up. Damn!

But then she lifted her gaze and caught sight of him. Recognition lit her eyes and relief washed over her features. Nathan's chest swelled with wonder at the grateful smile she cast him. He felt like a hero. Her hero. And nothing had ever felt better in his life. He could do this, he told himself. He could be kind and caring with this woman.

"I settled things with the admissions people," he said softly so as not to wake Adam. "I showed them the birth certificate and they seemed satisfied for now."

"Thank you," she said. She rose from her chair, but her gaze never wavered from his. Her eyes drew him to her. He held out the bag of clothes as an excuse to move closer.

"Your mom sent some things she thought you'd need." He transferred the straps into her grasp, profoundly aware of the warmth of her skin as their hands slid by each other. "How's Adam?" he asked as he stared down at the sleeping boy, who looked so small in the big hospital bed. Small he might be, but he also looked like the biggest responsibility anyone should ever have to bear—and one he was completely unqualified to assist with. He'd never considered having children of his own. And yet, watching Adam sleep, he had an odd yearning....

"He's doing a lot better now," Rachel answered, breaking the flow of his thoughts. "He might be able to go home by dinnertime today."

Dawn was lightening the sky outside the window. "You must be hungry," Nathan said. "I could get you something to eat."

She shook her head. "Cafeteria doesn't open for another hour. I'll get something then."

He nodded, unsure what to say or do next. Should he leave her alone now? He didn't want to do that, but his job was complete and he could think of no reason to stay other than that he wanted to be with her. Then he remembered to tell her the rest of what he'd done. "On my way over here, I called a friend of mine who works on dependents' papers."

Her eyebrows shot up. "At this hour?"

He grinned. "He owed me a favor and this seemed like a good time to call it in. I woke him up and told him to find Adam's papers and send an ID card over here to you before noon. Is that soon enough, do you think?"

She chuckled and her eyes sparkled up at him, making him ache to put his arms around her. "Yes, that's soon enough," she said. "You're amazing and I can't thank you enough."

He shook his head, not wanting her gratitude but hard-pressed to identify exactly what he *did* want from her. "I'm glad to do anything I can for you and Adam." Looking at her swamped him with a confusion of feelings, so he turned his gaze to the boy and watched him sleep. He knew she was staring at his profile and he wondered what she was thinking.

"I'm sorry I had to wake you up in the middle of the night," she said. "You're probably tired and you have to go to work in a few hours. Which reminds me to request the day off, sir."

"Granted," he said. Did she want him to go? Would she let him stay if he asked?

Very softly, almost reluctantly, she said, "You don't have to stay. If you don't want to."

He had to focus on her then, to gauge the true meaning of her words and the timbre of her voice. What he saw made his pulse skitter. Though her words told him he could go, her eyes begged him to stay.

He dared not show his happiness, given the circumstances that had brought them to this room together. So he calmly drew another chair alongside hers and said, "How about if I just stick around until the cafeteria opens. Then I can get you breakfast while you stay with Adam. I know you don't want to leave him." How he knew that he couldn't say. His own parents had left him and Julian in the care of nannies throughout their youth.

Her smile reassured him that he'd read the signals correctly. He sat down beside her and asked her how Adam's attack had begun. Soon, they were talking in hushed tones together and Nathan's arm had stolen across the back of her chair. When she rubbed her sleep-deprived eyes with her fingertips, Nathan's hand went to her neck to massage away some of her fatigue. She gave an appreciative groan, so he stood behind her and kneaded her neck and shoulder muscles until she let out a sigh of pleasure.

That sigh made Nathan's thoughts run wildly over forbidden territory—fantasies of massaging her well-muscled body from head to toe. Her head lolled back against his thigh, and he knew he'd better stop before he had an erection he couldn't hide.

"Hey, how 'bout I go get you some coffee and eggs," he suggested, searching for an excuse to escape so he could reclaim his self-control.

"That would be wonderful," she said in a voice that sounded sultry and seductive to his wishful ears.

"Be right back," he said, and he dared not let her see the front of him as he slipped out of the room.

RACHEL SPENT THE REST of the day without sleep, watching over her son, making sure he ate his meals, tucking him in after trips to the bathroom, reading him stories. While he focused on a favorite cartoon on television in the afternoon, she took time out to shower—grateful that Adam's room had a full bathroom attached—and change into the clothes Nathan had been thoughtful enough to bring her. As she combed through her wet hair, she remembered the sensation of his hands working the tense muscles of her shoulders, recalling the scent and heat of him as he stood just behind her. She didn't need a Ph.D. to realize she could fall for this guy if she let herself.

He'd called twice to check on Adam and to reassure her that she could take as much time off from work as necessary to be with her son. The General hadn't seemed interested in finding out the reason for her absence. In fact, Nathan said Donner had apparently assumed it was Rachel herself who had suddenly come down with something.

"He probably thinks his behavior yesterday scared me into calling in sick."

"Well, I didn't disabuse him of that idea. I'd rather he didn't know about Adam for as long as we can manage it."

She had certainly agreed with that sentiment. The idea of anyone causing Adam to be upset—and possibly causing more asthma problems—made her stomach hurt.

"Hey, Mom," said her child from his bed. "The doctor's here!" Rachel smiled at the difference in her son compared with the night before. The medicines the hospital staff had given him through the nebulizer and IV had done wonders. Her smile grew even larger when she saw Dr. Fletcher sitting on the side of Adam's bed, showing him a plastic model that looked like a pair of lungs. "Hey, it opens up!" exclaimed her son as he worked the catch and parted the two halves.

"I want you to learn how your lungs are supposed to work and how the medicines will keep them doing what their supposed to," the doctor said. "How does that sound?"

Adam glanced at Rachel and she saw the doubt in his eyes. She didn't want him to worry that episodes like the one last night could attack him at random. She knew what that kind of fear could do to a person, given Donner's effect on her.

"Dr. Fletcher is going to give you medicines you can take at home that will help you breathe easily all the time," she assured him. "Won't that be a relief?" And she smiled, hoping to convey that everything would be okay now.

"Once we get you on the right medications, you probably won't have to spend another night at the hospital for asthma," Dr. Fletcher said.

Adam looked from one to the other and nodded once. Then he looked down at the model in his hands and pointed to a part on the inside of the plastic lung. "What's this?" he asked. And from there, Dr. Fletcher did a masterful job of explaining asthma to Rachel's eight-year-old.

She left the hospital that evening with her son walking at her side. She had an arsenal of inhalers and a vial of tablets with which to help keep Adam's lungs open. Dr. Fletcher said that the allergy specialist would order a home nebulizer and would show her how to use it with her son when the two of them went for their first regular appointment. Although she was exhausted, Rachel was very happy that she'd managed to get Adam the help he'd needed. She was well aware how deadly asthma could be. Now at least she felt she had tools to help keep it under control.

Between answering the many questions her parents had and giving Adam the attention he needed, Rachel didn't have a spare minute until she finally fell into bed at 2100 hours. Sleep overtook her instantly. She dreamed of the man who had come to her rescue the night before—the one who had been thoughtful enough to bring her clothes and fetch her food and call in a personal favor to make sure her son's ID card got delivered to her by noon. But her dream had a great deal more to do with the sensations his wonderful hands could produce as they massaged her tight muscles, and then stroked her naked skin, and then touched where few others had been given access.

She awoke with a start, flushed with the heat of her dream, then dashed through her shower and dressed quickly for work, determined not to be late. Yet as she drove to the Pentagon, she wasn't sure which made her feel more nervous—the idea of seeing Donner or the prospect of seeing Nathan.

The latter smiled warmly when she entered the office. She knew his eyes followed her all the way to her desk and she wondered if he didn't sense something of the connection growing between them, too. That thought made her happy, when it ought to worry her. But pleasant thoughts about Nathan lessened her dread of meeting up with the General. As long as Nathan sat at his desk, she felt safe.

The General, though, appeared at her side around mid-morning. "Feeling better today, Chief?" he asked with a knowing glint in his eyes.

"Yes, sir," she said, looking straight at him. She simply couldn't let him think he'd cowed her. "Thank you for asking," she added before turning back to her work as if he didn't matter.

"General Donner," Allison said from her desk. Rachel saw in her peripheral vision that the young woman gave him a brilliant smile. "I have those reports you asked me to gather for you, sir."

"Very good, Allison." He gave Rachel's shoulder a squeeze as he passed her and sauntered toward Allison. "Come into my office and we'll discuss them." The two of them disappeared behind his closed doors.

Rachel couldn't contain a growl. She swiveled her chair toward Nathan and glared. "We have to *do* something!" she whispered angrily. "Come with me to the POAC, where we can talk while we pretend to do PT," she said.

He nodded and grabbed his gym bag. "Let me just get one of the enlisted men from down the hall to cover the phones."

Fifteen minutes later, she walked out of the women's locker room and found him on the basketball court they'd reserved. She felt both cursed and fortunate to find no others in the gym at this midmorning hour to distract her from the man's lean and muscular frame, his broad shoulders and narrow hips, his devastating smile as he dribbled the ball in circles around his body—showing off.

"I have some serious frustration to burn off first, so play a little one on one with me," she called to him. She didn't tell him that her frustration was more about him than about Donner at the moment. He grinned and tossed her the ball. She dribbled it down the court toward the basket farthest from the doors. She decided it was safer to talk about the General than about the feelings that galloped through her when she looked at Nathan. "That bastard needs to leave Allison alone," she complained as she lined up her shot.

"You should worry about yourself. He's only toying with Allison to get at you." He jogged into position and made a halfhearted effort to block her.

She ducked under his arm easily and sent the ball swooshing through the net. Quickly he retrieved the ball, then moved slowly back onto the court as he bounced the ball with one hand. He eyed her with lifted eyebrows, clearly surprised by her skill. She laughed and stole the basketball away from him by lunging under his arm again. She made another basket, then laughed at his shocked expression. "I played on the team at Fort Bragg, remember?"

As he realized she meant to play hard, he smiled and the light of competition shone from his eyes. "Maybe so, but I'm taller and faster and you won't be able to block a single shot I want to take," he said. "All I have to do is keep the ball out of your hands."

"We'll see about that," she countered. And thoughts of General Donner and Allison faded as they began to play in earnest, burning off steam and frustrated desires.

She was only slightly more agile than Nathan and had to use her ability to feint and jump in order to block his shots. She succeeded only half the time. Then he made several baskets in a row, despite all her efforts to thwart him. The familiar lust to win began to sluice through her veins, so she called upon her arsenal of well-practiced tricks to foil his shots and retain the ball when she captured it. But he still made more baskets than she did. Twice, they found themselves locked in combat, her back pressed against his front and his arms around her, flailing to knock the ball from her hands as she tried to set up a shot. Rachel had to call on every ounce of will to keep from being completely distracted from her purpose by his nearness, his strength, his hard hot body.

She missed the next basket and he took control of the ball. Frustrated with herself for letting her mind drift toward sexual fantasies while playing a game she took very seriously, she dashed in to disrupt his progress toward the opposite end of the court.

"You can't win, Rachel," he taunted as he reminded her that he was three points ahead. That was when her frustration boiled over and she moved in, coming up hard against the forearm he held out to block her. He calmly dribbled the ball just out of her reach, edging toward his basket and grinning down at her.

The sexy curve of those lips awakened something inside

her, and all at once she thought she ought to just kiss that smirk right off his face. No, she couldn't do that. She didn't dare. But just the idea made her focus return over and over to his wicked grin. Nathan kept forcing her backward, even as she tried to dodge under his blocking arm to capture the ball.

"I'm almost there," he teased with laughter in his voice. "A couple more steps and I'll make that basket."

It was his amused arrogance—and perhaps the heat of the moment—that pushed her beyond good judgment. "Hey, handsome," she said as she abandoned all caution. She reached up to grasp him around his neck and then pulled his face down to hers. She kissed him hard on the lips—almost lost herself in the thrill of it—remembered her purpose just as his tongue swept with devastating effect across her lips, and then stole the ball from him as she abruptly broke away. She ran the length of the court unimpeded, bouncing the ball rhythmically before her. This time she made the basket.

Glancing over her shoulder to gauge the position of her nemesis, she saw him standing still in the center of the court, agape. "You can't do that," he complained. "That's illegal."

"Oh, really," she said with a sly smile as she collected the ball from where it had landed after going through the net. "In what way was it illegal?" She dribbled toward him warily, staying just out of reach, but teasing him with her nearness. "Was it an unwanted sexual advance?" she asked, referring to the definition for sexual harassment.

The meaning of her question dawned on him slowly, but as it did, a feral gleam came into his eyes and a predatory smile lifted the corners of his mouth. He lunged and knocked the ball cleanly out of her hand, but instead of taking control of it himself, he continued toward her. He moved quickly, stalking her as she backed away.

She laughed nervously. "What are you doing?" she

asked, glancing at the discarded ball and then at the man advancing upon her even as she retreated.

He strode with great purpose in her direction until she found herself pressed against the padded wall of the gym. "What am I doing?" he repeated as he neared. "I'm about to ask you the same question, Rachel." Then he pressed the length of his body to hers and swooped to plant his lips upon her mouth.

This was no playful ploy or clever trick. *This* was a real kiss, with sensual lips and wet tongue and labored breathing. The man had no ulterior motive and didn't dash away as she had. He kissed her with single-minded intent— to make her weak with desire and hot with passion.

He succeeded. She surrendered without a fight and wrapped her arms around his neck, clinging to him, ensuring he wouldn't suddenly stop doing such wonderful things to her with his mouth. But he didn't seem to have any intention of stopping. His lips continued to sweep across hers; his tongue continued to delve between her teeth; his body continued to press her against the wall, his hard chest against her breasts, his thigh between her legs. And then his hands began to roam over her body.

She whimpered with building passion when his fingers skated over her hardened nipple, making her body sing. She groaned when his mouth moved away from hers, then gasped when he trailed hot, wet nibbles along the underside of her jaw and down her throat. By the time his talented mouth reached her collarbone, one hand had ventured beneath her T-shirt to unzip the front closure of her sports bra. His hot palm cupped her breast while his lips made their way back to her eager mouth.

Between kisses, he asked breathlessly, "Now, tell me, Rachel. Is *this* an unwanted sexual advance?"

She moaned and squirmed against his touch—wanting, needing. But he suddenly froze in place and shushed her when she drew breath to beg him to continue. Then she heard it, too—voices outside the gymnasium doors. Then

the clatter of metal as someone opened them. The boister-
ous voices grew louder as people entered on the far side of
the cavernous room where Rachel stood in the throes of
passion with Captain Nathan Fordham.

CHAPTER NINE

"THAT'S CAPTAIN FORDHAM!" someone called. Nathan did his best to block their view of Rachel as he heard, "Woo-hoo, Captain, way to go!"

"Get out!" he barked to them, and although he heard laughter and catcalls, they obeyed.

"Oh, God," Rachel moaned. "What have we done?"

"We'll deal with that once you're safely away from here without being seen," he said. "This way." He pulled her along the wall, using his body to hide her in case some curious soul lingered. Then he opened an alarmed door and urged her through it, ignoring the whoops that rang from the box overhead.

"Hurry," he said as he led her down a flight of stairs. She followed willingly, taking the stairs with as much speed and agility as he did. He ducked into a laundry room and brought her in behind him.

"Are you okay?" He felt ridiculous asking her that, and even more foolish when, instead of answering, she reached under her T-shirt and reconnected the sports bra he'd unhooked. He remembered how her breast had fitted into his palm, and he had to look away before his blood began to heat again. He ran his fingers through his hair. How could he have lost control like that with her? "I'm sorry. So sorry. I shouldn't have kissed you like that. I just—" He stopped speaking when he turned back to find her staring at him, her expression blank.

"How should you have kissed me?" she asked, looking

for all the world like a balloon with the helium leaking slowly out of it.

He blinked. Confusion mingled with his regrets. "How should I...?"

"You said you shouldn't have kissed me 'like that.' But never mind." She waved her hand in front of her face as if wiping a chalkboard clean. "I understand you." He detected a slight catch in her voice and his heart ached. He didn't want to be responsible for her pain.

He ran his fingers through his already mussed hair again and tried to think what he ought to say, how he could explain. His head swam with too many emotions, too many conflicting truths. "I...I should be more respectful," he began. "I...I outrank you. We shouldn't...you know...I'm not like that." He jabbed his hand upward toward the gym. "I'm not like *him.*"

Her eyes lit and she took a step forward. He knew he should retreat, but he wanted her back in his arms too much to force himself to do the proper thing. He stood still as he watched her hand rise slowly so she could put her fingertips over his lips. "Shh," she said softly. "You're not like Donner. You're a good, honorable man—an officer and a gentleman." When she took her hand away, he ached to recapture the warmth of it. It was all he could do not to reach for her. But she spoke again—quietly, thoughtfully. "You're right that we shouldn't let ourselves be distracted now, Nathan. We have to stay focused on Donner, on keeping him from hurting Allison—"

"Or you," he interjected.

"Or anyone else." She glanced away, and he wondered if she was thinking of how Donner might try to use her family in his schemes. "But I want you to remember that you're not in my chain of command." She looked up into his eyes again. Her cheeks were flushed. "So what we did isn't illegal, even by Army standards."

With that, she bolted through the door of the laundry out into the sunshine. Before the door swung closed, he saw her running full tilt past the day-care center, taking the path they'd jogged with Donner and the others.

AS IF HER DAY HADN'T ALREADY been complicated enough, Rachel returned to the office to find Mrs. Donner standing near her desk, tapping her foot impatiently. She recognized the woman from the pictures in the General's office. Nathan was nowhere in sight. In fact, the room was empty except for the General's wife.

"Hello, Mrs. Donner," Rachel said as she approached. "I'm Chief Southwell. May I help you?"

She looked Rachel over slowly, with a disdainful eye. "Why, yes," she said in a cold, silky voice. "Where is Captain Fordham?"

Rachel's eyebrows shot up involuntarily, but she corrected her expression immediately and hoped the woman hadn't noticed. "I'm not certain, ma'am. He might still be doing PT or he could be running an errand."

Mrs. Donner shifted her weight to her other hip and shook an errant strand of hair back from where it had dared to drift along her cheek. "Well, never mind. Just find my husband for me, please." She sniffed delicately and looked away dismissively.

"Isn't he in his office?" Rachel asked, glancing toward the closed door.

"I knocked, but there was no answer."

"I'll ring him on the intercom. He might not be in there."

"Then his door would be open, wouldn't it." It was a statement, not a question, and her voice dripped with condescension.

Because the woman had a point, Rachel said nothing. She sat down at her desk and worked the intercom, holding the phone to her ear for what seemed like a long time before the General answered. He sounded irritated and a little breathless.

"Sir, your wife is here. She'd like to speak to you. Should I send her in?"

An empty pause followed. "Ask her to wait a moment. I'll be right out."

Rachel hung up the receiver and met the gaze of the woman standing in front of her. "He said he'll be right out."

Mrs. Donner glared at Rachel, then examined her watch. "We're to be at a luncheon in fifteen minutes. We'll never make it there in time."

"I'm sure the—" But Rachel was saved from making further excuses when the door to the General's office opened. Donner stepped out, straightening his tie.

"Good afternoon, dear," he said. "Shall we go to lunch?"

"We'll be late," she retorted with a sour expression. But Donner walked to her and kissed her on the cheek, which she tipped up to him as if this gesture of affection was her due. She smiled ever so slightly at her husband and they departed.

Rachel turned to her computer, but in her peripheral vision she noticed someone else coming out of Donner's office. Surprised, she swiveled in that direction. Allison Fitzpatrick went to her desk and sat down without looking left or right. She swished her computer mouse back and forth to reactivate her monitor. Rachel stared, astonished and mute.

Allison began typing. Her cheeks were pink and her eyes bright—like someone who had just faced a very difficult experience. Rachel's heart went out to her. She must have been alone with the General. God only knows what had gone on in there. She searched for something to say to the younger woman.

"Allison, are you okay?" she asked.

The woman didn't take her eyes from her monitor. "I'm fine," she said in a too-cheerful tone.

Knowing this woman so little, Rachel got the feeling that

she shouldn't push her for more right now. She wouldn't win Allison's help with the case against Donner by pressuring her into withdrawing completely. If only Rachel could think of a way to persuade her to testify against the man, Rachel's own story would be corroborated.

Very gently, Rachel abandoned more questions in favor of an offer of friendship. "I can help you, if you're worried about anything."

"No, I'm not worried about anything," she said. But she wouldn't make eye contact.

"I know what the General is like. We could help each other if we—"

"You do *not* know what he's like!" she shouted as she turned suddenly, stabbing Rachel with an angry gaze. "You don't know anything!" And she ran from the room, on the verge of tears. Rachel decided to let her go. Before she tried to do more, she would need to go see the post psychologist to find out what her best approach should be.

Clearly, things were much worse for Allison than Rachel had realized. Something had to be done before the General could do any more harm to the poor girl. But no plan formed as the hours of the day wore on. When Allison returned to her desk, she said nothing, and Rachel held her tongue and tried to wrap her brain around a strategy to end the General's tyranny. But strategic thinking eluded her— largely because she couldn't stop reliving Nathan's kiss and analyzing the powerful feelings that had surged through her while he'd held her in his arms.

When the man with the searing kiss finally came back to his desk in the afternoon, giving no explanation for where he had been, Rachel found herself glancing his way every few minutes and wondering if he'd felt anything similar to the heart-stopping, breathtaking passion she'd experienced. But he never gave away a single hint about his state of mind. He sat behind his computer and worked steadily, never glancing at her, not even speaking.

After a while, she began to imagine she would go insane

if she didn't escape his nearness for at least a few minutes. She stood and announced, "I'm going to the drugstore. Either of you need anything?"

Allison gave her an absentminded "No, thanks." Nathan looked her way without answering. His gaze was nothing less than piercing. In his face, Rachel saw all that he'd been hiding these past few hours. His lips were a straight line of tension and his eyes burned with something hot and barely contained. Clearly, he felt at least a hint of what she'd been suffering. The thought made her blood run hot and thick. Her mouth suddenly seemed overmoist and she swallowed. Then, without thinking, she dampened her lips with the tip of her tongue. Nathan's eyebrows lifted for a split second as his gaze dropped from her eyes to her mouth. He stared at her lips, making her skin tingle and her breath catch. Making her unable to move.

"I could use something to cool me down," he finally said very softly. Rachel wondered if he intended to sound so provocative, but she didn't ask. She just stood still and noted the way his body moved as he took out his wallet and produced a dollar. "A Coke or something."

"Sure," she managed to say as she moved closer. She felt ridiculously out of control as she reached for the money with a shaking hand. Nearly snatching it from him, she turned and headed out as fast as she could go without running.

NATHAN WATCHED HER DEPART and knew he was going to die of frustration before the week was out. Rachel Southwell kissed better than any other woman he could remember. And now that he'd had a taste of her, he wanted more. Yet, once again he acknowledged that pursuing her would complicate things beyond what either of them could handle. If only he hadn't discovered how that athletic body of hers felt pressed against his length. If only he could forget the silky-soft texture of her lips and slick heat of her tongue.

He groaned and ran his fingers through his hair, found

that his brow was hot and wished the ice-cold can of Coke would materialize before him so he could hold it against his overheated face for a few seconds. Glancing at Allison, he reassured himself that she paid him no attention, then he shifted in his seat to adjust the discomfort of a partial erection trapped inside his pants. He would have to get a grip on his libido before he'd be able to stand up without embarrassment.

Just as that worry skipped through his mind, General Donner and his wife entered the office. The sight of the older woman eliminated his aroused condition faster than a bucket of icewater.

"Good afternoon, sir, ma'am," he said with a smile he hoped didn't appear as false as it felt.

"Captain Fordham," purred Lydia Donner as she sidled toward his desk with a predatory smirk on her shiny, painted lips. The cosmetics she wore made her seem beautiful from a distance, but up close she looked as if she wore a mask, and Nathan had a hard time hiding his revulsion.

"Where's the Chief?" the General asked.

Allison spoke up from where she stood at the filing cabinet, putting folders away. "She's gone to the drugstore, sir."

Donner nodded as he headed toward his office. "Send her in when she gets back." He didn't bother to turn toward his wife as he said, "I'll see you this evening, my dear." Then he disappeared behind his door.

Summarily dismissed, Lydia stood where she was, staring at the closed door with a slightly startled expression on her face. "He seems preoccupied. Is it this problem in Hawaii, do you think?"

Normally, Nathan knew better than to give the woman a single morsel of information about his boss. She might have heard about Hawaii from her husband, but quite possibly she had heard rumors she hoped to confirm. Since she'd brought the subject up, maybe he could suggest that she use some of her frequent-flyer points to go along with them on their trip to the Pacific.

"The trip could be weighing on his mind. Maybe you should consider joining him on this TDY. You could help keep him on an even keel."

The woman's expression grew thoughtful. Then she looked at him again with a sly grin. "What's this new Chief like?" she asked conversationally as she wandered toward Rachel's desk and then swept the tips of her fingers across the surface of it as though she meant to check for dust. "I've heard she's done miracles with the computer systems."

"Yes, ma'am," Nathan said, hoping he wouldn't have to say anything more. Lydia's interest in Rachel could not be a good sign.

"I met her earlier. She seems capable."

"Yes, ma'am." He couldn't keep himself from recollecting just how capable a lover Rachel would be, if her kisses were any indication. Desperate to avoid such thoughts, he focused on Lydia.

"Will the Chief be going to Hawaii with you?"

"Yes, she will."

"Perhaps you could make the arrangements for me to tag along. Hawaii is such a lovely place and it's been years since I've been there."

Satisfied that the General's wife would convince her husband she should go, Nathan agreed to include her in the arrangements. "I'll e-mail you the itinerary, ma'am. We'll be leaving Friday."

"I suppose I should be getting home now," Lydia said. Her wistful tone almost made him feel sorry for her, so he offered her a slight smile. Her life had to be incredibly tedious, with no occupation other than to serve as the General's wife. The occasional lunch with other generals and their wives, a few parties and social obligations and infrequent trips like this one were just about all she had to keep her busy now that her children were grown. He actually felt a modicum of pity for her. But thoughts of Lydia Donner's lack of fulfillment evaporated the instant Rachel returned.

She carried a small plastic shopping bag from the drugstore and a large, capped cup with a straw sticking out of it. She put the cup on the desk in front of him and dropped a nickel beside it—his change from the dollar he'd given her. Without a word, she went to her desk and sat down. He took a swig from the straw and closed his eyes to fully concentrate on the cold, fizzy liquid sliding down his throat. Anything to keep from staring at the beautiful woman a mere ten feet away. Needing to once again eliminate thoughts of Rachel, he turned to his e-mail list and chose the one he should respond to next. His hand moved with the mouse, his finger clicked the left button and his fantasies were tamed for the moment.

AS SOON AS SHE SAT DOWN, Rachel noticed the envelope partially tucked beneath her desk blotter. It was off-white and the size of a greeting card. It hadn't been there when she'd left for the drugstore. For a fleeting moment, she thought it might be from Nathan, but she dismissed the idea almost before it had fully formed. The Captain might be indecently talented with his mouth and hands, but he wasn't the type to write little notes to women. No love sonnets would spring from Nathan's pen, she was certain. Especially when he clearly felt guilty as hell over their kiss.

Perplexed, she picked up the card even as she asked her office mates if anyone had come by to see her while she'd been gone.

"The General and his wife came back," Allison volunteered. "And I just remembered—he said he wanted to see you in his office as soon as you got here." Her expression was somber as she delivered this unwelcome news. Allison must have understood that she was sending Rachel into a wolf's den.

Rachel didn't get up to comply immediately. She hated

being alone in Donner's office with him and welcomed any excuse to delay. The envelope she held between her hands provided such an excuse, at least for the moment. She caught Nathan's gaze. Without an exchange of words, he seemed to understand that she sought confirmation from him. With a worried expression, he looked pointedly at the envelope, then shook his head slightly to assure her that Allison was right—no one else had stopped by. Rachel could feel his gaze linger upon her as she slid a letter opener under the seal and slit the paper.

REPORT THE GENERAL AND YOU'LL BE SORRY, the note read in bold, black capital letters. I KNOW ABOUT YOUR BASTARD SON. Rachel sucked in a breath, then eased it out so as not to let her co-workers realize the depths of her shock. She read the words again to be sure she wasn't mistaken, then she put the thing back inside the envelope with trembling fingers.

She would have been better off facing Donner in his office than reading such a note. Her head swam with half formed fears and illogical suppositions. Who would do such a thing? What did it mean?

She didn't want to betray her horror to Nathan, but she knew he would see it the instant she met his gaze. So she kept her eyes averted as she tucked the envelope into her purse beneath her desk. She would take some time to collect herself before she told him about it. Besides, the office wasn't the place to discuss something like this. Her last effort to find a safe Pentagon location where they could talk things over had ended in a passionate embrace. Clearly, she should avoid talking to him face-to-face—at least until the memory of their kiss had dissipated some.

Right now, she needed to call home and assure herself that all was well. Her mother answered on the third ring. "Hi, Mom. How is everything?" she asked, trying not to betray her worry.

"Everything's fine, dear. Adam is outside playing with that boy, Brian, from down the street."

"Oh. I was hoping to talk to him."

"I could go get him, if you want me to."

"Could you see if he's busy, maybe take the phone to him if he's in the driveway?"

"Hold on a minute." But her mother's voice returned a moment later. "He's on the sidewalk, putting on his helmet to go for a bike ride with Brian. Should I call him over?"

"No," she said reluctantly. "Just make sure he stays near the house. Has anything out of the ordinary happened today?"

"Is there something wrong, Rae?"

Rachel hadn't decided whether she should tell her mother about the note. She didn't want to alarm her unnecessarily. "I don't think so. Maybe just mother's intuition or something, but keep an extra-sharp eye on Adam today, okay?"

"I'll do that. Don't you worry, Rachel."

As Rachel hung up the phone, she wondered how she would manage to do anything *but*. Her stomach churned with worry, her brain screamed with it; her pulse pounded with it. Worry was something she wasn't used to feeling since she'd joined the Army. She'd been trained to take charge and work solutions rather than worry. But this situation was so far beyond her training she had no idea what to do next. And that sense of groping for elusive answers began to make her angry as well as worried. For God's sake, she was an officer in the U.S. Army. As an enlistee, she'd been trained to kill. Every year, she qualified as a sharpshooter. She knew how to accurately fire a wide range of lethal weapons. And she was Airborne! Defeat had no meaning for her.

Bolstered by these thoughts, Rachel tried to think rationally about the note, even as she opened her database and pretended to work. Who could know she intended to report the General's harassment? And who would take offense at that plan? She could eliminate most women from her list of suspects because all the ones she'd met so far would almost unanimously applaud her efforts regarding Donner—unless there was a woman from the General's past who feared she'd be called as a witness or something. Would a person like that threaten her son?

That last question brought the fear for her child surging back tenfold. She couldn't think objectively when her mind was clouded with such concerns. Before a half hour was out, she recognized she needed help. Her gaze lifted and collided with Nathan's as if he'd been waiting for her to look up at him. Clearly, he wanted to know what the mysterious note contained.

She retrieved the note and went to his desk. Except for when she'd quickly grabbed his money for the soda, this was the closest she'd been to him since their encounter in the POAC. "I need to, um, show you something, uh, in the files next door," she improvised.

He didn't hesitate at this strange suggestion, but got up immediately and followed her into the hallway. "What's wrong?" he asked in a hushed tone as soon as they were in the corridor.

"There was this note on my desk." She handed it over to him so he could read it for himself. After watching those sexy brown eyes scan the words, she said, "I called home and everything seems to be okay. But I was hoping you could check with your brother and see if he couldn't have people drive by the house a few times, just to be sure. I don't think the police would do anything at all based solely on this vague note."

"You're right. Asking Julian, instead, is a good idea," he said, nodding as he stared at the note with a knitted brow. "Who would have put this on your desk? Who had the opportunity to do it without being seen?"

"I don't even know who realizes what I'm up to regarding the General. Or who knows about Adam."

He looked as puzzled as she felt. Then the light of realization came into his eyes. "It must be his wife," he said. "Who else would care what happens to him?"

That made some sense. A close family member would

be ruined if the truth about Donner's behavior ever got out. "But I was here when she came in today. I would have seen her put a note on my desk."

"You were at the store. She wandered near your desk. I was watching her most of the time, but it's possible she slipped this out without me noticing. I have no idea how she would realize we want to report him. And if the General doesn't know about Adam yet—and I'm pretty sure he would have used that information against you by now if he *did* know—then how could Lydia know about your son?"

"Is she likely to bother Adam or cause trouble?"

"I don't think so, but I'll call Julian, anyway, to be safe."

"Thanks, Nathan."

He gave her a half smile, then looked at his feet. "I'm glad you felt you could still come to me with this. I don't want...what happened at the gym...we can't let that get in our way. We need to work this Donner thing together." He raised his gaze to hers again but still had that sheepish expression. She watched with fascination as his cheeks went slightly pink.

To reassure him, she smiled back—despite the unyielding concern for her son that darkened her heart. "I'm getting plenty of practice asking you for help. What happened between us this morning can't change our goals in regard to the General."

He nodded and said, "Agreed. It's too risky to talk here, though. I'll call you at home tonight to tell you what Julian thinks we should do about this." He glanced at his watch. "Why don't you go home and make sure everything is okay there."

"The General said he wanted to see me," she said, wishing with all her heart she could do what Nathan suggested.

He scowled in apparent disgust. "Probably just wants another opportunity to mess with you." He brightened slightly as he said, "But you can't help it if you aren't feeling well again. I'll cover for you."

Relieved, she didn't hesitate to accept, even though she hated making him lie for her. Or was it just going to be another omission of the truth like the many others they'd perpetrated since her arrival at the Pentagon? God, how she wished this nightmare would come to an end soon. But at least she wasn't alone. She had Nathan conspiring with her, helping her, caring for her.

"Thank you," she said, feeling that the words were inadequate. A tremulous smile was the only other thing she could offer him just then and she gave it to him as she collected her things quickly and fled before the General could detain her.

Later that night, after she'd tucked Adam safely into his bed and kissed him on his soft brow, she went to her own bedroom, stripped off her bathrobe and climbed between the cool sheets. She looked at the phone, wondering when he would call. Silly to feel so eager for his voice, his reassurance. She picked up a magazine from her nightstand and thumbed through the pages, not really reading anything. The ring of the phone made her jump and her heart began to pound as she reached to answer it. "Hello?"

"Rae," he said, using her parents' nickname for her. "I hope there's nothing to report from your end except peace and tranquillity." The sound of his voice soothed her and excited her at the same time. Somehow the deep tone made her remember the taste of his mouth, the heat and pressure of his kiss.

"All's quiet," she managed to say. Then she forced herself to talk to him as if this were an ordinary military assignment, a soldiering problem they'd been told to solve. "Adam was glad to have me home from work early. We took a walk so I could look around the neighborhood to see if anyone was watching the house or the area. I couldn't find anything out of the ordinary."

"Julian thinks the note writer just wanted to scare you off. There's not much we should do right now except keep on trying to get some evidence on Donner. But he's gonna have someone drive by a few times a day for a couple of weeks—especially while we're in Hawaii—just to be sure."

This was more than she could have hoped for. Julian took a risk having MPs keep an eye on things outside of their Fort Belvoir jurisdiction. "I really appreciate anything he can do. I'd forgotten we're flying out Friday. It would ease my mind to know that Julian's guys were coming by. I told my mother that I just had one of those maternal instinct things going on and she said she'd keep a closer watch on Adam until it passed."

Nathan chuckled into the phone. "That's a pact that only a pair of mothers would understand."

"Probably," she agreed. "Listen, Nathan, we have to do something about Donner sooner rather than later. The faster we move, the quicker my son will stop being his wife's target—if she's really the one who left the note."

"I agree. But neither Julian nor I has come up with a plan other than to get Allison to press charges along with you or get Donner to say something in public to give himself away."

"He's too clever for that. But I think I've got an idea."

"As long as it doesn't put you in more danger than you are already, I'm listening," he said, but he sounded doubtful.

"Anything that gets this behind me will be less dangerous," she countered. "Here's the idea. We get Julian to give us a small recording device I can hide under my clothing—'

"No."

"And we take it with us to Hawaii—"

"No."

"And look for an opportunity when the General seems likely to be particularly awful, so we can hook me up and get the hard evidence on tape."

"No way, Rachel. That's unbelievably dangerous. What

if he found the device on you? What do you think he'd do then?''

''He won't find it and you'll be nearby to protect me even if he does.'' She knew she wasn't playing fair with such a blatant appeal to his ability to protect her, but this was the best idea any of them had thought of and she needed his cooperation.

Nathan was silent and Rachel could tell he was comparing the dangers of her plan with the risks involved in waiting for some other idea to materialize. ''I don't like it,'' he said at last.

''I don't like anything about this whole thing, but we need to do something soon. He's affecting Allison badly and my bet is it won't be long before she's in the same condition as Sergeant Walker. Already she's too unstable to rely upon, even if we could actually convince her to press charges.''

''Allison isn't the one who'd be at risk if Donner catches on to this scheme,'' he growled. Then he was quiet for a moment. ''Look, I'll talk to Julian about it, see what he thinks.''

''That sounds fair.'' Rachel's spirits rose at the prospect of bringing this problem to closure. At the same time, she recognized the risks and felt a healthy measure of trepidation. What if Donner caught her in the act of trying to trap him? He could send her to the war zone in a heartbeat. She didn't fear such an assignment, but Adam would be devastated. He couldn't travel with her into an area of conflict.

''How's Adam's asthma?'' Nathan asked.

''He's doing well on the daily medications. He has so much energy now. He says he can't wait to show you and Major Julian how well he can run the basketball down the court.''

''I wish I could see that, but we'll be in Hawaii by next Saturday. Julian will have to run the basketball program without me.''

''I've never been to Hawaii,'' she said.

"Well, I wish you were going under different circumstances. It'll be difficult to enjoy it with Donner panting after you the whole time and... Sorry, I shouldn't have said that. I don't want to make this harder on you by reminding you of him all the time."

"That's okay," she said. Then a long pause clung to the phone lines. Rachel didn't want to let go of the conversation—she would feel alone and worried as soon as she said goodbye—but she couldn't think of what to say next.

"I should let you get some sleep now," he said, but he sounded nearly as reluctant to end the call as she was.

Taking a breath, she dared to ask, "Could you talk to me for a while longer? I'm not going to be able to sleep if I hang up now. I'll just dwell on what could happen next."

"Sure," he said, sounding like he might be glad the conversation didn't have to end. "What should we talk about?"

"Anything that will take my mind off my troubles."

"Well, let's see...tell me where you are in the house right now."

She smiled at this effort, feeling that she was in high school again. "In my bedroom. Under the blankets. I've brushed my teeth and washed my face like a good girl. Everyone else is asleep, so the house is very quiet. Where are you?"

"I'm in my bedroom, too, but you haven't been to my apartment, so you probably can't imagine it."

Rachel didn't dare tell him that she could easily imagine him in his bed, propped up against some pillows, bare chested and well muscled, and... "What are you wearing?" she asked impulsively, hoping she didn't sound as young and ridiculous as she felt. But as she waited for him to respond, she realized that her question might have seemed provocative, and her heart tripped over itself. She should take it back, she thought. She should change the subject...

"Uh, boxer shorts. That's what I wear to bed." His voice

had gone low and smooth, and she wondered if his boxers were silky, like his tone. The timbre of his voice made her feel all fuzzy inside and she forgot about changing the subject. "What about you?" he asked. Now there was a distinctly seductive note to his voice.

Rachel shivered but didn't feel cold. "A T-shirt and underpants. That's what *I* wear to bed." She copied his tone and fought the urge to giggle at the sophomoric tension permeating the conversation. Yet she nearly held her breath as she waited for him to say something else. She thought of his kiss and her pulse quickened.

"Um…listen, Rae, about that kiss this morning…"

He'd pulled the thought right out of her head and she gave a little huff of amusement. Before she could think better of her words, she said, "*That* topic is guaranteed to take my mind off of my troubles. It's been a long time since I've been kissed like that." This was not the way to talk to a man who confused her, she chided herself. This was not the way to stay detached and in control. On the other hand, it certainly seemed like a good way to keep him on the phone.

"Really?" he asked as if he couldn't quite believe she'd said what he thought she'd said.

She couldn't quite believe it, either. But, what the hell. She needed to keep talking to him, desperately needed to be safe from the torment of her own worries for a while. "Oh, yeah." And she waited on pins and needles for what he would say next.

CHAPTER TEN

"I'M, UH, GLAD YOU LIKED IT." He sounded very uncertain and a little breathless.

"Didn't *you* like it?" Her heart began to pick up speed as she recklessly probed for his thoughts on the issue of their kiss. It had rocked her world. She wanted to know if it had done anything to him. Or did she? This unexpected frankness about sex challenged her equilibrium, and once again, she wished she could take the words back. Once again, he responded before she could.

"Oh, I liked it," he said with enthusiasm. "More than I can say. But we really shouldn't—"

"Yes, I know," she interrupted. "We can't be seen together behaving intimately. Because we work in the same office. And we need to stick to dealing with Donner. Kissing like that was very wicked of us. Especially in public. A dreadful mistake." She wished she had the courage to ask him if he wanted anything to happen between them when things were resolved with Donner, but her gumption suddenly evaporated. And she wasn't sure she was ready to commit herself to finding out where their kisses might lead. The very thought scared her to her toes. What if she fell in love with this guy and he didn't return her feelings? Her voice came out decidedly sulky as she added, "You won't let it happen again and all that."

He moaned softly. "Rachel," he said. It sounded like a lament. "If you only knew how much I wish I could be there with you right now, taking your mind off your troubles with a hundred passionate kisses. You can't begin to know how much I want that.''

With her blood thrumming in her veins, she risked the question that swelled and swirled inside her. ''What would you do exactly if you were here right now?'' And as soon as the words were out of her mouth, she couldn't believe she'd uttered them.

''Hmm. What would I do? Are you sure you want to hear this?''

Her hand rose to her chin and then her fingertips trailed down the sensitive column of her throat to her collarbone. She could feel her pulse throbbing with anticipation. Did she dare? ''Yes.''

He hesitated only a moment. Then his voice came to her, deep and gravelly. ''First, I'd kiss that perfect mouth of yours. It would taste like the mint of your toothpaste. Your lips would be warm, your tongue slippery and—'' He stopped abruptly, as if he remembered he shouldn't say such things.

''You're doing an excellent job of taking my mind off my troubles,'' she whispered.

He chuckled, a little nervous—or excited. ''I…I've never talked to anyone like this before—on the phone, I mean.''

''Me, neither.'' She glanced toward the door to make certain it was securely closed.

''We shouldn't…''

''I know. We shouldn't.'' Shocked at how much she wished they could, she had to lighten the moment. She searched her mind. ''So, first you'd kiss me and then you'd…take me out dancing.'' She would like to go dancing with Nathan almost as much as she'd like to stay home kissing him.

''What?'' She heard the laughter in his voice.

''Don't tell me you can't dance. A man as graceful as you…'' She trailed off, remembering that men probably didn't like being called graceful, even though it was a very sexy attribute.

"I can dance," he admitted a little reluctantly. "I took lessons for years."

"You're kidding!" She couldn't keep the surprise out of her voice.

"My mother said that Julian and I needed to learn ballroom dancing in order to be well-rounded gentlemen of the world. I think it had something to do with shaping us into leaders of men, who must be capable of holding their own at formal affairs."

"Wow" was all she could think to say.

"So if we went dancing, I'd have to teach you to tango," he said in a low, seductive voice.

She laughed. "That would certainly get tongues wagging about us."

"We'd have to find an out-of-the-way dance club where no one knew us," he admitted. The suggestion held the breathless allure of a clandestine rendezvous. "Then again, we'd probably never find anyone within the tri-state area who could actually play the right music."

"We'd improvise," she said.

"I'd sweep you into my arms," he added.

"And my flowing red skirt would flutter around our knees with each spin..."

"The crowd would be amazed at how well we moved together..."

"Like we were one person..."

"And when you step away toward the end of the dance, I'd pull you back to me to hold you hard against my chest..."

"I'd look into your eyes..."

"Are you ready for the final dip? You have to trust me as I bend you back, back, back over my arm." His voice had gone so soft and raspy she strained to hear every syllable.

"You won't let me fall," she said quietly. The power of this realization—that he would be there for her—stole her breath away.

"I'd never let you fall," he agreed. The charged silence seemed full of excruciating promise. It stretched on, aching with possibilities.

She knew this conversation had to end here, on her revelation of trust and his promise of security.

"Thank you," she whispered. "I think I can sleep now."

"Sweet dreams, Rae."

"They will be. And yours, too, I hope."

He huffed a small laugh. "No doubt about it. I'll be dreaming of the tango."

So wretchedly sentimental, yet so romantic and tender. She sighed contentedly. "Good night, Nate."

She waited for him to softly say, "Good night," and then put the receiver gently onto its cradle. Replaying their words over and over in her mind, wondering at all they implied, she forgot about the troubles that plagued her and finally fell asleep.

THE NEXT MORNING she realized that the troubles hadn't forgotten about her. By leaving early the day before, Rachel hadn't escaped a confrontation with General Donner. She'd merely delayed it. After spending an hour getting ready for work and hoping she would find the courage to face Nathan without embarrassment when she saw him at the office, she stuffed her confusion over him into the recesses of her mind and headed to the Pentagon. First thing upon her arrival, Donner demanded that she appear in his office.

"I hope you're feeling better."

"Yes, sir," she said woodenly. To be in this man's presence after the magical sweetness she'd experienced with Nathan the night before seemed grotesque. The way he sat perched on the edge of his desk, with his ankles crossed casually in front of him, put him far too close to her chair. His nearness made her queasy with dread.

"Good. I need you to be in top form for what I have in mind." He paused and the glint in his eyes suggested things she didn't want to consider. But then his expression shifted to something more businesslike. "Remember when I mentioned before that there's this female Senator who thinks she needs to single-handedly bring the DeRussy incident to closure?" He said the word *female* as if it were an insult to the federal government. "The woman needs to be reassured that she doesn't have to continue her caterwauling about the National Guard. I need her to understand that I'm working on it! You're the perfect emissary for the job. I want you to go in person."

Rachel blinked a few times. "You want me to talk to Senator Zemin and assure her you're working on the Fort DeRussy case?" she asked, trying to separate his orders from his insults.

"Yes. Go talk to her and make sure she knows I'm doing everything humanly possible." He squinted his blue eyes at Rachel speculatively. "You *will* make me out to be a hero, won't you, Chief?"

"Of course," she said, but she silently wondered if this Senator disliked Donner enough to be trusted to help fight the General's harassment. That Barbara Zemin had no love for Donner was common knowledge.

The General uncrossed his ankles and leaned forward, putting his face closer to hers. "Because if you even think of expressing any accusations about allegedly unprofessional interests I might have in you, you'll be in Afghanistan faster than you can say goodbye to your sickly father."

Rachel sucked in a breath. How had he found out about her father? Did he know about Adam, too? Surely the person who'd put the note on her desk would have told him. Damn! Still, there was hope he didn't know yet, given that he'd never mentioned her son.

Donner smiled, showing his pearly teeth. The light in his eyes, though, was not of amusement but satisfaction. Then those eyes turned decidedly lustful. "And speaking of my interests…"

His hand snaked out, and before she could flinch, he slid his index finger over her cheek and down her throat to where the pale-green blouse of her uniform lay open at the collar. He pressed the pad of his finger against her skin at the vee above the second button that joined the two halves of cloth. She shuddered, and he smiled as he stared at that button as if he could slip it open with the power of his thoughts.

Attempting to draw away, she came up against the unrelenting chair back. It dug into her spine. "Don't," she said.

"Rachel, Rachel, when will you learn that resistance is hopeless. And in the end, you won't want to resist." He chuckled. "But I won't demand too much of you today. It will be far more pleasant to insist upon your cooperation when we're in beautiful Hawaii." He withdrew his touch and crossed his arms over his chest, grinning at her.

Sickened, Rachel glanced sideways to gauge the distance to the door, only to realize that his outstretched legs blocked her way. She would have to step over them to get out of the room. She knew without a doubt that if she tried, he would grab her. The thought of becoming trapped in his embrace made her skin crawl.

Distraction seemed the best option. If she'd learned anything about the General in the time she'd spent working for him, it was that he wanted the National Guard to flourish under his command. He had to resolve the issues in Hawaii before he could move forward with any of his other plans. Perhaps she could make him focus once again on that instead of on her.

She forced her revulsion aside and spoke as though he were not a hideous creature who made her stomach roil. "Sir, perhaps before I talk to Senator Zemin, you'd like me to make some calls to the women involved in the incident. Then I could truthfully report to her that we'd begun our investigation. It will look good to her that you've assigned a woman to the delicate matter of speaking with the female officers who claim to have been accosted."

His eyebrows shot up in surprise at her proposal. Clearly,

he hadn't expected her to be helpful voluntarily. "Yes," he agreed as he shifted to his feet. "Yes, that would be a very strategic move. Talk to as many of the women as you can reach. Send e-mails to the others so we have a record of our effort. Then make an appointment to see the Senator. She'll agree to see you right away, I'm certain. Just let her know you're heading out for Hawaii on Friday and she'll fit you in so she can give you the benefit of her guidance before you go." He emphasized *guidance* with acidic sarcasm. Then he walked around his desk to his executive chair.

Relief coursed through Rachel as her path became cleared of his loathsome body. She stood up and sidled closer to the door. "I'll get right on it, sir."

He grinned up at her. "You do that, Chief. But don't forget what I said about your cooperation in beautiful Hawaii."

"I won't forget," she said through gritted teeth. It was all she could do not to shout her indignation, to rail at him for being such a pig, to scream with outrage and disgust. God, what a monster he was! Before she found herself spitting in his eye, she bolted out of his office.

And ran smack into the tall, hard body of Captain Nathan Fordham.

CHAPTER ELEVEN

NATHAN CAUGHT HER BY HER waist before she ricocheted into the wall. Somehow, he ended up with her pressed to his entire length. In the seconds he held her, his mind flooded with memories of the night before. He heard again her seductive voice admitting she liked his kiss, and then he relived her sighs as he swept her into their imaginary dance. He'd tossed and turned half the night thinking of the seduction of the tango, and that led to vivid dreams of all the other ways he wanted to have her body pressed to his. Oh, how he wanted to kiss her, touch her, make love to her.

And guilt choked him, even as desire set him on fire.

He let her go and turned away, hoping to hide his arousal and the blush he knew had crept over his face. She didn't say anything, but stood still a moment, as if catching her breath. Then she mumbled something about making some phone calls and went to her desk. The awkwardness set his teeth on edge. He wanted to talk to her, somehow put her mind at ease about what had transpired between them. But he had no idea what he could say to accomplish that.

Taking his seat, Nathan went through the motions of starting his day, even though his head throbbed over the daunting task of sorting out his feelings. The night before had been an exceptional experience, and the part of him that wasn't swamped with disgust that he'd let himself drift so far from professionalism rejoiced that she'd so willingly shared the unexpectedly romantic moments with him. Yet he didn't know what to say to her about that, either. *I love you* popped into his mind as a possibility. But he dismissed this immediately. He couldn't really be in love with her. Could he?

Glancing toward her as she made a series of phone calls, he noted her expressive eyes and the way her lips moved as she talked. Those features revealed her intelligence and her caring heart. They reminded him of her determination to protect those for whom she felt responsible. And she had more than her fair share of responsibilities. Luckily, she had an extra-large measure of determination.

Hoping Allison hadn't noticed the tension or his inability to keep his eyes off Rachel, Nathan opened his e-mail and began wading through messages, while his mind wandered where it would. Rachel, always to Rachel. Sometimes he wondered at his obsession with her. How would he protect her if he couldn't stop lusting after her? And protect her he must. Already he could see the dread in her eyes whenever she had to be alone with Donner. The wild, hunted glint in those amber depths after each encounter she endured made him nearly insane with the need to keep her safe from the monster their commanding officer had become.

So he wouldn't let her out of his sight, he decided as he finally finished reading incoming mail and turned his attention to confirming with the Hawaii hotel. Working the reservations so that the General and his wife were assigned to an executive suite on the floor above, he deliberately put Rachel into the room adjoining his own. Only so he could watch over her, he told himself. The adjoining doors had locks. But all she'd have to do is open her side if she needed him for anything. Anything at all.

"Do you have a number for Senator Zemin's office?" she asked him just as he completed the arrangements related to their trip. Those were the first words she'd spoken directly to him since she'd left Donner's office. A professional request, but Nathan was glad to know she wouldn't go out of her way to avoid talking to him.

He gave her the number, wondering what she was up to. Without a shred of guilt, he listened as she explained her purpose to the staff person on the other end of the line. Alarms went off in his head as he realized Rachel intended to meet with the Senator in person.

The instant she replaced the receiver, he confronted her. "What are you doing?"

She gazed at him with those soft brown eyes, causing him to lose track of the issue for a moment as he wondered how they would look while he made passionate love to her.

She yanked him back to reality quickly enough. "The General told me to meet the Senator and make him look good." She raised one eyebrow and smiled slightly. The irony was inescapable.

He tipped his head toward the door. "Let's get lunch and talk over your congressional strategy." The need to be alone with her overcame his good sense.

To his relief, she nodded and picked up her purse. "Can we get anything for you, Allison?" she asked.

The younger woman muttered something incoherent as she shook her head. She didn't make eye contact, but just kept on typing. Rachel told her they'd be back in half an hour so she could take a break, too. Then she joined him in the hallway.

"Her behavior reminds me of Sergeant Walker's," he said. To talk about Allison for a minute or two, rather than launch right into a discussion about the Senator, seemed prudent. Especially since he had every intention of telling Rachel every last pitfall she would face if she met with that particular politician in person and alone. "You're right that the General is having a bad effect on her."

"That's why we have to do something soon to end his reign of terror. I've spent the morning speaking with some of the women involved in the Fort DeRussy incident. When I identified myself and said I was calling for the General, two of them volunteered that they had worked under Donner's command in the past. They didn't come right out with anything specific, but they were both very clear that they don't ever want to deal with him again.''

"But would they testify against him?" They walked slowly through the halls.

"I think they might. But we'd have to get him as far as a trial first. Did you talk to your brother about the recording equipment?"

Reluctantly, he nodded. "I called him before I left for work. He's no happier with the idea than I am. He says it's not only dangerous, but he's not sure it's legal."

She came to a dead stop in the center of the wide corridor and scores of people passed them. "What choice do we have?"

"It would be risky, but maybe you could persuade Senator Zemin to help us." He hated the idea, but desperation led him to at least suggest it.

She shook her head. "I thought of that, too, as soon as he told me I should go talk with her. But he threatened to send me to Afghanistan if I decided to say anything to the Senator about his less-than-professional behavior. If it wasn't for Adam, I wouldn't worry about a deployment like that. But now isn't a good time."

"Trust me, there's never a good time to go to Afghanistan. Been there, done that." And the memories were grim. His experiences in that hellhole were largely responsible for why he'd asked for a quiet, laid-back job as a general's aide. And his accomplishments in that back-of-beyond country made more than one general request him as an assistant. Only the best officers got to be aides.

Rachel started walking again toward the cafeteria. "It's bad enough I'm going to Hawaii."

The mention of their upcoming trip made him think of the adjoining rooms he'd booked. And that led once again to fantasies about the future based on his detailed dreams of the night before. As he opened the cafeteria door for her, his gaze momentarily escaped his control and drifted to her backside. As it had so many time before, his mouth watered, but his hunger had little to do with the aroma of food wafting from the grills and hot plates along the food-service bars. Then he remembered where he was and quickly refocused his eyes—and his thoughts—before other parts of his body joined in the fun.

"On the other hand," she added, as she smiled at people she knew and waved to one of the female officers he remembered she'd had lunch with a few times. "If the Senator seems predisposed to helping, maybe I could explain the bind I'm in, ask for her discretion. I heard she doesn't like him. Maybe she'd agree that he wouldn't have to know I was the one who steered her in the right direction."

"You'd need to be very careful. Politicians can't be trusted."

From her place in front of him in the food line, she turned to looked at him with a knitted brow. "What makes you so jaded about politicians?"

"My father was a congressman."

She gawked at him. "Well, why don't we ask *him* for help! With his contacts we could—"

"No."

She blinked at him. "No?"

He sighed and realized he was not going to escape telling her his life story. At least he could opt to make it the short version. "Okay, it's like this—my mother died in a drunk driving accident when I was about thirteen." He couldn't bring himself to reveal that his mother had been the one drinking that awful night. After a fight with his father, she'd stormed out of the house and peeled down the driveway in the sports car she'd purchased in an attempt to give her life some meaning. "But we'd had a lot of nannies growing up, so not much changed except that she wasn't there anymore. My father continued to be a busy congressman and we hardly ever saw him. We grew up certain that he had more important things to do than spend much time with his sons. Then suddenly my father had Alzheimer's disease. Pretty soon, he didn't even remember he had sons. It took about a year for him to get bad enough to go into an institution.''

He saw the sympathy in her eyes, didn't like seeing it there. He shrugged and said, "It's not a big deal. These things happen.''

To his relief, she somehow swept her face clear of pity. She turned her attention to filling her cup with lemonade. "And that's where he is today?'' she asked as he followed her along in the line.

"Yup,'' he said casually, not wanting to dredge up any more old hurts. He had a feeling that if he started confessing to Rachel, he wouldn't stop. So he changed the subject back to the original topic. "He was one of the better ones in Congress. At least he tried to behave with some measure of integrity. But the truth is, most politicians would sell their grandmothers if it got them where they wanted to be. That's the nature of the beast.''

"All right. I'm forewarned,'' she said as she paid for her meal and headed toward the tables. "Any other bits of advice before I face the Senator in her lair?'' She scanned the cavernous room for empty seats.

"Don't tell her anything personal. Don't let her trick you into talking about anything you aren't prepared to discuss. Don't fall for her friendly—''

She set her tray down and held up her hands as though asking for mercy. "Okay, okay! I get the picture. Sheesh! You really *are* a politician's son.''

He smiled at her, surprisingly relaxed, considering their earlier awkwardness. At least Donner had given them plenty to talk about to ease them through any residual embarrassment. Or at least so he thought until their knees collided beneath the tiny cafeteria table.

"Sorry,'' he muttered as he repositioned his legs. But the damage was done. The tangle of limbs raised memories too recent and powerful to suppress. He shifted uncomfortably and stared down at his food.

"About yesterday,'' she began in a soft, gentle voice.

He raised his gaze to hers and prayed she wouldn't speak apologies or regrets.

"That kiss…and then…the tango…" She grinned shyly at him. Her cheeks were charmingly pink. "I don't know what possessed me to coax you into a conversation like that, when I know full well—"

"That we shouldn't," he finished for her. "Well, I know what possessed me," he added, determined to cut off any opportunity for recriminations. "You're intelligent, witty, brave and beautiful. I can't help myself."

Her gaze lifted and her eyes went wide. Surprise wiped her face clean of expression. She didn't seem capable of speech.

Nathan shared her surprise for a moment. Had those words really come out of his mouth? Would she make more of them than he intended? And what would she do with such information? Nathan felt the blood drain from his face as he realized he'd just laid his heart on the table for her to destroy, if she chose. Not even his tour in the war zone had made him feel so vulnerable.

Her mouth moved, but no words formed. Her tongue flicked out to dampen her lips. Nathan couldn't take his eyes away from the sight of their moist shine.

"I…I thought you said we couldn't…" she began.

He forced himself to look into her eyes. "We can't," he said, noting that she hadn't mentioned anything about returning his admiration. No sense in tormenting himself with false hopes, he decided. And they couldn't act upon such feelings even if she shared them. He had to just bottle up his emotions and his libido and stick to business. Putting thoughts into action, he pulled back from her physically to the extent the chair would allow, ready to set the record straight about there being any repeats or expansions of the previous night's exploits.

But just as his hand slid to the very edge of the table, she reached out and rested her fingers over his. They were warm, the gesture tender. Regardless of who might see, he had a nearly uncontrollable desire to raise her fingertips to his lips. The soldier in him prevailed and he remained motionless. The warmth of her touch seeped into him, melted him, made him hope for something he couldn't name. He waited, barely breathing. Perhaps she would express some return of his feelings after all....

"When this is all over?" she said like a question. But her gaze skittered to the left, as if the possibilities unnerved her.

Still, it was something, and he stifled the urge to gasp for air his relief was so great. It meant she was thinking about what might happen between them in the future. That had to be good. Right? "Yes," he rasped as he turned his hand over beneath hers and gently clasped her fingers. Then he remembered where they were, and let go as he glanced around them to see if anyone had noticed. He cleared his throat. "Yes," he repeated in a more businesslike tone. "When this is over." He wasn't sure what he was agreeing to, but he certainly wanted something to happen between them when things settled down. "Or as soon as you transfer someplace else so we're not working in the same office."

She grinned. "Now, that's a mighty powerful incentive to transfer." Sobering, she said, "But you know I can't do that until we're sure he won't hurt anyone else."

He nodded. "I forgot to mention 'responsible' and 'determined,' among your most attractive characteristics."

She gave him a sweet, disarming smile. They shared a moment of comfortable silence until he worried his hunger for her would be visible to anyone who happened to look their way. "Eat," he said. "And tell me the latest about Adam and your parents."

She picked up her sandwich and began to recount her son's recent exploits.

BY THE TIME SHE WALKED INTO Senator Zemin's office the next day, Rachel's stomach was in knots. If her mission to make Donner look good was not daunting enough, Nathan's dire warnings about politicians had put her on edge. She tugged on the dark green jacket of her class A uniform and took some comfort in the many ribbons bedecking the front. Remembering the Airborne medal pinned over her left breast, she squared her shoulders. She would not allow the Senator to intimidate her.

"Welcome, Ms. Southwell," said Barbara Zemin as she moved gracefully from behind her desk with a hand outstretched. The staff member who had announced Rachel quietly slipped out of the room and closed the door.

Rachel mustered a smile and clasped the Senator's hand firmly. "It's good of you to make time for me, Senator."

"Well, the matter you've come to discuss is of great importance to me and my constituents. These are troubled times and we can't have our National Guard running amok. The public won't stand for it. Especially when the perpetrators are the same people securing our nations' airports and train stations."

Rachel stared at the woman, who sounded for all the world as if she were delivering a prepared speech. "Yes, ma'am," she managed to reply.

Zemin indicated a grouping of armchairs and Rachel moved toward the one facing the door. The Senator claimed another one and then took Rachel's measure. "Why are you really here?" the older woman asked.

"P-pardon me?" Rachel stammered. Nathan had been right about politicians. The tricks of this one already had her unbalanced.

Zemin smiled the way she did in all her pictures, except that her eyes held the light of speculation. "You're not really here to tell me that Major General Walter Cornelius Donner is the salt of the earth," she said.

"I'm not?" Rachel asked, stalling for time and probing for clues.

The Senator grinned. "You're good at this, Chief."

Rachel blinked. Did Zemin think answering questions with questions was some kind of ploy? There seemed no sense in enlightening her to the fact that she was simply trying to regain her equilibrium, so she said nothing.

The Senator waited a moment, then filled the void by saying, "Look, we both know that Donner will do anything to maintain the good image of the Army National Guard. I'm sure he'll get to the bottom of what happened to those women at Fort DeRussy eventually. Meanwhile, he's the biggest misogynist in the history of the military."

"Do you think so?" Rachel asked, figuring she was getting more from sounding stupid than she would if she actually spoke her mind. And hearing the Senator peg Donner so precisely rocked her enough to make further commentary impossible.

"I hear a lot of things, being one of so few female Senators these days. People seem to think they can confide in me. You can, too," she urged.

Rachel knew she had to be careful. This woman was just as dangerous as Nathan had warned. "I'm sure I could confide in you, ma'am," she said. "And I'd be willing to provide the whole truth about anything I have firsthand knowledge of at any trial for misconduct. It wouldn't matter to me if the person on trial was a private or a general." There. That sounded cooperative without giving too much away.

Zemin laughed. "You should go into politics when you're done with the Army. You'd be great dealing with the press. You're well able to dance around the truth very nicely without actually committing yourself to anything concrete."

Screwing up her courage, Rachel said, "I'm prepared to commit when the time is right. Right now I have a career to protect."

"So you do. If you find yourself with any sort of evidence—obtained in whatever way you see fit—please remember that I can lend you protection in exchange for putting the bastard behind bars instead of wearing stars." She stood and Rachel followed her lead. "Thank you for coming, Ms. Southwell. I'll be in touch. Or you get in touch with me." She smiled and added, "When the time is right."

And just like that, the interview was over.

Rachel left Capitol Hill and headed back to the Pentagon, wondering what Nathan would say about Senator Zemin's promise to provide top cover if they could catch Donner on tape, even if doing so was not entirely by the book.

But when she finally found Nathan at the Pentagon, he didn't need much persuasion that desperate actions might be required.

"That man is going to drive me to violence any minute now," he said through gritted teeth. "We simply have to stop him."

"What did he do now?" Rachel asked, guessing she probably would wish she hadn't inquired.

"Allison ran out of his office in tears and hasn't come back."

CHAPTER TWELVE

RACHEL LEARNED THAT NATHAN had made every effort to contact the young Specialist to ensure she would be okay, but Allison didn't answer her cell or home phones. Following up with calls of her own from her home in the evening, Rachel had no better luck reaching her. When Specialist Fitzpatrick reappeared at work the next day, she was composed, but she wouldn't speak of what had troubled her. Rachel was too pressed for time to spend more than half an hour trying to coax information out of her. They were to depart for Hawaii in the morning and she had a hundred things to do before she left.

Adam had an appointment at noon with the allergist, who would be seeing him regularly from now on. Undoubtedly, there would be prescriptions to fill, since the samples she'd received at the hospital, which had improved his health so dramatically, were nearly gone. At least she wouldn't have to pony up the cost of the medications now that Adam had an ID card and was listed as her dependent. Rachel had Nathan to thank for that. No telling when she would have met with success on that count if the Captain hadn't intervened.

She stole a peek in Nathan's direction as she sat at her desk feeding commands to the database for delivery of a report she needed to finish before she left for the Pacific. He really was the best thing that had come her way since Adam's birth. So why didn't she just tell him so instead of making vague references to what might happen between them when this mess with Donner was resolved? After his declaration in the cafeteria—and she sighed at the memory of him saying those nice things about her, ending with how he simply couldn't help himself—he'd surely like to hear something more concrete about what she thought of *him*. But she couldn't seem to make herself speak what was in her heart. Fear, she supposed. Fear of being rejected, abandoned, left behind. Again...

"Allison, will you be okay if Rachel and I go off to a meeting for a few hours?" Nathan asked the Specialist. Rachel looked up with raised eyebrows. This was the first she'd heard of a meeting this morning. She hoped it would be over in time for her to take Adam to his doctor.

"I'll be fine. Everything's under control," she said, offering a shaky smile. She would probably never willingly reveal what had happened with Donner, and Rachel knew she would make a lousy corroborating witness.

"You can reach me on my cell phone if you need me," he said. Then his gaze rotated to Rachel's. He smiled. "Let's go."

Oh, what that sexy smile could do to her! Without a single question about where they might be headed or how long it would take, she picked up her purse and beret and followed him out the door. Just to spend some time with him would be wonderful.

"No more threatening notes?" he asked.

"No. But I didn't look for one, either. If you're right that it's Mrs. Donner, then I don't expect I'll see another one until she comes around again."

"Don't you want to know where we're going?"

"I figured you'd get around to telling me eventually."

He nodded grimly, deflating her fantasy that this outing would be a pleasurable one. He led her through the corridors to South Parking without explaining. He asked about her parents and Adam, then assured her, when she inquired, that they would be back in time for her son's doctor appointment. Construction equipment of every shape and size stood to the right of that exit, and the noise from the machines already in operation made it impossible to converse. Rachel didn't mind. The machinery was helping to rebuild the damage wrought by the terrorists, and the roar of their engines lifted her confidence in the resilience of America.

They paused to put on their berets and then headed toward the vast sea of parked cars. He led her to his silver Audi S4 and tripped the lock mechanism on his key fob. Then he opened the door for her. Rachel couldn't remember the last time a man had opened a car door for her. Before meeting Nathan, she might have scowled over how the gesture emphasized that she was female rather than just another part of the military team. But she found herself smiling when it was this particular man treating her with the courtesies reserved for a lady. She grinned up at him as she drew her legs into the car. He looked appreciatively at her limbs for a second, which suffused her with sudden shyness, then he lifted his gaze to her eyes and returned her smile.

When he got behind the wheel, his expression grew serious again. "We're going to see my brother at Fort Belvoir. He said he might be able to hook us up with a taping device. I shared with him what you told me about Senator Zemin, and for some odd reason, he's convinced her support will be enough to get us past any questions about exactly how we acquired the tape once we submit it as evidence."

"That's great!" The prospect of finally resolving this mess with Donner made her feel much better about going to Hawaii. She would undoubtedly find the opportunity to record what they would need while she was there.

"Actually, it's dangerous as hell. If he catches you with this device on your person, your career will be doomed. *After* he makes you suffer through a tour in some godforsaken location, far away from your family."

She sobered immediately and nodded. Nathan was right. Encouraging as it was to think an end might be in sight, she couldn't overlook the risks. "I'm counting on the good Senator to keep me out of Afghanistan, at least."

"Don't bet on it. She has her own agenda."

"So you said."

They arrived at the offices of the Criminal Investigation Division in less than thirty minutes. Julian was waiting for them. He scanned up and down the hallway like a spy on a clandestine mission before closing his office door so they could talk in privacy. When he turned and saw them staring, he must have realized how paranoid he seemed, because he said, "I'd rather that no one associated your visit with the recording device I signed out of the equipment closet. It would be better all around if any recording you're able to get just materializes on the desk of your Senator friend."

"Wouldn't the lawyers have to show where it came from if they admitted it as evidence in court?" Nathan asked.

Julian grinned at his younger brother—the first smile he'd cracked since their arrival. "You've been paying attention to the things I tell you about the law," he remarked. "Yes, if the tape was going to be used as evidence, they'd need to know its source and chain of control. But then you'd have other problems—like, Rachel would have to go to court and verify the recording and subject herself to questioning by defense."

"I wouldn't mind doing that if it meant stopping Donner from hurting other women," she said.

Julian looked her in the eyes. "But you would go through hell, with no guarantee that you'd really stop him. There are a hundred ways his lawyer could tear up your testimony—and destroy your reputation—if you had to testify against a two-star general."

"So, why are we here?" Nathan asked, making no effort to hide his impatience.

"Look," Julian said. "If you get something incriminating on the tape, I think you should send the thing to the Senator and let her do the rest. From what you've told me, she wants to put a stop to the General, too. She might be able to do that without all the fuss and bother of a court case.''

"How?" Rachel asked, as she exchanged confused glances with Nathan.

"All she really has to do is play the tape to a few other ranking generals, maybe a couple of other Senators. His career would be over. He'd be forced to retire. No fuss, no bother.''

Nathan nodded. "Yeah, that might work," he said. "I've seen senior officers forced to retire for far less.''

Rachel squinted and growled. "*That* is not a satisfactory outcome," she announced. She could see from their expressions they had no clue why she would say such a thing. "This guy messes with any woman he can control, so he does *not* deserve to retire honorably. He'll collect his fat retirement check and just move on to a high-paying civilian job where he'll terrorize civilian women. The man needs to be in prison for what he's done already!''

"Whoa there!" Julian said. Then he focused on his brother and said, "You've got your work cut out for you, Nate. She wants to rescue the entire world.''

Nathan's eyes were flinty and his mouth set in a thin line when he met Rachel's gaze. "You can't seriously think you are obligated to protect the women who *might* work for him in a civilian job he *might* get. For that matter we might not get the evidence or it might not be sufficient to get him suddenly retired, never mind behind bars.''

She scowled. "Are you saying it's okay with you if he hurts women as long as they're not Army women?''

His eyebrows drew together. "Of course not!''

She softened toward him when he gave this correct response. More gently she said, "He belongs in jail, right?''

"Yes.''

Rachel smiled at this second appropriate answer. "So we need to get the Judge Advocate General guys to prosecute, right?''

Nathan began shaking his head even before she finished the sentence. "Not if it means dragging your reputation through hell, ruining your career, hurting Adam and your parents, no. There's a limit to how much you're expected to sacrifice to stop this guy, Rae."

Julian stood up from behind his desk. "Okay, you two. Enough. You need to get the recording before you bother to argue about what to do with it. Rachel, just keep in mind that civilian women have more laws protecting them and therefore more opportunity for prosecuting someone for sexual harassment than do women in the military." He gestured for her to stand up, too. "Come over here so I can show you how you use it. You can wear it tucked into your waistband under your sweater, where it won't be noticed."

SHE WAS IN THE CAR, HEADING for the doctor's office with Adam, by eleven-thirty. "I know I said I wasn't going away again, but this is just a short trip. I'll be back in a few days, a week at most."

"You packed a suitcase," Adam said in an accusing tone. Glancing at his profile, Rachel saw that his lower lip stuck out just enough to alert her to the onset of a serious sulk.

"It's one very *small* suitcase. You know everyone with a job has to take a business trip now and then. I'm not moving away again or anything."

"You said I could go with you if the Army sent you somewhere. I want to go to Hawaii, too."

"I can't take you with me this time. And it's a terribly long flight. It won't be any fun at all."

He turned his face toward her and she saw that his expression had gone from belligerent to worried. He dropped his voice to nearly a whisper, but she heard him. "What if your plane flies into a skyscraper?"

Now, *that* question made her heart stumble. She stared ahead at the road they traveled while her thoughts tripped over one another searching for some reasonable response.

The image of those airplanes plowing into the twin towers in New York kept flashing across her mind's eye. Adam had seen the video reel hundreds of times on television. Even all these months after that terrible day, the pictures of the attack appeared periodically. They were unavoidable. Despite the awful reality of that fateful day, she had to find a way to reassure her son.

"My plane will not fly into a skyscraper. I'm sure of it." *Very weak,* she assessed. But what else could she say? To tell him that all the bad guys who might do such a thing again had been captured would be a lie. To tell him that air travel was safe now would be false. Yet she didn't want him to be afraid for her.

She drove into the parking lot of the doctor's office, found an empty spot and pulled in. When she shut off the engine, she stayed in her seat a moment, clinging to the steering wheel and staring out the windshield. She knew that Adam still gazed at her with fear haunting his youthful eyes. He was waiting for her to say something more reassuring than her vague promise that nothing would happen.

With her heart in her throat and the threat of tears stinging her eyes, she turned to her son and met his gaze steadily. She wanted him to see the determination in her eyes and the set of her mouth. "Adam, we can't let terrorists make us too scared to do what we need to do. If we stop doing our jobs or stop going to school or stop having fun because we're afraid something scary could happen, then the bad guys will win. We can't let that happen, right?"

Adam nodded, and grew thoughtful. Rachel continued, even though her uncertainty nearly suffocated her. "So even if we're afraid sometimes, we still have to go on doing what we're supposed to do or what we like to do. Now, the Army thinks that the plane I'm taking will be safe enough for me to fly on. I'll be with Captain Nathan and our boss, General Donner. He's a two-star general. The

Army wouldn't let such an important man on a plane if they thought something terrible could happen.''

Adam looked out the passenger side window a moment. Rachel waited with bated breath for his reaction. After a moment, he pushed the button to unlock his seat belt and said, ''Okay.'' Then he got out of the car.

Rachel let out her breath and joined him as he headed to the building where his new doctor had his office. Halfway there, Adam did something she rarely got to enjoy now that he was a big eight-year-old. He slipped his fingers into hers and walked with her hand in hand. He was silent until they were on the elevator. After he'd pushed the button for the appropriate floor he said, ''I still think you should take me to Hawaii. They have cool volcanoes there.''

Rachel smiled. ''Maybe I *will* take you there someday. Just not this time.''

Adam grinned and Rachel knew this latest parenting crisis was over.

AT DULLES AIRPORT THE NEXT morning while they waited in line to go through Security to catch their commercial flight, the General actually pinched her bottom when she preceded him through the security checkpoint. She jumped but suppressed a yelp. The guard looked at her intently after that and scrutinized the contents of her purse, pulling the taping device partway out. For a sickening moment, she thought the General would notice it, but his attention was on his wife.

''Remember not to play that during takeoff and landing,'' the guard said, apparently thinking it was an MP3 disk player. Relief washed over her until it occurred to her that if the guard didn't recognize this device for what it was, there could be other devices that got by him. So much for stringent security.

''What's wrong?'' Nathan asked when he moved alongside her for the long walk to the gate.

''How can you tell something's wrong?'' she countered.

Apparently she wasn't as good at hiding her emotions as she wanted to believe.

He scowled. "I can just tell. Did he do something?"

They both knew who "he" was. "The guard almost took the tape recorder out for closer inspection. That certainly had my heart pounding harder."

"You should have given it to me to carry. Let me have it now and I'll put it in my carry-on bag."

"That's okay. I'm fine. I don't want anyone seeing me pass it to you. We may be in uniform, but suspicions are high and I don't want to draw attention."

"Donner didn't see it?"

"No, but he pinched my butt when I went through security ahead of him."

She watched Nathan's expression turn deadly and his cheeks flush with anger. "I'm gonna håfta knock his lights out eventually," he muttered. Fortunately, the General heard none of this. He lagged behind with his wife so he could continue to harangue her about why she shouldn't have come on this trip with him. He'd been at it almost since they'd arrived. Rachel noted that Mrs. Donner had little to say, but got her way nonetheless.

"You will do no such thing," she admonished Nathan. "They'd end up court-martialing *you* instead of him. And I don't need you defending me every second."

"The hell you don't," he shot back.

"You're not my protector, Nathan."

"The hell I'm not."

She eyed him as they walked, feeling she'd just discovered a whole new side to the man. Something in the way he said he was her protector—all indignant and with exaggerated manliness—warmed her heart and irritated her at the same time. She shook her head at the confusion of emotions this guy brought out in her.

"You know, he could really hurt you, no matter how capable you think you are." He was deadly serious.

"I realize that. And I'm glad to have your help. It's just

that you sound downright archaic sometimes. I'm not a helpless medieval woman in need of a champion.''

He was silent a moment, seeming to ponder her observation. "But I'd like to be your knight in shining armor.'' He said it so softly she almost didn't hear. Then he added, "Stay in front of me as you board the plane and make sure you sit in the window seat you were assigned to, even if there are a lot of empty seats.''

"Okay.'' She wasn't sure why this was so important, but he obviously had his reasons. Glancing at Donner as he came up on their heels, she decided this was not the time to challenge Nathan's orders. And once she finally boarded, she understood the Captain's strategy. She took the window seat she'd been assigned and then Nathan sat right next to her. He'd obviously planned it this way so the General wouldn't be able to cozy up to her for the long flight to their stopover in San Francisco.

The General came into view just as she found the buckle of her seat belt. He leaned over Nathan with one arm casually draped along the back of the seat. "Let's trade seats, Captain. I need to discuss some things with the Chief and my wife would rather talk to you than to me.''

Nathan blinked up at his commanding officer as if this request took him by surprise, but as soon as he spoke, Rachel knew he'd been prepared for such a suggestion from the General. "Sir, I'd be glad to talk to your wife, but the Chief and I need to review the list of people we'll be interviewing and go over the information we've already collected. Otherwise we won't be ready to get started when we land in Hawaii.''

"It's a long flight. You don't need the whole trip to plan your strategy, do you?''

"No, sir, but I'd like to get started on it now while I'm wide-awake. These long flights tend to make me dog tired after a few hours.''

Rachel jumped in with, "We don't have very many days to get done everything we need to do.''

The General's mouth pursed as he thought about this. Then, to Rachel's deep relief, he nodded. "Fine. I suppose your preparation for the interviews of the Guardsmen is more important."

The flight attendant asked the General to take his seat, and in a flash, he was gone to the front of the plane where Rachel couldn't see him.

Suddenly alone with Nathan, Rachel found that her tension did not abate, although the man beside her made her nervous for completely different reasons. She became aware of the faint scent of his aftershave. His shoulder was so close to hers she could feel the heat of his body. If she didn't keep her knees pressed together, their legs would collide.

"That was close," he said casually, as if he felt none of the edginess she suffered from.

"Do we really have stuff to review before we get to Hawaii?"

"Yes, but it can wait."

"You had your exchange with Donner all planned out before we sat down. You knew how to get rid of him. Thanks."

"Actually, I only came up with it when he started heading toward us." He grinned. "I may not be the athlete you are, but I'm smart," he said as he tapped his forehead and winked.

Rachel laughed. It felt good. Some of the tension eased out of her. "If you're so smart, why aren't you wearing your seat belt?"

He leaned away from her a bit and looked down between their seats. "Because you're sitting on half of it and I didn't want to go reaching for it without your permission. You've already been groped once today. I didn't think you'd appreciate it a second time."

She was tempted to shake his complacency by saying she wouldn't mind if *he* took such liberties, but she didn't dare. That would be far too forward, notwithstanding their romantic phone conversation. That intimacy had lasted only as long as they'd talked. Now they were back to searching for what to say to each other and how to behave.

She reached beneath her thigh and pulled out the loose end of his seat belt, saying nothing. His fingers slid over hers as he took it from her, and the contact did not go unnoticed by the rest of her body. She thought Nathan was irritatingly unaffected until she noticed he fumbled with the belt buckle and had to try three times before he got the thing connected.

He didn't glance her way at all during the preflight instructions, and during takeoff he ignored her completely, even though she could not seem to escape an intense awareness of him. Not even the fleeting thoughts about the airplanes that had gone down at the hands of terrorists could take her mind completely off the man beside her.

Once they were comfortably airborne, Nathan said, "The General got one thing right—it is a long flight. We ought to try to sleep." Then he settled his head against the headrest and closed his eyes.

After staring at him a minute or two in disbelief, she reached for the novel she had tucked in her purse at her feet. When she straightened up again and glanced in Nathan's direction, she noticed a faint pinkness to his cheeks that hadn't been there before. Had she somehow been the cause of that?

To test the possibility, she loosened the leash on the devil inside her and shifted in her seat as though to get comfortable. In the process, she let her leg casually press against his. Her reward was a gradual brightening of his blush and a barely discernible sheen to his brow. Rachel smiled and left her leg snugly leaning against his.

CHAPTER THIRTEEN

AS THEY FLEW OVER the Pacific after taking off from San Francisco, Nathan saw General Donner walk down the aisle toward them again, and wondered what had taken him so long. He'd expected Donner to make another bid to sit next to Rachel before now. Perhaps the General had been distracted by the in-flight movie, or maybe his wife had found a way to keep him by her side. Until now.

Nathan wasn't worried that the General would get his way. But he had to concentrate hard on keeping his anger hidden. Concealing his disdain for his commanding officer had become increasingly difficult since Rachel had entered the picture.

"Well, well, well," said Donner as he moved alongside their row of seats and peered down at the Chief. "Don't you two look cozy." He made it a statement rather than a question, and annoyance dripped from every word.

"Yes, well, she sort of tipped this way after she'd fallen asleep and I didn't see the sense in waking her," Nathan said to explain how she'd ended up snuggled against his arm and sleeping peacefully.

"If she sleeps through the whole flight, she ought to be wide-awake and ready to party all night," Donner said suggestively.

"I don't think so, sir. We worked on things on the first leg of the flight. We put our stuff away when we changed planes in San Francisco, but she's been reading during most of this leg. She only went to sleep about fifteen minutes ago." This was largely fiction—she'd probably been sleep-

ing for more than an hour and his shoulder ached from lack
of movement—but Nathan felt justified given the importance of keeping the General at bay.

"Same with Lydia," he grumbled. "Just fell asleep five
minutes ago." His eyes proclaimed his disgust for the situation. Nathan nodded as if he sympathized with the General.

After a little more small talk, the General apparently decided that Rachel was not going to wake up. He finally
went back to his own seat, once again strategically booked
far from his and Rachel's.

"Is he gone?" Rachel whispered after a moment.

"Yes. I had a feeling you woke up while he was standing
here, but I didn't want him to realize that."

"I figured as much." She sat up, noticed that her arm
had entwined with his, slipped it away and stared at the
shoulder she'd used for a pillow. "Sorry," she mumbled
as she smoothed the wrinkled sleeve of his uniform shirt.

"I didn't mind," he assured her gently, but he also
flexed his shoulder to ease the cramp that had set in.

Her gaze lifted to his and those big brown eyes of hers
were misty. "You're a very nice man, Nathan," she said.

"Ugh! Please don't say I'm nice!" He exaggerated his
outrage for her amusement. "Nice men are weaklings. Tell
me I'm brave and strong and tough as nails."

"You're brave and strong and tough as nails," she said
dutifully.

He gave her a lopsided grin.

"And very nice," she added with a soft smile.

He lost himself in those eyes of hers, falling deeper and
deeper into them until he felt he was drowning. Instead of
struggling against the sensation, he found himself sinking
into it, giving himself over to it. Gradually, something only
vaguely familiar began to churn inside him until sentimental words were on the verge of bubbling out. He wanted to
tell her how full his heart felt, how much he longed to be
part of her life, how intensely he needed her.

He parted his lips. He saw her eyes widen with expectation, as if she knew he would say something important.

But he was saved from making any sappy declarations when a flight attendant announced over the speaker that they would be landing on time in sunny Hawaii and that they were currently flying at thirty thousand feet.

His heart thudding fast and heavy, he clamped his mouth closed and turned away. He felt her settle back against her reclining seat as if she had deflated.

God, that had been close! He'd almost said things that he couldn't possibly be sure of!

Because the truth was, he knew nothing about love, nothing about how it felt or what the signs might be. And he had no right to tell her he loved her when he wasn't sure if he could love anyone at all.

EXHAUSTION SUFFUSED RACHEL by the time she finally made it to her hotel room at the Hale Koa on Fort DeRussy. Remaining constantly aware of Donner in order to avoid giving him any opportunities to touch her had been a tiring chore. And she'd found herself equally aware of Nathan's nearness, whether she wanted to be or not. Whenever the Captain stood within five feet of her, something went singing along her veins, and to pretend otherwise tuckered her out.

Without even looking out the window at the view of the beach and the clear blue Pacific, she dropped her suitcase and collapsed onto the bed. Her eyes drifted shut, but then she remembered she should call her parents and Adam to let them know she'd arrived safely. Craning her neck, she eyed the clock. What time would it be back in Virginia?

Before she could do the math, she heard a tapping on a second door near the windows. Lifting her head, she stared at the door, too tired to think what it was there for. The tapping came again, sounding a great deal like someone knocking. An image of the General standing on the other side made her heart skip a beat. She sat up.

Then she remembered that Donner and his wife were in a suite on the floor above, while Nathan was in the room next to hers. An adjoining room, apparently.

She stood and moved cautiously across the room. An image of Nathan standing on the other side of the door made her heart trip again. She put one palm on the smooth, wooden surface and fingered the knob to the dead bolt. "Nathan?" she said softly as she pressed her hot forehead to the cool doorjamb.

"Yes" was the whispered reply.

Fully aware that she was opening the door onto monumental temptation, she turned the dead bolt and pulled on the knob. He stood across the threshold looking so good she nearly sighed.

"I got connecting rooms in case you need me," he said. Then he grinned and held his hands up, palms out. "I know, I know, you can take care of yourself, but I just thought—"

"Thank you," she said, interrupting him. "I appreciate having you watching my six." It was an Air Force term, but he nodded his understanding that he was covering her back.

"Teamwork," he said. Then he retreated a step, looking young and unsure of himself. "Well, you can keep the door locked on your side," he said, gesturing toward it. "I just wanted you to know I'm never far away."

"Donner wouldn't dare approach me here in my room, would he?" She glanced over her shoulder at the living space. It seemed very confined suddenly. There was a balcony, but it was high enough up so that escape out the sliding doors would be dangerous. If Donner trapped her in here, she would have nowhere to run.

"All you'd have to do is scream and I'd be through the door in a heartbeat, locked or not," he assured her. His tone was deadly and she had no doubt that he would do whatever he had to do in order to protect her. "I got you into this mess and I'll be damned if I'll let anything happen to you because of it.''

Having been completely on her own for such a long time, Rachel was slow to identify the emotion that settled inside her as she listened to his vow. But after a second or two, she understood that what she felt could be described as relief. Or whatever the opposite of loneliness might be. And to her surprise, she didn't feel weak or somehow less capable. Knowing that Nathan stood firmly as her partner in this whole sordid experience made Rachel stronger and more confident.

She smiled but couldn't think of anything to say. So she did what her heart demanded of her. She stepped over the divide between their rooms and slipped into his arms as if she belonged there. He drew her against him and wrapped his strength around her. She could feel his heart beating against her cheek.

Safe. Warm and safe.

She heard him sigh, felt him dip his head and nuzzle her hair, realized his palms stroked along her spine. But he made no demands on her. He simply held her for a long moment.

Just when she began to think of lifting her face to his to see if he would kiss her, Nathan released her and stepped back. ''I'm hungry,'' he said.

Rachel realized she was hungry, too, but not for food. Still, she understood that Nathan was making an effort to behave himself. They had agreed that nothing could come of their attraction until things with Donner were closed and he was attempting to honor that bargain. So she nodded and said something about calling home and sleeping off her jet lag. As she spoke, she sidled back to her own room, said good-night and closed the connecting door.

She leaned against it for a few minutes, fighting the urge to open it again and beg him to make love to her all night. But she knew she couldn't—or at least shouldn't—do that.

Long, sleepless hours followed. The next day was mostly

business, although she found the time to visit the surprisingly interesting Army Museum on post and to wander along the beach as far as the Duke Kahanamoku statue, which was nestled amid tall palm trees. Even though it was Saturday, Donner felt it was important to get right to work. There were people employed at the hotel and stationed on the island who had witnessed the altercation they were investigating. Rachel was sent in one direction and Nathan in another. She didn't see him again until Sunday afternoon. And he didn't see her at all.

She spotted him from her balcony as he stood on the beach in front of the setting sun practicing his tae kwon do. He moved with such grace and deadly speed she found herself holding her breath as she watched, grateful she wasn't so high up as to need binoculars. After a few minutes, he did exactly what she had unconsciously hoped for. He took off his shirt.

She leaned forward in her chair, sitting right on the edge of the seat, and clung to the railing as she stared. He wore long, loose white pants and a solid black sash around his waist. From television, she knew they were the traditional clothes for martial arts. The shirt was probably a loose wraparound thing, but apparently it was too warm for it out in the sun.

For all his talk about not being the athletic one, Rachel couldn't find a single thing wrong with the man's body. He was lean and tanned and full of muscle. His flesh rippled fluidly as he practiced. Suddenly, he performed a series of kicks and punches at blinding speed and she gasped. Then she noticed that two young women stood near him, also watching him avidly. They were bikini-clad and clearly intent on what they saw. Predators, Rachel thought as jealousy rose like bile, choking her. Abruptly, Nathan stopped his workout and stretched to pick up his shirt from the sand. One of the women approached him brazenly and spoke to him. She heard his laughter, then hers. Dusk crept over them while they chatted and Rachel squinted hard in their direction, trying to see what would happen. To her deep relief, she finally spotted Nathan's white form nearing the hotel—alone.

That didn't mean the woman wouldn't meet him later, mocked the green demon of jealousy that had awakened inside her.

Shaking her head in disgust at her own thoughts, Rachel went into her room. As she passed the connecting door, she took note of the dead bolt, securely locked. Temptation seized her, nagging her to turn the knob so he could enter if he chose. She resisted, feeling foolish because she knew he wouldn't try the door. He wouldn't enter her room under cover of darkness. Not without an express invitation, at least. What would he do if she issued such an invitation? No doubt gently remind her that this was not the time or the place. The man had a great deal more willpower than she did. Or he simply didn't feel as strongly about her as she wanted him to.

She sighed and went to brush her teeth. Another night of tossing and turning lay ahead of her. At least the General had been too busy to harass her so far. She hadn't even bothered to wear the tiny tape recorder, since their itineraries for the day didn't intersect. Still, she had no doubt that he would try something eventually. She almost welcomed it. Perhaps tomorrow she ought to start wearing the recording device. She almost wanted to seek the man out and provoke something incriminating out of him so she could capture it on tape and bring an end to the case.

Then Donner wouldn't stand between her and Nathan.

BY MONDAY AFTERNOON Nathan couldn't tell if he was living a fantasy or a nightmare. Every minute he spent near Rachel was an impossible struggle with self-control. That no one noticed his interest in her amazed him. From his perspective, it was extremely obvious.

Yet he couldn't get enough of the woman.

He told her that his hovering was for her protection, and

she seemed to accept this excuse. But Nathan knew it was only that—an excuse. A reason to be around her every waking minute. That he could keep the General from harassing her was a welcome bonus.

Even when she wasn't nearby, like now, when she was off interviewing witnesses, he found himself thinking about her and wishing—

"Captain!" came the General's strident voice through the haze of his daydreams.

"Sir!" He got immediately to his feet and stood on the carpet in front of the hotel lobby chair he'd been occupying until Donner's arrival.

"I called you three times before you answered. What's wrong with you?"

"Nothing, sir. My mind had wandered off. What can I do for you?" Nathan eyed Donner, searching for clues to whether he suspected anything between him and Rachel. Not that there *was* anything between them yet. The sleepless nights since they'd arrived in Hawaii attested to the fact that she wasn't sharing his bed.

General Donner waved his hand in the air as if trying to shoo a pesky fly. "That Senator is here!" he cried. "That woman! Who does she think she is?"

Nathan's full attention riveted on the General now. "Senator Zemin is here in Hawaii?"

"That's what I said, isn't it? Get your head out of your butt, Captain."

"But Congress is in session. Why would she come back here now?"

"To give me a hard time, no doubt. She knows I'm here. I had the Chief tell her we'd be making this trip. I thought it would appease her. But, no. She decided to come stand over my shoulder and watch everything I do. She has no business being here."

"Well, sir, this *is* her home state...." Nathan dared to say as he rubbed the back of his neck thoughtfully.

"I know it's her state, but she has no business being

here *now!*'' The General's face had gone red as his agitation mounted. "She should be in Washington, where she belongs, working on the Defense Appropriations Bill." He paused, clearly rethinking his last words. "Or better yet, she should be in a kitchen or bed, where *all* women belong."

Nathan couldn't believe the man had just said that out loud. What he wouldn't give to have had Rachel's tape recorder strapped to his body to capture the sexist comment. "Sir?"

Donner waved his hand in the air again. "You know I didn't mean that. A bad joke. She just has me upset."

"Yes, sir," Nathan muttered. "What can I do to help you with the situation?" He hoped he'd get to leave Donner to struggle with Zemin alone. That would teach him.

"There's nothing you *can* do. She wants to follow me around and see what I'm up to. It will be one long schmoozing session."

"How many days will she be here?"

"Two or three, unless she decides I'm not doing all that I can do. Then she might stay for the duration. Have you and the Chief finished with your interviews of the people involved in the incident?"

"Almost," he said. "I was waiting for one of the waitresses to come by and tell me what she knows." He checked his watch and noted that the woman was twenty minutes late. "Looks like she's not going to show. I can get you the files we've put together so far."

"You do that," said the General as he paced impatiently. Then he glanced over his shoulder at his wife, who had appeared across the lobby. The woman was dressed in a very small bikini with a transparent shirt over it. Many male eyes turned to fasten on the scenery she provided. Donner barked, "I'll be back," and stalked in Lydia's direction. He grabbed his wife by the arm and ushered her away quickly.

"Well, he's certainly an interesting man" came a

woman's voice from behind him. Nathan turned and saw the Senator herself, not five feet away. "How do you stand working for him?"

As a congressman's son, Nathan knew better than to respond to that question. There was no good answer for it, anyway. "The General wants what's best for the Army National Guard," he said.

"At least, the male part of the Guard," she bit off. "Doesn't have much use for women, does he?"

Again, he knew better than to rise to her bait, so he remained silent.

"You're the General's briefcase carrier, aren't you?"

"Pardon me, ma'am?" If he'd heard her right, he was about to be highly offended.

"I remember you from the hearing. You sat behind him and handed him papers so he could hoodwink the other members of the committee. And you carried his briefcase."

He squared his shoulders. "I'm an officer in the United States Army, ma'am. I do my job. Currently, I'm the General's aide." Had he ever thought this woman might help him or Rachel? Not likely.

She gazed into his eyes with as much steel as he imagined his own must contain. Lowering her voice, she whispered, "Does your job include finding him weak-willed women to work for him? Does it include making sure the General has plenty of fillies in his stable to choose from?"

Nathan struggled to keep the shock out of his eyes and off his face. He lowered his voice to match hers, but made sure his tone was ice-cold. "No, ma'am, it does not."

She seemed to take his measure for another few seconds, then she smiled. "Good! Perhaps we'll talk again soon." With that, she and her attendants, who had remained standing several yards back from them, drifted away across the lobby.

Nathan felt the pent-up air rush out of him. Although he would never admit that the Senator could intimidate the hell

out of him, he fervently hoped he would never talk with
her again.

Shaking his head, he gave up trying to figure out why
she had approached him at all and what she was planning.
One thing he knew for certain: theirs had not been an idle
or chance encounter. The only good thing he could hope
for from her presence was that she might keep the General
too busy to bother Rachel.

He carried that hope with him for about two hours.

Right up until he found out just how wrong it was.

CHAPTER FOURTEEN

SINCE SHE COULDN'T SEEM to find the time to sight-see, Rachel made certain she escaped long enough to go swimming in the warm, clear water that lapped the smooth sand of the beach near the hotel. The General had conscripted Nathan to take Lydia Donner shopping while Donner himself spent the day with Senator Zemin. So Rachel had a free hour to enjoy the water, jumping waves and searching for sea creatures with the mask and snorkel she'd rented. It was a well-deserved respite from the tension she'd been suffering, and as she headed back to the hotel, she knew she should try to find the time for more outings like this.

A chill ran over her damp skin as she padded down the corridor of the hotel toward her room. The air conditioner was be pumping out plenty of cold air, making her shiver. She thought about the hot shower and sweatshirt that awaited her inside her room, one swipe of her key away. Then she'd curl up on her spacious bed and read through the notes she'd collected since she'd been on the island.

Crossing the threshold, she sensed immediately that something wasn't right. Even before the door clicked shut behind her, she noticed the curtains near the balcony door billowed slightly in the afternoon breeze. She was sure she had closed the glass before she'd gone out. And if she'd forgotten, then the maid should have done it. Yet she could see no sign of anyone out there. The sun was bright and unobstructed through the sheer curtains. The hum of motors wafted through the opening, telling her that repairs and maintenance in the yard were still ongoing outside.

Cautiously, she moved a few feet farther into the room and glanced sideways into the bathroom. There were fresh towels on the rack and she could even see inside the tub because the maid had pulled back the shower curtain. No one stood there.

She peeked around the corner toward the headboard of the bed to make certain no one hid there, waiting to pounce. Nothing. Feeling foolish, she began to relax. Obviously, her imagination had run away with her. She supposed this was to be expected, given the strain of dealing with General Donner, of waiting for him to manipulate their daily agendas so he would have his opportunity. But her duties hadn't overlapped with his yet. She wondered if she'd have to wait until she got back to the Pentagon before she'd make use of the tape recorder. If she could capture him talking to her as he had the last time she'd been alone with him in his office... She shuddered at the memory. Then she began to shiver.

She dropped her towel onto the floor and walked toward the balcony door to close it. Just as she neared, a shadow moved quickly from the right and blotted out part of the light beyond the curtain. Rachel nearly came out of her skin with fright and she jumped back, losing the precious second when she could have shut and locked the door against the intruder.

Her blood ran cold when Donner's voice came to her from beyond the sheers. "Hello, Rachel," he said smoothly as he pushed the door fully open and stepped into the room. The curtains slid over him slowly as they parted where he passed. Just as slowly, he raked her body with his lascivious gaze. Despite her shock, she noticed he wore casual civilian clothes. And he was in the process of peeling latex gloves off his hands.

Registering that the gloves meant he'd *planned* to break into her room, Rachel fought against her horrified immobility and spun away. In another heartbeat she was fumbling at the exit doorknob, knowing that getting to the hallway was her only chance. She had her fingers wrapped around the smooth metal and could taste freedom as the latch rasped open.

She didn't make it.

He grabbed her from behind and hauled her backward against his body. In despair, she watched the knob turn back and heard the lock reengage with a loud click. As he twisted her around to pull her into the room again, a scream broke from her throat, but it sounded more angry than afraid. This gave her courage, and she kicked and twisted and clawed at the arm pinioning her to his length. In her struggle, the back of her head connected with his nose. He howled and she could smell the stale reek of alcohol. Only a few more well-chosen moves on her part and Donner loosened his grip. She wrestled herself free.

He was now between her and the exit, so she lunged to the other side of the bed, putting the expanse of the mattress between them. The General rubbed at his nose, but still looked as if he enjoyed the game. He grinned from ear to ear. "You're every inch the challenge I'd hoped for," he said.

"Get out!" she cried, anger and revulsion warring for dominance inside her. "How dare you come into my room." She glanced down at his hands. There were no gloves in sight. "You planned this!" she accused.

"Seduction takes careful preparation," he said easily as he looked at his hands, too. "But I don't need to worry about where I touch now. I'll only put my hands on your skin, after all." He looked back up into her face and she saw he was glassy-eyed.

Rachel stared at him, horrified. He sounded so coherent, yet she detected a slight slur to his words. "Are you drunk? This is madness!" she cried, but this time she sounded weaker, almost desperate. She cleared her throat and got hold of her courage. "If you come near me, I'll start screaming and I won't stop. Someone will hear, and then where will you be? I'll struggle and you'll have to hurt me to get your way. How will you explain the bruises?''

He continued to smile and she noticed he was flushed. ''No one outside is likely to hear you because of the work they're doing. And if you scream, I'll stuff that little swim-suit of yours into your mouth and tape it shut.'' So saying, he indicated the roll of duct tape he'd left sitting on her chest of drawers. He must have brought it with him and she hadn't seen it when she'd entered the room. ''If I have to bruise you, so be it. I like it rough. Maybe you do, too. Who will know whether I put the bruises there or some other man? And in the end you'll enjoy what I do to you, so you won't report anything. They always like it and never report it.'' He took a few steps to the right as if to skirt the bed and Rachel quickly moved an equal distance, keeping him at bay. ''If I get so much as a hint that you might try to tell anyone about what goes on between us, you'll be sent to Alaska or Afghanistan or Africa.'' He grinned. ''I like the ring of all those *A* places, so far away.''

Oh, dear God, she thought. The man really must be in-sane. Had he actually convinced himself that the lack of reports on him from other women must mean they'd liked it? He was sicker than she'd thought. And far more dan-gerous. Sexual harassment was one thing, but Donner was talking about rape. Bile rose in her throat at the very thought. ''I won't consent to sex with you. Not ever,'' she said, needing to be sure he understood that she was not just being coy. ''I'll fight you every second, and *not* because I like it rough.''

He laughed, giving her time to realize that the dance they'd been doing around the bed had put her on the op-posite side of the room near the balcony again. With one glance, she noted the proximity of the connecting door to Nathan's room. The minute Donner began to crawl across the bed in her direction, she made for that door, opened her side of it and began to pound on the second one on Na-than's side.

Nathan didn't come for her.

But the General did. He took his time, letting her beat desperately on the barrier between her room and Nathan's with her fists until they hurt. When he stood directly behind her, he pressed himself against her, pushing her to the door, trapping her there. Slowly, he started to rub his erection against her hip.

She smothered a whimper and took action. Reaching back with her fingers bent into claws, she tried for an eye, but only managed to scratch a cheek. At least that brought another howl from the beast and he backed up slightly. It was enough for Rachel to escape for the moment.

Without thinking, she ran for the balcony. Somehow, freedom seemed to lie in that direction, even though her room was at least fifty feet up. The afternoon breeze felt freakishly clean and wholesome, given the gravity of her situation. She wanted to call for help, but the General had told the truth about the noisy repairs going on below. No one was likely to hear her and the consequences Donner would inflict made her decide against the attempt. With growing desperation, she leaned out over the railing, searching for some way to escape. She was willing to put her military training to the test if she had to.

"Don't be stupid, Rachel," the General said from the threshold. "There's nowhere to go from here. It would be exceedingly dangerous to try. Why not just accept your fate and come to bed with me."

The calm proposition, said in such a reasonable tone, as if there was truly a possibility she would comply, made Rachel more frantic than before. She *had* to get away, *had* to escape.

He was behind her again, this time groping for her breasts. Her swimsuit felt like no clothing at all and her stomach roiled with nausea. He tried to hold her steady, but she twisted away. Unfortunately, she could go only a few feet on the confining balcony. Donner didn't appear disturbed by her repeated escapes. They were fleeting, after all. It dawned on her that he might be toying with her, letting her struggle out of his grasp so he could have the pleasure of capturing her again.

As he approached one more time, she found herself looking once more over the side of the railing. It was a long way down. There were no handholds, no ledges.

"Remember what you were taught in the military, Chief. Endure what you must so you live to fight another day. Isn't that right? You don't want to consider going over the edge. It's a sheer drop to the pavement. Certain death. I'm not planning on killing you afterward, Rachel, if that's what you're worried about. That wouldn't be sporting of me." Then he put his hands on her anew, smoothing his palms over her shoulders and down her arms, taking one swimsuit strap down, too. The damp cloth peeled away from one breast almost to the nipple.

That was when she decided she'd had enough. Terror sometimes brought uncommon courage, and there was nothing like jumping out of airplanes to indelibly imprint the idea of fear as a tool. Just as his fingers grasped the edge of her swimsuit to pull it down farther, Rachel leaped up and back so she sat on the edge of the railing. Horror crossed the General's face as he contemplated the possibility that she meant to jump. She used the moment of his initial shock to sidle the rest of the way to the end of the bar where she could touch the cement wall that divided one balcony from the other. Then she got her feet under her, curling her toes around the metal railing and clinging with her hands to the stones embedded in the wall.

She didn't have much time to assess her options. The General had shaken free of his stunned immobility and wanted to coax her down. He held his palms out to her in supplication. "Come down from there," he said. Then in a firmer voice, he added, "That's an order!"

Realizing she had the upper hand now, Rachel laughed maniacally, hoping to give the General pause. At the same time, she leaned way back and to the side, inspecting the distance to Nathan's balcony. Her fingers slipped slightly on the jutting stones and her laughter choked off as she jerked back to find her balance again.

One balcony was surprisingly far from the other. She'd have to make the leap exactly right and let go of the dividing wall before she'd secured her hold on the other side. Her gaze shot downward and she morbidly contemplated how long it would take her body to reach the pavement. Seconds were passing as if they were hours while Donner continued to stalk her, alternately pleading and demanding. Soon he'd be able to grab her leg and force her back into the room, where she would be helpless.

Then God only knows what he'd do to her.

Already, he'd moved too close. "If you touch me, I'll let go and fall. How would you explain *that*, General?"

He stopped and blinked at her, bewildered. There was a sheen of sweat on his face and a dark patch on his formerly clean linen shirt where perspiration had soaked through. Just then he turned his head toward the inside of her room, as if he heard something from within.

She didn't hesitate to take the chance his inattention offered. In less than a second, she got into position, reached one arm and leg out as far as they would go and sprang for the other balcony.

She nearly slipped on the second railing, but grabbed onto the jutting rocks on Nathan's side of the cement wall just in time. She teetered on her toes atop the upper bar of the balcony, then willed herself forward. Tumbling to the rough floor, she knocked over a plastic lounging chair but scrambled to her feet and lurched ahead. She yanked hard on the handle of the glass slider, only to wrench her shoulder muscles. The door into Nathan's room was locked tight.

Trapped! If the General broke through the connecting door, he'd only have to unlock the slider from the inside to get at her. Even as she made this discovery, a crack sounded inside Nathan's room. The General must have gotten through. He was coming for her. Panic seized her. Heart pounding, she glanced over her shoulder in the direction she'd just come and guessed she wouldn't be able to force herself to make the leap for freedom a second time.

In the same moment that she turned her head, she heard a welcome voice on her own balcony. "Son of a bitch!" Nathan cried.

Rachel leaned over the railing far enough to see what transpired. Donner still stood by the patio furniture, staring stupefied at the place where she had disappeared from sight. He seemed incapable of turning his attention to the threat Nathan posed. And Nathan looked gloriously dangerous as he stood behind the man with fury etched in every muscle.

"Rachel, come back here!" Donner cried, spotting her on the other side.

As the General uttered her name, Nathan's face contorted with rage. He stepped forward into a stance she'd seen him take before. "In your dreams," he growled as he lifted his two hands and brought them down hard on either side of Donner's neck, striking the nerves with precision and sending the man instantly into unconsciousness.

Nathan didn't bother to catch the man's body as it fell. He simply stepped back with a look of primitive satisfaction and watched Donner crumple.

"Rae!" Nathan called as he stepped over the inert form in an effort to get to her. He reached out, but was stymied by the expanse of the wall that divided them. Understanding brought horror into his eyes. Then he began to swear. "You could have fallen! You could be dead," he railed at her.

"I wouldn't have tried it if I hadn't been trained for such things. But thank God it was you crashing through the door instead of Donner coming this way to get me." She felt herself sway. "I have to sit down." Suddenly light-headed, Rachel retreated and righted the chair she'd fallen over. Pain flared as her abraded fingertips slid over the plastic. She ignored the hurt and sat, taking a deep breath and letting it out slowly. Adrenaline was a terrible thing to have flood your body, because when it stopped flooding, it left your limbs weak as a kitten's. Before long the trembling would set in.

Nathan appeared at his glass door just as she started to quake. Then suddenly he was beside her, lifting her into his arms, holding her against him, sweeping her into his room, mumbling soothing words. She couldn't stop shaking, and even though she knew this was a normal response to the danger she'd experienced, she loathed exhibiting such weakness.

Nathan eased her down so she sat on the edge of his bed, then he grabbed up the bedspread and pulled it around her. He held it tightly beneath her chin as he squatted before her, looking into her eyes with worry in his.

She shivered uncontrollably. And she didn't feel completely safe. Not even with Nathan scooched down right in front of her. Not even with him crooning reassuring words, coaxing her into believing that everything was okay now. Not even knowing the General was unconscious in the next room.

"Th-the—G-G-General," she stuttered. "H-how—l-l-long—will—"

He took mercy on her and answered her before she finished. "Not long. I'll need to tie him up. But not before I'm sure you're going to be okay."

"I-I'm—f-fine," she said, feeling ridiculous making the assertion when she could barely even speak coherently. "Y-you c-c-came ju-just in time."

He eyed her dubiously, but in another minute, she had warmed enough to send him a shaky smile. "Really," she said in a steadier voice. "I'm okay. What are we going to do about D-Donner?"

"*You're* not going to do a damn thing," he said as he stood up and sat down next to her and put a strong, protective arm around her shoulders "You're going to stay right where you are and warm up while I cart his criminal ass to the authorities."

She shook her head. "You can't do that. There's nothing to prove what he did. He'll deny everything we say. And he's still a general. Who would believe us over him?"

"He forced his way into your room! He touched things, left fingerprints! He touched *you!*" It was obvious that this last part disturbed him deeply, and Rachel felt a little of the horror ebb as she arrived at the certainty that Nathan Fordham cared about her.

"He wore latex gloves when he broke into my room. He was so smug about it. There won't be any prints. There won't be any proof at all. He was very careful."

"Where are the gloves? Maybe someone could get his prints from the inside. That should count for some sort of proof that he—'

She held up her had to stop him. "He could have tossed them over the balcony, for all I know. And even if they turn up, they won't be enough. Should we risk our careers on the possibility that we can prove he wore latex gloves, that the authorities will believe our story against his?"

He glared at her. "Son of a bitch!" he exclaimed for the second time since he'd come upon the scene.

"Yeah," she agreed, sharing his frustration. "I think we need to do something with him before he wakes up, though. Maybe we could drag him to his own room. He's been drinking or something, so maybe he won't wake up until we dump him off. If we're lucky, he won't remember much."

He leaned back a bit so he could look into her face. He blinked a few times. "Are you crazy? He would have raped you if he'd gotten the chance! We can't just put him into his room all cozy like nothing ever happened."

She didn't say anything to that. Nathan had every right to be outraged. There was no sense in arguing when she shared his sentiments so completely. And she knew that even without her help, Nathan would come around to understand the futility of pressing charges now without better proof.

He tried another approach. "We could call the police now and when they come up here, they'll see him in your room. That and the gloves ought to count for something. And I'll testify to what I saw when I came in here. It's two against one."

She stared at the floor a few seconds "He's a general, Nate. Do you have any idea how many cases of harassment and rape end in acquittal in the military?" She spoke in a soft voice, not really wanting to hear this particular awful truth herself right now.

She felt him shudder as he said, "I don't want to know."

"That's right, you don't. But the reality is, we have no real proof. His fingerprints are nowhere to be found, I'm not bruised, there's no semen." The last concept made her stomach turn over again and she thought for a moment that she would be sick. Swallowing hard, she eyed the two unmoving feet of the General, which she could see through the connecting doorway and her glass slider. If they so much as twitched, she would take that as an excuse to go knock him out again. How satisfying that would be.... "All he'd have to say is that we manufactured the scene to discredit him for our own glorification."

"That's ridiculous! No one would believe it!"

"No one would believe this well-respected, upstanding two-star General would attempt rape, either."

"Fine!" Nathan barked as he surged to his feet. "I'll drag him to his damn room and leave him there. He might find a few boot prints on his rib cage when he wakes up!"

She looked at him, half amused despite the grim situation. "You would never kick an unconscious man, Nate."

He squinted at her, and his bleak expression confirmed her assessment of him. "I could make an exception in *his* case and no one would ever question my honor," he grumbled.

"You'd question your *own* honor."

He shook his head and looked down at the floor, seeming both disgusted and frustrated. He presented an incredibly handsome figure, posed with his hands on his hips and his muscles tense with coiled anger. "I need to get him moved," he said as he rubbed the back of his neck. He eyed her skeptically. "Are you up to playing lookout for me?"

She nodded. There was no way on earth she would let Nathan leave her alone with her thoughts right now. "Let me get some clothes on," she said, remembering that beneath the warm bedspread, she still wore only her swimsuit. She was grateful when Nathan followed her into her room so she wouldn't be alone with the General's inert body. Glancing at the clock, she realized with no small measure of shock that less than twenty minutes had passed since she'd first come back from the beach. It had seemed like hours. With a shake of her head, she grabbed some clothes and went into the bathroom to change.

TWO HOURS LATER, Nathan eyed Rachel across the dinner table in the quiet restaurant they'd decided to try. A meal in a public place had been her idea. She'd said something about getting in touch with normal activities and things to help ease the lingering shock.

"That's what people are supposed to do after trauma. Like after the terrorist attacks," she'd said. "The President told us to get back to our normal lives and put the bad stuff behind us. That's what I need to do."

Nathan thought it would be more complicated than that, but figured now was not the right time to say so. She seemed far too fragile. For the past hour and a half, she'd been telling him she was fine, but nothing she said convinced him. There was a slight tremble to her fingers when she reached for her wineglass, and he thought her smile was a little forced. He wished he could do something to take her mind off what had happened—off what they still had to do.

Somehow, they had to find a way to pretend nothing *had* happened. They could only hope the General was smart enough to go along. If he tried to accuse Nathan of striking a superior officer, things would get ugly very fast. They'd be forced to make their case against Donner before they were ready. Anything could go wrong. It all hinged on what Donner would do once he woke up. Their discussion so far had centered on their plans, depending on what the bastard did next.

"Thank you for switching rooms with me," she said very softly. "That was a really good idea. I'm not sure I'd sleep tonight if I had to be in the room where he...where he..." She trailed off, then took a sip of her wine.

Nathan looked across at Rachel and wished he could make her forget. But he had trouble forgetting himself. Something had snapped inside him the instant he'd seen Donner in Rachel's room. By attacking Rachel in this overt, aggressive way, the General had crossed a line Nathan hadn't even realized he'd drawn. To stand by while the man taunted and harassed, objectified and stalked had been hard enough. Attempted rape was quite another thing. Nothing would stop him from seeing to Donner's total destruction now that he'd tried to physically harm Rachel.

Rachel. He took a bite of his steak and then looked up at her again. She'd tried to be so strong. For the most part, she'd succeeded—except for those few minutes when shock had taken hold of her and made her shake. God, that had been a horrible moment. Witnessing her like that had nearly broken him. But then she'd rallied and calmly explained that Donner still held too many cards. At least Rachel had been operating on all cylinders. He was mortified the clear thinking had come from the victim rather than the rescuer.

"I wouldn't be able to sleep, either, if I had to worry about you all night," he said. "At least this way, I'll know immediately if he comes to the room he still thinks is yours."

"It's a good thing we could make it seem that we were helping Donner to his suite. I thought I was going to go into cardiac arrest when we came across that hotel maid," she said, talking casually about their escapade in getting Donner to his room.

"It helped that he stank of alcohol. Telling her we needed to put him to bed to sleep it off certainly solved the problem." He eyed her, wondering if he should change the subject until she'd had more time to regroup. Deciding she could handle it, he said, "When I fished in his pocket to get his room key, I also found the latex gloves you saw him wearing. I kept them. They were wadded up and wrong side out, so I'm not sure how much use Julian will be able to make of them. Prints might be smudged, but, if we're lucky, we can use them to help corroborate our overall story when it comes time to present it."

She stared at him with candlelight and admiration shining in her eyes. "That was good thinking on your part."

He shook his head, denying that he'd done anything worthy of her praise. "I just want this all over with as soon as possible. The strain will be so much worse for you now that you know what he's capable of." He didn't say out loud that he was afraid for her safety and that he would be hard-pressed to let her out of his sight for so much as a second. He found himself chewing the inside of his lower lip as he thought about how he would manage to remain glued to her without making her feel like a prisoner.

"Since he'd been drinking before he showed up in your room, I wonder how much he'll remember of what he did."

She shuddered. "I'm hoping he'll just pretend nothing happened, whether he remembers or not. He'll have enough explaining to do to his wife without dragging us into the picture."

"Where was she when we brought him to his room? Last I heard, you had to take her shopping." Rachel wore a slight smile as she said this and Nathan was glad she could see humor in any part of the day.

"I left her on the beach watching some young Marines play volleyball. I was praying she'd still be out there, but

if she'd been in the room, I would have told her pretty
much what we told the maid.''

Her expression grew serious again. ''I dread coming
face-to-face with him again.'' She lifted her glass and
drained the remainder of her wine. She poured more from
the bottle they'd ordered, but filled her glass only partway.

He wanted to hold her, and finally couldn't resist putting
his hand over hers where it rested on the linen tablecloth.
Softly, he said, ''I wish there were a way to get you home
early, but I can't think of a good excuse. We could claim
Adam had an asthma attack, except I don't believe Donner
knows about him yet and I'd like to keep it that way for
as long as possible.''

She turned her palm upward under his and then gently
rubbed the back of his hand with her thumb. ''Someone
knows about Adam or I wouldn't have gotten that note. I
called Julian yesterday to make sure everything was okay
and he said things have been quiet.''

He nodded, glad she'd thought to make that call to his
brother. ''From now on, you'll need to wear the tape recorder every day, so you'll be ready in case—'' He stopped
before he blurted out ''he comes after you again.'' He'd
been dead set against the recording device, but now he saw
no other way to end the nightmare quickly. ''And, well,
I'm going to have to be your shadow from now on. I'll find
a way to work around any of his orders that take me away
from you. Until we bring this to an end, I'm stuck to you
like a tick on a ten-year-old.''

She smiled at that quirky little expression he'd learned
from one of his nannies many years ago. His heart lightened
at the sight. And he was relieved her first reaction wasn't
to protest.

''Yes, that sounds like a good plan,'' she said as she
continued to trail her thumb back and forth over his knuck-
les. The sensation began to make him think about things
he had no business considering, given her ordeal.

After a moment, she surprised him with a change of subject. "I learned some self-defense in training," she said. "But nothing like the martial arts you know. We mostly focused on weapons, stuff women don't usually carry around in their purses."

He raised his eyebrows, wondering where this line of conversation could be headed.

She looked into his eyes. "You promised once that you'd teach me some martial arts. I want to get started with that, if you don't mind. And let's get right to the deadly stuff so I won't ever find myself at anyone's mercy again."

He noticed her eyes were bright and her cheeks were slightly flushed. He shifted in his chair and thought about how he should deal with this surprising turn of events. Somehow he suspected that she wouldn't be satisfied with assurances that *he* would protect her.

"Okay," he said. "But don't expect too much of yourself too soon. I've been studying for years." He paused a moment, remembering. "Actually, I've been at it for almost two decades. My brother convinced our nanny that we needed the classes for the discipline." Julian had privately explained to Nathan that studying the martial arts might help him cope with the pain of losing their mother. And it had. Because he'd done tae kwon do every free moment of his youth, time had passed more quickly. Grief had been relegated to the recesses of his heart, until one day Nathan found he could remember his mother without weeping. He'd been all of sixteen years old by then and well on his way to his first black belt.

"I only want to learn the stuff to get out of someone's grasp and then deck them so they can't grab me again."

He couldn't suppress a smile. "Is that all?" he asked, intending for her to hear the irony in his tone.

"Yes," she said with a firm nod. "I'm particularly interested in the way you knocked him out." She slipped her fingers from beneath his and demonstrated with a sharp chopping motion, nearly tipping over her water.

Nathan caught the glass before it toppled. "You know,

a little knowledge can be a dangerous thing. That's why you're supposed to learn martial arts slowly from the beginning without skipping steps.''

Rachel put her hands in her lap and looked down at her plate. ''Could we start tonight?'' she asked as if he hadn't uttered his warning.

''Rae, I'm not going to be able to teach you everything you want to know in one night. You're small,'' he began, then held up his hands when she took a breath to protest. ''But strong and agile,'' he added in anticipation of her objection. ''You'll have to learn to compensate for your size with speed and flexibility. It'll take a while.''

She nodded, accepting his softly spoken counsel. ''But at least if we get started I'd be in the *process* of helping myself. I need to feel I'm doing everything I can to ensure I'm never a victim to a scumbag like Donner again.''

That made perfectly good sense to Nathan. ''Well, then, let's call for the check and we'll go out to the beach for your first lesson.''

CHAPTER FIFTEEN

SHE STOOD ON THE NEARLY deserted beach near the hotel with the man she'd discovered to be one of the biggest temptations of her life and wondered what the future would hold for them. Earlier, a relationship had seemed impossible, with all that remained between them. But somehow the moonlight and salty breeze and tolling waves conspired to make anything seem possible. She watched him from her perch on a small sand dune as he demonstrated a simple series of kicks and blocks. He was beautifully graceful and unerringly precise.

She watched—and she wanted.

"Okay, your turn," he called to her.

Lost in her observations about his body and memories of his kisses, she needed a moment to recall her purpose in coming out to the beach at night with him. Remembering that she was here for a lesson, she stood and brushed sand off her slacks, then went onto the harder packed beach near him. The darkness and the palm trees shielded them from the hotel. The last thing they needed was for the General or his wife to see them. Nathan must have had this in mind when he'd chosen their secluded spot a short way down the beach.

"Stand like this," Nathan advised. She tried to emulate his pose and then to follow his movements. His nearness was a distraction, but after a while she managed to forget her attraction so she could concentrate on the steps.

"You're a quick study," he said after twenty minutes of practice.

"I'm more motivated than some," she said, and the stomach full of anxiety that had started to feel too familiar made itself known again. She shook her head to refocus her mind, refusing to let Donner's attack keep her from making the most of this time alone with Nathan. Finding a smile, she offered it to him. "And I have a very good teacher."

He returned the grin. "You think so? Let's see what you've learned," he said. "Face me and get into that stance we just worked on."

She did as he told her and he lined himself up similarly so that the outside edges of their right wrists crossed and touched gently. "Now, do what comes naturally to you," he advised, and without giving her more than a nanosecond to consider what he meant, he started to tap at her arms with a series of light chops and punches.

She found that if she stayed alert and moved fast she could use the blocks she'd learned and ward off many of his maneuvers. She only tasted defeat when he grabbed both her wrists and stepped forward to yank one of her legs out from under her with his foot. "No fair!" she said as she looked up at him from her unexpected seat on the sand. "You didn't teach me what to do with my feet."

"I want to be sure you're not deluding yourself. You've made excellent progress, but the instant you put yourself into a martial arts stance, everyone around you will assume you know what you're doing. And they won't pull their punches. So a little knowledge can be dangerous. I want to be sure you know your limits and use this stuff only when you're sure you'll be effective."

"Yes, Sensay," she said, using a word she'd heard once on television to refer to a martial arts teacher. "I'm duly warned." She accepted the hand he offered and got to her feet. As their hands clasped, her awareness of him tripled. She felt her cheeks go hot and worried he'd notice the youthful reaction. She tried distracting him by saying, "I don't suppose I can hope for that to be the last time you knock me over."

Amusement danced in his eyes. "If you want to learn to defend yourself, you're going to have to expect to take a few falls."

She nodded and assumed the proper stance again. They practiced until her wrist bones throbbed from the gentle but constant blocking. Nathan seemed to know exactly when she'd had enough. He stood back from her and bowed in respect. Feeling a little foolish, she did the same.

"Let's try something different before we call it a night," he said. "I want to show you a little jujitsu. You might be able to use this stuff right away because it's easy to learn and strictly defensive." He moved so that he stood right behind her. His position made her stiffen as she remembered Donner doing the same, but she held her ground. This was Nathan, after all. He bore no resemblance to the General. She would not let herself confuse the two.

As if he sensed her wariness, Nathan spoke softly to her, explaining what he would do. "Now I'm going to grab on to you and then tell you how to escape. Okay?"

She nodded. Then suddenly his strong arms snaked around her, encircling her completely. She felt trapped as vivid memories flooded her mind, despite her determination to keep Donner from tormenting her even when he was nowhere near her. Nathan didn't hold her tightly, but in that moment, she couldn't breathe. It took her only a second to begin to struggle for all she was worth and a few more seconds for Nathan's soothing voice to penetrate her confusion.

"Easy, Rae. I'm not going to hurt you. Take it easy, now."

Rachel forced herself to relax. It was one of the hardest things she'd ever asked of herself, and given her Airborne training, that was saying a lot about Donner's effect on her. But then she focused on Nathan's voice and concentrated on associating the sound of it with the warmth and pressure of the body behind her. In another moment, she recognized with both her heart and her mind that it was Nathan holding her. And the strong arms surrounding her gradually became warm and safe...and sensuous.

He continued to whisper soothingly into her ear. "You're not in danger now. I'll let you go whenever you tell me to. But you need to understand that you'll never get away from an attacker by twisting and kicking. See? All I have to do is pick you up." He did just that, lifting her off her feet and fitting her back more snugly against his broad chest. She was even more helpless than before. Although being pinned against Nathan had enormous appeal, she understood that it was a good thing Donner hadn't tried something like this.

Brute force was not the answer to getting out of an attacker's hold, so she made herself go limp and wondered why she hadn't received this kind of training in basic. She supposed it was because most of the time the soldiers carried weapons when there was likely to be an assault. Getting away from a common mugger or potential rapist wasn't what the Army was all about. "Okay," she said as he put her back onto her feet. "What should I do?"

"You're going to move fast enough so that your opponent won't have time to think of lifting you up. So, you'll be on your feet when you feel someone try to grab you." His arms tightened around her again. "The minute you sense the attack, you'll jab with your right elbow—go ahead and do that."

She followed his instruction with gusto and he grunted in pain and bent slightly. But he didn't let go.

"Did I mention that when we're practicing you should try to not actually hurt the instructor," he said as if through gritted teeth.

"Oh. Sorry."

"Right. Okay, so after you jab with the elbow, you can also stomp your attacker's foot—no, don't actually *do* that." He did a two-step to keep his foot from being trod upon, laughing softly. "Just make the motion as if you were going to slam your heel down on my toes. Now, flex your knees so you dip down and out of my grasp."

Miracle of miracles, when she bent her knees, she slipped right out of his hold.

"That's it. Good! Now jump around and reverse your stance so you can do the punch I taught you a few minutes ago. Aim for my nose." He had to pull his head back about a foot to avoid having his nose broken by the heel of her hand. "Geez! You're a natural," he said.

"Let's do it again!" she demanded as a sense of blessed control and power surged through her.

He smiled. "Turn around for me so I can grab you."

She did so but didn't feel his arms encircle her immediately. Anticipation made her impatient. But just as she started to look over her shoulder to see what the holdup could be, he pounced. Stunned, she didn't react as instantaneously as she would have liked. But in another heartbeat she had jabbed, stomped and ducked. Spinning to deliver the final blow, she saw Nathan already bent at the waist, holding his side with one hand and his foot with the other, which caused him to teeter on the one leg he balanced upon.

She went to him with outstretched hands. "Sorry, sorry, sorry! I forgot to pull my punches. Are you hurt?" She put one hand on his shoulder and dipped slightly to look into his face.

In a flash, he had her in his grasp again. But this time, she found herself crushed against him face-to-face. "Ha!" he cried. "I've got you now!"

She laughed and so did he, but then their amusement suddenly gave way to something much more intense. Her senses came alive; her pulse quickened. He stared down into her eyes. And she couldn't have broken from his gaze even if she'd thought to try.

"Rachel," he said in a soft, husky voice. His focus dropped to her mouth and her breath caught. He would kiss her now, she thought. She wanted him to kiss her very much.

Instead, he loosened his hold on her. "I...we..." he began. He pulled away abruptly, turning from her. "I can't believe I did that, given what you've been through today."

"A kiss from you would have nothing to do with what Donner did earlier," she assured him.

But he stood stiffly apart from her and rubbed the back of his neck. "Maybe we should call it a night," he suggested as he took a hesitant step away.

Rachel knew with abject certainty that she did not want to leave Nathan just yet. Common sense had no chance to prevail against the desperate need to keep him with her.

"Don't go!" she blurted as she took a step in his direction. She barely managed to keep from throwing herself into his arms again. In a calmer voice, she said, "Can we practice the jujitsu a few more times? I don't feel I would do the move automatically yet and I need to have just one thing I can do to protect myself if Donner tries anything else. I promise not to actually make contact this time."

She heard him take in a breath and let it out slowly. The seconds stretched, until at last he faced her. "Turn around again and we'll practice a few more times."

Once again, his arms snaked around her, but instead of immediately jabbing and ducking, she found herself savoring the moment of complete safety. As if he couldn't help himself any more than she could, he responded to her hesitation with a defeated groan and dipped his head to nuzzle her ear.

"Rae," he whispered as his hold shifted. One strong hand splayed over her rib cage just below her breasts, pulling her more firmly to his chest. The other lifted and the backs of his fingers brushed down her cheek. Shivering with renewed excitement, she tipped her head and his touch slid down the side of her throat. All thoughts of what they were supposed to be doing evaporated in the heat of anticipation.

Rachel felt his warm breath tremble along her nape. A sigh slipped from her as his lips made gentle contact just behind her earlobe. Ever so tenderly, he began to kiss along the side of her throat and tease the ticklish swirls of her ear with his tongue. At the same time, she felt his hand inch lower on her ribs, then over her stomach—slowly, slowly—down to her abdomen, pressing her to him, making her aware of the heat pooling inside her and the rock-hard erection nestled against her backside.

Raising her arm and reaching back, she slid her fingers through his hair and encouraged him with every subtle shift of her body. But his fingers ceased their downward progression toward the part of her body that ached the most for his touch. So she half turned and tipped her head back against his shoulder, searching for his mouth with hers, instinctively seeking heightened arousal and forgetting all the reasons why she should not.

He groaned just before his lips pressed to hers, then he sought a deeper connection and pulled her all the way around to kiss her more thoroughly. His tongue was hot and slick. His touch roamed, kneading and stroking her from neck to tail. When he splayed his hand over her bottom and gently urged her against him, the undeniable fact of his arousal made her a little light-headed. And suddenly, it was imperative that she feel that proud erection inside her body.

No clear thoughts intruded anymore—there were only images flashing through her mind. One of them had her bending her knees the way he'd taught her and dipping down until she lay upon the sand. She would draw him down with her. The next image had him hovering over her, wildly impassioned and desperate. The prospect made her legs begin to give way, and her fantasy might have evolved into reality if he hadn't lifted his mouth from hers just then.

He gazed down at her, searching her face. His breaths came fast and every muscle in his beautiful body flexed with tension. His eyes flashed with desire. But instead of kissing her some more as she wanted him to, he spoke softly to her. "I want you, Rachel. There's no denying it. But I need you to think about what *you* want first."

He kissed her cheek, then seemed to forget himself as he kissed along her jaw and down her throat and suddenly back to her mouth again, leaving her breathless and trembling, leaving her more sure of what she wanted than ever before in her life. She would have said so if he'd given her the chance. But as soon as he lifted his lips from hers again, he whispered, "Come to my room tonight, Rae. I'll leave the door unlocked. Be sure it's what you want and then, please—come to me."

Then he sucked in a breath and stepped back, looking for all the world as if this was the hardest thing he'd had to do in a long time. He held her at arm's length until she was steady on her feet, then he let her go. He gestured in the direction of the hotel. "Go back now."

"But I..." she began until he held up his hand to stop her.

"Don't say anything right now. Go back to the hotel. I'll follow you to be sure you're safe."

She hesitated and he added, "If this is really what you want, it'll still be what you want in a little while. And then we'll know we've made a rational choice instead of an impassioned one." If there was more, she didn't hear it as he stepped back several paces into the shadows of the overhanging tropical trees. She could barely see him and she knew that was his intention. God bless him, he struggled to do the right thing.

So she forced her legs to move her toward the bright lights of the hotel. He would follow her, as he'd promised, until she'd made her way to her room. And once there, she would have to decide—without lust drugging her, without the heat of the moment coaxing her.

AS HE PACED THE ROOM that had been Rachel's until this afternoon, Nathan thought of all the reasons he should not have asked her to come here tonight. He could give himself credit for not dropping her to the sand and making love to her on the spot, as he'd ached to do, but he'd certainly failed to resist her completely. Was he little better than Donner, taking advantage of Rachel's vulnerability? Her need for comfort could easily overcome her better judgment. And he knew better than anyone that better judgment would require them to stay away from each other physically.

Yet he found himself standing still and staring at the bed Rachel had slept in the night before. He couldn't help picturing her there.

Other thoughts along those lines began to stream through his consciousness. No one knew them here in Hawaii— except for Donner and his wife, and he suspected they'd be too preoccupied to bother them right now. Lydia would be focused on her outrage at the General behaving like a drunkard, while Donner himself would be trying to figure out how to explain the scratches on his face to Senator Zemin at their morning meeting. If Nathan and Rachel were ever to have a time alone together when they wouldn't be caught, this was the best opportunity. This could be their moment to discover each other, he told himself. And there were so many things he wanted to discover about Rachel...

He groaned as he realized he was making excuses for going where his desires led him. Frustrated, he began to pace again. He hated his inability to better control his need for Rachel. This periodic flaring of his passions seemed to thin the line between Donner and him. Wanting her so desperately was nothing less than barbaric in the wake of what she had just gone through at that monster's hands. She didn't need him lusting after her while she was recovering from the trauma Donner had caused.

He stopped in his tracks as another terrible thought assaulted him. Although he would like to count himself a hero for taking that painful step away from her out on the beach, he recognized that he'd also put the burden completely on her shoulders as to what the outcome of this night would be. He'd laid an awful temptation at her feet and then walked away. *She'd* have to decide for the both of them whether they'd make love or not. Because he knew for certain that if she opened that connecting door, he wouldn't be strong enough to step away from her again.

He looked at that door for a long time, willing it to open and for her to come through it. She would turn his dreams into reality. And there had been plenty of dreams about Rachel since their arrival in Hawaii as he'd lain in his bed thinking of her in the room next to his.

God, he needed her—and not just for one night. Though he'd sworn to remain single after he'd realized how unhappy his selfish father had made his mother in their marriage, he wasn't sure he could hold to that promise. Rachel had changed him. She'd made him think he might be able to overcome his father's legacy. She'd rearranged his insides and now he saw things differently. Instead of being certain he would be just like his father—absent in all the ways that mattered to a wife and children—he'd begun to believe he could devote the rest of his days to Rachel. The hope of having Adam in his life on a permanent basis infiltrated his thoughts, too. Somehow, he suspected the daunting responsibility of being a stepfather would be worth the effort with a boy like Adam. The idea of making a brother or sister for the boy also had immense appeal. Yes, he wanted Rachel for more than one night.

Was that love?

Could he have fallen in love with her, beyond all expectation? Running his fingers through his hair and feeling his pulse speed up, he allowed himself to consider the possibility. Doubts immediately assailed him.

If he truly loved her, he would do what was right. He'd lift the burden from her shoulders about deciding whether they would be together tonight. He'd go to her and tell her once again that they needed to remain apart until things were settled, until they no longer worked in the same office, until Donner was no more than a bad memory, until she could be certain of her feelings.

Heart hammering, he steeled his determination to do the right thing, stepped closer to the connecting door and raised his fist to knock. But then he hesitated, questioning his true motives. If he saw her, wouldn't he forget everything he'd just sworn he'd say to her? He'd take one look at her and sweep her into his arms. His excuse would be the passion she evoked. And then how different would he be from Donner?

No different at all.

He groaned in an agony of confusion and self-doubt, then backed away from the door. Catching sight of himself in the dresser mirror, he groaned again. He was a mess, with his hair sticking up and a shadow of a beard beginning to show. There were dark circles under his eyes from worry and lack of sleep. His shirt was half unbuttoned and the tails half untucked.

Irritated with himself, he pulled the shirt off over his head in one, swift motion, then chucked it onto the top of his suitcase in the corner. He ought to lock the connecting door and go to bed. But he didn't dare go near it again for fear he'd turn the knob and open it, instead.

If he didn't feel the need to stay near Rachel in case Donner made another attempt, he'd go running on the beach to clear his head. But he couldn't leave her. So he finished undressing, brushed his teeth, clicked off the lights and climbed into bed.

As soon as he slithered between the sheets, he remembered once more that Rachel had slept here last. He knew the linens were fresh, but he couldn't resist the urge to smooth his palm over the place where her body might have been the previous night and where it would be now if she were here with him. Memories of their kisses replayed in his mind and he couldn't seem to hold back the flood of fantasies that followed. After only a few seconds of trying, he gave himself over to them and drifted on a sea of frustrated desire. Sometime thereafter, he stumbled fitfully into that place between sleep and wakefulness.

He dreamed the connecting door opened and Rachel came into his room. "Thank God," he heard himself whisper on a sigh of utter relief. Then he dreamed he pulled back the covers, inviting her to join him in bed.

RACHEL HAD SPENT HOURS agonizing over the choice Nathan had given her. But in the end, she hadn't so much come to a decision as given in to basic needs. She simply couldn't bear to be alone tonight, and he was the only person in the world who could make her feel safe. She needed his arms around her, she craved his touch and his strength and she knew that making love to Nathan would wipe away the nightmare she couldn't force herself to forget.

Yet, as she turned the handle of the connecting door, she'd been assaulted by second thoughts. What if he'd reconsidered his invitation? When the knob turned unimpeded, she felt slightly reassured. If he'd changed his mind, he'd have locked the door on his side. But again, as she pulled the door open on silent hinges, she wondered how he would receive her. All the reasons she should go to her own bed winged their way through her mind, confusing her, making it nearly impossible to move.

Then she heard him whisper "Thank God," and knew she was where she wanted to be, where she needed to be. Her heart skipped over itself as she watched him sweep the covers aside in welcome. Taking a few cautious steps toward him, she saw by the moonlight that he'd been asleep. Her indecision had kept him waiting a long time. As she slipped between the sheets, shivering within their cool embrace, she promised herself she'd make it up to him tonight.

With a slight rustle of linen, his warm hand stole over her waist and drew her against his heated body. His other arm pillowed her head and his warmth enveloped her. Despite the nervousness that had suddenly taken hold of her, she snuggled closer.

That was when he exploded with "For the love of God!" and every muscle of his body went rigid with sudden tension. He sucked in a breath and then let it out slowly on a series of mild expletives while she lay passively beside him with unexpected laughter threatening to make its way to the surface.

"I should have warned you that they're always cold," she said, daring to move her icy feet to a warmer place on his shins, making him tense anew.

"My God, woman! How do you stand it?" Still wincing as if in great pain, he gallantly captured her freezing toes between his calves, bravely sacrificing his body heat for her comfort.

"I don't exactly have a choice. No matter how much I exercise, my feet are always cold at night." She swept her hands gently over his chest as she spoke and he hummed his approval. "They're already warming. Thank you."

"I'll get you a pair of those electric socks or something." He kissed her brow and held her close for a moment while her palms roamed the contours of his muscles from shoulders to ribs. She explored this part of his body slowly, hoping she didn't seem too bold. For the first time in a long time, Rachel felt completely warm all the way to her soul. Yet she feared she would somehow break the spell and find herself alone with her nightmarish memories again. So she didn't utter another word.

As if he could read her thoughts, he said, "I figure you might not want to be by yourself tonight, Rae. If you'd like me to just hold you all night while you sleep, I can do that. I don't want you to feel as if you have to—"

She put her lips against his to stop the words. She couldn't bear to hear that he could lie beside without making love to her. What she needed was to have her nightmares cleansed from her mind by a tidal wave of passion from this man. So she swept her tongue over his lips and pulled him against her.

And after a stunned second, he responded with a surge

of interest that expressed very eloquently how hard it would have been for him to simply hold her while she slept. He moved over her and kissed her deeply with mobile lips and seeking tongue, until she was hot and breathless.

His hands skimmed over her from breast to hip and back again. She arched into his palm and cursed the barrier of her T-shirt. She wanted to feel his skin against hers and she writhed beneath him, seeking that elusive contact.

"Off with this now," he murmured as he tugged the bottom of her shirt toward her head. Working together, they got her out of it in only seconds. He went still as he hovered above her and his gaze drifted from her eyes to her lips to her breasts. "Oh, yes," he breathed, and she lost all shreds of shyness on the whisper of that last sibilant word.

CHAPTER SIXTEEN

NATHAN STRAINED AGAINST unleashing his self-control. He wanted to make wild, passionate love to her, but he knew better than to try after what she'd been through earlier. Determined to give her comfort and gentleness, he forced himself to go slowly, to make sure she knew she held the reins, to ensure she could move any way she chose. And he was richly rewarded for his restraint. Rachel's hands reached for him again and she touched him sensuously. She smoothed her palms over his shoulders, along his neck, across his chest—making him shiver with anticipation as he held himself above her on rigid arms and thought about taking her left nipple into his mouth to suckle.

"You're beautiful," she said, yanking his gaze to her face with that unexpected remark.

He huffed his amazement even as he shook with wanting. "I'm supposed to say that to *you*. And you are. More beautiful than I ever imagined." Unable to resist any longer, he dipped his head and kissed the rise of her breast, then slid his tongue roughly over one pink nipple. Oh, she tasted so good! When she curled herself upward, seeking and offering at the same time, he hungered to be inside her, to claim her, to possess her.

He nearly gave in to that yearning. He nearly unleashed the beast inside him. She seemed to want him to. The way she twined her legs with his, the way she touched him and kissed him—she gave all the indications of wanting him as much as he wanted her. But a vague unease kept him from letting go.

Sure he would lose control at any moment, he threw himself sideways and twisted onto his back, gasping for breath. "I need to slow down," he whispered more to himself than to her. But she heard him.

"Why?" She'd risen onto one elbow and there was a seductive smile curving her sexy lips, inviting him to let go of his control. The sheet had drifted to her hip, but she appeared unconcerned by her tantalizing exposure. Taking in her sparkling eyes, her well-kissed lips, her slender throat, her shapely breasts, her rosy nipples, he ached to throw her to her back and plunge into her. Instead, he threw his arm over his eyes and groaned. Perspiration trickled down his temple.

"Because you deserve it," he managed to say. He left unspoken his fear that he would turn into a lustful animal with little to separate him from the Donners of the world if he didn't take care. As he turned on his side to face her, he saw that her brow was knit in confusion. He stroked a finger over an eyebrow and down her cheek while he tried to think of what he should say. She couldn't possibly know the torment he struggled with and he didn't want to tell her. Doing so might explain why he'd suddenly stopped in the middle of one of the most intensely wonderful moments of his adult life, but it would also connect his lovemaking to Donner's attack. Bad enough he already suffered from that terrible association. "And…" he added without knowing exactly what he was about to say, "I've been determined from the minute I met you to be respectful of you, especially after you told me about Adam's father."

"But I've volunteered for this, Captain," she said with a reassuring grin. She traced an index finger in a circle on his bare shoulder. "I want you," she said softly.

And that would have been all he needed to soothe his troubled heart, except that thinking of Adam's father brought the other element of his unease to the surface: he wasn't prepared to make love to this woman tonight. If there were condoms buried in the depths of his shaving kit, they wouldn't be in very good shape. Growling softly in frustration, he knew he'd have to admit his lack of forethought. "I invited you here. So you'd think I'd be ready for you. But I'm not," he confessed.

She propped herself on her elbow and put her hand on his cheek, holding his gaze with hers. "Tell me what's wrong, Nate."

"Adam's father left you pregnant. I don't want to do the same. But I'm afraid I didn't think about buying condoms and…"

A warm and tender smile lit her face. "Don't worry about it," she said gently.

"Of course I should worry about it! I don't want to be like him! I don't want to be like—" He'd almost said "Donner" but managed to catch himself in time. If he said the General's name, the man would become an inescapable specter in the night, hovering between them, at least in their minds.

"You're not like him, Nathan. You're not like anyone else. You're just you," she said gently. "And I think you're someone who could help me forget Adam's father and…and…" She didn't seem willing to say the monster's name, either, but Nathan understood. The ache in his heart subsided a little at the idea that he might help her forget.

"But what about…" he began.

"I've been on the pill since I joined the Army…to…to keep me on a predictable schedule, you know? Not because…not for other reasons. Until now." Her cheeks went pink as she offered him this information. Was she embarrassed? She shouldn't be.

He found he simply had to reach for her. Pulling her close against his body, he kissed her lightly on the cheek. "The Army gave me a clean bill of health six months ago and I admit I haven't had any opportunities to contract any dangerous diseases since then," he confessed. This was the first time he could ever remember thinking that his abysmal sex life was a blessing.

"Same here," she said with a shy smile. "Guess we were saving ourselves for each other."

He laughed, and with a lighter heart, he nibbled along her throat to the softest part of her neck that had already become a favorite nuzzling spot.

"My feet are cold again," she said with laughter in her voice.

Warming her feet was so far from the lustful, Donner-like behavior he resisted that he welcomed the chore. As he slid his legs toward her chilled toes—nowhere near as cold as they had been earlier—an idea came into his head that he thought would help him separate himself from the General. "I know how to warm those ice blocks of yours," he said in a teasing whisper as he dove beneath the covers.

She yelped and drew away in surprise, but he captured her feet with his hands as he slithered crossways so his own feet stuck out the side. His head remained positioned where he could exhale onto her toes while he cupped them near his mouth. She laughed and tried to pull them away, but after a moment, she relaxed. Then he heard her hum little sounds of approval as he chafed her feet between his palms and breathed on them some more.

He nipped at her big toe, making her yelp again. But she didn't pull away this time. "Mmm," she murmured. "This is a very pleasant way to get my feet warm."

"That was the plan," he said as he nibbled on the inside of her ankle while he massaged the arch of one foot. The other one got similar treatment and she sighed deeply.

"You're a very interesting man, Nathan. First that very sexy phone conversation you instigated, now this…this thing with the feet…."

He laughed and put his teeth gently to her muscular calf, then lightly slid his index finger upward along the back of her knee.

"Oh, my!" she softly cried as he trailed gently over that most sensitive portion of her leg, just between her calf and her thigh.

Her reactions stoked the fire already burning inside him and he once again fought the urge to hurry. To think was becoming harder. Most of his overheated blood had forsaken his brain for a more demanding master southward, leaving him a mindless slave to passion. He operated on instinct now, and although he managed to maintain an even pace as he smoothed his hands over her sleekly muscled thighs, every movement proceeded incrementally toward his objective—to make passionate love to Rachel Southwell.

Needing to keep his mouth on her flesh, he kissed along the silky, inner skin of her upper legs. The higher his caresses trailed, the more she squirmed and whimpered. But she didn't try to get away. On the contrary, she slithered this way and that so as to make herself more accessible.

"Hmm." He came upon her skimpy panties, which had somehow remained on her person despite his earlier efforts to get her naked. "These will have to go."

One tug from him got things started and she took over from there, wiggling out of them in less than a second. He had to duck back so as not to be clipped on the chin by a flailing knee, and he used the moment to get out of his boxer shorts. But the minute she settled, he returned to his endeavor: kissing her everywhere that made her moan and sigh, making her ready for what he longed to do.

"Please," she said, but he carried on, suddenly finding the prospect of bringing her to the pinnacle more urgent than the prospect of getting there himself. He licked and tasted and felt her grow more restless by the minute. She was hot and wet and her limbs had begun to tremble. Still, he continued with his lips and tongue.

Rachel had other ideas. She suddenly pushed back the sheet, exposing him. Then she laced her fingers into the longer hair at his crown and pulled. She was strong and he had no choice but to do exactly what she wanted. She drew him upward until he covered her body with his. Effortlessly, his erection found its way unerringly into that warm, damp space at the apex of her legs and with a few more twists and squirms on her part, he was inside her and sliding home.

He heard himself moan. "You're so...so..." He couldn't find the words. There were none to describe what he felt in that first moment of joining with her. And then he went beyond words as she undulated her hips, taking him deeper still.

"Please," she begged, and he understood that she wanted him to find a rhythm that would take them both beyond reason.

He needed no other encouragement. In another few minutes, he found himself poised on the brink, tightly wound and quivering from head to toe. Yet he held back and watched her face as he somehow continued to drive in and draw out until he knew for certain that she teetered on the precipice herself. Only when he felt the uncontrollable undulations of her muscles did he release the reins of his self-control and plummet with her.

He seemed to fall forever through pleasure so deep he couldn't be sure he would survive. And then he clung to the life raft of her body, overwhelmed by a tide of emotion that had him swallowing hard and blinking furiously. He kept his face carefully hidden in the crook of her neck, shaken by the feelings that stormed him—and a little afraid. He'd never experienced anything like making love to Rachel.

Her hands drifted lightly over his back as she held him possessively. The gentle sweep of her touch eased his heart, helped him regain his emotional footing. And he knew there was no place on earth he'd rather be.

He suspected he would always feel this way about Rachel. She'd become as important to him as oxygen and sunlight. Should he tell her?

"That was wonderful," she said on a sigh.

He raised his head so he could look at her. He thought he saw moonlight pooling in her eyes as she smoothed her fingers over his brow, down his cheek, across his lips. But then she sniffed delicately and drew him down for a sweet, slow kiss.

"Make love to me all night long, Nathan. We don't know what tomorrow will bring."

Without hesitation, he began to oblige the lady's request, free of his earlier fears, liberated by her willingness and incomparable passion. Clearly, she saw no comparison between him and Donner, so he would follow her lead and pretend for one night that the General didn't exist, that they were free, that tomorrow wouldn't come.

As FIT AS SHE WAS, there were still muscles Rachel hadn't known she owned until she awoke the next morning and stretched. Glancing at Nathan sleeping peacefully next to her, she resisted the impulse to say "Ow, ow, ow" as unfamiliar aches announced themselves in no uncertain terms. But along with the tenderness in muscle and flesh, she recognized a deep, languid satisfaction suffusing her entire being. She smiled to herself and stared at the man who had made her feel this way. Her heart filled with a strange longing as she noted how innocent and handsome he looked in his sleep.

Nathan's lids lifted and suddenly she found herself staring into the depths of his brown eyes. It took him a second to focus, but as soon as he did, a smile slowly took over his features. She smiled back.

"We should get our day started," she said reluctantly.

"Must we?" he asked with a wicked lilt to his voice. His hand snaked its way beneath the covers until it found her waist and then her ribs, finally cupping her breast and gently fondling.

"Mmm," she said as she arched against his palm. "But we really should…"

"Later," he whispered. And it was a while before either of them had anything coherent to say again.

"It's getting late," she said, coming out of a satisfied stupor enough to notice that the sun was high.

"A good day to sleep in," he murmured.

She would have agreed, except that she had work to do and she'd be damned if she would get out of bed while he slept. So she swept a pillow from beneath his head and swatted him with it. He barked an incoherent protest and twisted away. "Okay, okay!" He sat up and dropped his feet over the side of the bed. She couldn't take her eyes from the picture he presented as he stretched widely, flexing myriad muscles in a glorious show of strength and conditioning.

As his fingers combed through his hair—making it stand on end in every direction—he asked her what she had on her agenda for the day. He seemed completely unaware that he'd done more harm than good with his hair or that he was naked or that he looked incredibly handsome in the streaming sunlight.

"I'm done with my interviews, but..." She groaned as she remembered exactly what her day included. "I have to meet the General and Senator Zemin today at 1100 hours to discuss our progress." She tried to keep her voice even and her tone neutral, but inside she quaked. Coming face-to-face with Donner again so soon would be very hard. All at once, her lips whispered words she never thought she'd utter, words she had schooled herself to avoid since the day she'd sworn in to active duty. "I can't do it. I can't." She dropped her chin to her chest, and felt her guts churn as embarrassment clashed with fear.

Nathan didn't speak at first. In the silence, the soldier inside her began to surface, silently protesting that she must do her duty or become something she never wanted to be. The shadow of cowardice that had made her say "I can't" began to recede. Then Nathan vanquished the fear completely when he said, "I'll come with you, if you want." He spoke as if he had no doubt she would do what duty required, despite her protests.

"Yes, that would help." She took a deep breath and raised her head. Then she lifted her chin a notch higher, wrapped the sheet around her naked body and stood up. "It's already ten. I'm going to take a shower." She headed for the connecting door.

"You can leave the sheet here," he said, and she caught the lascivious expression he wore just before she crossed the threshold.

With a laugh, she tossed the sheet back into his room with a flick of her wrist so that all he got to see was her bare forearm. Still—as she'd hoped—he groaned at the suggestion of her head-to-toe nakedness just on the other side of the wall.

Nathan was waiting for her when she stepped out of her steamy bathroom in her underwear. He leaned against the connecting door frame, already dressed in his short-sleeved class B uniform. *He* hadn't spent twenty minutes blowing his hair dry.

"Nice," he said with an appreciative grin as he looked her up and down.

She wasn't used to having a man present while she dressed, but she smiled at him anyway. Nathan was someone she'd definitely like to become accustomed to having around. But then she saw his expression turn sober and her gaze drifted to the device he held.

The tape recorder. Rachel's heart skipped a beat and her stomach went tight. He meant for her to wear the thing, of course. But now she was really and truly afraid of Donner and that made the recorder seem especially dangerous.

"I shouldn't be any more afraid of him than I was before," she said out loud. Nathan held her gaze with an intent expression in his eyes, but he said nothing. "I knew he might attack me physically. I knew what I was getting myself into. The fact that he made the attempt yesterday doesn't change anything. He failed. So, why am I shaking?" The last words were whispered through humiliation and she wasn't sure he'd heard. But then he tossed the tape recorder onto her bedspread and headed straight toward her.

Rachel froze. She had never found it easy to accept physical comfort from anyone and had become adept at standing on her own two feet, no matter what difficulty she faced. The idea that he would enfold her in his arms horrified her. He would make her weak, she thought. He would lend her his strength and she wouldn't be able to manage without his help after that. She would become dependent on him. Soft.

She took a step back and he stopped in his tracks two feet away. "I'm a soldier," she said as she squared her shoulders.

She saw in his eyes that he was sorting things out, processing her words and her actions. At the same time, she could also see he was startled and maybe a little hurt. She wished she could make him understand. He didn't deserve rejection. But she couldn't think what she should say. So she reached for her clothes.

"You wouldn't be human if you weren't more wary of Donner now than you were before," he said evenly. "You're a soldier, but you're a person, too. Let's not try to pretend otherwise." His tone and his words were exactly what she needed. He spoke to her as he would any other military member, male or female. Gratitude filled her. He understood what she'd needed and gave it to her readily, even though he might have wanted something different from the moment.

She nodded as she slid her arms into her short-sleeved uniform shirt. "Yes, maybe it's a natural reaction. I just didn't expect it. Regardless, I'll do what I have to do." She reached for her dark green slacks.

As she stepped into them, he asked, "Do you have a skirt?" He retrieved the tape recorder and began to unwind the wire.

"Not here in Hawaii," she said as she buttoned her shirt.

She watched Nathan lay the device out on the bed, stretching the wire to untangle it. "Why?"

"Because I don't think this is going to work with your class B uniform unless you're wearing a skirt so we can attach the thing to your inner thigh. Your slacks are too snug. The recorder will bulge noticeably."

She walked to the bed and stood beside him. Together, they looked at the device. It was small—narrow and about two inches long—but her uniform fit her closely, as regulations required, and the bulge of the recorder would be visible if they weren't careful. Julian had shown them how to secure it at her waist because she'd worn a sweater that day to ward off the chill of the ever-present air-conditioning. But a sweater would look ridiculous in Hawaii, where the temperature was an even seventy-two degrees year-round. And she'd purposefully left her skirts at home because, back at the Pentagon, Donner had commented several times on his appreciation of her legs. Pants seemed less enticing.

"I didn't think about this. I had that black cardigan with me the day we visited Julian. I should have brought a skirt with me. Stupid."

"It's okay, Rachel. You can't be expected to think of everything. Who would have thought about how it would look if we strapped it to your leg under your pants? Not me. But now that I'm looking at the device closely, I can see it's too thick."

"Maybe I could just put it in my pocket," she offered.

"No way. It would show and the General might ask what you have in there."

"Ah, the double standard rises to thwart me. Men can have wallets and keys in their uniform pockets, but not women. We can't have anything bulkier than a tissue or we get called on it." Though she felt annoyed in this instance, she had always accepted the unwritten rule against stuffed pockets without complaining, given that most of the other unwritten rules seemed to favor women. Umbrellas were frowned upon for men in uniform, while women could use them without disapproval. Men had to wear their shirts tucked firmly into their waistbands, while women's blouses were hemmed so they could be left untucked. Women could wear studs in their pierced ears and style their hair how they wanted as long as it didn't surpass the bottom of their collars. So the rules about pockets were no big deal.

"Well, I can't say I'm too heartbroken over this turn of events," Nathan said. "Much as I want to get the goods on Donner as soon as possible, I've never been thrilled with the idea of you taking the risk with the tape recorder, especially while we're here in Hawaii. There are too many opportunities for him to corner you alone when I can't be nearby and—" He stopped short when he glanced at her. Rachel was fairly certain her face had gone pale at the mention of Donner cornering her alone.

"Yes, I agree," she said in a rush, hiding the choking fear behind a cascade of words. "I think it would be safer to try for the recording while at the Pentagon. It'll be easier for me to get him to say something incriminating while I'm alone with him in his office because I'll know you're right outside the door in case he becomes too aggressive." Somehow, relying on Nathan to be outside the door in case she needed backup wasn't as weak as relying on him for a comforting hug.

He nodded and showed he understood the distinction by saying, "You can count on me to watch your six, Rae. Always."

She gave him as much of a smile as she could muster, then turned to finish dressing while he put the tape recorder away. Together, they headed for the lobby for her meeting with Donner.

CHAPTER SEVENTEEN

IF NATHAN HADN'T BEEN standing beside her, lending his silent strength, Rachel didn't think she would have managed to stay on her feet when General Donner appeared in the lobby and headed toward them. Her pulse thumped so loudly in her ears she wasn't sure she would be able to hear anything else. It was all she could do to keep her breathing even and her limbs from shaking.

"Good morning," the General said. "Has the Senator arrived yet?" He sounded for all the world as if nothing unusual had happened the day before. And if it hadn't been for the scratches on his cheek—faded now that the blood had been washed away—he would have appeared none the worse for wear.

"No, sir," Nathan replied, and Rachel detected the anger seething just below the surface. The General clearly did not. He nodded and indicated that they would sit in the Luau Garden. He led the way outside, donning his beret as he went. Rachel exchanged glances with Nathan as they followed their commander, pulling their berets on, too.

"I told her we'd wait for her here," the General said. "I decided we should have this meeting in the open to help keep the woman contained. How difficult can she be in such a public setting?" He smiled at them as if they shared in his clever scheme. He sat down, and Rachel and Nathan followed suit. "Why are you here, Nate?"

Rachel searched her mind frantically for a reason to keep him by her, shocked she wasn't better prepared. But Nathan had already thought things through. "I've helped with some of the interviews and I could offer a second perspective."

That seemed good enough for Donner. "And what *is* your perspective? We might as well talk about what we've found out while we wait for her to get here. I've read your reports, but where do you think all this is leading us?"

Rachel felt a little of her tension seep away. The General either didn't remember the incident of the day before or chose to pretend it hadn't happened. It was almost as if he were two different people—the one who could selflessly and tenaciously support the National Guard and the other who could abuse women. The two never expressed themselves at the same time. Rachel shivered at the thought. But she quickly got a grip. For now, the good General Donner was in control.

She found her voice. "I think the men were out of line, but the women seem to believe the apologies they received were enough." She didn't dare say that two of the women had reported experiencing worse at the hands of superior officers against whom they didn't feel they could safely complain. That part of the interviews rang too closely to Rachel's own story for her to speak of it. "We probably need to review the disciplinary actions taken against the men involved to be sure they were treated evenhandedly."

"Yes, that's good. You're sure none of the women wants more from us? I mean Zemin seems determined to—" The General stopped speaking as a shadow slipped over him from behind.

"Determined to what?" the Senator asked.

The General stood, making the Senator look up to maintain eye contact. He smiled and held out his hand to her. "Determined to see justice done, to leave no stone unturned, to do what's right for those poor women," he said as he shook the hand the Senator reluctantly placed in his.

Both Nathan and Rachel had risen, too, and greeted the Senator. Two men who looked very much like bodyguards stood behind her. They offered no greeting and did not join the group. They didn't so much as give anyone a nod. When the Senator took a seat, they moved casually into positions that provided them the best view of the surroundings. Though they looked nonchalant, they scanned the pool area, the outdoor bar and the rest of the scenery with intensity.

"What happened to you?" the Senator asked, gesturing toward the General's cheek.

Without so much as blinking, Donner blithely claimed he'd had a run-in with his razor. Rachel wondered whether or not he remembered how it had really happened. If only she could be sure he had no clear recollections, she might be able to let go of some of her worry. If he actually recalled what had transpired, he might make good on his threat to send her to one of those faraway A places. Worse, he might take his anger out on Nathan.

The presence of Barbara Zemin gave Rachel a respite from these thoughts as she concentrated on the research and interviews she'd done. For the next half hour, she and Nathan delivered the data they had collected, answered questions and finally provided their opinions of the situation at the General's request. As necessary, they produced documentation from the files they had brought along. Zemin nodded, asked a few more questions, nodded again, then stood up abruptly. The three Army officers stood, too, albeit with a slight awkwardness born of surprise.

"Good work," she said to Rachel as she shook her hand. "And you, too, Captain." She turned to the General, but did not hold out her hand to him. "If you'll excuse me, I have another appointment. Send your final report to my office in Washington." And with that, she quickly departed, her security guards following as though tied to her by an invisible string.

Only after the Senator had gone did Rachel realize the woman had been unforgivably rude to the General. "She's really a piece of work, that woman," the General muttered. "She seems happy with what we've done with the investigation, but she still has something stuck in her craw." He startled Rachel by swiftly turning to glare at her. "I want to know what it is." His gaze bore into Rachel. Her stomach somersaulted, but she kept her chin up and refused to let him see her quake.

"Sir, I could—" Nathan began, but the General cut him off with a swift movement of his hand.

"Do you see my wife hovering over there at the bar, drinking before noon and pining for my company?" he said in an acid tone. "Go and keep her out of trouble until I can baby-sit her myself."

Nathan hesitated, clearly unwilling to leave Rachel alone with Donner. Though she felt cold all the way to her soul, she managed to give Nathan a nearly imperceptible nod, urging him to do as he was told. There was no need for him to cross the General on this. The bar was within sight of where they stood. Somehow, she would find a way to stay put while the General vented his spleen.

But as she watched Nathan walk slowly away, her heart began to hammer. Surreptitiously, she took a deep breath and let it out. "Sir," she said to get things started. "I have no idea what could be bothering the Senator, other than this case."

"Don't you?" he said, eyeing her coldly.

She didn't speak, afraid he somehow knew the exact nature of her one private conversation with Zemin. He would catch her in a lie if she continued to claim she had no idea what issues still nagged at the Senator.

"Did you meet with that woman? Did you tell her things about you and me? Did you dare to suggest to her that I've been anything but patient with you?"

"Sir, I had one meeting with her at your insistence. You ordered me to go to her office to let her know how we'd be addressing her issues regarding this situation here in Hawaii." Oh, God, had he forgotten?

He glared at her. "What else did you talk about?"

She didn't want to claim that nothing else had been said

because that would be a lie. Besides, he seemed to know already. "I don't understand what you mean, sir," she said. It was all she could do to stay standing under the weight of his nearness. Malevolence seemed to pour off him in waves that nearly suffocated her. To breathe was becoming harder as memories of his hands on her body began to rise up inside her mind.

"I've tried to be reasonable with you, Chief. But I've just about had it with your stubbornness." He took a step closer, standing over her with a red face and sneering mouth. "You think you got out of it yesterday," he whispered. "But I'm not done with you yet."

Looking up into his eyes, she knew then that he remembered what had happened between them in her room. But did he recall Nathan's role? Cold dread enveloped her as she thought of what this man could do to Nathan's future.

"I assure you, I will have my way. I always do," he said softly. He took a step back from her then and his eyes lost their crazed expression. "Dismissed!"

Shaking from head to toe, Rachel moved on automatic when she came to attention and gave him the required salute. He returned it with an intense lack of respect. Then she did an about-face and marched back inside the hotel, determined to make it to her room without falling apart.

NATHAN HAD GONE RELUCTANTLY toward the bar, straining to hear every word spoken behind him until the gurgle of the nearby fountains overtook the voices. Lydia smiled widely as he approached. Prudence required he smile in return. He chose a seat on the far side of her so that he would be able to see everything that transpired between Rachel and the General, even if he couldn't hear them.

"Your Chief is going to get an earful," Lydia said. "My husband is none too happy with her."

Nathan needed a lot of willpower to school his features into a bland expression. "Why is that?" he said casually. He ordered an orange juice from the bartender.

"That Senator keeps hinting that she has something else on Walter, something that will embarrass him personally as well as professionally. For some reason, Walter thinks your little Chief is involved."

Nathan smiled at the server when the juice arrived, casually took a sip, then said, "She's not *my* Chief. And why would the General think she's had time to do anything other than the interviews he told her to take care of?"

"Who knows?" she said as she swirled the straw in her glass, making the ice clink. "He doesn't like her much. On the other hand, I suspect he likes her too much." She continued to look at her glass as she said this, so Nathan was able to study her expression in his peripheral vision.

What had she meant by that last remark? He glanced again to where Rachel stood, assured himself that she and the General were not going anywhere, then turned his attention back to Lydia. "Hmm," he said, as if he didn't have much interest in the subject but wanted to be supportive of whatever Lydia thought.

As he'd hoped, his lack of enthusiasm prodded her to say more. "I'm aware of my husband's peccadilloes, Captain. You might pass a word of warning on to your Chief. Tell her she really ought to just put in for a transfer. Things could get ugly if she doesn't."

Nathan looked directly at the woman and wondered at her audacity in making such a blatant threat. "If you know what your husband is up to, why would you defend him?"

She gave a long-suffering sigh. "I'm from West Virginia, and not a good part of that state. My father was a coal miner, as are all my brothers. Walter took me out of there, and still provides me with more than a girl with my background ever could have dreamed about. Why, I've had dinner with governors and shaken the hand of a king. Not bad for someone who barely made it through high school. He may not pay much attention to me physically," she said as she looked searchingly into Nathan's eyes, "but he gives me everything else I want. And I'll crush anyone who tries to take that away from me," she said calmly. Then she smiled, flashing her teeth before she took a sip of her drink through the straw.

"Ready, my dear?" the General said as he approached. Nathan quickly scanned the area for Rachel, but didn't see her. "We're going sight-seeing today," he explained pleasantly to Nathan. Nathan scowled, frantic to find Rachel. But he managed a few polite words before he hurried away.

SHE KNEW HE'D FIND HER quickly and he did. From where she waited for the elevator, she saw him searching the lobby as he came through it and relief seemed to suffuse him as he laid eyes on her. He approached quickly, but checked himself before he enfolded her in his arms, as he'd seemed about to do. Standing awkwardly in front of her, he asked "Are you all right?"

She explained that the General had made his usual threats, indicated with a rueful smile that she'd be looking for orders to Afghanistan any time now and assured him she was okay. "I thought seeing him for the first time would be a lot worse. But I lived through it. He remembers some of it. But I'm not sure he recalls your role in it all. I'm still hoping he doesn't."

"For God's sake, don't worry about *me*," Nathan said, then he told her about his conversation with Mrs. Donner.

"Then she *is* the one who sent that threatening note I found on my desk back home. I wonder how she found out about Adam."

"I don't know. She never mentioned Adam to me." The elevator finally came and they boarded it. "I think we should call it a day and change into civilian clothes. Let's put all this behind us for a while. The General took his wife sight-seeing. Maybe we could do the same, since it's our last day here."

"Let me call home to check on everyone first."

"Yes, that's a good idea. Then we'll pretend we're not even in the Army for a while."

"Speaking of Adam, his birthday is coming up. I promised to get him something from Hawaii to augment all his other gifts." She smiled, letting pleasant thoughts of her son overtake the residual distress of confronting Donner. "His grandparents spoil him."

"I'll bet his mom does, too," he said with a grin.

After changing and checking in at home, they inquired with the hotel concierge, who hooked them up with a local tour bus that took them all around the island of Oahu. In the early evening, they even found a club with decent food and musicians willing to play a few big-band tunes so Nathan could twirl her around the floor, proving that his childhood dance lessons hadn't gone to waste. Even though no one could play any tango music, Rachel had more fun than she'd had in a very long time. Nathan was excellent company, and despite the vague unease that constantly gnawed at the back of her mind, she spent the whole day laughing and taking in the awesome surroundings.

Returning late to the hotel, Nathan suggested dinner. "How about the Koko Café? If we eat in the Hale Koa Room we'll have to change into appropriate attire." He made a face to indicate his distaste for *that* rule.

"If we ordered room service, we wouldn't have to change into anything at all," she said, then felt her cheeks go hot with embarrassment.

He didn't say anything at first and Rachel wanted to retract the suggestive words. She opened her mouth to speak, but then noticed the slow grin curving his lips and eyes. "You take my breath away," he said. Then he gently grasped her by the elbow and led her hastily toward the elevators.

"Well, well, well, don't we look happy." Senator Zemin appeared out of nowhere and stood in their path. "I like to see our military men and women happy. But I'd have thought you two would have some serious matters weighing on your minds." She leaned toward them and lowered her voice. "I'd have thought you'd have the sense not to mess up a case against harassment by making this public display of affection for each other.''

Rachel blinked. To say something so blatant, or to even care, wasn't like Barbara Zemin. Cautiously, Rachel said, "I don't know what you mean, ma'am."

Zemin stared at her without expression, but Rachel refused to be the first to look away. Nathan said nothing at all.

A false smile slowly curved the other woman's lips. "As I've told you before, Rachel, you should consider a future in politics. Captain, I'd appreciate a little more discretion on your part. It was the eagerness on your face that captured my attention. Try to tone it down a little, for the sake of the greater good." And with that, she marched off. Only then did Rachel notice the Senator's guards as they moved out of obscurity to trail behind as they had before.

"We have to be more careful," Nathan said as soon as the elevator doors slid closed.

"Yes, that's probably true. Sometimes I think she's as crazy as Donner."

"And his wife," Nathan added as he turned to face her.

"We're surrounded by nutcases."

"I suspect we're the only two sane people we know," he said as he leaned closer to her, drawing her near without touching her.

"Is that a bad thing?" she whispered, caught in his seductive gaze.

"Let's not dwell on it," he said as he dipped his head and gently touched her lips with his. The elevator sped upward and her heart rate accelerated likewise. By the time the bell chimed and the doors slid open, Rachel trembled and the blood sang through her veins.

She gladly followed him down the hall to his room. It was a long while before they got around to ordering room service.

And after the lovely night they had, morning came especially early. They had to skip breakfast in order to pack and dress in time to meet the General's car for the trip to the airport. But Rachel didn't care. She was a little giddy with unexpected happiness, and even Donner's presence seemed inconsequential as she sat on the plane beside Nathan—once again out of sight of the General and his wife—and remembered the wonders she'd discovered in the Captain's arms the night before. She knew her euphoria wouldn't last, that as soon as they landed in Washington she would return to her worries about her future and about how to finish things with Donner. She would have to give up Nathan, too, once they were home—at least in the physical sense. They both understood that getting caught would be too easy, given that their bedrooms would no longer be one connecting door apart. But for now, Rachel was content.

HER CONTENTMENT LASTED UNTIL she set foot inside her house after parting from Nathan and the others and heading home by taxi in the pouring rain. Julian sat at the kitchen table, sipping coffee, while Adam played with toy trucks at his feet. Raindrops pelted the windows, and the house felt close. Her father sat next to Julian while her mother served up a batch of freshly baked cookies. The scene looked homey and sweet, except that Julian's presence could only mean trouble. But she had to wait to hear his reason for stopping by, because Adam saw her standing on the threshold of the kitchen and launched himself directly at her. He wrapped his arms around her waist and hugged her hard.

"You came back, just like you said you would!" he exclaimed. "And my birthday is in a week, so did you get me something from Hawaii, like a volcano or a coconut?"

She smiled at him and said she wasn't going to tell him anything or it would spoil the surprise. He seemed satisfied with the implication that some kind of surprise was coming and went back to his trucks. Rachel turned to the adults.

"I called your parents to make sure everything was normal," Julian explained.

"And I didn't want to lie to him," her mother confessed.

"Damn teenagers," her father muttered. "Damn eggs everywhere."

"Bernie, don't swear. Adam is sitting right here."

"I see him," he grumbled to his wife.

"Eggs?" Rachel said, confused.

"Someone threw eggs on your car," Julian explained. "Quite a lot of them. By the time your parents saw the damage—"

"Actually, it was Adam who noticed the mess," Virginia interjected.

"By the time Adam saw the eggs, they had dried on the car," Julian continued. "The rain didn't start until a couple of hours ago, or it might have washed some of it away. I'm afraid you'll have to have the whole car repainted."

"But who would do such a thing?" she asked.

"Damn teenagers," her father said again.

"Maybe," Julian said. "But I wanted to see things for myself, take some pictures. I'm done here for now." He turned to Rachel as he got up from his seat. "Sorry about your car." He turned to leave.

"Thanks, Major. I'll walk you to the door." Once out of earshot from everyone else, she said, "And thank you for coming over here. I'm sure it was just a teenage prank like my father says, but it's good to be careful under the circumstances."

Julian looked at her. "I don't think it was teenagers. But it's too soon to come to any conclusions."

She nodded. "Let me know what I can do to help you figure out who's responsible. Right now, I just want to play trucks with my kid."

Julian gave her a crooked smile. "Sounds great. You call me if anything else happens out of the ordinary."

"I will."

NATHAN PACED the confines of his apartment, padding in his stocking feet back and forth through the living area. He didn't want to be here. He wanted to be with Rachel.

He pictured her homecoming—Adam running into her arms and her parents beaming with pride at their successful daughter. She would be surrounded by love. Suddenly, he wanted to be a part of that more than he wanted to continue breathing. In the past few days, he'd come to understand that what she had was what he'd been looking for all his life—a family to love and support him.

He glanced at the photograph that stood on an end table. It was of his own family—his parents, Julian and him. They were all smiling for the camera, but he remembered that day hadn't been very happy. His parents had bickered endlessly even though they were out in public, strolling along a boardwalk at some beach. Except for the moment during which this picture had been taken, they'd never been a family.

That was probably why Julian had joined the Army after community college. He'd craved discipline, a code of honor and affiliation with a group of people he could be proud of. But his departure had left a gaping hole in Nathan's life. Julian was really the only family Nathan had ever known.

The ringing of the phone drew him out of his depressing reverie. It was Rachel, and the sound of her voice lightened his heart as nothing else could.

"Are you all unpacked?" she asked.

He looked over at the suitcases standing in his entryway. They were exactly where he'd left them when he'd first walked into his silent apartment. "Not a chance," he admitted. "How are Adam and your parents?"

"Adam is his usual self, only much more lively than my mother is used to. I think his medications are really helping. He's like a normal kid again. He gave me his list for possible birthday presents and you'll be surprised to know that a Hawaiian shirt was not on it." She referred to a playful argument they'd had while shopping in Waikiki for Adam's birthday. He'd wanted to buy him a horribly bright shirt with flamingos all over it. She'd informed him that eight-year-old boys weren't into the surfer look.

"You'll see. He's gonna love it."

"You bought it for him against my advice?" There was laughter in her voice.

"When your back was turned," he admitted.

"I should have known."

Feeling like a stray cat but beyond caring, he said, "So now you have to invite me to his birthday party, since I got him a present."

"Ah, now I see what you're up to. Finagling an invitation to a kid's birthday party. It's probably for the cake and ice cream. Or is it because you long to wear those little pointy hats with the too-tight elastic under your chin?"

He laughed at that. "You've found me out."

"Okay, you're invited. 1300 hours on Saturday. Julian can come, too, if he wants."

Nathan's throat tightened suddenly at her generosity. Her willingness to share her family seemed unbelievably kind and selfless. His experiences told him that most people hoarded what they cherished most. Clearly, Rachel didn't believe in doing that. "I'm not sure Julian will come," he said. His brother wouldn't want to intrude on a family event. Nathan was fairly certain he'd feel like an intruder, too, but he didn't care as long as he could be with Rachel and Adam.

"Well, he was just here earlier today," she said, and then she explained about her car and the eggs and how Julian had been to her house to see if he could find any clues. "The finish on my car is ruined. Apparently there's something in eggs that eats into paint."

"Does Julian think this is related to the note you got before we left?"

"He isn't sure, but he said it wouldn't hurt to collect evidence, just in case. He was particularly interested in the footprints that were left in the mud near the driveway.

When the police were here, they didn't even glance at those footprints. Your brother is a good detective. So you should invite him to the party for me. I think he's lonely.''

Nathan stifled a groan. Yes, Julian was probably lonely. And so was Nathan. He wanted her here in his arms so badly, his heart ached with it. ''I miss you,'' he heard himself whisper.

''I miss you, too. I'm glad I'll see you tomorrow at the office. It won't be the same as holding your hand as we walk along a secluded, moonlit Oahu beach, but at least I'll be able to catch your eye now and then.''

''I don't like having to hide what I feel for you.''

A long silence followed and his guts writhed. Did she share those feelings? At last, she said, ''We need to get this mess behind us, Nate. Bring the tape recorder to work tomorrow. We'll have to be prepared for any opportunities Donner might offer us.''

THE NEXT DAY, SHE FOUND another note sitting under the edge of her blotter as soon as she sat down at her desk. Cautiously, she slipped it out of its envelope, glancing around to be sure no one was watching her as she did so. Nathan had not yet arrived and Allison had returned to her typing after she'd offered a cursory welcome back to Rachel. The woman was even more withdrawn than before they'd gone, and Rachel's gaze shifted to Donner's office door—closed, indicating he was inside. What could he have done to Allison so early in the morning?

She opened the folded paper in her hands and read: ''Adam's birthday party won't be so much fun if his mother isn't there. Leave the General alone.''

Rachel sucked in a breath. The threat was so much more direct this time. Whoever wrote the two notes guessed that she would be doubly afraid at the mention of Adam by name. Someone not only knew about her son, but also that he was having a birthday party. And that someone wanted to protect the General. Why? And who?

Rachel's trembling fingers attested to how well the writer had succeeded in frightening her. But she set her jaw as she refolded the note and put it back into the envelope. She couldn't let this unknown person break her determination. As troubled as she was by the threat to her family, she wouldn't let herself be cowed by this manipulation. So, she schooled her breathing back to normal and dialed home, just as she had the last time. All seemed normal there. Adam was playing on his computer because it was too hot and humid for outdoor activities. He planned on having one of his friends over after lunch. Normal.

Nathan walked in then and dropped his briefcase beside his desk. His gaze zeroed in on Rachel immediately and he said, "Must get coffee. How about you?"

She nodded and rose to follow him out.

"Oh, don't mind me, I'll just answer the phones while you two go off together again," Allison said. Her tone was just light enough to sound like she might be teasing. But her expression seemed serious, even a little angry.

"Hi, Allison. Nice to be back. Good to see you, too," Nathan said with a teasing grin. "You want me to bring you something?"

"No, thanks." She turned away to shuffle some papers.

Rachel was too preoccupied with the note in her hand to pay much attention to Allison just then. She moved swiftly down the hallway, indicating that Nathan should follow. After ducking into a seldom-used stairwell, she led him to the basement, where she pulled him by his sleeve to the alcove beneath the bottom set of stairs. As soon as she turned to face him, he leaned down and kissed her. For a moment, she forgot everything except the feeling of his lips on hers. Desire swept over her like a brushfire, and within seconds she was breathing hard and deepening their kiss. Fortunately, Nathan had more sense and self-control. He eased them back gradually to a less-combustible kiss.

When he lifted his head, he continued to hold her tightly.

"Sorry," he said as if not even remotely sorrowful. "I just had to do that."

"Mmm," she managed to say. "Um, I didn't bring you here to…to…" Her gaze went to his mouth and lingered there as she thought about kissing him again.

He chuckled. "Keep looking at me like that and we might end up doing something down here that would make me blush whenever I remembered it later—which would be often, I'm sure."

She eased back, remembering why she'd wanted to talk to him in this secluded place. "There was another note on my desk when I got in this morning."

His expression instantly sobered. "Let me see it." He took the note from her and read it.

"Who knows about Adam's birthday?"

"Just me and my parents and one or two of Adam's friends from the neighborhood."

"Are any of his friends' parents in the military?"

"Not that I know of. Other than when I put in for his ID card and when we went to the hospital, I haven't told anyone in the Army about Adam or his birthday party, except…" She stopped herself in time, but Nathan knew what she'd been about to say.

"Except for me," he finished for her. Those brown eyes looked stormy.

CHAPTER EIGHTEEN

"YES," SHE ADMITTED. "But you aren't a suspect here, Nathan. Give me a break. I'm not accusing you."

"I told my brother about the party. He said he'd come, by the way."

"Good, I'm glad. He's not a suspect, either. Ask him if he mentioned it to anyone else."

"I'll ask, but it's unlikely. Julian is a bit of a loner. Damn!" He spun away on this last word and smacked his hand on the nearest wall. His frustration was almost tangible.

Although Rachel felt nearly as undone by this turn of events, she understood the need to be strong and level-headed, especially if Nathan could not be. "Did you bring the tape recorder? I want to wear it every day from now on. I'll complain about the air conditioner being too high so I can have my black sweater on all the time to help hide it."

"I brought it, but it's up in my briefcase. I had the foresight to put it into a lunch bag so you would get it from me later. Don't we need to talk to Julian about this new note? I mean, this is getting more dangerous than any of us bargained for."

"Yes, we should call Julian. But at least the note doesn't actually threaten Adam. It just mentions him to shake me up. The real threat is to me, and I knew there would be risks to this mission and—"

"The hell you did!" he shouted. "Not like this! It's bad enough that monster mauls you whenever he gets the chance, nearly rapes you in your own hotel room, threatens you with a transfer to God-knows-where. But this unknown nemesis was not in the cards.''

"Maybe not, but I'm not giving up now. We must be close to getting something on the bastard, or his champion—whoever she is—wouldn't be sending these notes. I'm not going to back down.''

"Stubborn woman," he muttered as he paced the small area in front of the stairs. "So you think the champion is his wife? You said 'whoever *she* is.' What makes you so sure?''

"I don't think a man would leave little notes on my desk. Guys don't do that.''

Nodding, he started to speak, but paused when he heard a door open above them, then footsteps on the treads. Then another door opened and closed. Silence followed. "I want us to see Julian," he insisted. "Maybe he can give us a clear perspective.''

"Okay. We can go tomorrow. Call him tonight from home to arrange it.''

"We should go see him now," he said. His mouth formed a thin line of tension and his eyes blazed with contained anger.

"We have to be more careful than that, Nate. You don't know if Julian is even available right now. And someone might be watching us to see how we react to this note. We need to try to confuse the enemy by responding in an unexpected way. Calmly.''

"Never let them see you sweat, right, Chief?''

"That's right, Captain. Now, let's go back and pretend we're not bothered by this latest psych operation.'' That got a grim smile out of him, at least.

"I still need that coffee.''

"Me, too. And we wouldn't want to return empty-handed or Allison might surprise us again by coming out of her shell long enough to comment.''

THE NEXT DAY IN JULIAN'S office, Nathan was relieved that his brother could assure Rachel he hadn't told anyone else about the birthday party. The last thing they needed was to have to open the field of suspects to casual acquaintances. Nathan handed over the new note and Julian examined it. Then photographs of the car-egging came out for inspection. They showed the footprints found near Rachel's car.

"The thing is, they're clearly military-style boots," Julian explained.

"Well, then they must be mine from the last time I wore my battle dress uniform to work. I would have worn my boots with my BDUs," Rachel said.

Julian rubbed the back of his neck. The gesture made Nathan smile slightly. He recognized it as something he did himself when he was thinking hard about something. "I don't think they're your prints," Julian said. "The only reason I was lucky enough to get them is that it rained pretty hard the day before the incident, then dried some in the heat the next day. It didn't start raining again until later. If not for the rain, that patch of ground would have been dry and solid. If you'd made any prints, first rain would have washed them out. These prints were made between the two downpours."

Nathan raised his eyebrows. "You're good at this stuff," he said. He'd never fully appreciate his brother's skills before now.

Julian grinned. "Yeah, well, it keeps me busy." He looked back at Rachel. "Got any enemies who're in the military?"

"Probably. But I couldn't name any. Besides, those clunky military-style boots are pretty common with young people these days. Maybe my father is right and it was just those damn teenagers." She said this last part in a gruff and mumbled way, imitating her dad and making Julian smile.

"We're no further along than we were before," Nathan complained. "The notes were typed and printed off a computer, so we don't know any CID voodoo to trace its origin without testing every printer within a ten-mile radius. There's no indication who it could be from, although we're fairly certain it's from the same person who sent the first one. We can't tell if the note writer is the same person as the egg thrower. All we're sure of is the person who left the notes sides with Donner and wants to protect him." He glanced at Rachel.

Julian nodded. "Make a list of all the people you know who would want to protect him."

"It's a short list, Jules. I can only think of one person. His wife."

"But she can't be the one who did the eggs, because she wouldn't be caught dead in combat boots," Rachel said.

"That's for sure. So that means the notes and the eggs aren't related," Nathan suggested.

Julian surprised them by shaking his head. "I don't think it's the wife who did the eggs or the notes. Call it a hunch. I just can't see her referring to her husband as 'the General.' From the psych profile you wrote up on her for me, she's not the type."

It was Rachel's turn to lift eyebrows as she turned to Nathan. "You did a psych profile on Lydia Donner?"

"It's what I do," he said with a shrug. Then another possibility came to him. "She could have hired someone to do the eggs for her and she might have called her husband 'the General' to throw us off the trail."

"Always a possibility. But I still want you two to look around more closely at the people you interact with each day. Consider everyone you know with a fresh eye. Think whether anyone has something to gain by keeping Donner in his position. Make lists."

Nathan looked at Rachel with a wry grin. "Julian is a great one for making lists." Turning back to his brother, he stood and said, "We appreciate you taking the time to help us, Julian. We'll try to come up with something that will help."

Rachel preceded him out of the office, and Nathan would have followed if Julian hadn't called him back with a whisper and a gesture. Oblivious to this, Rachel kept on going while Nathan backed up to hear what else his brother had to say. "Listen, Nate, I think you should do your best to stay near her night and day. I don't like the way things seem to be escalating."

"Yeah, I'd like nothing better than to glue myself to her side, but we can't be seen getting too cozy, Jules. You know what that would do to our case against Donner if we're lucky enough to get to a trial."

Julian nodded. "I'm still hoping it won't come to a trial. Just spend as much time with her as you can. That's an order," he added with a knowing grin.

"Yes, sir," Nathan said, and he gave his brother a salute as he left to catch up with Rachel.

"ARE YOU SURE YOU DON'T want to go with me to the coffee shop, Allison? We could talk," Rachel offered again. The younger woman had seemed shaken by an earlier visit Mrs. Donner had made and Rachel wondered if the General's wife could be putting threatening notes on Allison's desk, too. But instead of reaching out, Allison withdrew even more. Rachel was at her wit's end about how to help the younger woman. And Allison's increasingly sensitive condition made Rachel spitting mad at their commanding officer.

"Yeah, I'm sure. I've got a ton of stuff to do before I go home tonight." Allison smiled, but it was shaky and forced. Rachel didn't know how to persuade her. Not even a visit to the post psychologist had helped much. He'd advised patience and kindness. "Let her know you're available to talk," he'd said.

She made one last effort. "Okay, but if you ever feel like chatting—well, I could use some female companionship now and then. The testosterone in this place can be overwhelming sometimes."

Allison actually grinned at that, but then she returned to her filing.

Rachel headed for the door alone since Nathan was on an errand for the General. "I'm going to go pick up those files we need from down the hall," she said.

Just as she rounded the corner in the outer hallway, Donner showed up at her elbow.

"How's our report coming along, Chief? Any problems putting the facts together in a way that will shut down Zemin's complaints?" He kept pace beside her and there was no escape.

Rachel swallowed and surreptitiously pressed on the button beneath her sweater and waistband that would turn on the tape recorder hidden under her clothes. She couldn't be sure it clicked on. The thing was meant to be silent. "No, sir, no trouble with the report. It's shaping up nicely. I might need to do some follow-up with one of the people we interviewed. But otherwise, everything's fine."

"Good, good. How's the job these days? Got enough interesting work?" He sounded for all the world like a concerned supervisor. Where was the lecher when she needed to get him on tape?

"Yes, sir, the work is good. No complaints." She silently prayed that she was recording and he would say something awful. Her heart rate was high with both trepidation for what he might do and anticipation for bringing the case to closure. If only he would utter an incriminating few words the whole nightmare could be over.

Maybe he needed a little boost in the right direction, she thought. At the top of the long ramp leading to the concourse where all the shops were located, she stopped and faced him. "Sir, I've been meaning to talk to you about something," she began.

The gleam in the General's eye turned suspicious and cold. "What's that, Chief?"

"In Hawaii, when you came to my hotel room and…"

His brow knit and he held up his hand to stop her speech.

"I don't know what you mean, Chief." Then he leaned closer, almost to where the microphone hid beneath her lapel, almost as if he knew it was there. "And neither do you," he whispered as he reached around and squeezed her bottom.

Rachel jumped away, loath to have his hands on her body again. Embarrassment flooded her as she realized what he'd done, right here in this public place. He grinned at her and she saw the wickedness in his eyes. How could she ever have thought he was handsome? His classic features now appeared horribly distorted by the sickness that lay beneath them.

As he began to walk away without another word, Rachel had the sense to glance around her to see if anyone had witnessed the harassment. But, of course, the General would have made sure that no one had been paying them any attention before doing something so blatant. Not a soul looked her way. Everyone kept on heading to wherever they were going, oblivious of her distress.

Perspiration dampened her brow and her breathing felt labored. But she managed to start walking again, though she'd forgotten where she'd been heading. She went in the opposite direction from Donner, moving mechanically through the hallways, scanning this way and that as if searching for an escape route. A clear part of her mind told her she was behaving irrationally, that she should turn and go back to the office until she could remember what her errand had been. But the greater urge prevailed and she kept walking, weaving in and out of the corridors that were like spokes in the huge pentagonal building and trailing around the corridors that formed the concentric circles. A person could cover miles and miles inside without ever going down the same corridor twice, she thought idly. After a long time wandering, she finally reached a construction barrier that would not allow her further progress.

She stood there, staring at the signs and pictures randomly posted on the makeshift wall. They were remembrances of the terrorist attack—a copied photo of a lost loved one, a child's crudely made flag, a copy of the opening lines of the Declaration of Independence. One by one, she read them. To recall that there were people who had it worse than she did helped her. She told herself she should rejoice that she was alive and able to fight. At least she knew her enemy and would eventually get the chance to confront him. At the same time, she felt a certain affinity with the survivors of September 11—her situation, like theirs, reeked of unfairness. Like them, she recognized what had prodded her to meander through the hallways here today, searching for something elusive.

It was fear that nowhere was safe anymore.

But on that thought, Chief Warrant Officer Rachel Southwell squared her shoulders. She turned away from the wall and headed back to her office with determination in her strides. Awareness had dawned that her physical reactions and mental confusion were just manifestations of the insidious fear Donner purposefully inflicted. She was certain she could control them, use them, channel them. Her training made her capable of doing so.

And her resolve to fight renewed itself on the realization that her world would be safe once again—as soon as the enemy was neutralized.

"Where were you?" Allison asked when she returned. "And where are the files?"

"Files," Rachel said without inflection, suddenly remembering what had taken her out of the office in the first place.

"Ma'am, you've been gone for hours. I was getting ready to send out a search party."

Rachel glanced at the General's office door. It stood open and no lights burned within. "I was waylaid. I forgot what I'd gone out for. And it's late. We should call it a night."

"Captain Fordham already left. He said he had a date."

Rachel blinked at Allison. "A date?" She tried to think past the sinking feeling that enveloped her. But her mind wouldn't clear. Appalling disappointment swamped her. On top of everything else, she was alone again—the pregnant girl whose lover wouldn't marry her, the recruit whose teammates wouldn't hoist her over the confidence course wall, the soldier left behind.

"Yeah, he said he had a date with an angel." Allison watched Rachel carefully for reaction. But when Rachel just stood there, Allison began to pack up her things for the night. The younger woman must have been speaking, because her mouth moved and she gestured occasionally. But Rachel didn't hear a word. Like a machine, she helped Allison turn off equipment and shut down the lights. Then she picked up her purse and her beret and went out. Vaguely, she understood that Allison had bid her goodnight. Rachel raised her hand and smiled as she headed in the opposite direction to the parking lot where her car resided.

Dusk had fallen already. As if it mattered, she looked at her watch, surprised to note that it was 2000 hours already. Why had Allison stayed so late? That wasn't like her. But maybe she really *had* been worried when Rachel had not returned promptly from her errand. At least *someone* cared. At this point, she'd take what she could get, even if her ally was a mixed-up, depressed and very young Allison Fitzpatrick.

As she walked through the darkening parking lot, Rachel cataloged the signs of depression she herself seemed to be manifesting. Her periodic confusion and listlessness, the sense of defeat that overwhelmed her now and then, the lack of sleep and appetite. She wondered if she could be overreacting to what Allison had mentioned about Nathan's date. Maybe he had said that to throw off suspicion, given how much time he'd spent with her lately—following her around whenever he could. Or maybe he had a date with someone who could supply information to help against Donner. Anything was possible.

Except, it wasn't possible that he would betray her by

finding another woman to go out on the town with. It wasn't in him to do that.

Yet, as she drove out of the lot and made her way onto the highway, she couldn't shake the thought that he might have. That was the depression talking, she knew. And if he had gone out with a woman, there wasn't a thing she could do about it. In fact, that appeared to be the story of her life—bad things kept happening to her that she had no control over. She sighed. *That* was the depression talking, too.

She needed to shake it off, she decided as she turned into one of the neighborhoods that she frequently cut through on her way home from work. Right about then she realized the same headlights had been in her rearview mirror for a long time. Or was that paranoia talking?

Rachel laughed, noted she sounded a little hysterical, but kept an eye on the car behind her. To appease her need for reassurance, she made a left down a side street that she never normally took. The other car followed.

Coincidence? She turned again. The car followed. Now it had gained on her. The headlights were blinding. And just as she thought about the brightness of the lights, the driver clicked on the high beams, forcing Rachel to squint and reflexively raise her arm to shield her eyes. Damn!

She told herself to stay calm as she pressed the gas a little harder to see what would happen next. The car paced her. What the hell was going on here? It couldn't be a police officer or he'd have put on his siren and police light by now.

The high beams flashed on and off a few times, so she took a chance and pulled her car to the shoulder of the deserted stretch of road she found herself on, hoping the driver just wanted to get by. But as she idled at the side of the road, she saw that whoever tailed her had done the same. The car sat behind her with the bright lights on, waiting. No one got out of the car. Rachel's blood pressure rose.

Unarmed, she couldn't go over and confront the person.

So she cautiously started to drive again, hoping she would at least find a neighborhood or some office buildings. Being in a public place hadn't helped her earlier in the day with Donner, but she knew she'd have a better chance of surviving whatever maniac drove behind her if she was near other people. Could it be Donner? The General's champion? What did the driver want? To scare her? These tactics were succeeding!

Should she call the police? Yes, that seemed like a good idea. She reached for her cell phone, trying to think of how she would explain her predicament to the 911 operator, but suddenly there came a huge sound and her head snapped back and then her body lurched forward as the car behind her rammed the back of her vehicle.

"Shit!" she said as she tried to dial the phone and steer at the same time. Those three numbers should have been easy to punch in, but her fingers trembled on the surge of adrenaline. Another jolt from behind sent her hard against her seat belt and she applied the brakes, thinking she should stop the car before she was driven off the road. Before she could slow down much, she saw the headlights behind her swerve. The brightness shifted from her rearview mirror to her side mirror. They got larger and larger as she watched.

And then on instinct she braced herself because in that instant, those lights swerved again as the driver jerked the car over to slam into the side of Rachel's vehicle, sending it skidding wildly into a guardrail with the sound of metal screeching. The next thing she knew, she'd gone weightless. Her arms flew protectively over her face as she prepared for what had to come next. A scream surfaced within those elongated seconds before impact. A terrible squeal of crunching steel and a crushing pressure coincided with the discharge of the air bag, which slammed Rachel hard against the headrest.

Silence. The engine had stopped and the car rested at a precarious tilt, nose down in a ditch. The air bag had already lost firmness and she pushed at it listlessly, moving as if in slow motion. Then she heard the ding, ding, ding of a warning bell on her dashboard. It must have been going since she'd come to a stop, but she hadn't heard it at first.

An expletive burst from her lips as she remembered all at once that someone had caused this accident on purpose. That someone could be heading for her car to finish the job!

Frantically, she fumbled for the seat belt latch. Seconds ticked by as she tried to release it. As she struggled, she scanned the area frantically. Headlights illuminated the roadway just ahead of where she'd come to a standstill. They glowed ominously, then dimmed suddenly. The car sped off and faded into the distant darkness.

Rachel's whole body sagged with relief when she saw her nemesis drive off. She sat in the seat without moving, listening to the oddly comforting sound of the warning bell, and concentrated on getting her shaking body under control. It didn't take long. She'd become unusually well practiced at dealing with trauma and shock these past few weeks. After a while longer, she realized that the evening heat bore down on her. She needed to do something.

This time, the seat belt unlatched on her first try. Amid the rainlike sound of glass shards falling, she shoved the remains of the air bag out of her way and managed to get the driver's side door open, even though it groaned loudly as she pushed. The air that greeted her was thick with humidity, typical of Washington in the summer—even at night. But at least her car headlights remained on, offering a little help with her footing as she shakily made her way up the berm to the roadside. She had to figure out where she was before she called anyone for help. It felt good to be on her feet, to discover that nothing was broken, to flex traumatized muscles.

A road sign stood not ten feet from her position. It told her she had somehow gotten onto Route 15 and had traveled a good distance from home. But at least she had her bearings now. She trudged back to her car, noted the precarious angle at which it straddled the hill and gingerly retrieved her purse and the cell phone that had flown from her hands upon impact. The phone had 911 already punched in. She just had to press the send button to reach a dispatcher.

In no time, she explained her situation and was promised immediate assistance. The dispatcher began to ask her questions and Rachel answered them, hearing that her voice sounded dull and lifeless. The warning bell kept on chiming in the background as she stepped a few yards away from the vehicle, as the dispatcher advised.

"Stay off the highway, ma'am. Help is on the way," the woman told her.

"I'm behind the guardrail. Listen, I'm not hurt, so don't send an ambulance or anything."

"We'll need to check you out just to make sure, ma'am. It's standard procedure. You just let me know when you hear the sirens." And she chatted on in this way until Rachel *did* hear sirens.

"They're coming. Thanks. I have to call home now. They'll be worried and—"

"Don't hang up until the emergency vehicles arrive," said the kindly voice.

"No, but I have to call home and—" Rachel said, suddenly flooded with panic that she hadn't called already, that her first thought hadn't been for the safety of her son, that the person who had done this to her could be at her house by now. "I have to go!" she said as she pressed the disconnect button and then activated the speed dial that would ring her parents' phone.

Tension made her muscles rigid as she stood at the side of the road, shivering despite the heat and listening to the phone ring on the other end. It jangled on forever. Then a man's voice said, "Hello?"

"Dad?" she said, confused. In all the hundreds of times she had called home in the past seven years, not once had her father answered. He was embarrassed by his difficulty speaking since his stroke and would only come to the phone when Rachel's mother told him she was on the line.

But here he was saying "Rachel? Where're you?" into her ear and making Rachel's throat close on a lump of emotion that swelled from her aching heart to choke her. This was her dad and she was in trouble. Her eyes began to sting.

"I…" She couldn't speak, though, and the sirens were blaring in her ears now. She coughed and it sounded more like a sob to her. She put a finger in her other ear and tried again. "Dad, is everything okay there?"

"Hear sirens where you are. You okay?" he asked once again.

"I've had a car accident and…" Rescue workers swarmed all over her and she submitted when they led her to the ambulance. "I'm okay," she said both to her father and to the paramedics. To her dad, she added, "I just need to know Adam's okay, and you and Mom."

"Adam's fine. Mother, too. Where're you, Rae?" Her dad never called her Rae anymore. Not since her senior year in high school when she'd confessed her pregnancy to him through all those dreadful tears. New tears streamed down her face now, she realized. Somehow, she managed to tell her father where she was. He promised to come for her. It wasn't until after she disconnected that she remembered her father couldn't drive anymore. Should she call back and talk to her mother?

A paramedic pressed something white to Rachel's forehead, and when he pulled it back to dab again, she saw it was covered with blood. Her blood. All at once, her forehead began to throb and sting like the dickens. "Ow," she heard herself say as the wound was cleaned with something that felt like acid. Nausea welled as the adrenaline ebbed. But she was determined not to throw up. If she did, she was sure these concerned people would make her go to the hospital, and right now she only wanted to head home.

Hours seemed to pass, while a police officer asked her

questions. He gave her his business card in case she remembered any other details later. Eventually, the paramedics gave up urging her to go with them to the hospital. They departed more quietly than they'd come. She watched the tow truck hook her car to the winch that would drag it to the road.

Then new headlights approached and came to a stop nearby. A police officer intercepted the two people who emerged, but then let them by. Rachel stood up from her perch on the bent guardrail and waited to see who the new arrivals were.

In the inconsistent light, she made out the shape of a man who walked unevenly. A woman was hanging on to his arm. Then all at once the couple solidified into her parents. "Rae," she heard her father call, and the next thing she knew, she was pressed against her dad's shoulder, weeping. Huge, painful sobs were wrenched from the very depths of her. At the same time, she could feel her father's arms around her shoulders, holding her in his protective embrace. "S'okay, now, sweetie," he said. "Daddy's here."

"Adam?" she asked in between the other soothing words her father crooned.

"Fine, Rae. Don't worry. Taking care of *you*," he said.

Her mother stroked her palm over Rachel's back, lending comfort while also standing guard over the father and daughter, making sure no one interrupted them. When Rachel's tears finally slowed and she lifted her head from her father's shoulder, her mother spoke for the first time. "Let's get you two home now," she said. "That nice policeman that greeted us said we could go whenever we're ready."

Rachel swiped at her father's shirt where she'd left a large wet spot. "Sorry," she murmured.

"S'what dads are for," he said, and Rachel nearly burst into tears again. He kept an arm over her shoulder as they started off, partly for comfort and partly to help him navigate the uneven terrain on his less-than-trustworthy legs. Rachel's mother moved to his other side and the three of them made there way to the car in silence.

Not until she had finished telling her parents what had happened and they were nearly home did Rachel remember that the angel Nathan had taken on a date that night was Adam. They'd gone to the Globetrotters game in D.C.

CHAPTER NINETEEN

NATHAN PACED INSIDE THE Southwells' house like a caged animal. He tried hard not to alarm Adam, but the boy could probably feel the tension that seeped from every pore. The older Southwells had left a note on the kitchen table for them, but it hadn't made Nathan feel much better.

He crumpled the thing in his hand as he recalled the words: "Gone to get Rachel. Car trouble. Please stay with Adam. Be back soon." And he paced the family room anew.

"You said you'd watch me play Mario Brothers," Adam said.

"I *am* watching you," Nathan replied.

"No, you're not."

"Yes, I am." To prove it, Nathan lowered himself to the carpet next to Adam and pointed his face in the general direction of the television set.

"You're still not watching," Adam muttered.

Exasperation threatened to overtake Nathan. He looked down at the little guy, forced a smile and tried to focus. "You're right. But I'll pay attention now," he said. And he did try. But the game couldn't hold him. Worry for Rachel nagged at him. Surely something bad had happened for both her parents to go after her. All sorts of car-related disasters occurred to him. None of the imagined possibilities made him feel any better.

"You're still not paying attention," Adam accused softly.

Nathan surged to his feet and glared down at the child.

"I'm just a little distracted, okay?" he said more loudly than he'd intended.

Adam turned his face up at him, his eyes huge. "Okay," he whispered. Nathan immediately felt awful but had no idea what to say. So Adam stared up and Nathan stared down, holding each other's gazes, and neither said anything for a few long seconds.

"Something's wrong," the child finally said. He stood up, the top of his head coming only a bit higher than Nathan's waist. "You said my grandparents were picking up my mother. Is something wrong with my mom?" His eyes were round and liquid. But his jaw remained firmly set, making him look much like his mother.

Nathan's heart filled to overflowing with a strange ache. Though he wished he'd been able to hide his concern, he wouldn't lie to Adam now. "Yeah. Her car broke down and your grandparents went to get her. I'm sure everything's okay, but I'll feel better when everyone gets home."

Adam held his eyes some more, as if assessing whether or not this was the whole story. After a moment he nodded. "Me, too. Maybe we should go make some popcorn to pass the time."

Nathan had to laugh at that. "How could you eat again?" He had fed the kid almost incessantly throughout the entire basketball game. Hot dogs, chips, pretzels—there seemed to be no end to his appetite.

Adam shrugged and put his small hand into Nathan's. He'd done this many times during their wonderful evening together. The boy led the way to the kitchen and set himself to getting out an air popper, butter, a saucepan and an enormous bowl.

"Maybe we should just make some in the microwave," Nathan suggested as he eyed the equipment dubiously. "I'm not much of a cook."

"That's okay. You can just watch," Adam said confidently. Nathan wasn't sure if he should be relieved or worried to have the kid taking charge. But before he could put a stop to the proceedings, Adam had the popper whirring and the butter melting on the stove top. "My grandma taught me how to cook some things. She says I need to know how to take care of myself so I can be an independent man when I grow up."

"Smart grandmother," Nathan said. He himself ended up eating out or fetching carryout more nights than he cared to admit. He supposed his mother had assumed he'd have a cook to see to his needs in his adult life. He'd never known her to lift a finger in the kitchen the whole time she'd been alive. And she'd certainly never encouraged her boys to do so.

"You have to make sure the butter doesn't get brown," Adam said as he carefully swirled the melting yellow stuff around in the bottom of the saucepan. After a minute, he set the pan aside on a pot holder, carefully turning the handles in toward the wall, and remembered to shut off the burner. Almost simultaneously, the air popper finished spitting out popped corn and Adam shut that off, too. "Almost done," he said.

Just as Adam finished dribbling the butter painstakingly over as many of the popped kernels as he could manage, Nathan heard a car pull into the driveway. He went swiftly to the window and looked out. He saw Rachel emerge from the back seat and he breathed a sigh of relief when she moved to the front passenger side door to help her father. Clearly, she was okay.

"They're home," Adam said happily from where he stood, just beneath Nathan's arm. "Everything's fine now."

Nathan drew the child against him for a cursory hug, feeling awkward in this show of affection but needing to share his feelings. "Yup, everything's fine now," he agreed as he stepped back to await the three adults.

A shuffle at the door preceded its opening. Then Mrs. Southwell walked in, followed by Rachel and her father. The older woman looked slightly startled to see the boy and the man standing expectantly in her kitchen. But then she smiled and sniffed the air. "Fresh popcorn," she said appreciatively. "Let's you and me take it up to your room and eat it while we read a story," she said. "Give your mom a hug good-night first."

Adam went to Rachel and she got down on one knee to embrace him. She held him to her until he began to squirm. Her eyes were tightly closed and Nathan knew a little of what she was feeling. He'd experienced that painful-joyful ache in his own heart every time Adam had placed a hand trustingly in his tonight. When Adam managed to pull away from his mother, she began to plant little kisses all over his face until the boy giggled and then laughed and tried to hold her face still to get relief from the torment. "How were the Globetrotters?" she asked, and Adam launched into an involved explanation that he could see Rachel only half listened to.

Nathan laughed. At least he wasn't the only one who couldn't always give Adam undivided attention. But then he sobered as he watched the mother and child. It was a sweet moment to observe and he felt privileged to be there. But another part of him yearned painfully for memories like Adam would have when he was grown. Another part wanted Adam to go away soon so he could have Rachel to himself. She looked tired and Adam was wearing her down with his chatter.

Stunned by these less-than-charitable thoughts, Nathan turned aside and noticed Mr. Southwell observing him just as Mrs. Southwell reminded Adam that it was a school night and very late.

"Sir," Nathan said. "Is she all right? What's wrong with her car?"

"Totaled," Mr. Southwell said calmly.

Nathan's eyebrows shot up. "She? Totaled? What? How?" He knew he sounded ridiculous, but he couldn't quite make the leap to complete sentences.

"Accident," the older man said. "She'll tell you. C'mon, Ant. Bed," he said to Adam.

"Mom hurt her head," Adam said to Nathan as the boy tipped Rachel's face to the side so the butterfly bandage on the left side of her brow became visible. After exchanging glances with Nathan, Adam released his mother. He looked up at Nathan with big brown eyes so much like his mother's. "Thank you for taking me to the basketball game, Captain Nathan. It was a lot of fun." He said it like a robot. But Nathan was impressed he'd remembered to thank him in this formal manner. Obviously, the adults in his life had rehearsed him through this point of etiquette.

"It was my pleasure, Adam. I might need to borrow you again when I want to do something grown men are supposed to be too big for."

Adam smiled and headed out of the room with his grandparents.

"I've got the popcorn," Mrs. Southwell said as she herded the little boy forward.

"Let's read more Harry Potter," Adam's fading voice suggested.

"'Arry Pot-tah," Mr. Southwell muttered in an English accent, hamming for the child as he tottered gingerly down the hall behind the other two, walker clunking in front of him with every step. The man was speaking much more clearly since the last time Nathan had seen him. And walking more surely, too.

Losing track of the voices and footsteps, Nathan stood frozen in place as he stared at Rachel. His heart began to hammer as she looked back at him. Neither spoke. Neither moved. Nathan had no idea what he should say, how he should act. He wanted to sweep her into his arms, but he recalled that time in her hotel room when she hadn't welcomed his comfort. Would she accept his concern now?

Or would she want to be a soldier?

His answer came when she broke from her trance to move swiftly into his embrace. He held her, felt her heart beat against his, and knew a deep gratitude that she was safe, that she was here, that she let him hold her.

"It was awful," Rachel said against his shoulder.

"Tell me about it."

She nodded but didn't begin right away. "First, I need to get into a hot bath and then a warm bed. Come on." She slipped from the circle of his arms and took his hand so she could lead him down the hall toward her bedroom. "I sleep on this lower level. My parents and Adam have bedrooms upstairs," she explained. "That's why we had the little elevator seat installed on the stairway. Dad didn't want to move his bedroom down here. He's not good with change." She sounded nervous. Could she tell how uncomfortable *he* was about being led to her room while her parents were so near? The last thing he wanted was to find himself on the bad side of her father and mother.

"Um, are you sure...I mean..." He tried to find the words.

"My parents realize I need to talk to you about this. They know you'll help. I think they hope you'll secure my safety, even though you and I are aware I can take care of myself," she said. Nathan smiled at the defiance in her voice when she made that last statement. "So they won't mind if you come with me while I soak my sore limbs."

Instantly, a picture formed in his mind of her in a hot tub, steam wafting around her, her beautiful body all wet and soapy and... *Oh, geez, get a grip,* he thought to himself. "But..." He tried again, knowing he would likely seduce her before the hour was out if he didn't find a way to stay out of her bedroom.

"Besides," Rachel said with a saucy grin, "they'll never know what we're up to with Adam so wound up and chattering about his night out with you."

With a sigh, Nathan gave in. The truth was he really didn't want it any other way. And they had already reached her bedroom, where he was enveloped in her scent, her essence. He couldn't have made himself give up this immersion in Rachel's world for anything. When she led him to the bathroom and began to draw water into the tub, he swallowed hard.

Would she disrobe right here in front of him? Would she slide into the hot water while he watched? Would she let him help her wash? His heart beat harder as steam began to fill the room.

"Close the door, Nathan," said the woman of his dreams. "And if you're going to join me, you'll need to get out of those clothes." This suggestion was delivered in hushed, sultry tones.

Join her? In the bath? Naked? Oh, yeah. Except…

"But…your parents…A-Adam," he stammered.

"Pretend there's no one else home. Pretend we're not even in this house. We're at an exotic resort or something." She put her hands on his chest as she said this and then ran her palms up over his shoulders and around the back of his neck, while her breasts pressed against him and his blood went as hot as the water pouring from the faucet.

"God, you're beautiful," he said as every reason to resist left his head, to be replaced by an all-consuming desire. He bent his head down and claimed her mouth. "Rachel," he rasped as he felt her tug the bottom of his polo shirt upward. He cooperated instantly, raising his arms so she could lift the thing off. When she ran her touch over his hot, naked skin, Nathan shuddered and gave himself over to the inevitable.

In seconds, they had both abandoned every article of clothing. Hands and lips and tongues explored, while the air became thicker and the water deeper. At last, she broke away. Breathing heavily, Nathan watched her turn off the tap and slip into the water. Then she beckoned to him.

Cautiously, he joined her in the confining space. Displaced water lapped over the porcelain's edge, but she didn't seem to care. "I need you tonight, Nathan. I really need you," she said.

"I'm here for you, Rae. I'll always be here for you," he promised as he watched her maneuver her body so she straddled his thighs. The water licked over her breasts as she moved, making her nipples tight despite the heat. Before he could take one of those delectable buds into his mouth as he longed to do, she lifted herself onto him and then settled into place with a glorious sigh. Nathan held her still, loath for this exquisite moment to dash away too quickly. The pleasure of her body united with his made him moan and flex.

He ran his hands from her trim waist up along her ribs to her shoulder blades and heard her moan, too. The sound struck him somehow and he looked closely into her eyes. "Did I hurt you?" he asked, wondering how he could manage to speak when the sensations of his body demanded his undivided attention.

"Sore muscles, that's all. Your gentle hands feel wonderful." And she groaned again and closed her eyes as he softly kneaded the flesh along her back and neck.

She'd just been in a car accident, he suddenly recalled. She might be hurt. He should...

Rachel began to move over him, lifting and sinking rhythmically, making him forget everything except the pleasure of her body enveloping him. Sounds came from his throat as he fought within himself to prolong the wonder, but then she reached between their bodies to the place where they were joined and...

She came with such intensity he could feel every contraction of her muscles. And his body responded with equal enthusiasm, wrenching a roar of ecstasy from his throat as he let himself follow where she led.

HOURS LATER, RACHEL LAY deep under the covers in the safety of her own bed, wrapped in the comfort of Nathan's arms. This was something she could definitely get used to. She hoped she'd get the chance. It certainly didn't seem likely that she'd be able to make herself live without him.

"I should call Julian and let him know everything you just told me about your car accident," Nathan said.

"There's no way this could be unrelated to the whole thing with Donner. Someone deliberately ran you off the road tonight."

"Morning will be soon enough to call Julian. Right now, I just want to stay snuggled in bed with you, safe and sound."

He pulled her a little closer and rubbed his chin in her hair. "I still can't handle the thought that I could have lost you tonight," he whispered.

"I'm going to have to confront the General and press formal charges, ready or not. It isn't right for me to go on at this level of risk. I have to think of Adam."

She heard him huff softly. "You're talking like a soldier."

"Yeah."

"Well, this time I agree with you. We have to end this, one way or another." The hardened edge to his voice caused a vague unease to coil in her stomach.

"What do you mean, 'one way or another.' You're not going to try to take matters into your own hands, are you?"

"Not if I can help it," he said.

She abruptly lifted herself onto one elbow and turned to look down at him. "Now, you listen to me, Nathan Fordham," she said. "Don't you dare—"

"Marry me," he interjected.

She blinked. "What did you say?"

"Marry me. As soon as possible." He didn't wait for an answer. Instead, he lifted his head to seal his mouth to hers. Then he did any number of things designed to make her forget her own name, never mind whatever it was she'd been about to say to him.

Not until hours later, when he slept peacefully at her side, did she remember what had worried her. Clearly, she was out of time if Nathan had begun to consider independent action. She would have to bring matters to an immediate head with Donner before Nathan did something to ruin his future or risk his life. In the morning, she would have to put on her recording device and confront the General.

Morning arrived promptly at 0530, as it did every work-day, with Adam rushing into her bedroom to wake her up.

"Mom! Get up. Time to go running!" And he jumped on her bed, bouncing a few times.

Nathan groaned and put a pillow over his head and Adam suddenly went very still. He just sat on his knees on the corner of the mattress and stared at the man who was under the covers in his mother's bed. Rachel winced at her lack of forethought. Why hadn't she locked her bedroom door? A locked door might have been less of a shock for Adam than *this*. But at least she'd gotten chilly in the night and had put on a T-shirt.

"G'mornin', Adam Ant," she said, hoping that if she took this new development in stride, maybe Adam would, too.

"Is that Captain Nathan?" he asked quietly, still staring at the lump that represented the man.

Rachel feigned surprise, looked over at the lump, poked at it once or twice, evoking a grunt, then said, "Why, yes, I believe it is."

Adam giggled. "Does he need to get up to run, too? He's in the Army like you are, right?"

"Right!" she said. "I give you permission to get him up and running."

Adam took her suggestion to heart and delightedly began to jump up and down on the bed again. Rachel figured if Nathan really wanted to be part of her life—"Marry me," he'd said, and she still could hardly believe it—then he'd have to get used to an eight-year-old boy's antics. She waited to see what the sleepy man would do. She didn't have to wait long.

With a huge, playful roar, Nathan surged from beneath the covers and captured a giggling Adam in a bear hug. "Who dares to wake the monster?" Nathan growled, then he started tickling the boy breathless. Just before Rachel might have started to fret about his asthma kicking in, Nathan stopped and let Adam recover. "What's this about getting up to go running? It's barely dawn."

"Mom has to run every day to stay in shape. She told me I could help by making sure she gets up every morning in time to do her workout before heading to the office."

"I see," Nathan said as he eyed Rachel dubiously. "But maybe we should make an exception this morning since your mom had a rough time with the car last night."

"Oh, yeah. I forgot," Adam said. He looked at his mother speculatively. "Are you okay?"

"I'm fine. Just some sore muscles and stuff. But maybe we could skip the run just this once. What do you think?"

Adam raised his eyebrows and said, "It's *your* workout," in a tone that communicated she'd be sorry later when she had to catch up on the missed routine.

Nathan laughed. "He sounds just like you," he said. Then he grew serious and bravely broached the more difficult aspect of his presence in her bed. "Um, listen, Adam, you're probably wondering about me being here with your mom overnight and…"

"No, I'm not," Adam said with a mischievous grin. "I'm not stupid, you know."

Rachel barely suppressed a chuckle as Nathan blushed. "Uh, well, no, you're not stupid. I—I know that," the man stammered. "But I probably owe you some sort of explanation, anyway."

"Okay," Adam said, then looked expectantly at Nathan. The honorable Captain stared at the boy a moment as if at a loss. Rachel decided she shouldn't offer her assistance unless it was requested, so she waited.

"Well, sometimes men and women—" he started, then cut himself off abruptly. "I mean, um, your mother and I…" But again aborted his thoughts. Finally, he took a deep breath and said, "I love your mom very much."

Rachel's breath caught and her heart skipped a beat, but Adam just smiled and said, "I know," then jumped off the bed. "Let's have pancakes for breakfast since we have extra time."

"Great!" Nathan said. "Who here can make pancakes?" He cocked a brow toward Rachel as if he expected her to volunteer.

Adam spoke up. "Grandma can, but she's still sleeping. It's up to you, Mom. But I'll help."

With a groan of resignation, Rachel reached for her bathrobe resting on the hope chest at the foot of her bed. "Lead the way, Adam."

NATHAN COULDN'T REMEMBER the last time he'd had so much fun. And to think it wasn't even 0600 hours yet. When had he even been fully awake at this hour? Never. Or at least, not since his last military training, when he was forced to get up at reveille. But here he was, watching his two favorite people pour batter onto a flat skillet and churning out fluffy golden pancakes one after the other. And the experience was one he wouldn't have missed for anything. Not even for a few extra hours of much-needed sleep.

"The syrup needs to be warmed in the microwave, Captain Nathan," Adam advised. "Just put the whole bottle in there and set it for about a minute."

Nathan grinned at the idea of taking orders from an eight-year-old, but then did exactly as he was told. Just as he finished punching in the numbers, he heard movement behind him and turned. Coming face-to-face with Rachel's father first thing in the morning, wearing the same clothes he'd had on the night before, with hair that must surely look messed up from sleep—well, he wasn't prepared for that.

"'Mornin'," said Bernie Southwell to them all, but he didn't take his eyes off Nathan. That stare made Nate wonder if he'd ever be welcome in the household again after this.

"Good morning," Rachel and Adam chimed in unison.

"Want some pancakes?" Rachel asked.

"Sure," Mr. Southwell said, but his gaze, locked with Nathan's, didn't waver. Focused as they were on the cooking, Rachel and Adam were oblivious to the byplay between the two men.

"Sir, perhaps we could talk in the other room for a minute," Nathan said. It just seemed right to come clean with the older man—take responsibility for his sins, as it were. He *had* just spent the night with the man's daughter under his own roof, after all. He could at least soften the insult by announcing his intentions to marry Rachel, maybe ask her father's permission. That should go a long way toward appeasing him, Nathan figured.

Bernie nodded, dropped his steely gaze at last and shuffled out of the room behind the clump, clump, clump of his walker. He led Nathan to a small den with a desk and bookcases. "Sit," he said as he indicated the recliner near the wall. Bernie took the desk chair for himself.

Nathan sat. Then he rested his elbows on his knees, trying to think how to begin. He yearned for the morning coffee he had somehow forgotten to consume. Drawing a blank on what to say, he rubbed his hands over his face, then checked to see if the older man appeared any more sympathetic than he had a few minutes ago.

Not a chance. Mr. Southwell simply stared at him without expression. Waiting. Nathan rubbed the back of his neck.

"I plan to marry your daughter, sir," he blurted. "With your permission, of course."

Bernie didn't move or speak. His expression didn't change, at least not right away. Slowly, a distinct twinkle appeared in those seasoned eyes. The lines at the corners of them deepened. "You ask her yet?" he said at last.

Nathan blinked. He'd certainly mentioned marriage to Rachel, but he couldn't actually say he'd asked her. Demanded, was more like it. And he hadn't waited for her to agree. If the truth were known, Nathan had been afraid to hear a rejection of his proposal. So he'd made passionate love to her, instead, and they hadn't had a moment to discuss the issue further. "Not exactly."

Mr. Southwell chuckled now. "Not exactly," he murmured. "Not exactly." He got up from his chair slowly, clinging to the armrests. Nathan wanted to offer his assistance, but wasn't sure if this man would be as prickly as his daughter about accepting help. "Be sure to let me know what happens," Mr. Southwell said as he shuffled out of the room, laughing as he went. It was the longest string of words Nathan had heard the man utter.

Nathan stood in the room a moment longer, letting the man's reaction sink in. The implication was that Rachel might have something to say about whether or not she wanted marriage in her future. Well, of course she did. But did "let me know what happens" mean Rachel might refuse him? A scary thought. However, Nathan wasn't going to give up easily. He'd convince her somehow. He *had* to.

"Come eat, Nathan!" she called from the kitchen. The sound of her voice wiped away the gloom that had befallen him. If she could function normally after what she'd been through these past weeks, then so could he. He stamped a smile onto his face and headed back the way he'd come. He might as well try to enjoy the pancakes, because he had a feeling the day would be grueling.

CHAPTER TWENTY

AFTER GOING HOME to shower and change into his uniform, Nathan made his way to the Pentagon and was greeted by General Donner's decidedly unhappy growl. "My office. Now."

"Yes, sir," Nathan said as he followed the General into the inner sanctum, glancing over his shoulder to notice that although Allison sat at her desk in her BDUs, Rachel hadn't arrived to work yet.

"Sit. It's OER time," Donner said, referring to the officer's evaluation report. On this document, an officer's commander wrote up performance reviews. A bad one would ruin a career faster than lightning.

Nathan knew that his OER wasn't due for another month, and no one did OERs early, so his senses went on high alert as he took the offered seat in front of the General's desk and waited.

The General shuffled some papers, then put one particular sheet on top. "As you know, I expect unflinching loyalty from the officers and soldiers who work for me."

"Yes, sir." Uh-oh, Nathan thought. What had the General discovered?

"I have it on good authority that you haven't been loyal."

A series of angry expletives went through Nathan's mind as he realized that the jig was up, at least for him. This man was about to destroy everything he'd worked for in the military, yet all Nathan could think about was whether or not Donner also planned to destroy Rachel. "I have been loyal to the Army, sir. Every breath I take is devoted to the Army.''

"I *am* the Army, Captain!" the General shouted as he went red in the face. "If you're not loyal to me, then you're not loyal to the Army." And he clearly meant it. The man actually believed that he was the embodiment of the U.S. Army. Nathan couldn't think of anything to say in the face of such egomania. Donner eyed him. "Do you understand what I'm telling you?"

"Yes, sir, I believe I understand you."

At Nathan's calm response, the General's florid color deepened. But then he seemed to regain control of himself as he leaned back in his chair and slowly steepled his hands in front of him. "You're not terribly upset," he said without emotion.

"Getting upset will serve no purpose, sir." And Nathan realized that a strange calm had come over him despite the prospect of his entire military career going up in smoke. All he really cared about was Rachel and how badly she was likely to suffer. If only he could have persuaded her to transfer before now. If only he hadn't asked her to become a part of this mess in the first place.

"You won't be making major with this OER, I'm afraid." Donner smoothly turned the form in Nathan's direction and slid it across the desk toward him. Nathan had little interest in what it said. Anything less than the nearly perfect ratings he was used to would be a death sentence for his future in the Army. When he didn't look at the thing right away, the General demanded, "Read it."

Hiding an impatient sigh, Nathan picked up the form. That was when he noticed the antique revolver sitting on the corner of Donner's desk. It was in pieces, and a polishing rag and oil sat beside it. Nate had no doubt the weapon would be in good working order when it was put back together. How had the General gotten the thing past Security? But then, he'd probably had it here in his desk for years.

"Read it," the General demanded again.

Nathan read the OER. The scores were not so low as to appear outrageous, but just low enough in comparison with previous appraisals to destroy his chances for promotion. The narrative began with "While Captain Fordham has performed exceptionally well, he has occasionally chosen expediency over the chain of command, possibly due to so recently returning from a field assignment where he enjoyed considerable independence. Nonetheless, he has performed miracles with office organization and..." The document went on with the usual effusion of compliments.

This approach was despicably clever on the General's part. If he'd blasted Nathan throughout the document, the whole rating would have looked suspicious, given his previous exemplary record. But with only the one sentence intimating a single failing—and with an excuse offered for the behavior—Donner's evaluation had every appearance of being honestly delivered. Nathan would have a hell of a time getting the thing eliminated from his records unless Donner's true motives were somehow brought immediately to light.

He knew the General expected him to say something, and since the man could still do worse things to him—such as send him to the back of beyond for his remaining time in the military—Nathan felt he ought to oblige him. "Would you care to be specific about any occasion when I've avoided the chain of command, sir?" he asked.

The General's face went taut. His eyes glinted. He made no attempt to keep the emotion out of his voice this time. "How could you take Southwell's word for things and act upon them without even discussing the matter with me?" He sounded outraged, persecuted and deeply hurt. "I thought we understood each other. I thought we had a rapport. How could you betray me?"

But Nathan understood the psychology of this situation far better than the General did. And he would not allow himself to be duped into some confession of his activities by Donner's unspecified complaints. ''When did I take Chief Southwell's word over yours, sir? When did I betray you?''

''When you decided to help her get a tape recorder'' came the acidic reply.

Oh, shit. Nathan couldn't think of a thing to say to that. His thoughts circled endlessly around the question of how the General had discovered that part of their plan. They'd been so careful not to let him see the device. They'd taken every precaution.

The General shook his head as if in disgust. ''Before you're dismissed so you can get back to work, I'd like you to know that I figured out where you got the recorder and I plan to see justice done there, too.''

Oh, no, not Julian! God, how could this be happening! It was one thing to have his own career affected, but Julian had worked so hard. And his brother *needed* the Army in ways Nathan could only begin to understand. He only hoped Julian could use his connections to overcome whatever Donner tried.

''And if you think that little hussy Chief Southwell will be getting an easy ride, you should think again. The things I have planned for her...'' he said. Then he smiled. ''It'll be a ride, all right, but not necessarily an easy one. On the other hand, unlike you, I might give *her* another chance to cooperate and save herself. She's a good officer. She could go far, if she's willing to come around to my way of seeing things. And I just found out she's a mother, too. I'd hate to have to obstruct the ties she's only just begun to develop with her son by sending her away again. Yes, I think I'll give her another chance to make amends.''

Nathan's calm fled as sudden rage flared, barely contained. All at once, he knew without a doubt that he couldn't accept any of this without a fight. There was simply too much at stake. He'd call in any favors people throughout the military thought they owed to him. He'd go to Senator Zemin and beg for help. He'd talk to newspapers, if necessary. He'd do whatever it took to save Julian and Rachel.

Surprisingly, the General's eyes cleared of their earlier malice. He smiled as he put his hands flat on his desk and stood. "We have to prepare for General Collier's visit, Nate. He wants to take a tour and see those briefings we did for the others. He must have heard about them. He's bringing the usual entourage, so you'll need to coordinate with protocol."

Nathan stared at the man. It was as though he'd been one person and then changed into another before his very eyes. Rachel had mentioned something once about the good General Donner and the bad General Donner, but he'd never seen it clearly until now. The General standing in front of him now looked at him expectantly, as if he had no doubt that Nathan would continue to perform his duties to the best of his abilities, notwithstanding the OER that was about to go into his official military file.

"Yes, sir," Nathan said as he got to his feet. Because one of the most difficult parts of this was, he *would* perform his duties well. He was a soldier and he would act like one for as long as the Army allowed him to continue serving.

RACHEL HADN'T SEEN NATHAN since he'd gone home to dress for work. She knew he'd arrived because his briefcase was in its usual place. But the man himself was nowhere to be found and Allison was no help.

"He didn't tell me where he was going. He had a document in his hand when he came out of the General's office and he just took off down the hall," she said.

"Some urgent business for General Donner, no doubt," Rachel surmised, but the whole thing made her uneasy. This was the day she'd have to bring this whole mess to some sort of conclusion. Or go down trying. She'd feel much better about her prospects if she knew Nathan sat right outside the office where she would make the attempt.

As she eyed the General's door, closed at the moment while Donner made some phone calls, Rachel was struck by the fact that she didn't seem to mind relying on Nathan for support anymore. And she realized the change had occurred because she trusted him. She knew he wouldn't let her down.

Accepting this newfound trust felt surprisingly freeing, as though a burden had been lifted. She'd been on her own, depending only on herself for so long, she hadn't realized how heavy her load had become. Now she saw how much more effective she and Nathan would be together than either of them could have been independently. That thought strengthened her, so that when General Donner opened his door, she was ready to face him in his lair.

"Allison," he called out in a gruff tone. "Come in here."

Rachel watched the younger woman get up and head for the General's office without a moment's hesitation. "Allison, do you want me to come in with you? Or I could call on the intercom in a minute to interrupt, or..."

Allison turned puzzled eyes to Rachel. "Why would you do that?" she asked. "I'm fine." But her face was a mask of tension and her eyes glittered too brightly. She crossed the threshold. "Oh, I almost forgot," she said from the doorway. "They need your report on the airport security teams down at the Secretary's office by noon today." Then she closed the door, leaving Rachel to ponder the enigma of Specialist Allison Fitzpatrick as she headed to the third-floor E ring with the required report.

NATHAN KNEW HE ENTERED Julian's office like a hurricane, but he simply couldn't manage to slow himself down. Without ceremony, he threw himself into a chair across from his brother and then tossed a plastic grocery bag on top of the desk.

"What's all this?" Julian asked.

"Evidence. Everything we've been able to collect so far."

Julian leaned forward eagerly, the light of success in his eyes. "You got the tape recording?"

"No—at least, not the one you were hoping for." Nathan upended the bag and the contents spilled forth. "There's this tape of Rachel and Donner talking in the hallway of the Pentagon. He pretends to not understand what Rachel is talking about." He picked up the tape and set it aside. "I was thinking that the tone he used, together with Rachel's testimony, might help persuade someone he's not being honest."

Julian picked up a clear plastic bag in which a pair of latex gloves resided. "What's this?"

"Remember when we told you about how he attacked Rachel in her hotel room in Hawaii?"

"What?" Julian exclaimed. "He attacked her? Physically?"

Nathan blinked. "We told you," he insisted, but doubt crept over him even before he got out the last syllable. "Rachel said she called you afterward and..."

"Christ Almighty, Nathan, how could you not tell me something this important!"

"Rachel said she called you and I assumed—"

"She called to ask me how things were at her home and to see how Adam did playing basketball on Saturday now that he's on that asthma medication," Julian said. "Why didn't *you* call me?"

Nathan shook his head, trying to remember. "Things moved pretty fast after that. We were busy with work and trying to figure out how to use the tape recorder while wearing summer uniforms. I guess I thought she talked to you...."

Julian took a breath and let it out. "Okay. Okay. Sounds like you thought she told me and she probably thought you told me."

"Well, you couldn't have done anything about it anyway. It happened, we handled it the best we could and then I did my level best not to let her out of my sight.''

Julian nodded thoughtfully. ''And when you came home, we were distracted by the incident with the eggs on her car. So, tell me the details of this attack now.''

Nathan explained what had happened, leaving nothing out. Then he indicated the latex gloves he'd brought. ''So I kept the gloves he wore when he broke into the room because maybe his fingerprints are on the inside of them, maybe that would help support our story.''

''Those gloves usually have powder on the inside. But we'll take a look.'' Julian examined the items that had been in Nathan's bag of evidence, studying each one. ''Things have really gotten out of hand.''

''And there's more.'' Nathan told him about Rachel's car accident from the night before. ''She was purposefully run off the road, Jules. She could have been killed. There's no question in my mind that the person responsible is connected with Donner.''

''Enough! We've got to stop the whole case,'' Julian said.

''You need to be careful, too. He knows you're involved, because he found out about the tape recorder somehow. He greeted me with this OER this morning.'' Nathan slid the document across the desk.

Julian started swearing under his breath before he finished reading the first sentence. ''He's trying to ruin your whole career. God only knows what he'll do to Rachel.''

''And to you,'' Nathan reminded him.

Julian waved a hand dismissively. ''He's not going to get away with any of this, Nate. We'll pull the plug on this whole debacle and turn over what we have.''

''Yeah, well, that's what I was thinking, too. So, with all of this together, plus my testimony and Rachel's, shouldn't we be able to do something?''

''It isn't what we hoped for, but it'll have to be enough. We never expected Donner to become violent. Harassment is one thing, but a physical attack is a whole other ballpark." Julian scratched his temple. "The part I don't understand is who would try to run Rachel off the road. That just isn't Donner's or Lydia's style."

"Whoever it is, they're trying to scare her into leaving Donner alone. Because if they'd really wanted Rachel dead, they could have pulled it off with very little additional effort."

"You're probably right." Julian looked up suddenly and captured Nathan's gaze. "Where's Rachel now?"

Nathan held up a calming hand. "I called her house and asked her mother to make sure she doesn't go in to work. So she should be safe at home with her family now."

"Go make sure she is and that she stays there," Julian said. "I have to make some phone calls to get this whole investigation stopped."

Nathan stared at his brother as suspicion sneaked up on him. "Who are you going to call?"

Julian's expression went grim. "There are people a lot higher than us who have been trying to get hard evidence on Donner for a long time. They approached me because they knew we're brothers and you're Donner's aide."

Nathan felt as if he'd fallen off a precipice. "You've been working with other people on this mess and you didn't tell me?" He could barely get out the words.

Julian held his palms up as if to plead helplessness. "I was ordered not to, Nate. And it didn't seem all that important for me to go against those orders when you were already doing exactly what they wanted without any prompting from me."

"What do you mean by that? How was I doing what they wanted?" Pressure built in Nathan's chest. He stood up, as if the air a few feet higher might be easier to breathe.

"They wanted you to get evidence on Donner's harassment so that their case against him would be solid. And you had already approached me about the same thing."

"You found Rachel because these nameless higher-ups

told you to get a woman in on it, too." Nathan said this more to himself than to his traitorous brother. Things were starting to fall into place as he remembered certain details. "That's why you didn't want me to talk Rachel out of coming to the Pentagon."

"That's true, Nate. But we didn't know her then. We needed a good plan to put a bad man behind bars. And Rachel needed to come to the Pentagon anyway."

Nathan couldn't contain himself a moment longer. "You son of a bitch!" he shouted as he lunged for his brother, the only man in the world he truly trusted, the one he thought he knew so well. "You set her up!"

Julian jerked back, but he didn't try very hard to get away, so Nathan managed to grasp him by the shirt. "Calm down, Nate. It's not as bad as it seems."

"You should have told me!" he barked as he shook his older brother and then threw him back into his chair. "Instead, you let us believe we were on our own, that there were no choices, that we had to put up with all of Donner's shit until we got the evidence you said we needed."

"It wasn't supposed to go this far," Julian shouted back. "I didn't know about what he did to Rachel in Hawaii or I would have stopped everything right then."

"You should have told me that others were involved. I would have called these higher people who want to nail the General and explained that things had become too dangerous as soon as she got that first threatening note. Instead, Rachel and I behaved like soldiers, sticking it out for the sake of the greater good because we thought no one would believe our stories."

Julian looked down and sighed. "Maybe you're right, Nate. Maybe I should have told you. But that's easy to say with the clarity of hindsight. At the time, I decided to follow orders."

Nathan stared at him. An unfamiliar ache had taken him by the throat. But he managed to choke out, "I'm your brother...." And he blinked hard against an odd stinging in his eyes.

"I know," Julian said. When he looked up into Nathan's eyes, the expression said he'd just lost his best friend.

Maybe he had, Nathan thought as he grabbed his beret from the corner of Julian's desk and stalked out of the office and into the parking lot. If Julian had lost his best friend, that would mean Nathan had, too.

CHAPTER TWENTY-ONE

Donner called Rachel into his office as he returned to the suite from God knows where. She stood to follow him, but the phone rang. Allison was nowhere to be found, so Rachel turned to answer it.

"Leave it," Donner snapped. He gestured for her to come with him immediately.

She'd become fairly adept now at switching on her hidden tape recorder with one touch to her waistband. Doing so now seemed like a good idea. Donner's frustration was nearly tangible, and Rachel figured if he was ever going to give her something to record, now would be the time.

The bleating of the phone marked the cadence of her gait as she forced her legs to take one step after the other until she was on the threshold of the General's office. Remembering her experience with him the last time they'd been alone, she hesitated. He was a great deal stronger and he was angry. Anything could happen once she allowed herself to enter his domain. Still, this was a mission she couldn't retreat from, no matter the danger to herself. There were so many other people this man could hurt if her courage failed her now.

She walked through the doorway into the room and wondered if he would sense her fear. Surely he would see the trembling of her knees and the sweat on her brow. Determined to distract him from these signs of weakness, she moved to the chair in front of his desk and stood at attention. "Yes, sir," she said.

"Sit." He took his own chair and swiveled it a little to

the side so she viewed his patrician profile. He leaned back, seemingly at ease, but she could feel his tension and knew he was only pretending to be relaxed. "We need to talk," he said without looking at her.

His focus remained on the edge of his desk, drawing Rachel's eyes to what he was staring at. When she realized the object of his fixation, her throat and lungs constricted. On the corner of the mahogany surface lay a gun. It looked like a six-shooter, but it appeared to be in excellent working condition. Its silver metal gleamed and the pearl handle shone. She could see there were bullets in the chambers.

"What do we need to talk about, sir?" she heard her own voice say. The words had come out without even the slightest quaver. But her eyes remained steadily on the gun. And her mind rapidly considered her options if he reached for it. Then she considered her options if *she* reached for it.

"About your lack of loyalty and how you can make it up to me." His hand drifted toward the weapon. He didn't pick it up, but caressed the thing, instead. Gently, his finger slid over the handle, across the bullet chamber and down the barrel.

Rachel decided not to pretend ignorance. Better to cut to the chase. "How do you expect me to make it up to you, sir?" she asked, still managing that even tone and calm voice.

"Oh, I think you know what I have in mind," he said as he grinned and faced her, looking her in the eyes for the first time.

"I'd prefer that you spell it out for me so I know exactly what the terms are," she countered. The tape was silently turning in her tiny recorder, but he hadn't yet said an explicit word.

"Am I to spell it out for you so you can capture the details on your little recording device?" he asked with an amused twinkle in his eyes. "Where have you got it hidden?" His perusal up and down her body made it clear he realized it was somewhere on her person. "Shall I look for it myself? That would be interesting."

She refused to let on that his knowledge rocked her to her toes. Her heart hammered against her ribs, but she schooled her face into passivity and said, "You wouldn't find anything if you did. I was in a bit of a rush getting out of the house this morning." Would he believe she'd forgotten the recorder at home?

The General laughed. "You're as glib as that woman Senator said you are."

Fleetingly, Rachel wondered why Zemin would have been chatting with Donner about glibness. Then a sickening doubt came to her about which side the Senator was really on.

"But you're not nearly as clever as you think you are, Rachel." He chuckled softly. "Rushed out of the house and forgot to wear your spy equipment, did you? Was it your ailing father who distracted you this morning? Or perhaps it was that little boy you have." He paused, but Rachel refused to react. "And I see from your records that you've never been married. A child out of wedlock indicates a certain moral flexibility. I like that in my women."

Donner lost his smile as he looked at her dispassionate expression. Suddenly, he slammed his hand on the desktop. "You have a great deal of nerve and no sense at all, thinking you could take me on like this. Did you really believe I wouldn't find out?"

When Rachel could come up with nothing to say, he got to his feet. She watched with mounting horror as the man made his way around his desk and angled toward her. Before he came too close, she scrambled out of her chair and backed away. In the distance the phone rang and rang.

"Sir, consider what you're doing. If you touch me, I'll press charges against you. I'm not like the others you've done this to. I won't be intimidated. I won't back down."

"Do you think I care? Go ahead and press your charges. You won't be the first one to try. No one will believe you.

There are a hundred other women who will line up to say you must be mistaken, confused. Why, even Specialist Fitzpatrick will dispute whatever stories you try to tell.''

Rachel came to a stop when she backed into a credenza. ''Why would Allison do that?''

''Because the stupid bitch is in love with me. I told her a few lies and now she'll do anything for me.'' He sauntered closer, leaving Rachel no avenue of escape. If she darted one way, he would shift to block her path.

She stood still and braced for the inevitable physical battle to come. ''You're making a big mistake, sir. Don't come any closer.''

''I'm going to do a full-cavity body search on you, Chief,'' he said with a grin. ''I'll find that tape recorder, and when that's taken care of, we'll find other ways to amuse ourselves.''

Rachel went into a fighting stance and felt her courage solidify. She might not win against his superior strength, but she'd make sure he didn't come out of it unscathed. And if she could hold him off for a while, someone would surely hear the scuffle and help her. She heard the phone continue to ring incessantly in the outer office. Where was Allison?

''Now, now, Rachel. This doesn't have to be a violent experience, although I'm perfectly willing to go that route if necessary. We could do this peacefully if you prefer. I could sit in this chair and you could get on your knees in front of me and you could make it all up to me with that lovely mouth of yours. Then we could let bygones be bygones. What do you say?'' He was very close to her now. She could smell his aftershave and it nearly choked her.

''I say you're clinically insane and probably have been for quite some time. What's really remarkable is how you've managed to keep your madness from discovery for all this time.''

The General's lips compressed into a thin line; his face grew flushed; his eyes glinted with malice. He moved closer. "Rachel, be reasonable," he said. "I could help your career. You could go far."

"I want to go far on my own merits," she managed to say as she danced to one side just when he was about to grab her.

He laughed. "You won't get anywhere if I don't want you to," he said. "Did you see young Captain Fordham's OER yet? I put an end to his aspirations."

Rachel felt the blood drain from her face. "And if I cooperate with you, you'll retract your bad report on him?" For one awful moment, she actually considered negotiating with this madman in order to save Nathan's future. Then the absurdity of doing so caught up with her.

"It wasn't exactly a bad report, Rachel. It was just less than wonderful. The kiss of death in the competitive Army." He paused and put a finger to the side of his mouth as if thinking. "I hadn't fully realized that Nathan meant so much to you. I should have tried coercing you through him sooner instead of wasting my time on Allison. I was so sure you'd sacrifice yourself to keep me from going after her. But it was Nathan you were predisposed to protect. I should have guessed that."

Then he lunged and grasped her by the arm, yanking her against his body so fast she felt like a rag doll. With a half turn, he had her back pressed to the wall. He groped her for the recording device as he leaned in for a kiss.

The thought of his mouth on hers made Rachel want to retch and she reacted swiftly and with dramatic force. One of those knees that Donner had wanted her to be on made sudden contact with the part he'd hoped she'd put her mouth to. When he groaned and doubled over, Rachel remembered the additional martial arts moves Nathan had taught her and clubbed the General on the back of the head, her joined fists serving as a mallet.

Donner dropped to his knees with a grunt. She made for the door without hesitation but then came to a startled halt when she saw another person in her path. Allison stood there, her face pale and drawn. The door to Donner's private bathroom stood open and the light was on inside. The younger woman must have come from there.

"Alli—" Rachel began, but the General had recovered enough to grab her from behind in a choke hold. It was all she could do to keep him from cutting off her air supply completely.

"What the hell are you doing here!" Donner barked at Allison.

"I...you...you tore the buttons off my blouse earlier," Allison stammered. "You told me to sew them back on with the kit in your bathroom." She made a confused gesture behind her, but she didn't take her eyes off the General.

"I didn't mean for you to take all morning doing it!" he complained. "Now, get out!"

"But I heard what you said. I heard you tell her you were just using me to persuade her."

"What if I did?" the General mocked. He loosened his grip on Rachel just enough so she could breathe.

"Let go of me!" Rachel cried as she noticed Allison's face go even more pale. "Get help, Allison," she pleaded.

"Tell her you were lying," Allison demanded. "Tell her that you love me, that you're going to leave your wife for me. Do you think I would have let you do all those things to me today if you hadn't made those promises?" She clenched and unclenched her hands at her sides.

The General laughed heartily. "I'm not going to leave my wife for anyone," he said.

"But that's why I did everything. All for you. So you would leave her for me. I told you about the tape recorder." She looked at Rachel and squinted. "I knew you were trying to trap him. And I paid attention when you thought I wasn't. I saw you shift the thing to a more comfortable spot under your clothes one day. It didn't take long for me to figure out what it was." Her frantic gaze slid back to the General. "And I told you about it so you'd know how much I care. So you'd see how valuable I could be to your career.''

"Are you insane?" Donner asked Allison. Rachel tried to wrestle herself free while his attention was diverted, but he pulled her up against his side and held her tightly again. "Divorcing my wife would be the end of my credibility. The fact that I'm a happily married man makes me above reproach. Because this one has stirred up so much trouble—" he gave Rachel a shake "—and involved that young Major from CID, I'll have to be especially careful about my image now."

"It's because of her," said the younger woman as she moved quickly to the General's desk. From the corner of the mahogany surface, she lifted the revolver in surprisingly steady hands and aimed it at Rachel. "If she was out of the way, you wouldn't need to worry. You could leave your wife then." She smiled triumphantly and pulled back the hammer with her thumb. The sound made Rachel's stomach plummet.

Donner quickly let go of Rachel and shoved her behind his body. Stunned by this unexpected act of chivalry, Rachel stayed there. "Allison, put the gun down. Who do you think you are, taking matters into your own hands?" the General demanded.

"Get out of the way, sir. I don't want to hurt you."

Rachel inched toward the door, but the General gestured for her to stay behind him. Seeing that she risked being shot if she left the safety he offered, Rachel had no choice but to obey. Allison clearly didn't want to shoot Donner.

"Allison, Rachel isn't the reason I won't marry you. You're deluding yourself if you believe I'd leave my wife for you. You had to know I only said that so you'd give me another one of your superior blow jobs. You have a real talent."

Rachel realized immediately that he'd said exactly the wrong thing to diffuse the situation. He was thinking like a man—a mistake he couldn't afford while he was looking down the barrel of that gun. "Don't," she said from behind him.

Donner, however, had no idea that he was treading in potentially fatal territory. "You have nothing to gain by shooting anyone. But you have everything to lose," he reasoned. "Put the gun down and I'll explain it all to you rationally so you'll see why we can't possibly—"

As if it were happening in slow motion, Rachel watched the gun sight stop moving around to get a clean shot at her, only to zero in steadily on General Donner's heart. Allison's eyes had gone cold, her mouth compressed, her movements calm and sure. Without further warning, a tremendous pop rent the air. Slowly, Donner's body lost its sturdiness, turned to rubber. He slid onto his knees, then gracefully slumped forward. His head made a loud thud as it hit the floor face first.

NATHAN'S HEART RACED as he squealed into a parking space and then sprinted past the day-care center toward the north entryway. He'd found out fifteen minutes ago that Rachel had gone to the Pentagon while Mrs. Southwell thought she was still in the shower. Rachel never got the message to stay at home, despite her mother's frantic efforts to reach her by phone. He'd called Pentagon security as soon as he'd ended his cell phone conversation with Rachel's mother. But as big as the Pentagon was and with so many corridors blocked, they might not get there in time. Rachel...

He stopped before he went through the double doors into the building and tried to even out his breathing, passing a shaking hand over his sweating brow. To look flushed and anxious in front of the guards as he went through Security wouldn't do. After the terrorist attacks, no one was above suspicion in this building. So he walked sedately to the gate, even though his mind screamed for him to hurry. Clearly, something was very wrong in the Office of Human Resources and Readiness of the Army National Guard.

He'd been ringing the line there for his entire drive from Fort Belvoir to the Pentagon and no one had answered. The number hadn't even been switched over for pickup down the hall.

Rachel was in trouble. He could feel it. He had to get to her. Right now.

Yet he calmly put his identification card through the swipe at the gate. He even mustered a cordial nod to one of the guards avidly watching each person who entered. Cresting the ramp leading into the first-floor E ring, he managed a controlled walk until he passed through the next set of doors. Then, heedless of the people around him, he launched into a sprint again. Without pause, he ran up the first stairway he came to and bolted onto the second floor. He skidded to a halt, looking one way and then the other to get his bearings. He couldn't afford a wrong turn now. But in another heartbeat he tore down a corridor, thinking only of getting to Rachel.

"Slow down, Captain!" someone shouted. Half turning, Nathan caught a glimpse of a colonel's silver birds on the shoulder of the woman who'd called out. So he dutifully slowed his pace. Reaching the A ring, he headed left and, seeing no one along this route, broke into another all-out sprint.

The hallways seemed to lengthen before him while time ticked by more rapidly than it should. As if in a horrible nightmare, he sped around the corner into the familiar office suite in which he'd worked all these months. Where the hell was security? he wondered, just as he heard the unmistakable report of a gun from inside Donner's office. He remembered the revolver on the General's desk.

Without thinking to try the handle, Nathan kicked the door in and rushed forward. The first thing he saw was Donner's body, lying in a pool of dark liquid. The second thing that registered was the barrel of the revolver pointed at something in the dark corner of the room. Skidding to a halt only a few feet from the woman who held the weapon,

Nathan didn't dare take his eyes off a tearful but determined Allison Fitzpatrick even as he heard Rachel's gasp and understood her plea for him to get out, to save himself.

"I tried to get you to back off, Chief," Allison said without bothering to give Nathan's sudden arrival more than a flicker of attention and heedless of the cries from Rachel. "I found out about your son when Personnel called needing some information about him for his ID card. I sent you those notes about him hoping you'd get scared and just find another assignment or something. Then I ran you off the road. I figured that would put you in the hospital for a while. But not you. If only you'd just reacted like most people, I wouldn't have to kill you now."

He watched Allison as she slowly, gently, expertly squeezed the trigger, even as he lunged in her direction, determined to knock the sight off its target. "No!" he cried, but again he heard the report of the gun—so loud it must have broken his eardrums, because sound faded and his ears began ringing. At the same time, he was knocked off his trajectory as something sharp ripped at his left shoulder. All he could think was that he hadn't acted in time, that he'd missed his aim, that Rachel was shot. Then he was falling, falling, unable to catch himself as his awareness of his body fled and blackness swallowed him whole.

SHE FELT THE BULLET WHISPER past her face as she reached for Nathan. He flew backward and slammed into her, so that they both landed hard in a heap against the wall, then slid to the floor. Stunned, Rachel couldn't react to the sounds she heard all around her. In the distance, a screaming woman and the shuffle of many booted feet. Close at hand, the revolver being cocked again and Allison's promise not to miss this time as she leveled the gun once more.

On instinct, Rachel twisted Nathan's body to the side so she could put her own protectively over him. She squeezed her eyes shut, bracing for the inevitable.

The shot she heard was not like the others, and after a

second, she realized she was unhurt. Daring to open her eyes, she glanced over her shoulder, to see the room filled with burly men in BDUs, holstering their weapons and surveying the scene. Their mouths were moving, but Rachel couldn't make sense of their words. All she could see of Allison was a pair of legs sprawled on the floor. The rest of her lay behind the desk. Rachel knew she could only see those legs because she sat on the floor, rocking slightly as she clung to the inert body in her arms. Forcing herself to stop, she concentrated on easing Nathan to the floor so she could take his vital signs—if he had any.

A sob crept up her throat on the heels of that morbid thought. "Medic! We need a medic!" she shouted past the fear lodged against her vocal chords. "Get me something to stop the bleeding!" She glanced up, to see an MP standing over her. "Towels or something!" she ordered. "Hurry!"

The MP snapped to action and Rachel knelt beside Nathan, her fingers pressed to the side of his throat. His blood pulsed rhythmically through his carotid artery and Rachel barely contained a whoop of joy. She turned her attention to unbuttoning his blood-soaked shirt, ripping apart his formerly white T-shirt, and peeling the cloth away from the wound so near his heart.

Except for the trickle of blood pumping out of it at regular intervals, the bullet hole didn't look as bad as her imagination had conjured. When a wad of towels was offered, she took it without looking up and pressed it to the wound. Remembering that the bullet must have passed through him to whiz by her head, she tried to raise him to put some of the towels beneath him. He was too heavy for her, but the MP standing by must have realized what she wanted to do. He lifted Nathan gently. Rachel saw a great deal of blood underneath him. She screamed for medics again. Carefully, she placed a towel where it would stanch the blood coming out the back, and the MP eased him onto it.

Thinking only about keeping his blood loss to a minimum, she put a good deal of pressure on the upper towel.

"That hurts," she heard someone mumble.

A moment passed before she to realized the complaint had come from Nathan. By the time she shifted her surprised gaze to his face, he'd opened his eyes. "That hurts, Rae," he said, attempting to lift his uninjured arm in protest, but managing to raise his hand only a few inches.

"Deal with it, Captain," she said. She was so damn glad to hear his voice. Comforting words failed her. Only soldierly commands would form in her mouth now. "Just stay alive, you hear me? You'll need all the blood that's left to accomplish that. So you'll just have to deal with it."

He gave her a weak smile, then his eyes glazed over and he lost consciousness again.

"He's dead! He's dead!" she heard a woman wailing behind her.

"Shut up!" Rachel shouted. "He's *not* dead!" Then she understood the woman wasn't referring to Nathan but to the General, still lying on the floor.

Lydia Donner ignored Rachel's command and continued to cry that her husband was dead. An MP tried to pull her away, but she shook him off and continued her lament.

"He's not dead, ma'am," the MP told her. "He's not dead."

"My life is over," she cried. "I was so happy as a General's wife. It didn't matter that he had his other women. I was the only one he took to his dinners and on his trips. Now it's over. Over!" Then she succumbed to racking sobs that no amount of reassurance from the MPs could assuage.

That was when Nathan's body began to shake uncontrollably as if he were having a seizure.

CHAPTER TWENTY-TWO

RACHEL SAT IN THE HOSPITAL waiting room, wondering how she had gone her whole life never setting foot in one before, only to find herself in an emergency room twice in the same month. Her forehead rested in one hand as she checked her watch for the hundredth time. Odd the way time seemed to be passing so slowly. Only five minutes had gone by since the last time she'd checked, seemingly hours ago.

"Mrs. Fordham?" said a woman's voice from nearby. Rachel glanced up out of curiosity, but then realized the person wearing hospital scrubs looked right at her.

"Me?" she asked, confused.

The woman scanned the chart she carried and frowned. "Oh, I see you go by Southwell. But aren't you also Captain Fordham's wife? You came with him in the ambulance...."

Rachel wasn't sure these medical professionals would tell her anything if she wasn't related to him somehow. "Yes," she confirmed. Nathan had asked her to marry him, after all.

The woman nodded and shook Rachel's hand as she gave her report. "I'm Dr. Smith. I was the surgeon for Captain Fordham. He's doing fine."

Rachel went weak with relief, but once again she couldn't form any words.

"The wound was clean. No vital organs were involved," the doctor said. "The bullet went straight through. So we just closed him up, gave him some blood, started an IV. He should be all set for you to take home by morning.''

"That soon?'' Rachel asked as she quickly rejected the possibility of taking Nathan to his own apartment. Better to have him at her house, where she could tend him. Constantly.

The doctor smiled. "He'll be up and around in no time. You got him here soon enough for us to stabilize him quickly. Maybe he'll even be back at work by next week.''

Rachel's pleasant thoughts of caring for a wounded and needy Nathan evaporated. "Oh,'' she said. "May I see him?''

"Right this way.''

He looked undeniably wounded and vulnerable for the moment, and Rachel decided she'd make the most of it. She smiled as she reached for his free hand and squeezed his fingers. His other arm was bound to his body by a sling. An IV of clear liquid dripped into him. Eyes groggy, he smiled back at her.

"So *now* will you marry me?'' he asked.

She laughed at his impatient tone. "I guess I'll have to, Captain. You took a bullet for me. What more could a woman ask for?''

But Nathan's smile disappeared and he gripped her hand more firmly. "Seriously, Rae. Not out of gratitude.''

She saw that he needed to hear the words she'd repeated like a mantra during the entire journey in the ambulance to the hospital. "You were unconscious, so you didn't hear what I kept telling you on our way here,'' she said softly. Love for this man filled her to the brim and overflowed. To her embarrassment, she realized her eyes had filled, too. She wasn't sure she would be able to hold the tears back for much longer now that the crisis was over. She swallowed hard.

Nathan's gaze never wavered from hers. "What did you keep telling me, Rae?''

She leaned closer and wrapped her hands around his.

"That I need you so much it hurts. That you couldn't leave me now, at the very beginning of the life we're about to build together. That I love you."

The smile returned to his face, slowly and with a veil of tenderness softening his expression. "If I'd known all it would take was a bullet wound to make you say that, then I would have found a way to get shot sooner."

"Don't say that," she chided. "And don't you ever do anything that stupid again."

"If I were faced with the same situation, I'd do exactly the same thing. So many people depend on you. The world wouldn't be the same without you."

"But I depend on *you* now. How would I manage without you lending me your strength? So promise me you won't dart in front of loaded guns anymore."

"I'll do my best to steer clear of such opportunities in the future," he said, and Rachel figured it was the best she'd get out of him.

NATHAN'S LEGS WERE SHAKY, but he refused to let that show. He'd promised Adam that he'd be part of his birthday party, and damn if he wasn't going to make good on that promise. He was happy to be on his feet and to recover some of his strength before dealing with the details of the case against Donner on Monday morning. He and Rachel were to meet Senator Zemin and a Lieutenant General Carter to discuss Donner's case. There would be a bunch of lawyers in attendance, too, even though there wouldn't be a trial. And Nathan was pretty certain his brother would also be present at that meeting. Zemin and Carter were the people who had approached Julian about Donner, the people who had ordered him to keep their involvement secret. The last thing he wanted was to face Julian for the first time since their argument while in the presence of so many strangers. Better to see him here at Adam's party.

Sure enough, Julian was seated in the living room, sipping lemonade, when Nathan made his way down the hall from the bedroom he'd been sharing with Rachel for the past two nights. She and her mother had insisted on bringing him to their home and no one had seemed to think it even slightly odd that he would be ensconced in Rachel's room for his recovery—notwithstanding that their marriage was still several weeks off.

Julian spotted him standing in the doorway and stood. "Come over here and sit," he ordered as he stepped out of the way so Nathan could take the comfortable recliner.

"I'm fine," Nathan asserted, but he went to the chair anyway, thinking he really ought to sit down soon. When he got closer to his destination, he stopped and met his brother's gaze. "I'm fine."

"Damn stupid thing for you to get shot," Julian grumbled. Then he dropped his focus to the floor and mumbled, "Thank God you're okay."

Nathan couldn't stand it. This cold, unyielding wall that had built up between them just wasn't right. So he reached with his good arm to give his brother a quick hug.

Julian took the peace offering to heart and drew Nathan into an embrace that sent a lightning bolt of pain lancing through his wounded shoulder. But Nathan wouldn't let it show. He returned the hug, hoping that this would be the end of their rift.

"I should have told you Zemin and General Carter had approached me about Donner," Julian said as he let go.

Nathan nodded. "I'm not sure what I would have done in your place, Jules. I might have followed orders, too. So let's forget it." He eased into the chair with a weary sigh.

Julian looked as though he might have more to say, but a squeal of laughter pierced the air and Adam streaked into the room, followed by two friends he'd invited to the party. "I want to open my presents now!" Adam cried, but no one gave him permission to start on the brightly wrapped gifts, so he raced out of the room again, accompanied by his shrieking comrades.

Nathan watched them go. "I've asked Rachel to marry

me and she accepted," he announced when they were alone once more.

Julian's face broke into a wide grin. "That's great! I was worried you might let her slip away from you." He took a seat in the wing chair nearby. "When's the big day?"

"Not for a few weeks, but we can't wait too long or we won't get assignments together when we transfer."

Julian's face lost some of its joy. "What's going to happen to your careers after all this?"

"I'll let you know once we meet with Zemin and Carter. They seem to think we've done a good job, even though it feels as if we completely botched the thing. No one was supposed to get shot."

Julian nodded. "That's true, but at least there's no chance of Donner escaping the consequences of his behavior this time. Between the evidence you and Rachel gathered, your sworn statements and all the things his previous victims have been saying, there's no question that Donner will get the dishonorable discharge he deserves once he's out of intensive care."

"I'm afraid this experience has made me somewhat more skeptical of the system than you apparently are, Julian. I don't believe anything is beyond question until it happens. It's possible he'll just get a medical discharge because of that bullet he took to his guts. Then the whole mess can be covered up."

"We won't let that happen," Julian said. "Allison Fitzpatrick is dead because of him."

Mrs. Southwell called to them from the kitchen to come and join the group for cake and ice cream. Nathan pulled himself reluctantly from the comfortable recliner and went with his brother toward the commotion they could hear emanating from the next room.

"You're sure you're up for all this? You'll be a father as soon as you're a husband." Julian gave a visible shudder.

"Yeah, well, I'll be proud to call Adam my son if he

agrees to that. He might be too old to accept me fully as a father. I might just be his mother's husband. We'll have to wait and see. Am I up for all this?'' he repeated as they joined the ruckus. "I'll let you know in about thirty years. I don't think I'll know for sure until then."

As SHE DROVE TOWARD their meeting with Senator Zemin and General Carter, Rachel glanced at Nathan for the tenth time, checking to see if he looked pale or tired. This was his first day leaving the house since the shooting and she couldn't help but worry. He smiled at her, seeming to understand her concern. "I'm fine," he said.

"You were dead on your feet by the end of Adam's birthday party and you didn't say a word until you fell into bed that night. So you can't be trusted to tell me how you're really doing."

"It was a great party. I didn't want to miss anything. I told you Adam would like the Hawaiian shirt."

"So you did. I guess I don't know everything about him after all."

"Did you talk to him about how I'll fit into his life after we marry?'' he asked. Rachel noted the tension in his voice as he posed the question. To her complete surprise, Nathan really longed to be a dad to Adam, though he would never admit it. She suspected that this wish to be accepted by Adam had something to do with not feeling accepted by his own father.

"I did talk to him," she said. "He's thrilled we're getting married. And without any prompting from me, he asked if that meant you'd be his dad. I told him that it was up to him. He could call you Dad or keep on calling you Nathan, the way other stepchildren do with their stepparents."

"And?"

"And he said he'd talk it over with you, man to man."

Nathan groaned. "Am I ready for a man-to-man talk with him?"

"I'm certain you can handle it."

"You are?"

"He's eight years old. I'm pretty sure you can cope with whatever he wants to discuss."

He sat in silence for a while, looking out the window as they passed by the Jefferson Memorial and several museums, heading toward Capitol Hill. "What do you think he'll say?" he finally asked.

"I have no idea," she said honestly. "You're worrying too much about it."

The expression he shot in her direction seemed a little desperate. "I just don't want to screw it up."

"I have faith in you, Nate. Just be yourself. This meeting with a U.S. Senator and a three-star general doesn't appear to faze you, but you're tied up in knots over talking to Adam." She chuckled at the incongruity as she parked the car. "Come on. Let's get this meeting over with so I can get you home to face Adam's man-to-man talk."

Nathan quaked visibly at the prospect.

Inside, the Senator greeted them warmly. Introductions were made, pleasantries exchanged, preliminaries discussed.

General Carter addressed them directly when he explained the situation. "We want you both to know that the Army has not been blind to General Donner's behavior. We've been concerned for some time, but have been unable to persuade any of his victims to come forward or press charges. The officers in our fine Judge Advocate General's Corps were not going to let us do anything against a decorated General without something solid to go on."

Senator Zemin gave them her best smile. "We don't want you to think the Army or the Federal Government were in any way turning a blind eye to what Donner was doing," she said.

Nathan looked the Senator in the eyes. "You sound as if you're worried we'd try to take you to court for negligence or something. You might as well know we can't do that as long as we're in uniform.''

The woman smiled at him slyly. ''But you could always make a case to the newspapers and we'd rather not have that.''

Rachel felt obliged to say, ''We wouldn't do that, ma'am. We're loyal to our government. What kind of officers would we be if we betrayed that?''

''You're damn fine officers,'' General Carter said. ''I've had your OFR corrected, Captain, and I'm putting you both in for commendations for your efforts.''

''What will happen to General Donner?'' Rachel asked.

''He'll probably plead guilty and accept a dishonorable discharge—without retirement pay—in exchange for no prison time. He'll be on probation for the rest of his life,'' the Senator said.

''Unless those trial defense lawyers make a case for mental incapacity,'' Carter added.

''What?'' Nathan exclaimed. ''How could you say—''

Carter interrupted. ''There are some indications that the man has suffered from multiple personality disorder for quite a while. He appears to be addicted to some serious medications prescribed by a private doctor. Combine those with alcohol and the man may not have known what he was doing much of the time.''

''He's been slipping so gradually into his current state that the Army almost missed it,'' Zemin said. ''Fortunately, a few brave young women had the guts to make initial reports of his behavior toward them. Unfortunately, none was willing to go forward and press charges. Hard to do much without that.''

''I'll press charges,'' Rachel said. Nathan gave her a grim smile of encouragement.

''And if you do, so will Sergeant Walker,'' said the Senator.

''When do I do it?'' Rachel asked.

"We have attorneys standing by to take your depositions if you're willing," Carter said.

Both Rachel and Nathan agreed. They then spent hours in separate rooms, where they could give their sworn statements in preparation for the Article 32 hearing that would take place soon. When finally she saw him again, Rachel noticed Nathan's pale complexion. His eyes lit with a smile when he caught sight of her, but his mouth remained a strained line. Apparently, she was the only one who cared to recall that he'd recently been shot.

"Come on, soldier. Let's get you home again," she said as she grasped his arm and led him away. He made no protest and seemed to put his mind to walking the distance to the car.

Even when he was settled in the passenger seat, he talked sparsely about the depositions and what they'd learned from the Senator and the General. "I'm just glad it's almost over," he told her wearily.

As they finally pulled along the curb in front of the house, Rachel saw her son sitting quietly on the steps of their porch. By the way he watched the car, she knew he'd been waiting for them. Certainly, Adam didn't plan on wasting any time before having that man-to-man conversation with Nathan.

Nathan saw him, too, and came to the same conclusion. "Now, if I can only make it through this next trial without botching things," he muttered.

Perhaps he hadn't meant for Rachel to hear him, but she had. "Just be yourself, Nate. You're a natural," she assured him. But the man stood on the sidewalk looking as though he were about to be thrown into shark-infested seas. "I'll just leave you two alone," she said softly as she slipped past the boy who kept his gaze on Nathan the entire time.

NATHAN HAD NO IDEA WHAT to say to the child who gazed up at him with searching eyes. Exhaustion led him to suggest they sit on the porch swing together. "We probably need to talk about how things will be when your mom and I get married,'' he began.

He just about fell onto the seat of the swing. The prospect of having this talk with Adam, of having this very first parent-child interaction, of embarking on this role as a parent, which he'd never thought he'd dare to try—well, it took the wind right out of him.

Adam sat, also. ''So, you're really going to marry my mom?'' he asked. His voice came out sure and clear, but Nathan detected a note of insecurity hidden somewhere in the depths. He remembered well how it felt to be so vulnerable while trying desperately to hide it from the world.

''Yeah, I'm really going to marry your mom. I love her and can't seem to feel good about living without her.''

Adam searched his face. Nathan didn't know what else to say, so he held the boy's gaze, hoping for a clue to the next appropriate move.

''A lot of kids have stepparents,'' he said matter-of-factly. Nathan nodded, wondering if Adam would let things go at that. But, no, the boy had more to say. ''But they have real mothers and fathers, too—except for Jamie Dorrington, whose Mom died of cancer last year. He only has a dad. Maybe he'll get a stepmother someday. He probably won't call her Mom because he remembers his real mom and it would be weird to call his stepmother the same thing. His father says he doesn't want a new wife and that Jamie is the most important thing to him now. That's good, I guess.''

Adam paused, giving time for Nathan to take in this speech amid a whirl of unfamiliar emotions. That this child could talk about the death of his friend's mother so calmly wrenched his heart. And Adam had such a clear picture of relationships and how things could change when a parent remarries. He was a remarkable boy, and suddenly Nathan felt an overwhelming admiration for him. He fought the urge to scoop him into his arms and hold him, to protect him against knowing too many grown-up things, to reassure

him that he would still be the apple of his mother's eye.
But Adam didn't seem to have finished and somehow Nathan sensed the importance of letting the child get everything out in the open.

As the pause continued over long seconds, though, Nathan began to doubt himself. Should he speak or act? Did Adam expect him to interject something here? If so, what?

Then the boy sitting next to him moved. Nathan watched Adam scoot a little forward on the seat. Scuffing his foot on the floor of the porch, Adam got the swing gently rocking. He tilted his head to the side and appeared to be on the brink of speaking again, but a few more seconds stretched by in silence.

Nathan's nerves stretched, too. The creak of the swing stabbed at his composure; the scuff of the sneakers on the planked floor set his teeth to grinding. "Adam?" he said at last. "You can talk to me about anything that's on your mind. I hope you know that."

"We-ell." He drew out the word and ended it on a sigh. "When Mom told me she was gonna marry you, I got to thinking about how I never had a dad." He glanced at Nathan, who schooled his features so as not to reveal his emotions. They were too raw to share just yet.

Adam continued. "I saw my birth certificate once. My mom's name was in the place for the mother. But the space for the father's name was blank."

There came an instantaneous tightening in Nathan's throat and an unfamiliar sting to his eyes that took him completely by surprise. He blinked hard and stared at the boy.

"Grandpa did a good job filling in for a dad. He's been great." There was more scuffing of the feet, while Nathan's heart began to beat harder and his throat grew tighter still.

"I was kinda wondering if you ever thought about having a son," Adam said, so softly that Nathan almost didn't hear. The child tipped his head to catch a peek at Nathan's face. His eyes were hopeful, yet he seemed prepared for disappointment.

Nathan did not want to disappoint this boy who so generously offered himself as a son. And now was the time to speak. If only he could choose the right words. But hesitation would be worse than saying the wrong things. So, taking a breath, he plunged in. "Adam, until I met you, I never thought I would be a father. But now that I know you, I can honestly say I'd be honored to be your dad. If you want, I could have my name put on your birth certificate to make it official." Finding it hard to get the next words past the lump in his throat, he added softly, "And you could even call me Dad, if you want." Then he held his breath as he waited to find out if Adam would accept this invitation. He was shocked to his toes to discover how much he hoped the little boy would.

Adam processed these words. Then an enormous grin split his face. "Yeah, that would be great!" he cried as he threw himself into Nathan's arms and hugged him around the neck. No matter how much that hug tore at his wounded shoulder, Nathan would not have missed it for the world. With his good arm, he squeezed back, suddenly remembering how much he could have used a hug from his own distant father now and then. This moment in a child's arms made up for much of what had been missing in his life up until now and he closed his eyes to savor the sensation of healing that coursed through him.

When he opened them again, he saw Rachel standing in the doorway leading out to the porch. Tears streamed down her cheeks, but there was a smile on her lips and in her eyes. Clearly, she'd heard, and Nathan was glad he wouldn't have to attempt to explain this amazing conversation to her in words. His feelings were beyond articulation.

He held Rachel's gaze and said, "I love you."

Adam loosened his grip and pulled back. "I love you, too, Dad," he said.

Suddenly, there were tears falling out of Nathan's eyes, too, but he ignored them. He smiled at his new son. Then sent a silent prayer heavenward that he'd find a way to deserve the honor.

Adam smiled back, then went skipping toward his mother. "You get a husband and I get a father. It all worked out!"

She smiled down at him and ruffled his hair. "It all worked out," she agreed.

Adam paused another moment to add, "When I grow up, I'm gonna be an officer in the United States Army like my mom and dad."

The stricken look on Rachel's face probably mirrored his own. Adam had a long road to travel before he would be off on his own, but somehow Nathan missed him already. Knowing that there was always strength in numbers, he went to Rachel and slipped his good arm around her shoulders and they both watched their boy skip off toward the basketball hoop, where a friend had just appeared, ready to play.

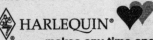

HARLEQUIN® Super ROMANCE®

Christmas is coming!
And Superromance is bringing you a gift...

The Gift of Christmas

These are three great stories by three great authors—
Jan Freed, Janice Kay Johnson and Margot Early.
They're all multiple award winners, and they all
bring something special to Christmas.

THE GIFT OF CHRISTMAS
is the perfect gift to give yourself
(and the romance readers you love!).

HARLEQUIN®
Makes any time special ®

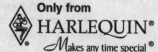